Praise for
Where A...

"Fans of well-written tales filled with ironic reversals will relish this quality collection of 34 stories (including 13 originals), the first of two planned volumes. The entries vary in length, but even the briefer ones, such as the vivid 'Desperate Times,' pack a punch. Many feature human beings in subservient roles, such as zoo exhibits for aliens ('The Henry and the Martha') or game animals for Earth's new masters ('Good Dog'). Other high points include 'Crickets, Everywhere,' a novel variation on the theme of an insect swarm apocalypse, and the creepy 'The Teddy's Touch,' in which a skilled government operative confronts an insidious conspiracy aimed at controlling thoughts and emotions...[Rand] consistently displays creative imagination as well as a gift for understatement...The deftly drawn characters and evocative descriptions will keep readers entirely satisfied.
—*Publisher's Weekly*

"I've belatedly discovered the remarkable work of Ken Rand in *Where Angels Fear*, first of a planned dulology showcasing his stories. What makes everything here so clearly the work of just one author is a particular sensory and emotional vividness that places the reader right in the middle of the scene—without exposition, stylized language, philosophical musings or any of the other strategies that create narrative distance. You are there, sometimes a little bewildered at the start but keenly aware of your surroundings, alert for the next clue, and in touch with the protagonist's mind whether the setting be deep space, an almost depopulated future Earth, Wyoming boondocks suddenly menaced by a plague of strange crickets, the mind of a man obsessed with an obscure '60s rock singer, or a disturbingly convincing dreamscape. There is also a nice bonus, 14 originals just as impressive as the reprints. Yes, Rand's a prolific writer, but I think those extras have more to say about the state of publishing today: not enough magazines and theme anthologies dealing with SF, fantasy, horror, weirdness (or whatever you want to call it) for a master of them all to appear as often as he should."
—Faren Miller, Locus

"Ken's reach seems to know no bounds. He tells stories about nearly everything in nearly every way possible. This collection goes on the special part of my bookshelf reserved for the authors who I want to read again and again."
—James Van Pelt, author of *Summer of the Apocalypse*

"Ken Rand's collection stirs that classic sense of wonder which is the hallmark of great science fiction. From the fearsome twist of 'Where Angels Fear' to the bizarre hopefulness of 'Gone Fishin',' and every sort of story in between, Ken's fiction delights and amazes. Don't miss this wonderful collection by one of the finest writers working in the genre today."
—Louise Marley, author of *Absalom's Mother*

"In *Where Angels Fear* Rand demonstrates yet again that we are in the hands of a creative and capable craftsman who knows his storytelling trade very well indeed."
—Ken Scholes, author of *Last Flight of the Goddess*

"There just isn't *anyone* else doing what Ken does, much less doing it better."
—Selina Rosen, author of *Recycled*

Also by Ken Rand

Fiction
Phoenix
Pax Dakota
Where Angels Fear
Bad News From Orbit
Through Wyoming Eyes
Soul Taster: Four Dark Tales
The Golems of Laramie County
Tales of the Lucky Nickel Saloon
Fairy BrewHaHa at the Lucky Nickel Saloon
Dadgum Martians Invade the Lucky Nickel Saloon!

Writer Reference
The Editor is In
The 10% Solution
From Idea to Story in 90 Seconds
Human Visions: The *Talebones* Interviews

The Port Chicago Books
Port Chicago Isn't There Anymore
Dan Colchico: In Defense of Port Chicago
In Their Own Words: The Port Chicago Letters

THE GODS
PERSPIRE

THE GODS PERSPIRE

KEN RAND

The Collected Short Fiction
Volume Two

FAIRWOOD PRESS
Bonney Lake • Seattle

The Gods Perspire

A Fairwood Press Book
November 2008
Copyright © 2008 by Ken Rand

Fairwood Press
21528 104th Street Court East
Bonney Lake, WA 98391
www.fairwoodpress.com

Cover and Book Design by Patrick Swenson

ISBN: 0-9789078-9-2
ISBN13: 978-0-9789078-9-1
First Fairwood Press Edition: November 2008
Printed in the United States of America

For Lynne, with love

Copyrights

CONTENTS

Foreword

by Ken Rand

I traveled with the Olie Anderson Auto Daredevil Thrill Show in the late 1970s (my mainstream novel titled *Dare*, about those days, is looking for a publisher). I was the announcer and PR guy, not a stuntman, but I did things I'd never done before, some pretty daring, interesting, and exciting things. It was an adventure.

I've never written a foreword to a collection of my own short stories before, but it's an adventure like any other. Strap in and take off; that's how it gets done.

Every story is an adventure. Each starts with a blank page, an idea, anticipation. A thrill. Every one ends with "the end" at the bottom of the last page and "What's next?" right after, facing the next blank page.

In January, 1996, I attended the two-day Kris & Dean Show in Utah. Husband and wife writer-editor-publisher-teacher-mentor team Kristine Kathryn Rusch and Dean Wesley Smith created the workshop to "pay forward," or "raise the floor" as they say, to teach new writers stuff they wished they'd known when they'd started out.

Kris and Dean emphasize productivity and practice, practice, practice. "If you write a story a week," Dean said (I'm paraphrasing here), "within two years, you'll sell one of those stories professionally." I did it; my first professional story sale was to *VB Tech Journal* ("The Nine Billion Names of Arthur C. Clarke") in July 1996.

In 1996, I got into an industrious groove, writing a story a week. I developed a way to conjure up a story idea on the fly, out of thin air (*From Idea to Story in 90 Seconds: A Writer's Primer*, from Media Man! Productions, details my method). I'd come up with a story idea Saturday night, start writing Sunday morning — my goal was 1000 words a day — and finish, edit, and mail the story by the following Saturday. Wash, rinse, repeat.

Late that fall, I realized that if I redoubled my effort — wrote two stories a week — I'd have 100 stories in my parfleche by Christmas. I liked the symmetry and the challenge. It seemed doable: I often finished my story-a-week goal on Thursday or even Wednesday and didn't write anything new till the following Sunday, focusing instead on editing and marketing at the end of the week. And in 1995, I'd accepted one of those dare-to-be-bad challenges to write three short stories in a week and I did it ("Imagine That," "Good Neighbors," and "The Gods Perspire"). So I knew I could do it.

I didn't quite make it to 100 stories by year's end, but I got close and I learned about productivity, focus, turning idea into story, and craft.

I also learned about tuning out the critic — inner and outer — and why I write.

I write because it's fun.

In compiling this collection, I came up with a lot of numbers — how many stories written, how many words, how many sold, how many rejections, and so on. I considered including that trivia here to impress you, but I've decided against. Readers don't care how hard writers work to make it look easy and writers already know so there's no point.

Readers want to know: is this a good story? The only thing I can control is "finish." "Good or bad" is somebody else's lookout. You may find some of these stories pretty good and some duds. You may decide you don't like a story that I think is keen. I've long ago stopped trying to predict how people will react to what I write. So this book comes with no money-back guarantee. I write. You read. End of contract.

Of course, I hope you like these stories, most of them. I hope you're entertained, thrilled, enlightened, educated, awed, impressed, and so on. That's what I hope — but all I expect is that I finished each story. Anyone can say you can't write; let nobody say you don't.

The writing is where the fun is.

Most of these stories are sort of daredevil stunts — challenges, new territory, experiments in some form or technique. "Breed Apart" was my first attempt to write from a female point of view. "Sawk" was my first fantasy. "Geezers" was my first mystery. I wrote "Doubles" aiming to go under 150 words. "Snowflakes, One by One" was my first shot at an alien point of view. The *Lucky Nickel* stories are an experiment in voice. And so on.

When Patrick Swenson asked me to put together my short story collection for Fairwood Press, it soon became clear that I'd been having way too much fun to put it all in one volume. We'd need two volumes. But how? Some order must be imposed. Another stunt. Cool.

I toyed with chronological order but set that aside when I noticed two trends in my writing. One is that my prose divides semi-equally between science fiction and fantasy, and the other is that my prose divides semi-equally between humor and dark stories. I have a reputation as a humor writer so I opted to divide the collection into the dark and the light.

Each volume flows naturally in a way, each story linked with the next, from extreme space opera at one end to extreme fantasy tropes at the other. In between are experiments in point of view (the alien stories), setting (I spend a lot of time, literarily, in Wyoming), voice (the Old West), and theme (home and family permeates everything I do). You'll see the clusters, I hope, and the flow.

Some stories were omitted for several reasons: space considerations, Paramount owns them (I wrote three *Trek* stories besides "I Am Klingon!" which appeared in *Star Trek: Strange New Worlds*, volume 2), they're collaborations (I wrote five stories with my friend Dave Felts), they're workshop stories not intended for publication, they didn't fit the light-dark motif, or — because I said so. (I omitted the *Bad News From Orbit* stories because while some are dark, most aren't, really. Besides, Silver Lake Publishing did an excellent collection for me. And I needed the space.)

These orphaned stories may one day appear in print from my own publishing company, Media Man! Productions. (I'm toying with the title: *No Story Left Behind: the Orphaned Tales*.)

So the adventure continues.

Writers know the story you start with isn't always the one you end with. Discovering the story is part of the process of writing the story. In a way, that's how we discover who we are.

I write because it's fun. Writing, like life, is an adventure. Nobody knows what's going to happen next — in a story, or in life — whether you're going to nail the landing on ESPN or break your damn fool neck. Every life is a story and every story is an adventure.

Enjoy yours. I've enjoyed mine.

Introducing
Ken Rand

by Dean Wesley Smith

N o matter if you hold the light side or the dark side of Ken
Rand's work in your hand right now, you are holding a real treasure.
Okay, right up front here, let me be honest.

Over the last decade or so, Ken has become known as one of the
field's strongest and brightest professional writers. His work spreads over
many topics, and is always unusual, well-written, and spellbinding. As a
reader, or as an editor, you always know you are in a real pro's hands when
you read one of Ken's stories.

And, to be very, very honest, I was completely honored to be asked to
write this introduction to his short fiction collections. I very seldom do this.
He could have gotten just about anyone, so when he asked me, I said yes.

Then, of course, I had no idea what to say. What could I say about a
writer who is so successful, so diverse, so talented that his stories speak
for themselves?

Ken, in his forward, gave his readers a fascinating glimpse into his
writing life, his work ethic, his push to become the writer he is now. You
can see why he has become so successful with his writing from that forward.

He mentioned me and Kris in there as a starting point for him, a
workshop we did in his home area. I'm always flattered when someone
says I had something of a hand in starting them on the road to their dream.
But I always remind the writer that he did the work, put in the years of
writing. I just sort of stood on the sidelines and pointed and said, "Go that-
a-way."

You can see from his forward, Ken did the work. Oh, wow, did he do
the work.

And great work, too. In fact, I bought his first professional short story
as well; it was that good. I bought it for a computer magazine that published
two science fiction short stories a month, usually by big name writers like

Jack Williamson, Harlan Ellison, Kristine Kathryn Rusch, David Brin, Gregory Benford, and so on. Right there, in that company, I put a first story by a writer by the name of Ken Rand.

And he deserved to be there.

Editors often can tell when a young writer comes into the field if they are going to still be around in ten years. I had no doubt Ken would be here. With Ken, I was right. And in spades, as these books prove.

I also bought another story from him that isn't in here, for a *Star Trek* anthology I edit for Pocket Books. That's how fantastically versatile Ken's writing is. He can move from horror, to funny fantasy, to *Star Trek*, and not miss a beat. Let me tell you, as a writer, that is very, very hard to do. Most writers never have the range you will see in these two books. Ken does, and he does it all at the top of the forms.

So, as one of Ken's former teachers, former editors, and still long-time fan, about all I can say to you, the readers, is go forward and read and enjoy. There is *a lot* of great stuff here. Take your time. You won't enjoy every story, remember, because only Ken (and maybe his fantastic wife) likes every word Ken has written. But you will enjoy most of them, of that I have no doubt.

And be warned. Some of these stories, both in the lighter book, and in the dark book, will stick with you, haunt you long after you have read them. That shows the power of a top professional writer like Ken Rand.

In these volumes, Ken will make you laugh, he will make you shudder, he will make you think, and most of all, he will entertain you.

And I guess that's the best I could ever say about any writer. Thanks, Ken, for the great work, the great stories, and the hours of enjoyment in reading. It's an honor to be your fan.

DOUBLES

His experiment to see if he could alter the future worked, says he, as I pour him another double.

Time runs in a straight line, like a train, says he, skipping the technical stuff about quarks and quantums. Bump it hard and derail it, says he, you change the future.

It worked, says he. But time isn't going straight anymore. The bump made it curve and I can't stop it, says he.

Says he, time will spiral back to the bump again and the curve will get sharper and sharper with each bump until the Universe spirals in on itself and collapses.

How long before that happens, says I.

Maybe 10,000 years, says he, give or take a few hundred.

He looks up and sees himself walking in and realizes he's figured wrong.

Last call, says I, as I pour myself a double.

THE NINE BILLION NAMES OF ARTHUR C. CLARKE

The great writer had just settled down to tea when, before him in the room, a shimmering light hovering just above the floor, caught his eye. Puzzled, he watched as the shimmering intensified, and a form gathered in it. The form coalesced into the shape of a man.

Then the shimmering light faded and the man remained in its place. The man smiled and looked around.

"Mr. Clarke, Arthur C., I presume," the man said, stepping forward and extending a hand.

The writer, startled, took the offered hand, found the grip firm and businesslike.

The visitor was a small man, narrow-shouldered, dapper, crisp. British. The dark suit, correct tie, the bowler, vest, pocket watch and chain, and the shoes. The accent, of course. And the umbrella tucked under one arm.

"How did you—" Clarke began.

"Bell Teleport, of course," the little man said, sitting, crossing a leg over a knee. "Technology that Earth science won't have until—well, you won't be around."

"But what about—"

"Not to worry, Mr. C. Nobody saw me. Nobody will. Guaranteed. Procedures and all that. Quarantined planet, Earth is."

"Quarantined—"

"Why all the hush-hush. Not due to join the Hegemony for—well, you won't be around."

"But why—"

"Proctor, I am," he produced a device from a shirt pocket and set it on the table between Clarke and him. "Confirm test results and all that." He took out a notebook and a pen. "Won't be but a minute."

"What the devil—"

"Oh, this." The man nodded at the device on the table. It resembled a travelers alarm clock with a face composed not of numbers or a digital readout, but of cryptic symbols chasing each other about on a tiny screen Some kind of screen saver, or— "Timer. Goes off to let me know when the boy makes his count. Supposed to keep an eye out when it does. Any minute now."

"What are you—"

"Chatty sort, aren't you?" he said, frowning his disapproval. "Some time left, I suppose." He checked his watch, nodded, clicked it shut and put it back in his vest pocket. He leaned forward.

"You are *the* Arthur C. Clarke, yes?"

"Why, yes, I—"

"Fellow who wrote 'Nine Billion Names of God?'"

"Yes, I wrote—"

"Mind, science fiction's not my field. Too flight-of-fancy. But I've read your stuff. Had to. Proctor, you know. Part time job. Pays tuition. Grad student from the University of— well, you wouldn't recognize the name. Far off planet. Figure Earth is in the galactic arm? I'm from the armpit."

The little man snickered. Clarke did not.

Instantly sober, the man continued. "Young fellow read your story, figured it could be done."

"What could be—"

"Count the names. Silly. But." He shrugged. "His thesis."

"You mean to say—"

"Thesis."

"But my story—"

"Ended with the stars going out, quite. Read your stuff. Told you."

"And someone actually thinks that—"

"Can be done. Modern science. Counting that many names and all that."

"But the ending—"

"Course not. Flight-of-fancy, stars going out. No, our chap thinks—"

A beeper sounded from the device on the table.

"There you are. Count's done."

And Arthur C. Clarke winked out of existence.

THE GODS PERSPIRE

A granite-jawed muscleman out of an old Russian propaganda poster stood across the counter from Jack. "Mister The Pipe," he said, "I have come to place a wager."

Who was this guy? Nobody never came to Jack "The Pipe" Lombardo unless they was regular guys. This guy sure as hell wasn't regular.

Course, enough came to Jack's Pipe Shoppe to just buy butts and papers and stuff that the IRS never paid him too much mind. It was the other customers, the ones who seemed to be trying to look over both shoulders at once when they slipped into the shop off the street real sudden like, like they was playing hide and seek from cops or their bosses or wives, that The Pipe was dead set on doing right by. They was his meal ticket. They was the ones who called him "The Pipe." Most he knew personal, some was one-timers. They brought in regular white envelopes with all the necessary stuff in it — which horse, which team, whatever — and sometimes money if they was owing, slipped it across the counter at him, yakking about the weather, politics, women — but never sports, not even the Superbowl or the World Series — got an envelope when they bought their newspaper or whatever, gave him a knowing smile and left. Some looked grim. Others, with fatter envelopes, left whistling.

It was an okay life. Course, the regular payoff to Big Augie was a pain in the butt, cause Augie would tack on what he called "special fees" whenever he knew Jack had had a pretty big day. So Jack never got to sock away much of a nest egg to move to Wyoming like he'd wanted for the past — Geez, ten years now? But Augie and his boys never gave Jack no trouble so long as he paid and the shop got along okay, so it was an okay life. It would do till Jack could go where the picture was taken, the one by his cash register, the one of the Teton Mountains reflected in a lake. Then, life would really be okay.

A couple of kids leafing through his comics looked over at the giant customer and muffled giggles.

"Hey, you kids," Jack yelled. "You bend the merchandise, you buy it, you got me?"

The kids tossed the comics on the floor, gave Jack the finger, and left, laughing.

Jack looked back up at the guy in front of the counter. Up. Six-ten, maybe seven foot. The giant's barrel chest, shoulders — maybe four-foot wide — and thigh-thick arms strained his suit fabric, a cheap off-the-rack Sears job. He had long yellow hair that looked like straw made up in two pigtails that hung over the front of each shoulder, down to his lapels. Clean-shaven. The guy looked like some Norwegian skier just off the boat. He smelled a bit fishy.

Jack wisely refrained from laughing out loud. After all, the guy was big, and he didn't look nervous at all.

Maybe this is Augie's new runner. Naw. Spencer is doing okay. And Augie would have brought a new runner by personal, to intro-duce, if he'd replaced Spencer. And Augie's runner wouldn't be laying no bets with The Pipe. Maybe Sabatini sends me his enforcer, still wants to bust into Augie's territory. The putz. Never learns.

Jack reached a casual hand under the counter. He touched the cold metal of the shotgun and released the safety. It was already aimed at the guy's gut.

"You got me wrong, buddy." Jack forced a smile. "I don't do no book."

"I am not here to purchase a book, Mister The Pipe," the big guy said. "I am here to place a wager."

The guy's voice was flat, his eyes steely, no expression. *Don't never play poker with this one.*

"Who you working for, bud? Sabatini send you? You ain't one of Big Augie's boys."

"I work for no one. I am not Bud. I know no Sabatini, nor one of Big Augie's boys. I am from Valhalla. I am Thor."

Suddenly, it hit Jack. Somebody was playing a joke on The Pipe. There was a theater right across the street, a rag-tag outfit where any number of his cronies could buy themselves use of an actor for a couple of twenties. And the gym down the street where the pro wrestlers worked out. Some was more hard up for cash than others. This guy looked like a wrestler — a new guy, cause The Pipe knew them all, it was his business to know — and new in town, judging by the ridiculous new duds.

But no, Jack decided, looking at the hair. A wig. Too yellow, too long. Too fruity.

"Thor, huh? God of thunder and all that crap, huh?"

"Of thunder, it is so. But not of crap."

Jack laughed and reached up to grab one of the pigtails. He intended to whip it off the actor and toss it and him into the street. If he was an actor, he was likely a fag despite his size, and he'd squeal and run. Fun joke, though.

But the wig didn't come off. Instead, the big guy was pulled forward a few inches when Jack tugged on the hair, a surprised look on his face, the first change of expression Jack had seen on the guy. Then the guy straightened, Jack let go of the hair, and the guy's gunmetal eyes turned hard, like Jack had seen in boxers when they went berserk.

Jack took a step back, the shotgun forgotten. He could run pretty good, out the back door, into the alley —

"Mortals do not touch gods," the guy — *Thor* — said. "It is forbidden. The punishment — "

"Look, uh, Mister Thor. Pal. Buddy. It was a mistake. Honest. I saw this, uh, bug on your shoulder and I was trying to get it off. Wouldn't want it to bite you or anything like that, would I? Give The Pipe a bad reputation, if I let things like that happen to my customers. Augie'd be pissed. I don't know squat about this god business. I ain't read the rulebooks. It ain't like Thor is a Catholic god, you know? Jesus, maybe I ought to go to church more often — "

"Cease talking."

"Right, you bet. Bet. That's what you came for, isn't — "

Thor slid an envelope across the counter.

"Great," Jack said extending a hand, "let's shake on — "

But Thor had already turned and walked out the door, ducking under.

Jack let out a sigh and was amazed he hadn't wet his pants. He sat on a stool behind the cash register and glanced at the picture of the mountains. *Someday. Someday.*

Then he opened the envelope, his hands shaking. Some nag named Thunder Hooves. To win, in the third, this afternoon. A twenty-to-one glue factory. Ten K. In cash.

"Jesus H."

He hung up the Out To Lunch sign on the door, locked up, and called Spencer, Augie's runner.

While Spencer was coming over, Jack called Augie, told him Spencer would be by with a package.

"How much?"

"Ten K."

"No friggin way."

"Friggin way."

Spencer was at the shop in a flash. A fresh black kid with no gang contacts. Didn't shoot, snort, or smoke. Stayed away from the babes. Raising money for college. Smart kid.

He took the envelope, smiled and waved at Jack, and left on his bike.

Jack watched him pedal across traffic, down the street, around the corner. Just another city bike courier, lost in the crowd. With ten grand.

Jesus H.

Big bets scared Jack cause they always drew Augie's attention, and even though he needed a big score to retire out West, he didn't need no attention from Augie. Last time he'd taken a big bet was back at Superbowl XXXV. Some guy with a diamond on his pinkie and a thousand-dollar hooker on each arm. Bet five grand. Said if he won, he'd be back. Jack smelled a fix, turned him to Augie direct.

Now, here was this, this — Naw. It had to be a gag. Had to be. Jack shrugged: Augie's business. He done right.

Jack put on his coat cause it'd started to get cloudy out, locked up the shop, and walked across the street to the theater. The Egyptian, they called it. Old, run down. Used to be a movie house. "Opening Soon: The Gods Aspire," the marquee said. Avant-guard, artsy-fartsy, fairy stuff.

The front door was open. Inside, some guy was on a ladder on the stage, tinkering with the lights.

"'The Gods Perspire,' huh?" Jack said, loud.

The ladder-guy looked down, squinted into the dim house.

"'The Gods *As*pire,' yes." The guy started down the ladder. "Our new show. Opens the 20th."

"The 20th? But there's a title fight that night. Mountain Rivera and — "

But it was clear to Jack that the tall, skinny, hippie-looking guy walking toward him down the narrow aisle didn't know from sports, didn't know nobody would come see his show when there was a heavyweight title on the line the same night.

"How may I help you?" The theater guy extended a slender hand. Jack could tell a lot about a guy by his handshake. It was a talent. The guy shook Jack's hand with delicate grace.

"Don't tell me," Jack said. "You were a dancer. A pretty good one, too, right?"

"Yes. My knees gave out. How did you — "

"A talent. Comes in handy in my business. I got the shop across the street — "

"Ah, yes, the tobacco store."

"Yeah, that's me. Anyway, I just had a customer stopped by, bought a paper, left his, uh, coat. Didn't get his name, but he looked like maybe he was an actor. I wondered if — "

"What'd he look like?"

Jack described the man. The theater guy shook his head.

"But I figured maybe with this new show you got — "

The theater guy laughed. "It's a work of experimental theater. The gods, you see, rise up and contend with each other for control of — "

"Yeah, this guy, I remember now, said his name was Thor."

"God of thunder."

"So he's here?"

"No. Actually, we don't use live actors in this show. Just lights, audio, props, screens, visual effects. That sort of thing. Experimental. The flies are computerized. Would you like to see?"

Jack waved the guy off and left. *Computerized flies? What the hell was he talking about?*

He glanced across the street at his shop before turning down the sidewalk toward the gym. Two punks were spray painting gang stuff on the wall under his front window.

Damn city's going to hell. Where're the cops when you need them?

The gym was hot, the odor of honest sweat hung in the air. Dim, like the theater, only noisier. Guys grunting and panting. The rhythmic thump of fists on bags, running feet, jump ropes slapping floors, metal weights clanging.

Jack described the big guy to the manager, an old crony.

"Not one of our people," the manager said.

"Lemme just have a looksee."

The manager shrugged. "Have at."

No dice. All the gym guys looked like they belonged. The big guy — *okay, Thor* — would've looked as out of place as —

Jack frowned in thought as he walked back to his shop, hands buried in his coat pockets, head down thinking hard. It had become cold, overcast.

— About as out of place as a Norse god in downtown —

Jack almost bumped into the man standing in front of his door. The guy was big.

"Let me guess," Jack said, "You must be Zeus, right?"

The big guy nodded. His massive, curly beard arched around a rosy-cheeked smile that threatened to burst into a booming laugh. Not as tall as Thor, but rounder. Dressed just as cheaply, though. Smelled garlicky.

"I wish to place a bet with Mister The Pipe," Zeus said.

"Look, buddy, would you keep your voice down? We're standing on the for-gods-sake street."

"This is the shop of Mister The Pipe, is it not?"

"Yeah, this is — "

"Are you acquainted with Mister The — "

"I *am* Mister The goddam — "

"Cease talking."

The bearded man extended a thick envelope toward Jack, who took it in numb, shaking hands. Zeus turned to walk away.

"Now just a minute," Jack yelled. People on the street turned to look, and looked quickly away, hurrying past. Zeus stopped and turned back to peer through beady eyes at Jack, a puzzled expression on his face.

"Zeus, you say?"

Zeus nodded.

"Yeah? Look, buddy, I know a little about Greek mythology. I'm a high school graduate and I took me some college courses. And I figure no god is going to go around in the middle of the city in the middle of the day placing his own bets. I mean, you got Mercury, for chrissake. Isn't he your messenger or something? How come you don't get him to do your running for you? Why — "

Zeus laughed a gut-jiggling bellow, shook his shaggy head, turned, and walked away.

Jack gritted his teeth. He opened his shop, locked it behind him, and went into the back room to open the envelope.

A bet on a marathoner in a track meet in Oregon. Guy with a Greek name Jack couldn't pronounce. *Mercury, I'll bet. That's why Zeus was busting his britches laughing.*

Jack had forgotten about the meet. Not much action there.

But now —

Twenty grand. Cashier's check. On the Greek runner. Fifty-to-one.

"Jesus H."

He called Big Augie immediately and Augie sent one of his boys over. Not that he didn't trust Spencer, but this was big.

"Next time one of these friggin god fellows come by," Augie said, "you call me. Hear? Nobody bets like this. Unless they got the friggin fix on."

If Jack was lucky, there wouldn't be no gods coming back.

The nag won, and the Greek in Oregon. Both set records.

When Thor came by the shop to collect the next day, Jack immediately threw out a couple of straight customers, closed shop, and phoned Augie.

"The one named Thor. He's here."

"I'm already on my way." Augie hung up. It was then that Jack noticed two of Augie's boys hanging out, real casual like, across the street by the theater, shoulders hunched against the rain that had just started. Watching. Just in case.

Augie arrived in two minutes flat, another record.

"You have my money," Thor said as Augie walked into the back room of Jack's shop, flanked by two of his best boys. It wasn't a question.

"Sure, I got your money, wiseguy."

"I am not Wiseguy. I am Thor. God of thunder."

"Yeah, right. And I'm the friggin Duke of Windsor."

"Give me the money, The Friggin Duke of Windsor."

"I saw your nag run today. I don't know how you did it but either the fix was on or my name is John friggin Wayne."

"I know of no Fix On. I thought you were The Friggin Duke of — "

"Enough of this. My associate, Gino," Augie nodded to one of his boys, "will now proceed to teach you better than to friggin mess with Augie Costello. Gino?"

Gino took a step toward Thor —

— and turned into a fish.

"Jesus H." Jack smelled urine, but it wasn't his. He'd already gone to the bathroom, just in case.

Augie's jaw dropped as he looked at the fish flopping around on the floor and his other guy, Orville, made a noise in his throat like it was being cut.

"What the friggin hell have you done?" Augie squeaked.

"Your Associate Gino has just been taught better than to friggin mess with Thor, god of thunder."

"Turn him back, mister," Orville whimpered, eyes brimming with tears. "Please turn my buddy back."

"I got the money, Mister Thor, sir," Big Augie said, reaching into his coat pocket. "Will a cashier's check do, sir? Or would you prefer cash?"

Augie extended a cashier's check toward Thor. Thor took the check, looked at it, nodded, and Gino changed back from a fish into one of Big Augie's boys.

Nobody spoke as Thor turned to leave the back room and go out the front way.

But as he did so, the little bell over the front door chimed, announcing another customer. *But I locked the door.* Jack shot past Thor into the front room, followed by Thor, Augie, and his two boys.

There stood Zeus.

"Mister The Pipe, I've come for my — "

Then Zeus saw Thor.

Outside, lightning flashed and thunderous peals shook the building as the two gods glared at each other.

"I don't think they like each other, boss," Orville said.

"What the friggin — "

But Augie's comment was drowned in cacophonous noise. Without their lips moving, Jack heard the gods yelling at each other in what sounded like several languages, none of them English. They stood six feet apart facing each other, brows knit in anger. They didn't move, stiff as birdshit covered statues in the park, yet Jack's head ached from their guttural screams and barks.

He, Augie, and the boys covered their ears. To no avail.

"Hey, gods, why don't you take it outside, for cris — "

A sudden silence left Jack's ears ringing. The two gods turned to him as if seeing him for the first time.

"Oh, shit," Jack said.

"Mister The Pipe," Thor said. "The Greek and I have reached an agreement to settle our differences. First, John Friggin Wayne will pay Zeus what is owed to him."

Augie took out a checkbook and began writing frantically. He handed the check to Zeus.

"It won't bounce, I swear," Augie said as Zeus eyed the check with a frown. Zeus nodded, put the check in his pocket and folded his beefy hands over his stomach.

Zeus nodded to Thor. "Continue."

"We now want you, Mister The Pipe, to hold our bets until we settle our differences."

"Yeah, sure," Jack shrugged, "but Augie here's got a nice big safe and a lot of muscle — "

"We trust *you*, Mister The Pipe," Thor said.

"That's why we placed our bets with you in the first place," Zeus said. "It may appear a coincidence that we both came to you, but in fact we both have shopped around."

"Independent of each other, of course," Thor said.

"We both require honesty in our gambling," Zeus said. "You are a crook, but you are an honest crook. The only such one we could find at present. Hence our both coming to you was not a coincidence."

"A coincidence that we were both on the Earthly plane to recreate at the same time — " Thor said.

"But in choosing you — "

"Thanks, I guess," Jack said. "I didn't realize you gods like to gamble."

"Some do," Thor said. Zeus nodded agreement.

"You've done this a lot?"

"Yes," Thor said, "but we seldom cross paths."

"Seldom? You mean — "

"The last time," Zeus said, "was World War Two."

"You guys had something to do with — "

"We argued," Thor said.

"Petty, I realize now," Zeus shrugged. "But."

"World War Two," Thor said. He nodded at the downpour outside.

"But, really, guys, gods, when it comes to big money — "

"We do not wager cash," Zeus said. "This time."

"We cannot risk future chance meetings between us," Thor said. "Too hard on the furniture."

"You will write down our wager, Mister The Pipe," Zeus said. "And you — " he caught Augie and his boys with steely eyes, "will witness."

"Yeah, sure, Mister Zeus," Augie said. The boys nodded vigorously.

"Okay," Jack said.

Zeus dictated, with frequent interjections from Thor. Jack wrote the wager being made between the Norse and the Greek in cramped, stuttering lines.

The two would wrestle on the 20th, on stage at the Egyptian during the opening of "The Gods Aspire" — they'd "rewrite" the script, so to speak, using their godly powers — and the winner would take all.

All.

The stakes were the universe and everything in it. The loser was to retreat — to Valhalla, if Thor lost — to Olympus, if Zeus lost — and never enter the affairs of the world again, forever. The universe, and everything in it, would then become the domain of the winner. Forever.

The agreement went on and on page after page, until Jack's hand cramped and his writing became illegible. When Jack complained, Zeus waved a finger and Jack's hand became uncramped, his handwriting became as legible as type, and he stopped sweating.

Rules of the match. Illegal holds defined. Boundaries of the ring. Number of rounds. Time per round. Point system. Zeus agreed to shave off his beard and hair. Thor would clip his golden locks. They'd wrestle nude. All the details.

Jack, of course, would referee.

"Can we watch?" Orville asked.

Augie interrupted. "Is it okay with you gods, sirs, if we take some side bets? You don't mind? Sirs?"

Both gods shrugged.

Augie and his boys left quickly, before anything else weird happened. As they hustled through the downpour to Augie's waiting car, Jack heard Augie say: "Get the friggin word out. I'm giving the Norse a five to one edge over the Greek. That Thor, he's friggin big."

"Good day, Mister The Pipe," Zeus said, a slight nod.

"Until the 20th," Thor added.

Both turned to leave.

"Just a sec, gods," Jack said.

They stopped and turned to him.

"Hows about a handshake," Jack said. "For luck."

"Mortals do not touch gods," Thor said.

"It is forbidden," Zeus added.

"Yeah, I know. But this is a special occasion, don't you think? I mean, it's for all the marbles, right? So how's about a break with tradition, just this once? For luck. Do it for The Pipe. You guys said you trust me, right? Right?"

The two gods looked at each other, shrugged and extended a hand to Jack.

Jack shook Thor's first. "Cause I met him first," Jack explained to Zeus. "And he's before you in the alphabet, too."

He then shook Zeus' hand.

"See you gods on the 20th," Jack waved as they left.

The sun was coming out.

When they'd walked down the street and turned their separate ways, Jack went back behind the counter and picked up the phone. He dialed.

"Lemme talk to Sabatini," he said.

A moment passed, then Sabatini came on the line. "The Pipe is turning or what?"

"Just placing a little side bet, Sabatini," Jack said, glancing at the picture of the mountains. *Soon. Pretty soon.*

"The Pipe gambles? Has the world come to an end or what?"

"Just listen — " and Jack told Sabatini about the match at the Egyptian on the 20th. He laid down his shop, all his savings and his insurance money on Zeus to win. He knew a few loan sharks. Maybe he'd add to the bet later.

"You know this Zeus fellow or what?" Sabatini asked.

"Let's just say I got a grip on some pretty good information," Jack said, kneading his aching hand, the one he'd used to shake hands with Thor. And then with Zeus.

BRIDGE OVER TROUBLED WATERS

Charon tapped skeletal fingers on the gunwales as he stood at the head of the gangplank waiting for the last passenger to board. The last was a fat mortal with rubbery white skin, like a slug, who whistled a happy tune Charon didn't recognize. The boatman was annoyed at the mortal's impertinence and because he didn't recognize the tune.

The passenger had a patch of white hair in the center of his chest that Charon grabbed in bony fingers as he passed. The whistling turned to a yelp.

"What's that tune, mortal?" Charon hissed.

"Hey, lemme loose," the fat man whined.

Charon complied with obvious reluctance. The mortal muttered thanks. Then: "Bridge on the River Kwai."

"What?"

"The tune. It's from the movie. Don't you remember? But I guess you don't see many movies down here. Do you show movies on the trip over?"

Charon kicked the mortal in his ample keester and sent him sprawling into the mass of sweaty bodies filling up the ferry's hold. The doomed mortals writhed like so many herring, fresh-caught and tossed into a net. Sailor-demons shoved others among the just-arrived dead into places on the bare wooden benches. Banks of oars waited for the doomed to heave to.

In the dim light afforded by a few lamps fore and aft, Charon scanned his ship as he took his place at the bow. Something was wrong, he knew, but he didn't quite know what. The happy mortal was a symptom, not the cause of his uneasiness. A clue, part of the — *wrongness*. He'd dealt with jovial mortals before. He recalled one who hummed "Michael Row The Boat Ashore." He'd keelhauled him.

No, that wasn't it. Something else, something —

"Ready to shove off, cap'n," a sailor said. Charon accepted the demon's clawed salute with a bob of his hood and the anchor clanked up from the

Styx. Whips cracked and sailors ran about. A wail of grief chorused from steerage.

"Shaddup," Charon commanded, his baleful voice booming across the dark river like the voice of doom itself. Relative silence ensued, broken by occasional involuntary whimpers, and voiding of bladders and stomachs.

No, it wasn't the fat mortal's sappy tune. But what?

Charon, deep in thought, scratched a non-existent itch on an arm long skinless.

The boat lurched away from the near shore, prompting renewed moans from below decks. Charon decided to stroll the planks and listen to the crew and passengers chatter. Maybe he'd find some clue to his vague malaise.

He found it. And it stopped him cold.

" — lights off the starboard bow — " a rower in the dark boat said to someone nearby. The unseen voice came strained, intense, between clenched teeth, between pulls on the oar.

" — must mean — more than one boat — traffic picking up I guess — more coming across each day — "

No! There's but one ferry — mine!

But the truth was evident. On the horizon, several faint lights twinkled yellow just above the flat river. Charon had seen them earlier — the source of his unease — but he'd dismissed them as illusion caused by boredom. Nothing had changed in the millennia he'd been ferrying cargo from the mortal shore to Hell, no lights but his own boat's had pierced the Stygian darkness. So the lights — those other lights — couldn't be real.

But now, he saw, they were.

" — maybe so, maybe not — " another voice grunted. " — look how they're lined up — spaced apart evenly above the surface — I used to be a civil engineer — used to build bridges — what you see — it's a bridge — "

" — how come a bridge — " the first voice panted, " — when they got a boat — "

" — my guess is — they got to modernize — a hundred lanes one way — more efficient than an old boat like this — "

Old boat!

" — what do you reckon — the old boatman's gonna do?"

What can I do?

" — used to be a union organizer — if I's him, I'd strike — "

Strike?

Charon rolled the word around his empty skull for a moment. He remembered the concept, from long ago.

"Strike," he muttered, testing the sound. He liked it.

"Strike!" he bellowed, and the boat's timbers quivered in sympathy. He stomped aft, pushing aside crew-demons too slow-witted to make way for him. In a few swift moves, he tripped a lever releasing the anchor, which rumbled and splashed into the water. The ship snapped about, jerked suddenly in the chain's grip as the anchor found bottom. It tipped dangerously.

Mortals moaned and screamed in terror, the boat's spine groaned in protest at the sudden stop, and oars snapped and splintered in their locks. Whips cracked, crew-demons barked obscenities and scrambled about, confused.

"Strike!" Charon roared.

A demon ran up to Charon. "Call from HQ, sir," it said, holding out a telephone. Charon grabbed the phone and backhanded the demon, who fell over the side.

"Charon."

"What in Heaven's name is going on out there?" The tinny voice on the phone was Hades himself.

"A bridge! You're building a bridge!"

"Congrats, Char, baby. You win the lottery."

"A bridge!"

"Look, Char," Hades sighed, "we put out a memo, we had a meeting. You never come to the staff meetings — "

"A bridge!"

"Mephisto's mustache, what are you doing? We got customers stacked up on the other side, we got quotas to meet. Why'd you drop anchor?"

"I'm on strike."

"Strike? You can't strike. Nobody's done that in Hell since — since — "

"First time for everything, boss."

"Including bridges. Times change, Char, ol' buddy. You got to change with them."

"Whatever happened to our traditional family values?"

"Discussed at the meeting you didn't show up for — "

"Oh, go to Heaven." Charon threw the phone into the Styx.

Minutes later, a low rumble vibrated the boat like an earthquake. Lightning arched from three black, man-shaped clouds rising aft of the boat. The Furies had arrived, lightning flashes illuminated their serpent-tangled hair and bloody eyes.

They carried scourges.

One Fury aimed her scourge at the anchor chain, snapping it like twine. The anchorless boat cascaded forward on a swell of water as the three Furies whipped it relentlessly forward. Charon stood helpless. He looked on in mute anger as Hades' enforcers cracked whip and broke his resistance like straw.

When he landed, Charon received a brief memo from Hades giving him the afternoon off while the boat drydocked for repairs and a new anchor was forged. In the memo, Hades offered no rebuke, Charon noted; the Furies' action sufficed.

Charon mused while he waited. *What to do?*

In the hour it took to get the boat Styxworthy again, Charon had found an answer. He made a few phone calls and returned to his command elated.

Midway through the second return trip, Charon got another phone call from Hades.

"Who in Heaven put you up to this?" Hades barked.

"I beg your pardon, sir?"

"Dammit it, Charon, don't play coy with me — "

"I'm afraid I don't know — "

"Those are *your* demons sabotaging the bridge!"

"Sabotaging the — my, what a shocking development — "

"Tools broken, pylons splintered, turnbuckles loosened — "

"How dreadful. Maybe you should stop work, conduct an investigation. Maybe even drop the entire project — "

"Damn you, Charon — "

Suddenly, Hades interrupted himself, covered the phone mouthpiece, and spoke to someone else in his office. Charon couldn't hear the brief, muffled conversation.

When Hades came back on the line, his tone dripped nectar. "Charon, my dear captain, would you be so kind as drop by my office at your soonest convenience after you deliver your cargo?"

"I'd be more than delighted to do so, sir," Charon said, his cheery voice almost cracking with dread.

A change of events, no doubt. And it doesn't sound good.

Charon hung up and phoned his demon contact on the bridge sabotage crew. The news could not have been grimmer —

Poseidon!

Hades' brother Poseidon would take over the job and bring in his own loyal work-demons. He'd dismiss the others, including Charon's. Work would progress nonstop, efficiently.

Well, better Poseidon than Zeus, I guess. Now what?

Deep in thought, Charon paced the ferry boards, inbound and overloaded with doomed mortals, stepping on the occasional hand or foot. As he'd done earlier, he let his mind wander, picking up bits and pieces of talk from crew and passengers. Perhaps a plan would reveal itself to his subconscious. If not, he'd at least let the wails, moans, and curses lull him into a semblance of peace.

" — yelled at me, so I yelled right back," a mortal grunted between heaves on his oar to another rower.

" — then he hit me," he continued, "with his fist — and I hit him with a bat — and then he shot me — "

"You shoulda quit — " another voice said, "at the yelling stage — then you wouldn't be here."

"Couldn't quit, no way — the guy pissed me off."

"If everybody thought that way — we'd have World War Three."

Bingo!

Charon dashed to the helm, grabbed up a phone. He hesitated a moment to collect himself and took a deep breath. He called the operator.

"And to whom do you wish to speak to, sir?" the phone demon asked.

Charon heard the demon's involuntary gasp when he said the name.

"But, sir, such a call cannot be placed — "

"And why not?"

"Well, I've never heard of anybody — "

"First time for everything, my dear. Besides, you don't have the authority to *not* place the call."

The demon sighed and placed the call.

Charon was humming the theme to "Bridge On the River Kwai" when a voice came on the line.

"Yes?"

"You probably don't know me," Charon said. "We've never met. I'm Charon, boatman on the River — "

"Yes, I've heard of you. What do you want?"

Charon described the problem and his plan to resolve it.

"You're right," the voice said. "A bridge would upset the balance of power. And you're right about them being unable to use a bridge consecrated as holy. You're also right in believing I'd want to help stop their scheme. I do. But we've never worked together before — "

"My dear St. Michael," Charon said, "there's a first time for everything."

WITH FORKED TONGUE

I never pick up hitchhikers.

I quit picking up hitchhikers long ago when I quit being a hippie, cut my hair, got a job, got married, had a couple of kids, and got involved in politics. I'm divorced, the kids are gone, and so is most of my hair. I'm not in politics anymore and I started picking up hitchhikers again.

Especially Indians.

It began last summer. At the time, I was on the candidate's campaign staff — You Know Who. I handled things, you might say, in the Utah area, generally. With his usual foot-in-mouth candor, he said something stupid about Indians. You can't get elected president doing things like that. It prompted a protest rally in Wendover, and I went to try to put out the fire.

My boss, of course, was "regretfully unable to attend."

I think I did a good job, considering. I'm a good bullshitter. I got some press and maybe a few votes back in his pocket that he'd pissed away. Sometimes you can't tell.

It was a clear, cloudless day when I headed back to Salt Lake, the air above the Salt Flats shimmered in the heat. I had the top down on the Caddy and I was in a hurry to meet some damn deadline or other. I saw the Indian with his thumb out at the on-ramp.

I figured four things: One, this guy is just another bum looking for a hand-out, in which case, screw him. Two, he was one of the protesters and maybe I should pick him up and kiss ass for a few more votes. Three, he was planted there by the competition so that he could report that I was callous enough not to pick him up and therefore all the stuff I said back at the rally was a bunch of crap, or something along those lines. Four, he was planted there by the competition so that, if I did pick him up, he could maybe trick me into saying something stupid that could be used against my boss.

I'm quick. I knew the score. I picked him up.

He was a fat guy, maybe six-one, 300 pounds.

"Hi," he said, getting in. "I'm an Indian."

His skin was almond-brown and sweaty. Shiny blue-black hair tied in two braids hung to his shoulder blades. He smelled of cheap cologne. Not bad, just cheap.

He wore a pink plaid cowboy shirt, the kind with the pearl snaps. Clean jeans, scuffed cowboy boots. Pot belly. If he wore a belt, I couldn't tell.

"Hello," I said, starting back onto the road, "I'm — "

"A white guy. I can tell." He laughed. It sounded like the make-believe gun sound-effect kids make when they play cowboys and Indians. "Huh-uh-uh-uh-uh." You remember. "All you white guys look alike to me."

I laughed, dryly and a bit apprehensively, although his cheery smile showed no sign of hostility.

"You want a drink?" he asked, offering a bottle-shaped paper sack I hadn't noticed before.

"No, thank you."

"I like my wine," the hitchhiker said reverently. He took a long swallow, "Ahh"'ed, and wiped a dribble off his chin. Okay, so that wasn't where the tape recorder was hidden. I couldn't spot it. The guy was a pro.

"This is Mogan David," he said, eyeing the paper sack critically. "Too sweet and heavy. I like it light, dry, and slightly tart. A good Chablis. You know what I mean?"

"Uh huh." I know less about wine than I do about Indians. "Where're you going?" I asked.

"Delta Center. We're having a big pow-wow. All the tribes are gathering, sending delegates. It's pretty important. I'm a delegate."

I hid a smile. If there was a rally or something at the Delta Center, I'd have known. Maybe he wasn't a pro.

He told me the name of the tribe he represented. It sounded unfamiliar. Too many syllables. It wasn't Ute, Navajo, Bannock, or Shoshone. I couldn't place it. His name? Leon something. He mumbled. I let it pass. Probably phony.

"Uh-huh," I said.

"Funny thing," he said, taking another drink. "Indians have a thousand languages. So does the whiteman. The whiteman never learned how to talk with his brother. Indians invented the pow-wow and sign language. And smoke signals."

"Uh-huh."

"You got a smoke?" I gave him one.

"The Indians never really killed each other, you know. Not like the whiteman, I mean, big wars and all. We understood each other. You got a match?"

I handed him my lighter.

"Oh sure," he continued, lighting his cigarette and putting the lighter in his pocket, "we had our little spats. Naturally, people got hurt. But not many. Do you realize how difficult it is to kill a man on a horse with a little-bitty, home-made bow and arrow? Killing buffalo was tough enough. Mostly, for people, we'd count coup. That's where you slap them up 'side the head with a stick. Didn't hurt much but it sure would bruise the ego."

"Uh-huh."

"But that changed," he said, taking my lighter out of his shirt pocket and handing it back to me. "When the whiteman came, he gave us a lot. Smallpox. Beads. Funny hats. Firesticks. Firewater. Want a drink?"

"No, thank you."

"Custer. Kevin Costner. Christianity. We don't hunt buffalo anymore. We have 7-11 and food stamps. We don't count coup either. We're unionized. Today's Indian is really changed. We're busy with politics, bingo, minority rights, mineral rights. That sort of thing."

"What's the big pow-wow all about?" I asked, as casual as you please.

There was a pause, a long one. I thought: here it comes.

"Who're you voting for?" he asked.

"Nobody."

"Me too."

"Uh-huh."

"Ever heard an Indian say, 'Whiteman speak with forked tongue?'" He said it in a phony deep voice like a late night movie rerun Indian chief.

"Uh-huh."

"Indians invented that too." He took another drink.

"So, what's the pow-wow all about?" I pressed.

Again, the silence dragged on. But I was cool. I waited him out.

Finally, "You want a drink?"

"No, thank you."

He shrugged, finished off the contents of the bottle with a gurgle and a sigh, and tossed it onto the salt encrusted hardpan along the road.

"There was a time when Indians didn't litter," he said wistfully. "This land was our land. Now it's everybody's. So, it's okay. Know what I mean?"

"Uh-huh."

"Got a smoke?" I gave him one.

"Marlboro," he said, eyeing the cigarette critically. "Okay, I guess. But I prefer Newports. Prettier box."

"Uh-huh."

"Got a light?" I handed him my lighter. He lit up and put the lighter in his shirt pocket.

"So, what's the — " I began.

"Got a knife?" he finished.

"A knife?" I said, trying to keep cool. This was too much. I'm afraid my voice cracked. "No. I have some fingernail clippers. Why do you want a knife?"

"The pow-wow is strictly an Indian affair. Top secret. Only Indians allowed. I can't tell you about it unless I make you an Indian, a blood brother. Then it'd be okay."

"Uh-huh." Did I mention that I felt a little queasy?

"I take a knife and cut my thumb," he said. "Then you cut your thumb and we mix the blood. That makes us blood brothers so I can tell you our secrets."

"Uh-huh." Queasy. It was that damn rally barbecue.

"Just like the Lions, Kiwanis, Elks, or Mormons. Secret handshakes, that sort of thing. Only messier. Fingernail clippers wouldn't do. You have nice upholstery," he said.

"Well, if you can't tell me — " I began.

"What the hell, why not?" he finished.

He paused. I waited. The airport was just ahead, and downtown was just a few minutes beyond. The silence again dragged on uncomfortably long, and I wondered if he was going to say anything at all before we reached West Temple.

Finally, he said, "Have you ever noticed the president?"

"Uh-huh." Here it comes.

"Hell of a job. Strict requirements, not like the old Job Corps. You have to be rich, middle-aged, male. White."

"Uh-huh."

"And American. No foreigners allowed in the club. No, sir. There'll never be an Arab president. There won't be an Indian one either. We're the lost tribe, you know. You think voters would accept a Jew in the White House?"

"I don't know."

"Never happen. Catholic maybe, even Mormon, but not a Jew. Look at this guy who's running — "

"Which one?"

" — His family goes way back to the founding fathers. That's always good for a politician, founding fatherhood. Know what I mean?"

"But which — "

"Back then, before Manhattan, things were pretty good between the whites and Indians. We gave the whiteman corn and tobacco. Taught him how to plant, hunt, fish, trap, baste a turkey. He gave us beads and Bibles. Everybody got along just fine."

"But — "

"We taught the whiteman a lot about medicine too. When he came over on his little wooden boats, he didn't know a lot. They didn't have Medicare in those days. So when somebody got sick, they'd just cut him open to let all the bad blood and demons out. Sometimes that didn't work.

"So they'd call in the local medicine man. He'd come by, dance around, sing a few medical songs, shake his rattles, and give the patient something to drink. Usually cougar piss, owl or bear shit, or something foul like that. And the patient would usually get well. They probably got well just to avoid drinking any more medicine, but what the hell," he shrugged. "It worked."

"Uh-huh."

"My ancestors," he said, "they had a hell of a medicine man. A guy named Coyote Breath or something. He treated a lot of white people in the old days. General practitioner. Made teepee calls. Reasonable rates." He laughed.

"Uh-huh." I didn't laugh.

Another long pause. Then he said, "I bet you don't believe in magic, do you?"

"Well, no — "

"Figures. Most white people don't. You ask where the light comes from and they say, 'Flip the switch.' You ask why is there air and they say 'To blow up volleyballs with.'" Another laugh. "An old Bill Cosby joke. But when you get right down to it, nobody really knows. God, the Great Spirit, Lady Luck, the Tooth Fairy. Maybe black magic. You know what I mean?"

"Uh-huh."

"Anyway, according to the legend, this Coyote Breath gets called in by a white family who had a sick little kid. The kid looks like a terminal case, but the good doctor gives it his best shot. Dances up a storm, sings his best tunes, rattles, drums, and whistles the latest hits. Gives the patient his best raccoon turds or whatever. But the patient dies anyway. Que sera, sera. The white family gets angry and won't pay old Coyote Breath. They can't sue for malpractice, so they just refuse to pay."

"What did he want?"

"Probably just a couple of chickens or some beads or some firewater. Maybe he just wanted to sleep with their daughter. Something simple like that."

"What did he do?"

"Well, he gets pretty pissed off. He doesn't charge much, but he still has an overhead. So he lays a curse on them."

"A curse?"

"Yeah. And not just the family either — on the whole white settlement. Really pissed. Dances his nastiest curse jig, sings his foulest curse songs. Splatters animal crap all over everything and everybody. Shakes his rattle so hard it breaks and scatters beads everywhere. Really pissed."

"What happened?"

"It worked."

"Uh-huh."

"You know, the whiteman breeds like rabbits. They say that about Indians, but it's really the other way around. The whiteman's population goes up, the Indians' declines. Know what I mean?"

"About the curse — "

"It worked. Come spring or so, a lot of babies get born in the white settlement. Deformed, the whole lot. The white people get really pissed, so they massacre a few Indians, including old Coyote Breath."

"Uh-huh."

"Tough about those white kids. Deformed, really messed up. Different things. Some with too many fingers, not enough toes. Others cross-eyed, knock-kneed, double-jointed. Even hunchbacked. Weird stuff. No good, except as bell-ringers or circus freaks. And there weren't many bells back then and no circuses."

"How horrible."

"Yeah, I know what you mean. The outer deformities were weird, but the inner ones were worse. That wasn't clear until after some of the kids grew up. Sure, some died young but some grew up, got married, had kids. The kids had kids. And so on. With each generation, the deformities decreased. At least the outer ones did. The eyes became less crossed, the knees less knocked, the joints less double, the backs less hunched. And so on. You hardly notice it anymore."

"You mean — "

"Whiteman speaks with forked tongue," he pronounced in his late-night TV Indian voice.

"You mean — "

"Yeah. There's a little bit of truth in every legend. The unicorn, Santa Claus, gremlins. Know what I mean?"

"But who — "

"So we got an election coming up — "

"You mean — "

"That's why we're pow-wowing — "

"But who — "

"Family goes way back. Founding fatherhood, all that."

"But who — "

"Yes sir, big pow-wow. All the tribes are there."

"But who — "

"You know, there's no picture of this guy with his tongue stuck out? Not one."

"But who — "

"We could go on the war-path, count coup. But all that's changed. We'll hold rallies, news conferences, protest marches, maybe blockade a road. That sort of thing. Get the media there and get the word out."

"But who — "

"We'll demand he prove it ain't so. We'll force him to go on network TV. Can you imagine the guy, on election eve, with his tongue sticking out, on the six o'clock news?"

"But who — "

"'My fellow Americans: blaah!' That'll do. Got a smoke?"

I had a few left, so I gave him the pack.

"Thanks," he said, eyeing the pack critically. "Marlboros. Okay, I guess. I prefer Newports. Prettier box, you know." He put the pack in his shirt pocket along with my lighter. The Delta Center was just ahead. "Anywhere along here," he said, gesturing vaguely.

I stopped the car and he got out.

"S'cuse me," I said, "but who — "

"Thanks," he said, shutting the door with a little wave and walking briskly away. For a minute, I considered chasing him down, but there was traffic and I had this deadline.

Later, I watched the candidates on TV, all of them. I turned the sound down and watched their lips move. None of them really opened their mouths enough to tell for sure.

Nothing in the newspapers or magazines either.

And there was no pow-wow. I would've known.

Okay, so the guy was a phony. Phony tribe, phony name. No doubt, he was pulling my leg. Hell of a gag. Sometimes I laugh too.

But after I quit the campaign — I quit the next day, in fact — I kept trying to see. When they'd show up on TV — the candidates, I mean — I'd watch them, real close.

One is now president. Yes, I know who won — *but which one is he?*

THE BRASS BOTTLE

The elephant tiptoed as best he could on his hind legs toward his office. He wanted to get inside before being spotted by his secretary who wallowed in gossip in a small herd of secretaries at the water cooler down the hall.

It didn't work. Tiptoeing past the efficient Miss Crabtree was hard for anybody and even harder for the President of Hellucinations, Inc. J.S. Peck's pink pigmentation further handicapped him.

The door gave only a faint squeak as Peck eased it open, but Crabtree's tiny ears perked up, scattering a small cloud of tsetse flies. She looked up from her gossiping and waved a jolly blunt foot at him, flashing a massive jaw full of crooked teeth by way of a smile. He saw her excuse herself from the other hippopotami and start waddling toward her desk outside his office door.

Pretending not to notice his secretary, and cursing himself again for forgetting to fix the door squeak, he hurriedly entered his office and shut the door.

No expense had been spared in Peck's office. Deep bear skin rugs muffled his steps. Polished hardwood paneling reeked of wealth, influence. A huge desk sat like an altar at the far end of the cavernous room. The desktop held an intercom, cigar decanter, ashtray, pen set, and the Brass Bottle. The high-backed leather chair behind the desk sat a subtle one-inch higher than the low-backed wooden chair in front of it.

On one wall certificates, degrees, and awards hung in tasteful frames around a small, well-worn cat-o'-nine-tails mounted on a polished walnut plaque in the center.

On the other wall, a large window gave Peck an executive's view, when he wanted it, of downtown Hell thirty stories below.

Above the desk, always looking over Peck's shoulder, the Chairman's portrait dominated the room.

As he unbuttoned his overcoat, the intercom buzzed.

He sighed. Another day in Hell began.

He tapped the intercom "on" button. "Bad morning, Miss Crabtree," he said in his Happy Voice, the one he used in staff meetings, when he had to fire someone, when he had to grovel before the Chairman while getting his ass chewed, or when he had to make nice with Crabtree, "How are we today?"

"Bad morning to you too, sir," Crabtree bellowed. Peck winced, tapped the intercom volume down a few notches with his trunk, and flapped his ears in irritation.

"The Sanitation Department was spreading ashes and garbage neck deep to a giraffe all over Hell, right in the middle of commute traffic this morning, sir," she prattled. "It's a good thing you came in late — I mean, later."

"Yes, well." Peck buffed a tusk with a handkerchief. "Got held up in a massacre. Have I missed anything?"

"I heard Recruiting is expecting some big shot today."

"Oh? Who?"

"Well, sir, I don't know— "

"You don't know? Beelzebub's beard, Crabtree, you're *supposed* to know."

"Well, golly, sir, I — "

"Stop blubbering and find out. If Recruiting has snared a bigwig, there'll be a reception. I want to know who, when, and where. I'm no doubt invited. A memo from the Entertainment Committee — "

"There's been no memo, sir — "

"No memo?" His tail snapped with irritation. "Nonsense, Crabtree. Heavens, if they're expecting important recruits, I'm always invited. You ever heard of a general, president, or a pope who didn't have nightmares?"

"Well, I can't say — "

"And guess who in Hell is in charge of nightmares. And psychoses, neuroses, hallucinations, and delirium tremens and — "

"You, sir?"

"Look, Crabtree." Peck snorted a blubbery sigh through his trunk. "Somebody screwed up somewhere. Maybe Mail Service. Get on the phone and check it out — "

"Yes, sir. Right away, sir."

"And stop calling me 'sir,'" he shouted, slapping the "off" button. He began pacing.

Must remember to call Personnel, see if they can get me an aardvark or a sloth. Something that didn't wallow in mud, wasn't green, and didn't smell like swamp gas.

Peck hated when she said "sir." She whistled through her forest of teeth and it hurt his ears. At first, he tried to train her to use the more subservient "Yes, Mr. Peck," or the informal "Yes, J.S." But she whistled on those too, so he gave up.

He finished removing his overcoat and hat and picked up his beloved old cat-o'-nine-tails from its wall mount. He gave it a sharp crack. *Haven't lost my touch.* He smiled.

"Bigwig coming to town, huh?" Crack. "Greetings, general." Crack. "Hello, Your Excellency." Crack. "Howdy, Mr. President." Crack. "Good day, Comrade Chairman." Crack. "How's it hanging, Your Holiness?" Crack.

For an instant, Peck fantasized about whipping Crabtree. Instead, he walked over to the desk and used the whip butt to deftly pop the "on" button. His satisfied grin became a grimace as Crabtree bellowed at him before he could turn the volume down.

"Yes, sir?"

"Crabtree, I'm in a bad mood. I am 'in' for all callers."

"Yes, sir."

"Great. Now, what's on the calendar for today?"

"Nothing, sir — "

"Nothing?"

"Yes, sir — "

"No appointments? Meetings? Calls? Letters to sign?"

"No, sir — "

"What about that reception?"

"Still working on it, sir."

"Well, let me know first thing. What about the mail? Anything for me? My new whip catalog come in yet?"

"No catalog, sir. A few bills. Shall I bring them in —? "

"Nononono, that won't be necessary, thank you, Crabtree. Just call me when you find out about that reception. Or if I have any visitors. Or whatever."

He punched off the intercom, returned the whip to its mount on the wall and began pacing again, tail swishing in agitation.

"Third day in a row," he honked.

He picked up the Brass Bottle and looked at the legend on it without really seeing it. He grunted, a disgusted noise in his throat, and plopped it back on the desk.

"Big promotion, big job, big salary, big office," he muttered. "Big deal. I should have told them to stuff it up their proboscises."

He walked to the window. He could smell the sulfur, and through gaps in the smoke and shimmering heat, he saw movement on the street far below. He watched a herd of naked lawyers digging holes in the street with silver spoons. A bull supervised. The bull sat on a slagheap reading a Daredevil comic book, now and then absently flicking his whip at a lawyer.

Look at them. Dig a hole, fill it up, twenty-four hours a day for eternity. At least they're not bored.

The intercom interrupted.

"Yes, Crabtree, what is it?"

"It's about the reception, sir — "

"Ah, yes, the reception. What did you find out?"

"There is no reception, sir," she said, as meekly as she could. "It was just a civil war somewhere in Africa, and a drought. A few hundred thousand Ethiopians are coming down. I made a mistake, sir."

"Crabtree, in this business you don't make mistakes."

"Well, I misunderstood, sir — "

"Crabtree, in this business you don't misunderstand."

"Well, I'm sorry, sir — "

"Crabtree, in this business you never have to say you're sorry."

"You have a visitor, sir."

"Crabtree, in this bus — What?"

"You have a — "

"A visitor? For me? I mean, who is he? Or she? Or it? What do they want?"

"It's a Mr. Horn, from Advertising. He says it's urgent." Peck tried but couldn't remember him.

"Shall I tell him you're busy?" Crabtree asked.

"Nononono, don't do that. Just a minute." Peck snapped off the intercom, grabbed some papers from a desk drawer, and scattered them across the desk. He pushed the Brass Bottle off to one side, rolled up his sleeves, loosened his tie, and flicked on the intercom.

"Miss Crabtree," he said in his Very Important voice, "I can take a minute to see Mr. Horn now, if you please."

He popped off the intercom before she could answer.

There was a gentle knock at the door.

"Come in, come in," Peck trumpeted.

The door squeaked open a few inches. Through the crack a polished horn protruded, followed by its owner, a blue rhinoceros wearing wire-rimmed spectacles.

Mr. Horn, from Advertising, crept into Peck's office like he was entering a shrine. He wore a simple, conservative brown suit. He kneaded a matching, unimposing brown hat in his hooves. Peck stifled a temptation to yell "Boo!" just to scare the Beelzebub out of him.

"M-m-mister — " the rhinoceros stuttered.

"Peck," Peck finished for him. "I know. And you're Horn, right? From Advertising, right?"

"R-r-right."

"Right. Have a seat, Horn. What in Hell do you want?"

Horn sat on the edge of the seat in front of the desk. He pushed his glasses higher on his horn and nodded at the clutter on Peck's desk. "If you're busy — "

"Nonsense." Peck opened a drawer, swept papers into it with his trunk, and closed the drawer. "Well, I'm always busy, but no executive is worth his sulfur if he can't spare time for his workers. My door is always open, that's my motto."

Horn smiled and nodded, silent.

"Well, what can I do for you, Horn?"

The rhino dabbed at his forehead with a crisply folded handkerchief. "Well, sir, I hoped you could help me — " He gulped. " — get a transfer."

"Transfer?"

The rhino almost jumped. The pale blue hide around his snout darkened a few shades. He nodded.

Peck felt himself flush and his muscles tighten. He lowered his tusks as if for combat. He snorted. He didn't recognize the feeling at first, and it frightened him a little. Then he remembered — an adrenaline rush. Long ago, while in the field, he lived for that rush. Danger, it meant — a challenge, or a predator.

But that couldn't be. Horn is a gazelle in rhino clothing. No threat. So why the heady rush? Age, maybe?

Still, a transfer request was routine, handled at the department head level, or by Personnel. Why would Horn bring such a routine matter to him? Unless...

The rhino sat tapping a hind leg, kneading his hat, sweating. Peck stifled a smile, enjoying the thrill of potential danger, a sensation he hadn't felt for a long time. If Horn represented a threat, even in some way he didn't fully recognize, so be it, Peck decided. He was ready.

"Have a cigar?" Peck said. Again, the rhino almost jumped.

"No, thank you — s-sir."

Peck scooped a cigar from the decanter with his trunk and lit it with a gold pocket lighter. "Please, Horn." He blew little smoke rings. "Call me Peck. Just between us boys, I hate being called 'sir.' Too formal. Call me 'J.S.'"

"Call you J-J — "

"Yeah. J.S."

"Gosh, I never expected — "

"Cut the crap, rhino," Peck barked. "I'm onto your game."

"G-game —? "

"Figure on jumping the chain of command, getting my help to boot your boss so you can move up the corporate ladder, huh? Let me tell you something, rhino. We have places in Hell for snitches, brown-nosers, and snakes-in-the-grass — "

"Sir," Horn puffed, "I am a rhinoceros, not a snake."

The vehement interruption surprised both Peck and Horn. Both sat gap jawed, blinking. *He knows I can roast his ass for a rogue*, Peck thought. He decided to hold his ground, find out what Horn was made of.

At last, Horn sputtered an apology. "I'm sorry for my outburst, sir. I meant no disrespect. I hold you and your office in the highest regard, believe me. I've been under a lot of stress, so I'm afraid such an outburst was long past due. I'm afraid my usefulness to the company has been compromised. So, by your leave, I'll submit my resignation."

Horn's response was contrite, but it wasn't the groveling, sniveling panic Peck had expected. Instead, it was delivered calmly, with dignity and pride. *He looks like a sheep, but he's standing his ground like an alpha male.*

Horn rose and turned to exit, but Peck rushed around the desk and intercepted him, putting himself between Horn and the door, putting an arm around the rhino, making soothing noises, and herding him back to his chair.

"Well," Peck began again when they had both sat, "did you talk to your department head about a transfer?"

The rhino shook his snout, dabbed at his forehead with his handkerchief, and blubbered.

"Relax," Peck said, "and tell me all about it."

Horn took a deep, ragged breath and began his tale. Peck didn't interrupt.

"I'm chief script writer in Advertising," Horn said. "I supervise a 30-demon staff writing nightmares for ad executives. The department is overworked due to satellite and cable TV proliferation and the Internet. We even have our own website.

"A few weeks ago, a soap company announced plans for a new product: 'New! Improved! Lemony Fresh! Washes Whiter Than White! Gentle on Your Hands! Environmentally Safe!' Routine stuff. I assigned two alligators, new to the staff, to slap together some nightmares for the ad people doing the account.

"The job was ideal for cub nightmare writers. Since it was a routine task, it'd be good practice for them, until they got the hang of the job, and

I'd get a feel for how they handled it. I gave them an old TV script to use as a model. A classic, safe, tried and true. It had prompted several suicides in 1952."

Horn sighed. "It should have been simple, but it wasn't. One of the two junior staffers was the nephew of the department head, a purple alligator named Lessard."

Peck knew Lessard. He was surprised Lessard had relatives that Lessard hadn't eaten yet.

"Huey, the little reptile," Horn said, "went over my horn and complained to his uncle. Lessard came to me with the script written by his nephew and complained it was too routine a task for a rare talent like Huey.

"I admit I was frightened, sir. I reassigned Huey to a more prominent job — one involving political advertising in a presidential election. Things fell apart. Huey got the wrong person elected, the ad people slept well, voter turnout was high, and so on.

"Meanwhile the rest of the staff grumbled at me for pushing Huey to such a job, bypassing more talented senior writers. And Lessard blamed me for both his nephew's failure and the erosion in staff morale."

"A disturbing development," Peck said. "I appreciate you coming forward, Horn. I'll start an immediate, thorough, and discreet investigation into Lessard's qualifications. Then fire his ass. Relax, Horn. I won't betray your confidence. You did the right thing in coming to me. Things will run smoothly in Advertising from now on, I assure you."

Horn had relaxed during his narrative, sitting back in the chair. "That's big of you, sir. Now, about a transfer — "

"Transfer?"

"My original reason for coming to see you."

"Or is it really Lessard's job you want?"

Horn shrugged. "Well, I'm surely more qualified than — "

"Aha!" Peck slapped the desk with a front foot. "So you want Lessard's job after all. Diabolical, Horn, I have to admit. You had me going there for a while — "

"But, sir, I don't want Lessard's job. Really. I want a transfer."

"But with Lessard out of the way — "

"Lessard isn't the problem. He's just the last human over the Styx. I've been in advertising for eighteen hundred years, but I hate it. My creativity is being wasted."

Horn scooted forward on his chair as he explained his hobby. "After spending eight hours a day writing ad executive nightmares and supervising other writers doing the same, I go home and I write — delirium tremens."

DTs. Peck's old field.

"DTs huh," Peck said, his interest piqued. "Why DTs?"

"Well, I realize writing hallucinations for alcoholics is dirty work, nothing compared to the prestige of advertising nightmares or even psychotic delusions — "

"Nonsense, Horn. DTs doesn't have the reputation it deserves among the other departments, but there's great work to be done there, believe me. I used to be a rank and file hallucination myself, you know."

"I know."

"You do?"

"I got bored with advertising after only two hundred years on the job. Then I read one day in a supermarket tabloid about Hell's newest sensation — the daring, handsome, swashbuckling Pink Elephant. I became an avid fan, following his every adventure. I even tried to dye my hide pink.

"You were the greatest, sir. I decided I wanted to be a great hallucination like you were."

"I was pretty good then, wasn't I?"

"From alley bum terror to President of Hellucinations, Inc. in under a century." Horn shook his head in amazement. "And you received the Brass Bottle, too."

"Yeah, I did. Ever see it?"

"I've seen pictures, but — "

Peck nodded casually to the Brass Bottle on the far edge of the desk, still half buried in papers. "There it is."

Horn gasped. He removed his glasses, buffed them, put them back on, and leaned forward to peer at the Bottle.

"Here in the room with me," he whispered, jaw slack. "How could I have missed it?"

"Bad lighting." Peck shrugged. "Nerves. I hardly ever notice it myself."

Horn was in rapture.

"Go ahead," Peck said, feeling magnanimous. "Pick it up."

Peck was sure Horn was going to wet his pants. But the rhino hesitated only a moment, then tenderly raised the Bottle to the light.

He solemnly read the legend printed on it. "To Johan Sebastian Peck, The Pink Elephant. The Best Damned Barroom and Alley Hallucination Producer, Designer, Director, and Performer in Hell."

Peck said nothing, puffing on his cigar, basking in Horn's admiration, another sensation long missed.

At last, the rhino set the Bottle back on the desk. He dusted it with his handkerchief and sat back, a rapt glow on his face.

"Horn, you've flattered your way into a transfer." Peck reached for the intercom. "I'll have you out in the field by lunch."

The rhino let out a yelp, startling Peck. "This is the most exciting moment of my life," Horn cried, clapping his hooves together.

He stood and sat, stood and sat.

"Mephisto's mustache, Horn." Peck laughed. "Get a grip on yourself."

The rhino sat on the chair edge, his excitement barely under control. "Sir — *J.S.* — I wonder if — that is, would you mind if I asked — "

"A question? Advise? Ask away, Horn. Like I said, my door is always open."

A pause. "What was it like?"

Peck's mirth faded in a wave of maudlin nostalgia. He walked to the window, looked out, and spoke as if to himself, lost in reverie.

"I started work when I was about your age, restless for glory, action, adventure. I felt destined to be a big star.

"Boot camp was Rome; my instructor, Bacchus himself. But I was unimpressed with the sodden old wino. I was ready to set Hell aflame with my new ideas."

"I was naive." Peck turned, facing Horn.

"One man's hallucination is another man's reality, somebody once said. I got hit with a strong reality dose on my first solo. A humbling experience.

"I worked an old soldier, a Gaul vet. The legionnaire told war stories to some unemployed, drunk young plebeians in a pub.

"The old soldier was a damn good storyteller, a natural liar, even when he was drunk as Hell. He had his audience's attention as he related daring feats in the First Punic War. Just as he reached the bloody climax of his story, I leaped into his line of vision, screaming blood-curdling curses.

"The old vet stopped and stood frozen, eyes popped open, wine dribbled down his sagging chin. The room went quiet. I expected shrieks of panic, maybe heart attacks.

"Instead, the soldier pointed to me and said, 'Now you know why Hannibal lost,' and everybody laughed.

"I slunk from the pub, blushing pink in embarrassment. I never lost the color.

"It was a humbling experience, especially in group critique afterwards. Laughable, my peers called the phony Greek accent. The makeup was hopeless. And the ridiculous pink skin couldn't scare a rabbit.

"I almost quit.

"Instead, I gave it one more try. I went back to the same pub naked, pink, and scriptless. I spoke simple Latin — and scared the shit out of an old patrician. Nothing spectacular. But it gave me the confidence to go on and become The Pink Elephant, President of Hellucinations, Inc.

"Lesson number one, Horn, is be yourself. Copywriter, hallucination, demon, human, rhino — whatever."

Horn nodded, rapt.

"Lesson number two: A famous demon once said, 'Success is getting up more times than you get knocked down.'"

"I'll remember that," Horn said.

"The third lesson is the most important."

"What's that?"

"Have fun!" Peck gave a little skip as he remembered the fun he'd had. "The thrill of taking on a whole roomful of drunks at once! The travel! The pubs of London! Paris when it gets plastered! New Year's Eve! An Irish brawl! Octoberfest! Prohibition! The Superbowl! Worldcon! Oh, and not just Republicans, lawyers, bankers, TV talkshow hosts and other bums, mind you! Artists! Poets, painters, movie-makers, rock stars! Van Gogh, Edgar Allen Poe, Twain, Ellison, King, Hemingway, Hendrix, Morrison! I was there!"

He paused, ears and trunk drooping, his euphoria suddenly gone. "Was." He sighed and slumped back into his chair.

"Was?"

"It's changed." Peck reached for his cigar, thought better of it, and slumped back again. "I don't know. I haven't been in the field since the Cubs won the pennant. I can remember it was exciting, vital, stimulating, creative — pick an adjective. I can remember how it felt, but I can't feel it anymore."

Peck sighed.

Horn ahemed in the sudden silence, shifted, pushed his glasses back up his horn, and tried a weak laugh. "Well, J.S., you've certainly earned your reward. The Brass Bottle, the biggest job in Hell, this office — "

"Kicked upstairs."

" — Influence, power, prestige, a pretty secretary — "

"Hell of a reward."

" — and peace and quiet. Lots of quiet."

"And boredom. Don't forget boredom."

"Well, look at it this way, J.S.," Horn chirped, "you've earned a rest — "

"Rest, my ass." Peck frowned. "Do you think I've lost my touch, is that it?"

"Oh, no, not at all. It's just that, well, time passes, things change — "

"Horn, no matter what time it is, I'm still the best. Always have been, always will be."

"Oh, I know, sir. It's just that, well, when the body ages, reaction time slows down — "

"Slows down?"

"An elephant your age, all the excitement — "

"I'm as good as I've ever been — "

" — the younger hallucinations are doing wonderful work — "

"Fairy tales," Peck shouted, slamming his trunk against the desk and standing. He paced. "They steal their stuff from Disney. Couldn't scare a butterfly. Don't know hyperbole from a hyena. Wouldn't know a metaphor if it bit them on the ass — "

"I'm sorry, sir," Horn cowered. "I didn't mean — "

"Nononono, Horn, no apology needed. You just made me realize how much I miss it. Lucifer, how I miss it."

"Too bad you couldn't — " Horn said quietly. He paused.

"Couldn't what?" Peck turned on Horn. "Couldn't go back? Why, Hell's bells, Horn, who do you think you're talking to? I could be on my way quicker than you could say 'Jack the Ripper.' Back where I belong. Back where I could be creative, useful — alive."

"Well," Horn squeaked, "I suppose it would make a nice vacation — "

"Vacation?" Peck bellowed. "Vacation?" He stood above Horn, front feet on hips, ears fluttering in agitation, tail snapping. Suddenly, he froze, entranced by some inner voice.

Horn cowered and gulped, waiting.

"So you want a transfer, Horn?"

"Please, sir, if you could — "

"Done." Peck moved around behind the desk. "Another lesson, Horn. Always listen to your hunches." He flicked on the intercom. Horn watched, blinking.

"Crabtree," Peck said, "take some notes." He spoke before she could reply. "I'm heading out, going back to the field. I'm transferring myself — permanently. Clear? Mr. Horn is also transferring. He's taking over my office. He's your boss from now on, understand? You handle the paperwork. I haven't got time. I have important work to do. Goodbye."

Peck snapped off the intercom without waiting for an answer and stood.

"I'm leaving the Brass Bottle for you as an inspiration, Horn." He put on his coat and hat. "Take over. You think you're clever enough to fool me, think you're being subtle. Right or wrong — and I'm not saying which I think it is — that tells me you've got alpha male stuff.

"Me, I guess I'm still a rogue." He shrugged. "My lot in life."

He picked up his whip and flicked it, smiled at the sharp snap. "But not a bad life. Goodbye."

With that, Peck turned and left.

*

Horn sat wide-eyed in the large, suddenly silent room.

At last he took a breath, stood and straightened his vest.

He smiled.

He paraded slowly through his new office, adjusting the Chairman's portrait, spitting out the window, adjusting the pen set on the already neat desk.

He sat in the large chair behind his new desk and caressed the thick chair arms. He took up Peck's forgotten cigar and sniffed it. He leaned back in the chair, put his hooves up on the desk, and puffed.

He turned on the intercom. "Helen?"

"Yes, Bobby," Crabtree crooned.

"It worked just like I said. A stroll through the swamp."

"I never doubted you, dear. Shall I come in?"

"First things first." Horn blew smoke rings. "Get a memo to Lessard. He's fired. Then get Maintenance to change the name on the door. I want it done by noon. Then come in. Don't bring your notebook. You won't need it."

Crabtree giggled and Horn grinned.

He turned off the intercom and his smile faded.

"You think you're clever enough to fool me," the elephant had said. *Was he, really? Had he?*

Horn thought about it for a moment. He finally shrugged —

— and tossed the Brass Bottle into the waste basket.

THE WAITING GAME

Six for poker, the usual Saturday night bunch. Peter, Moses, Adam, Gabriel, and Mary shuffle into their usual seats. Jesus' chair is empty.

"So, where's His Nibs?" Adam asks.

"Walkabout," Peter says. "Don't expect him to show."

The others grumble variations of their usual take on the subject of His frequent absences. Jesus does it a lot, taking time to visit the mortal plane, walk about among the natives, get a feel for what's going on among them. A game of His own peculiar design. He did it other days often enough, but He found walking about on the Earth, and going to and fro upon it, seemed to offer a particularly brilliant flash and zest on Saturday nights. Humankind seemed to tingle with leashed tension, but on Saturday nights, the tension often snaps and people do the most extraordinary things. Interesting things.

So Jesus walks about. And watches.

"Five to three he gets back before we fold." Gabriel favors his companions with a toothy smile, the gold incisor flashing like something from a pagan idol, a single gold loop earring bobbing from a fleshy ear under his bald dome, just touching his shoulder. Neckless. A black Buddha with a $1000 suit, a shit-eating grin, a pimp's jewelry and The Horn, ever within easy reach, balanced on one knee, clutched in many-ringed stubby fingers.

"Make it even up and you're on." Mary, sitting on a pillow to soften the hardwood chair bottom, shifts her weight, and sets a stack of chips aside. Gabriel matches the stack.

Mary is forever pregnant, symbolically but all too painfully, and the Saturday night game with the boys is one of few stimulating diversions available to her. She often chuckles at the irony of the ancient, chauvinistic role she's forced to play as the Mother Goddess — mixed metaphors — superimposed on her free will, and suppressing it, which, if turned loose, would permit her to jump Adam and screw his lights out.

She eyes the boy across the table and gives him her most alluring smile. She tries to make it seductive, but it comes out beatific. As usual. Genetics.

"Deal." Adam picks at a zit on his chin. He doesn't notice Mary. Not his type. Too old.

Adam is too young to be in the back room of The Half-Acre, the hottest nightspot in heaven, where Gabe and the boys hang out, killing time. Knocking back a few brewskis, shooting a little stick, talking trash, eyeing the babes. Playing a little poker on Saturday night.

Waiting.

But the boys let Adam in because while he isn't as old as the angels, and while he's forever sixteen, he's the oldest human in the ant farm. That gives him a certain status with the babes, and he picks them up and lays them down with ease and grace. Built, he is, and hung. The others are jealous, especially Gabriel, who cops to a stereotypical image that black guys are supposed to have huge dongs. Gabriel's dick is smaller than his pinky. He doesn't let on he feels inadequate, but he doesn't show up at the spa very often.

Adam, racist yuppie, looks for opportunities to get on Gabe's case. Gabe would like to choke the shit out of the pretty man-child, but everybody's actions are governed, dictated from An Unassailable Source, even angels. Gabe's digs at Adam are subtle and, he thinks, more satisfying.

Peter deals, green eyeshade bobbing above his narrow face. Moses cuts. Of course.

He manifests in an alleyway just behind Queen Bee Liquors, "Where the Ladies Can Shop," according to the small sign above the back door, faded and peeling with age. He inhales the smell of urine, stale booze, mildew, and rotting vegetation. The bleak street is more concealed in shadows than revealed by a small light above another doorway down the alley. Rows of overfilled trashcans, lumpy mounds of detritus lying here and there. Street traffic sounds from beyond the alley mouth.

It's a warm night. Los Angeles. Or maybe San Diego.

A shot rings out. As usual.

Almost every time He does a Saturday night walkabout, He hears gunfire. Sometimes it doesn't happen until just before He's ready to leave, sometimes He never sees who did what to whom, sometimes He doesn't hear the screams or wait around for the sirens, but it usually happens.

This time it happens seconds after His manifestation. He grunts in appreciation. It'll be a stimulating evening.

Two shots, muffled, from inside the liquor store, a small caliber handgun. Pop. Pop. Then a scream, a woman's, a wail of grief and anger, and two more shots. Pop. Pop. He walks toward the back door, bends down, pulls His long, straight hair back and presses His ear to the door.

He hears swearing in a cracked, adolescent, male voice. He hears shuffling on a tile floor, thumps and bumps in the night. He hears an old cash register *ka-ching* open, and rattles and scrapes as the bandit rifles it. Heavy breathing, swearing.

"Hold it right there, mister." A policeman silhouetted in the alley against the light from the street beyond, and the bubblegum machine atop a black and white pulsing red, red, red, red across the dirty jungle alleyscape. He sees light glint from the gun pointed at Him in the policeman's outstretched hands, hears the quaver in the man's voice. A rookie, maybe. Never shot anybody before. Maybe.

He straightens, careful not to move too fast, to avoid alarming the nervous cop. From inside the liquor store, He hears shouts. The other cop has confronted the robber, ordered him to surrender.

Sounds of rage and fear explode into the alleyway from inside the liquor store, and scuffling.

"Shit." The nervous cop points with his gun from Him to a spot across the alley, against a slimy brick wall. "Step aside. Away from the door."

He complies.

The nervous cop goes to the back door, tries the knob. He holsters his gun and bashes his shoulder into the door twice. The door cracks but holds.

Suddenly the door bursts open, so fast and hard it knocks the cop off balance and he falls on his ass. Out runs the robber, a skinny black kid in cheap tennies, jeans, an Oakland Raiders jacket, and his face a wide-eyed mask of fear. Five-five, maybe a hundred-ten pounds. Fifteen to seventeen years old. No facial hair, no visible scars or tattoos. The cop, looking up from where he'd fallen, in the light from inside the store and the fainter light from the street at the alley mouth, sees the boy's hands are empty. No gun; he'd dropped it.

He watches the cop and robber from across the alley, standing in shadow.

The robber turns to run, stumbles on a soggy trash glob in the alley and falls. He tries to get up again —

As the cop rises, reaches to unholster his gun, and calls out, "Hold it, kid — "

As the other cop steps into the doorway, braces himself with a wide stance, aims his gun at the robber —

As the robber tries to stand, falls back down on his ass, raises hands above his head, eyes wide, focused on the cop and the gun in the cop's hands, aimed at him —

As the robber cries in a fear-choked throat, "Don't shoot, please don't shot, pleasepleaseplease — "

As the cop lets fly.

Pop. Pop.

And the boy's chest explodes in a fine mist, visible as a flash of silvery rain in the light from the open liquor store back door and the lesser light from the street beyond the alley mouth. The boy jerks back at the impact of the .38 caliber slugs smashing into his sternum at less than fifteen feet. He twitches a moment, gasping and gurgling, and dies.

"Omigod." The nervous cop stands, clutching his mouth, ready to puke. "You killed him, Frank. You didn't have to — "

"Little fucker did the old man right in the face. Then he did the old lady, point blank. He almost did me too."

"Frank, he didn't have a gun. You shot him in cold — "

"Self defense, Thad-me-boy. I saw him pointing a gun at me. I saw him. Didn't you?"

"Frank, I don't know — "

"Didn't you? See him aim it at me? What looked like a gun? You saw it too. Didn't you?"

"Uh, yeah, Frank, I saw it. Yeah. Looked like a gun. But, Frank — "

"No witnesses. Just us. Okay? Okay?"

"But, Frank — " the nervous cop tilts his head toward Him, still standing in the shadows.

Watching.

And Frank notices Him for the first time.

"Jesus," Frank mutters through gritted teeth, and He answers; "Yes?"

Frank doesn't hear, or chooses to ignore what he heard. "Who is he?" he asks Thad-me-boy.

"Lookout for the perp, I think. I saw him standing by the back door when I got here."

"Shit." Frank starts to holster his gun, hesitates. Then, deliberately, he aims it at Him.

"Frank, don't — "

"You. Over here." Frank gestures with the gun.

He walks the few steps from across the alley to within half dozen feet of Frank and Thad-me-boy.

"What's your name?" Frank's tone is husky with menace. He's still breathing hard from the struggle in the liquor store. A slight paunch and too many years on the streets.

He doesn't answer Frank, plays it dumb, expression neutral, unchanged. Frank holsters his gun, reaches out and grabs His collar, jerking hard. Frank's breath smells of mustard. And alcohol.

"I said, what's your name, punk."

"Not our job, Frank." Thad-me-boy pulls at Frank's fists, knotted in His robe front. "Let's just take him in. Why don't you make the call? I'll cuff him. Okay, Frank?"

Frank is still nose-to-nose with Him, Frank's grip still firm on the robe, eyes narrowed, panting breath rank.

"Okay, Frank? Okay?"

"Get his gun." Frank says it without taking his glare off Him.

"Whose gun? You mean — "

"The perp's gun, Thad-me-boy. Get it."

"The perp's gun? What do you want with — "

"Get it."

Thad-me-boy mutters something in a shaky voice, goes into the liquor store, and gets the gun. Frank holds Him steady all the while, locked eye to eye, unflinching. But then, He hasn't tried to make him flinch. He's been trying to hold His breath.

"Here it is, Frank. What are you going to do with it, Frank? We should have left it right there — "

Eyes still locked on Him, Frank grabs the gun from Thad-me-boy's hand and extends it, butt first, toward Him.

"Take it," Frank commands.

He plays the dumb game, expressionless, as Frank repeats the command.

"Hey, what are you doing, Frank?"

"Don't worry, Thad-me-boy. It's jammed. That's how come the perp didn't do me, like he did mom and pop in there."

Frank grabs His hand, presses the perp's gun into it. He doesn't resist, holds the gun limply, pointing toward the ground, toward His own bare feet.

Frank backs up two steps, unholsters his gun.

"No, Frank, wait a minute, you can't do it, you can't shot him in cold blood, c'mon, Frank — "

"Punk saw me do the perp." Frank aims the gun. "I got to do the punk."

"Frank, please."

"Am I going to have a problem with you, Thad-me-boy?" Frank looks at Thad-me-boy, eyes murderous. The gun barrel turns away from Him toward Thad-me-boy —

"No, Frank, just — "

— just a little toward him —

"Am I?"

— just enough.

"No, Frank. No problem from me. I saw the gun, just like you said. I saw it. No problem. No problem."

Frank turns back toward Him and points the gun. He keeps the hand with the perp's gun aimed at the ground while He raises the other hand, the left one, the empty one, palm out.

"Jesus." Thad-me-boy points.

"Yes?" He answers, adding a slight smile, for Thad-me-boy's sudden illumination.

"Frank, look at his hands. Look at his feet. Look at his face." Thad-me-boy just begins to realize; and in an instant, his whole life changes. "Frank, I think I know who — "

Pop. Pop.

The gun's bark startles Thad-me-boy and he stifles a scream.

In the instant after he fires his gun, Frank's eyes go wide, his jaw drops and he lowers the gun, hand shaking.

"Jesus — "

"Like I said — "

"Can't be. I saw — "

"I saw it too."

"What did you see?"

Frank thinks a moment, watches as the two butterflies that emerged from his gun barrel when he fired it at Him flutter away down the alley toward the street and the strobing red lights beyond, watching the empty spot a few feet away where the punk had stood a moment before, a punk who looked like —

"Nah." Frank shakes his head. "I didn't see anything. The perp acted alone."

"He acted alone. Right. Just him. Just the perp, alone. We didn't see, we didn't see — what we thought we saw."

"Didn't see anything."

"Yeah. Right." But Thad-me-boy will never forget.

He materializes in His usual seat, hands folded in His lap, expression serene.

"Just in time for one last hand." Peter shuffles.

Peter and Moses have the largest stack of chips in front of them.

Adam sits scowling behind a meager stack. Mary is down a little, and Gabriel looks like he'd broke even.

"You owe me." Gabriel favors Mary with his shit-eating grin, scoops up the chips they'd set aside earlier.

Moses cuts.

"So, what's happening down there?" Peter deals. "They still busting my balls at the Gate to get in?"

Gabriel loses his grin, looks serious, one hand caressing The Horn, a nervous gesture. "Yeah, what's going down?"

Adam snorts. "Dog eat dog." He scowls at his cards. "Man eat man. Same old shit, I'll bet."

Jesus is silent, looking at His cards.

"Well?" Moses strokes his beard.

"Yeah, out with it." Mary looks annoyed.

Jesus sighs, shakes His head, brow furrowed, looking at His cards with disgust. He waggles the fingers of one hand at the cards, a magician's gesture, looks again and nods in satisfaction, smiling.

"He's bluffing," Adam says.

"He knows the rules," Moses says.

"He can't cheat," Peter says. "Can't do it."

"Yeah, but he can bluff," Adam says.

"C'mon, play cards," Mary says. "It's just a game."

"Yeah," Jesus says. "Just a game."

MURPHY'S LUCK

Okay, I guess you could call me a fairy godfather if you want to, or maybe a guardian angel, whatever. Me, I call myself Terrence O'Brian, and I'm a professional murphy. A pretty good one too, if you ask me.

Sometimes, us murphys act in strange ways our wonders to perform. Let me tell you about the murphy I done for my joe that got us here in the clink; makes me glad to be dead.

A murphy. I don't know where the name came from but it stuck. Maybe from back when whoever thought up murphys first thought them up. Maybe some guy named Murphy thought it up. Maybe they did it to have something for us to do after we croaked if we wasn't into harps or choirs. I don't know. I flunked reform school and I got a C-minus in murphy school.

Anyways, I sure as hell wasn't cutting it as a dead person so I'm glad they put me back on the street murphying. I hate harp music. Bor-ring. I guess somebody noticed and took me under their wing and steered me toward the murphy school.

Don't get the idea it's been easy. Murphying takes some skills your average spirit don't got. And I got them skills, I learned on the street.

So when I latched onto him, my "joe" as we call them, I thought I'd picked the perfect candidate who needed some luck.

He's a pretty average joe, most ways. In fact, that's his name. Joe. Joe Murphy, in fact. Hell of a coincidence. Maybe that's why I decided to be his murphy. Makes me laugh every time I think about it.

Let me tell you how I found him.

I'd been cruising the Downs where I used to drop a few on the ponies, figuring maybe I'd find somebody down on their luck, pockets turned inside out, shoulders slumped, shoes holey. I'd know the look, being as I'd had it myself a few times back when.

I heard somebody call his name — " Hey, Joe Murphy! " — and there he was. Needed a haircut, needed a shave, needed to get his suit pressed. Needed a good meal and a bath. He was getting ready to pick some guy's pocket.

Now, us murphys, when we get out of school, what we do is this: we got to find ourselves somebody to get attached to, which is where the guardian angel bit that folks believe in comes from, I guess. A joe, like I said.

Anyways, murphying is as like guardian angeling that it don't make much difference what you call it. And when we hitch ourselves to a joe, we're stuck with them through thick and thin, come hell or high water. Like marriage but without all the smarmy crap and they don't know we're here, see.

We're invisible. And once we hook ourselves to a joe, we don't get to talk with other murphys no more, or any other spirits neither. Nobody. It's the rules. This ain't a job for just anybody. But I work good alone.

It sure as hell beats playing harp.

Anyways, I'd spent a while I guess — time don't mean diddly to spirits — after I got out of murphy school casing prospects, looking for the right one. Taking my time, making sure I didn't get stuck with no bozo.

So when I saw this Joe Murphy guy trying to pick this other guy's pocket at the Downs, I figured I found my mark.

Did I say "mark?" Sorry. Old habits. Did I say I used to pick a few pockets myself back when?

Maybe that's what caught my eye when I seen ol' Joe trying for this guy's wallet — besides the name. Plus he was doing it wrong and he was about to get busted, I could see. And right then and there I decided I'd be this joe's murphy.

My first murphy was to make a raindrop — it was cloudy — fall right in the mark's eyeball. Splat. Distracted the mark long enough so my joe could score and fade out clean.

We got ourselves enough. I ain't saying how much. We played the horses all day, hit it pretty good on a 20-1 nag in the fifth and called it a payday.

As for the mark, cry me no tears. He was a lawyer.

My joe, he was pretty happy. Got himself shaved, cleaned up, bought some new duds, ate at a fancy restaurant. Smiled all day. Paid the rent.

We even had a few bucks to go cruising downtown. Mind you, I don't mean we had no car. We took a cab. Cruised for chicks. Hookers, mostly. You don't see too many straight chicks downtown, and if you did, they had dates. Chicks hanging on rich guys are out of our league, high class stuff.

But some hookers downtown weren't bad. Some was lookers, and my joe, he knew a few cause he went downtown now and then when he could spare a few bucks. And he was good to them too. Didn't play favorites, always paid up front, didn't go for kinky stuff. The chicks, they liked my joe all right.

And it made me feel good to see him happy. I guess there was some-thing in it for me, though I couldn't feel squat being a spirit and all, like maybe I was making up for those times when I'd done what Joe was doing and remembered how good I felt back when. But it never happened to me often enough, getting lucky, I mean, so I figured to do my best to make sure my joe was the luckiest stud ever had a murphy.

We went on for a long time I guess, a few weeks or months. We was careful. I'd usually let my joe case the mark on his own and make the snatch without getting up a murphy. But when I saw stuff he didn't see, like a real rich mark or a bust ready to go down on him, then I'd step in and steer him the right direction, being subtle all the time, of course, which is the murphy way.

Never let them figure they got murphy's luck, is the murphy way. But ol' Joe, he sure as hell figured right when he figured his luck had changed. One time, it'd be his shoelace would break, and he'd bend over and catch this glimpse of a money belt on a guy, which he wouldn't of seen if he'd been standing because of the angle and stuff. Another time, I'd make a phone ring in a phone booth right near where Joe was making a hit, and it'd happen just as this cop walked by, who, if I hadn't of rang the phone and made the cop go answer it, would of caught my joe red-handed.

A close one, but like I said, I'm a pretty good murphy.

But I never murphy at the Downs. Took me a while to figure there was too many other murphys there trying to make things go right for their joes. I couldn't see them, of course — like I said, we're invisible — but I knew they was there cause things got tricky. It got real complicated. Like what if you get ten murphys all trying to make sure their joe's horses all won? Ten different horses? Hell, I seen a three-way photo finish once.

Okay, I been delaying talking about Joe's chick. It's not like I want to even talk about her or nothing. Hell, when Joe saw her behind the twenty dollar window, I figured he was just scoping out another fox, like usual. Like he always did. Looking, you know what I mean. All guys do it, even us spirits.

But the day wrapped up with Joe down a hundred or so but he was still smiling and whistling, like he was happy he'd lost, I guess. And he goes and meets the chick. Name of Dolores. Stacked, yeah, but not his type, I swear.

They go out and have dinner and end up at her place, and I figure my joe'll get himself a piece and go home. An easy score. Roundheels. No big deal.

If I'd of known, I'd of stepped in and run a bus over her foot or what-ever. But who can figure? Maybe she had her own murphy looking to get her hitched.

Yeah. Hitched. They got married a month after they first got laid. In a church, flowers, her mom crying, sisters, a cake, pictures, the whole she-bang. All her idea. I could of puked.

Believe me, I tried to break it up, but nothing worked. I gave her the hiccups once, and he stayed with her all night giving her glasses of water, tickling her, going "boo," all the stuff supposed to make the hiccups go away. I finally gave up and stopped the hiccups, and they got so pleased they screwed the rest of the night away.

So I broke the bed. Damned if they didn't keep at it, humping on the floor. Hell, she liked it.

Of course, he quit going downtown, which made a few hookers un-happy, let me tell you. And Joe missed the hookers too, I could tell, though he didn't say diddly to his chick. And when she talked him into getting a regular job, I knew I had to get serious. Him, a cabby. Jesus H.

She was happy as a peach, I swear, and my ol' joe was so damn miserable it made me want to puke. But spirits can't puke because we don't eat nothing. But you get my point.

Well, what could I do? My job was to murphy for my joe, to make him happy, and here was this broad making him miserable, and him pretending he liked it. "Do you love me, honey?" she'd say and he'd say, "Yes, my dear-est," and I knew he didn't mean it. She was so happy and he was so —

If it was another murphy doing their job better than me, then I was really pissed. Maybe it was a chick murphy. I had to do something but I couldn't figure what.

Well, I guess I did figure, cause here we are.

I wonder what ol' Droopy Drawers, my teacher back in murphy school, would of said about the way I figured to make my joe happy. Five to three he'd of raised his bushy white eyebrows and said, "Well, Master O'Brian. Unorthodox, but effective." Ol' Droops, he liked guys that thought for them-selves. Hell, we didn't have no textbooks.

So here we are, me and Joe. We're in the outside corner of a 18-month stretch. The missus is hanging in there, but I been murphying the conjugal visits. Keeping her on the other side of the glass. And Joe don't miss it. He was never really, you know, hard up.

As for Joe and his pickpocketing, that last time, the one I murphyed that got us in here, is the last time he'll ever get caught, I swear.

Oh, he lifts now and then. Something from the guards, staff, visitors, or a couple of inmates who are real shitheads anyway and deserve it. Just enough to keep from getting rusty. Mostly the guards though. I did some finagling, got him on as a trustee, and he gets outside to do some shopping now and then, if you know what I mean. And we don't get caught. No more.

And Joe's happy. No broad nagging him to go to work, quit eyeing the babes, sit up. (Did I tell you she made him quit the ponies? I swear.) Got a cell all to himself. Just like he likes it. Course, he don't know his murphy had a hand in getting him his own, whereas everybody else in this lockup shares with some pervert or fag.

Just one thing.

Seems the warden likes Joe. I heard talk about letting him out early for good behavior. Maybe in a few weeks. I wonder how my joe will take it? He'd be able to get to the track instead of betting on the sly like he does here in the joint. Not to say he don't like laying a bet or two in stir, but actually being there when the horses run, he'd like that more.

So what will I do when they give him his walking papers? He was happy when we first met, then he got miserable when he met Dolores, and now he's happy again. I know he'd like to get back to the ponies and the chicks, but Dolores will be waiting. I don't know if he could handle it. Me either.

So maybe I got to murphy again, maybe get us in solitary, extended sentence. Whatever. I'll come up with something. Bet on it. Some guys are luckier than others, like my joe and me.

THE BELL
OF SANTA YSOBEL

The bell of Santa Ysobel stopped ringing at the same time the ringing in Father Ramón Ortiz's head stopped. He had been kneeling at morning prayer when it happened. So startled was he by the instant cessation of pain that he stopped praying in mid-word.

Was this, he wondered, a prayer answered, this sudden relief from pain? It was a blessing, certainly, but did it also signal a miracle? Was he to live, after all, despite his doctor's dire prognosis?

"Two weeks," Dr. Lopez had told him the day before, sympathy making her voice tremble. "Maybe two months. And the pain, the ringing, I'm afraid — " She sighed. It could not be stopped.

Ramón had prayed. Not for a change in his fate, but for an end to the pain, so he could serve until the end.

Now, the pain had ceased. For a moment, Ramón dared to hope that the tumor had somehow disappeared.

For the pain to end, even for a while, is a blessing. But for my life to be spared — He dismissed the thought. He rose, bones creaking. A blessing, yes. A miracle, no. He had no right to believe he'd been visited by a miracle.

After all, he was Father Ramón Ortiz, and this was, after all, only Mission de Santa Ysobel. Nothing remarkable every happened here.

He rose and patted his vestments into place over his ample stomach. He turned to leave the chapel and cross the courtyard toward the bell tower to investigate. He'd call the doctor later about his changed condition. Right now, he'd see to the more mundane task of finding out why the monks stopped ringing the bell.

Brother Enrique Maldonado intercepted him at the chapel door, panting for breath, his eyes wide with concern.

"What seems — "

"Father Ortiz," the big monk gasped, "something had gone wrong with the bell."

"Why isn't it ringing?"

Enrique wrung his hands and gulped. "You wouldn't believe. You must see for yourself."

Ramón went with Enrique across the courtyard to the bell tower, where two monks stood by the bell rope, looking bewildered. Wordless, Enrique pointed to the stairwell and started climbing up. Ramón sighed, followed, and remembered there were 143 steps to the top.

Long ago, Ramón used to run up and down those steps each morning, to keep in shape. But he'd long ago quit playing football, quit exercising.

"What could be so urgent — "

"Please, Father," Enrique shook his head, "you must see for yourself."

Ramón counted the steps. He stopped mid-way up the narrow wooden stairs. The shaft was windowless, and he expected to be out of breath, expected to feel his sweat-soaked vestments cling to his round chest. He cringed, waiting for the blood to pound in his head again and the pain to resume. But it did not.

Enrique waited a few steps ahead, hiding impatience. Half Ramon's age, Enrique appeared rested, not sweating much or breathing hard. A mountain goat.

As did Ramón. *But that can't be. I'm old, fat. And dying.*

He wiped a pudgy hand across his forehead, only slightly damp. He touched his heart, felt the beat strong and regular, as it had been so long ago. He felt — exhilarated.

Something was happening to him, he concluded, something —

Enrique coughed, a gentle prodding. Ramón nodded but didn't move, deep in thought. But thinking about what was happening to him seemed self-indulgent. Ramón forced his thoughts away from his own body toward the steps in front of him, concentrating.

One hundred and forty-three steps, he mused. The number had no spiritual significance. But neither, it seemed, did anything else about Mission de Santa Ysobel. Other churches boasted weeping statues, returning swallows, rich histories, Papal visits, prosperous villages, a paved road bringing tourists looking for ancient Spanish missions.

Little, dusty Santa Ysobel, just over the border from the U.S., boasted none of these. The village was poor. The church was built in 1902. Not even Spanish.

And 143 insignificant steps up the bell tower. How long had it been since he'd climbed these steps, let alone ran up them?

"Please, Father," Enrique urged. "It's not far now."

In fact, Ramón counted fourteen steps left. He'd already climbed a hundred and twenty-nine. No significance in that either.

At last at the top, he looked out at the countryside around the village.

Desert and sagebrush, deserted and burnt, as far as he could see. By-passed by civilization.

Uninspired by the dismal view, he responded to Enrique's silent urging and looked at the bell in the small tower's center.

Santa Ysobel had only one bell, not particularly beautiful or important in any respect. It wasn't large — one could wrap one's arms around its mouth and touch fingers — and it sounded a bit off key, as if it had been cast with a hidden flaw. Whatever the cause, the peal of the bell of Santa Ysobel had always sounded a bit odd to Ramón. Others had confessed the same when pressed for candor on the matter.

But the bell had stopped ringing this morning, stopped at the same time his headache stopped, and Enrique had urged him to climb those stairs to see — what?

"Now, Enrique," Ramón said, aware he wasn't panting, "please tell me why you have brought me here."

"Come see," Enrique pointed again to the bell, hanging waist high in its wooden carriage over the rope hole in the tower floor.

Ramón took two steps forward, all he needed in the tower to bring him an arm's length away from the bell. He bent forward and rested his hands on his knees, peering at the bell.

"So?" he said.

Enrique called to the monks at the bottom of the tower to ring the bell. They did.

At least they pulled the rope and the bell swung to and fro as it was supposed to and, when he looked under the swinging bell, Ramón could see the clapper bounce off the inner lip, but —

Nothing happened. No sound came.

"Stop pulling," he called down to the monks. They did. Ramón and Enrique stopped the swinging bell between them with their outstretched hands. Ramón again bent to examine the bell's underside, closer this time.

Running his hand over the bell's inner surface, he found no padding that would dampen the peal. The clapper was also unpadded. He tapped the clapper with his ring.

Tink.

He tapped the bell's inner lip with his ring.

Tong.

Then he swung the clapper against the bell's inner wall.

No sound.

"Hm."

"You see?" Enrique said. "You wouldn't have believed, I'm sure."

Ramón stood, expecting his bones to creak. They did not.

From the village, he heard a car horn blare, and a radio, and some kind of engine chugging. A dog barked. A breeze rattled the leaves in the cottonwood grove near the tower. He smelled corn cooking.

He heard one of the monks below cough.

"Something unusual — " Ramón muttered.

"A curse?"

"Hm." *The bell went silent at the same time my headache stopped.*

"Father Ortiz," Enrique said, "if this is a curse — "

"I've never heard of its like anywhere in the world," Ramón said, in a whisper, to himself. "Imagine. Something unique, as amazing as this, something of interest, maybe even of value, right here in the bell tower of the Mission de Santa Ysobel."

Enrique sighed, a desperate tone. He tugged on Ramon's sleeve. "Father Ortiz, if this is a curse — "

"Let's not be too hasty, Enrique. This requires study. Surely, you see that. Maybe it's a blessing in disguise — "

"The bell calls the faithful to prayer. How could its silence be anything but the work of — "

"Nevertheless," Ramón raised a thick finger. "We'll wait. Nothing ever happens in Santa Ysobel, as you know. This, this is just — "

"But if it is a curse — "

"A day. Or two. Be patient. We must see. If the pain comes back — "

"The pain?"

"I mean the ringing. Of the bell, I mean. If it comes back on its own — "

Enrique hesitated, frowning. He finally nodded in agreement.

"Meanwhile," Ramón said, "we don't talk about this. To anyone. Agreed?"

"But if it — "

"We might frighten people. You see?"

Again, Enrique nodded agreement.

Ramón followed Enrique down the narrow bell tower steps reveling in a physical vigor he hadn't felt in years, his mind in a whirl. He passed the monks at the foot of the stairs, ignoring their mutters of concern, and walked briskly toward his office.

If the bell was indeed cursed, as Enrique feared, it could be exorcised. He'd done it before, long ago, and he could do it again, if need be.

But if the bell went silent at the same time the ringing in his head had gone silent, would restoring the bell's ringing also restore his own ringing pain, the pain that tolled his coming death? Were the phenomena linked?

Blessing or curse? Or both.

He'd have to call Dr. Lopez and see her immediately. But he already had a good idea what another examination would find. And what his choices would then be.

In his office, alone at last, he lifted the phone receiver to his ear. And hesitated.

Slowly, he replaced the receiver. With a smile, he got down on the floor and did a hundred push-ups.

THE ADVENTURES OF AFTERLIFE AL, THE DEAD DETECTIVE!

Epidsode 216: The Quest for the Golden Spleen

I awaken.

Slowly, I regain, if not exactly life, at least consciousness and a dim awareness of my surroundings.

Awareness and memory return in small increments, like waking from a dream.

I'd been dead.

Now I'm not.

No; I'm still dead, but —

A voice.

"When outlaws turn to *death* to flee the long arm of the law, *who* you gonna call?" A woman's voice, familiar, husky, urgent, coming from a tiny speaker, a cell phone.

"*Afterlife Al!* The *Dead Detective!*"

*I'*m Afterlife Al. Was. Who's this woman, speaking like a TV cop show announcer? Through a cell phone by my ear. In my coffin.

"Yes, *Afterlife Al! I'*m who you call when you got to — bring 'em back — *dead!*"

I used to say that.

The voice: Ellie's.

I lay in my coffin, in my crypt. Dead, yes. But Ellie revives me. Again. Why?

Ellie's voice buzzes by my ear from the cell phone. I'm conditioned to respond. Ellie conditioned me, I remember, so she can revive me. The words are like a post-hypnotic suggestion. Magic stuff.

"You awake, Al?"

I remember. Some. Enough.

I will my corpse chest to pump so I can speak. "What?" I say, voice raspy. I haven't spoken aloud in — how long?

Ellie, once just Officer Eleanor Atwood, now Lt. Atwood, thank you very much, Las Vegas Metro. Of course. Ellie is the only one who has my number. She'd always had my number.

"Al, I need your help." Ellie sounds tired, like I sound when I have to talk to the living.

Ellie had been my partner, and yes, my lover, when I was alive and me and her worked patrol. Long and short: I got killed and she didn't. Ellie got promoted and I'd stayed dead.

I remember more as I awaken, in tiny increments, but I don't remember — what happened, exactly, back then. I don't think about that, now.

"What's up?" The phone telltale reads just after three a.m., Friday, and eighteen months, I remember, since Ellie's last call.

We have a deal, me and Ellie, I remember. I'll help when I can with detectiving where she can't detective — and she's good, make no mistake — and she'll keep people from giving me grief, opening my grave, disturbing my rest.

Live people, I mean. Dead people don't bother me. Live people? Keep 'em.

Except Ellie. She understands death. Cajun. Knows magic shit you wouldn't believe. I didn't, before.

The problem with magic shit is that I keep forgetting. Ellie keeps tabs, but I forget. Then when she calls, I remember, some. Then — I forget again.

"What do you know about the Queen Qutkushuk Traveling Exhibit?" she asks.

I will my body into more corporeality, something Ellie taught me, just enough to push open the coffin lid, oiled and hinged to respond to light pressure from inside. I sit up, spirit and corpse, and hold the cell phone to my emaciated, papery cheek in my near-skeletal right hand. Ellie'd done some magic stuff so my corpse can move.

The polished mahogany coffin frames my hips and legs as if I'm sitting in a kayak. I look around my crypt and remember my funeral, my burial. Our arrangement.

"Egyptian," I say. "I read in the papers. They found a crypt in the desert, undisturbed and full of treasure, a couple years before I — well, back then."

Nothing has changed. Too dark to see much. Narrow and cramped. Solid rock. The crypt had cost Ellie a fortune, but she paid. We have a deal.

"You say 'Traveling Exhibit?'"

This, I recall, is how each episode began. I sit up in my coffin, my sidekick — you remember Marta Sage; she won an Emmy for Best Supporting in our second year — summons me for the next adventure before the first commercial break.

"Touring the U.S., Al. It's scheduled to open at the Luxor for a one-month show. Opens in five hours. But."

"Tell all." My crypt is probably cold, dank-smelling, but I don't notice. Dark, but I don't expect guests.

"Al, there's a life-sized statue of Qutkushuk, made of gold and silver and encrusted with jewels — "

Ellie babbles over the tiny speaker as I ease from my coffin and struggle to stand. The statue, Ellie says, is unique, priceless. It's designed to be dissected, like a pharaoh's idea of a freshman anatomy class dummy. You can take it apart.

My corpse obeys my will, and I don't seep into the floor like it's quicksand. Mating spirit to body is tricky; it's like riding a bicycle. Your spirit can walk through walls but your body can't and, if you forget, you'll just detach from your body when you hit the wall. You look silly.

Your spirit can seep into floors if you don't pay attention; you lose contact with your corpse and it falls apart like a puppet with cut strings. I learned from Ellie after I died.

Going corporeal makes me queasy. It's psychological, I know, because I don't have a stomach anymore, but the queasiness is real, believe me. Nothing Ellie's magic shit can do about it. I don't go more corporeal than I have to. Except when Ellie wants me to. Needs me to.

The top of Qutkushuk's head, made of one piece of hammered white gold, comes off and reveals the brain; polished jade. Twin raw diamond eyeballs. Removable arms and legs. A gold plate covers her chest, hinged.

I ease out of the coffin and stand on the floor. I listen to Ellie's problem. I'm ready to help, corporeally or ethereally, whatever she needs. Love to hear her voice on the playback.

When you open Qutkushuk's chest, all the organs are there. The heart is a giant ruby, nothing like it in the world; the lungs a plump cluster of grape-sized emeralds, the stomach and intestines and all the organs — emeralds, diamonds, rubies, silver, gold, sapphires, lapis lazuli, garnets, jade, turquoise, pearls, opals — a fortune in an anatomy lesson. The spleen is solid gold.

Cool prop.

"You say only the spleen is gone?" I ask.

I'm ad-libbing. We're not on the set. No script. This is real.

The thieves snatch the whole body in a daring, well-crafted raid the scriptwriters would have envied. They almost get away. Cops stop them fifteen miles south of town. There's a shootout on I-15 and almost all the loot is recovered.

"Yeah. Just the spleen."

"And all your baddies are dead."

Ellie sighs. "We're searching, but it looks hopeless." The baddies blow themselves up, deliberate or accident, the cops don't know. "We open at eight a.m., Al. We got a fake gold spleen on its way here now, got an artist guy down in Henderson — "

"So what's wrong with that?"

I wobble a few steps in the crypt's close confines. Two short steps next to my coffin one way, two back, remembering how to walk. I'm ready if Ellie needs me to mingle with the living. The crypt has a door. Opens from the inside. I can walk my corpse about if I need to.

"Al, we're not sure it'll work, and we can't stop the press from prying. There was a shootout, an explosion. It's been on TV. They'll find out about the theft."

"So?"

"Qutkushuk is an Egyptian national treasure, Al." Ellie sounds irritated, frustrated. "Think international incident. Think global. Hell, you think *inter-dimensional*. I taught you."

"Right."

"We got Egyptian diplomats and security and — *you* know."

"You can't delay the opening?"

"Pick a big name in Vegas, Al. *Big* name. All there."

"Right." Vegas is the most security conscious place on the planet, but the thieves made the snatch anyway. Impressive.

"President Mugoshik and Vice President Harkness. I got big people watching me. *Big* people."

"Right." Ellie's ass is on the line, and I'm the only hope.

I don't want to go. Don't remember why, but I damn well know I don't want to go.

"It's like episode 92, Al." Pause. I can almost hear tears in her voice. "Remember?"

"Right." I remember. And it's Ellie. I have to go.

Who you gonna call?

"Give me pictures."

Ellie downloads the dead thieves' pictures onto the phone. Five Egyptians, three Saudis, and one Frenchman. I memorize their faces and names and other details but don't bother to save anything. I can't take a cell phone where I'm going.

"Now, Ellie, one more thing."

"What?"

"Send me a picture of a spleen."

*

I memorize what a spleen looks like, then I set the phone back in its socket in my coffin; Ellie installed a clandestine solar cell rig to power it. The rig is hidden in filigree atop the stone monument under which my body rests. It's tiny because the rig's only use is to power that one phone when Ellie calls.

The statue over my crypt is unusual for Silvercrest Eternal Repose Acres. Ellie ordered it. It's a life-size statue of *Afterlife Al, the Dead Detective!*, posing as he does — did — in the Saturday morning cartoon opening credits for which I did voice-overs after the live series I starred in wrapped — we went seven glorious seasons — and before I re-joined the force, and found Ellie. Caped and masked, granite-chinned, chest puffed out, fists on narrow hips. Baddies, beware. Eight a.m. Saturday, ABC. Brought to you by Toyco Corp., exclusive makers of Afterlife Al, the Dead Detective! Action Figures.

I'm the one that says, "Who you gonna call?" The *Ghostbusters* folks made lawsuit noises but nothing happened.

I became a cult classic — Afterlife Al, I mean; not me — and I get visitors to the monument and crypt now and then. *Allies*, they call themselves, like *Trekkies*. Fans. A bit late. Where were they when I was alive? I don't *feel* like Jim Morrison.

I had me three good careers; cop, then actor, then cop again. Four. Now I'm a dead detective. It's a living.

I'm thankful I don't need to go corporeal for this job. I doff my partial corporeality like sweaty gym socks and I go to Hell. That's where the thieves will be.

In his play "No Exit," Jean Paul Sartre says Hell is other people. There's something to it. I don't care for most people, dead or alive. Except Ellie. My theory is that people make their own Hell, and as no two people are alike, no two Hells are alike. When you die, your Hell will be different from mine, and my Hell is different from Qutkushuk's statue's golden spleen's thieves' Hells.

And, I've learned, no two visits to Hell are the same. It's like dreams. Or nightmares.

Still, we have things in common, the thieves and me. We're dead. It's a start.

There's this — I call it a "waiting room." It's outside Hell's main entrance. It's for those who don't know they're dead yet or who're fighting it, protesting. Unlike Hell itself, this — *purgatory*, you could call it — doesn't change much from visit to visit or from person to person.

We had a waiting room set back then, but it was no match for the reality.

It's like a dentist's office waiting room only so big it dwarfs the Astrodome, crowded with a zillion people, all watching "I Love Lucy" and "Happy Days" and "Afterlife Al" re-runs on flickery TVs, and reading old magazines and napping in plastic chairs in crumpled clothes, and everybody needs a shower. I don't smell, but I remember. Kids run up and down the aisles screaming while harassed parents try to shush them and nobody makes eye contact, just like in an ordinary dentist's office. Only these people are waiting for their number to be called so they can "move on," so to speak.

They all want a lawyer. "I ain't supposed to be here! There's been a mistake!" "I'm gonna sue!" Take a number, bud.

Based on how the thieves died, sudden-like, I figure I'll find one or two in the Universal Hell Waiting Room.

I saunter through the room till I spot a mug from the mug shots I'd memorized. Takes a while, but to the dead, time don't bode diddly.

It's not like the perp can run or hide, being dead. He's disoriented, how well I know, doesn't know the ropes. He doesn't know me from Nick Adams, so I act like I'm on staff. I wear a lab coat, horn-rimmed glasses, fake Freud goatee. I got a clipboard, pocket protector filled with pens, and I even got a slide rule.   "Just a few routine questions, sir," I say in a feigned German accent; I used to be good with accents. "Standard procedure, for our files, for new arrival in-processing, legal department client assistance, blah, blah, blah." He spills what his bunch did with the spleen, I scribble it down, thank him, and leave.

Simple as that.

I float back to my crypt and call Ellie.

"You're not going to like this," I say.

"Spill."

"It's not political or profit. It's religious. Some cult — " The guy I interrogated said his bunch were after the spleen alone, not the whole enchilada. The statue theft was a diversion. The police would focus on the statue while the spleen was spirited away, north into the desert for a ceremony.

Dark cults and secret societies that worshipped scorpion gods and two-headed goats and vampiric sorcerers and undead wizards from dimension X and golems and evil pagan spirits and golden, jewel-encrusted statues and beautiful dead Egyptian queens were routine fare in all 195 "Afterlife Al" episodes. But those were just stories.

After I died, Ellie clued me in; this stuff is real.

I don't recognize this cult but I'm not surprised Ellie does. Can't pronounce the name. Not important.

"This ceremony," she says, "it must be stopped."

"Like episode 56?"

In that show, some outfit from the Amazon wants to open the Gates of Hell. The Gates of Hell look like your regular, suburban, split-level ranch style door. Double doors, painted red, hinged, with a brass doorknob and bell and knocker. But big. As big as the hanger gates they use at Cape Canaveral where they store the Space Shuttle. Bigger.

I closed those gates, I remember now, and saved humanity.

Danny Glover guest-starred.

"Close enough," Ellie says. "Episode 56."

That urgent.

"Okay, Al." She takes a deep breath. "Here's what you got to do — " She tells me.

I don't want to do it, but I do.

Who you gonna call?

I make sure my body is resting okay in my coffin. Then I project myself astrally to the desert north of town to locate the golden spleen from the astral plane. Easy to find. Magic shit gives off a spiritual odor. Magic shit smells like — well, like magic shit. You don't want to know; but one day, like it or not, you'll find out.

When I find the spleen, I got to go corporeal, borrow a convenient body, and snatch it. Ellie doesn't tell me what I got to do then. I got to find a phone and call her is what. Then she'll say.

I got to hurry; we're short on time, Ellie says. The clock keeps ticking on the material plane.

So I go astral, go north, sniffing for the spleen.

I find myself hovering over Area 51. I wait for sirens to wail and interceptor jets to buzz me, firing missiles, but it doesn't happen. Rows of lights below mark buildings and runways. Searchlights and vehicles move here and there.

Nobody sees me.

I spot the golden spleen.

There's an abandoned warehouse — there's *always* an abandoned warehouse — at the south end of the secret government complex, magic shit stench rising up like it's a camel dung heap. I descend, float through the roof, and reconnoiter.

A cabal of baddies stand in a circle in the center of the bare warehouse, like an old hangar. They wear dirt-brown monk robes and hoods, and they chant stuff. Incense floats up from burners, and they got symbols scrawled in blood on the floors and walls. A guy at this podium reads gibberish from a dusty old book as big as a suitcase. Before him on a card table with a purple cloth lies Queen Qutkushuk's golden spleen.

A little distraction ought to do the trick.

I float outside a side door and find me an overflowed Dumpster. The warehouse, I see now, used to store computer and electronic stuff. Boxes and paper crap in the Dumpster. Should make a righteous fire.

I hate going corporeal in my own body, I hate it when I have to inhabit and animate another person's body, something else Ellie taught me, and you can't get me to *think* about animating an animal; but these are desperate times, my Ellie is in trouble, and I have to move quick.

Rats can do amazing things if you get inside them and make them do it: stuff you won't see on the Discovery Channel. For example, you can get them to pick up a wooden match in their paws and strike it on something rough, light the match, then drop it in a kindling pile. You can do it, but it leaves a sour taste on your tongue, believe me.

In a second — Voila! You got your baddie-distracting fire.

The baddies distract, run out to put out the fire. I drop the rat like a, well, a rat — and float back inside, grab the chief priest — guy named Preston Quackenbush, IV, a frustrated and bankrupt ex-software designer and now an electronics component contractor for the government. I use Pressy — he hates the nickname — to grab the spleen. I head for the door.

Robed cult henchmen spot me and holler an alert — cue chase theme music — and come running, but I have a plan. I run right at a wall, discorporate at the last second, run through it. Pressy bounces off the wall with a meaty thud — cue SFX — and the guys right behind me also bonk themselves on the wall. I discorporate again, go back inside, reanimate poor ol' Pressy, stand him up; he's got a knot on his head big as a walnut. I grab the spleen that I dropped as I discorporated, conk the other baddie henchmen with it, just to make sure they're out, then I saunter through the door opposite the still-distracted fire brigade.

I'm two steps away from the warehouse when I see four guys holding Ellie between them. They're two hundred feet away, at the far end of the warehouse. All four hold her in ropes stretched taut so she can't move, like she's a wild mustang they're trying to break. She holds a cell phone in one hand.

The guys are wearing military uniforms, Marine, I think.

"Ellie?" I say. She can't hear me.

I hear buzzing in Pressy's robe pocket. A cell phone.

"Hello?"

"Do as they say, Al." Ellie.

Now I understand why I found that baddie so easily in the waiting room, why he spilled so quick.

"Okay."

"Go back inside the warehouse."

"Okay."

Now I understand why I had no problem spotting the spleen over Area 51.

"Bring the spleen," Ellie says.

"Okay."

It's a trap.

I go.

Inside, the baddies have reassembled around the altar, robed and uniformed, all the same fraternity. Pointed M-16s direct me to replace the spleen on the altar.

I do.

"How about an — "

"Explanation?" Ellie says. Her face is twisted in agony, an internal pain. Her pretty eyes are red-rimmed and her cheeks are streaked with tears.

Ellie is released from her rope prison and she starts to climb atop the altar. She stops, one knee up exposing a tantalizing hint of thigh, and looks pleadingly at her captors.

As one — they're zombies, single-mind; we'd had zombies in episodes 42 and 43, a two-parter — they shrug assent.

As Ellie starts to explain, I suddenly don't want her to. Because I remember.

"Episode 195," I whisper. "The last — "

I remember what I don't want to remember. Why I'm dead and she's not. Why we have our agreement. Why I'm here.

I power up Pressy's lungs and let out a scream that breaks his ribs and rattles the warehouse walls. The zombies ignore it. They have a ceremony to conduct. A comrade to recover.

I remember.

I'm undead. Ellie is unliving.

One day, long, long ago, Ellie decides she doesn't want to be a demon anymore. It was the hours, she says, and the boredom. And the food. And the stupid job, stupid boss — the whole thing.

So she deserts her post, leaves the Gates of Hell, where she'd manned — or demoned, rather — the entry desk, checking photo ID, taking finger-prints, patting down women "patrons," searching for hidden contraband. "Anything to declare? Weapons? Flammable or toxic items? Drugs?"

She evades them for a short spell, joins the department, meets me — my acting career is long gone by then and I'm settled back into being a cop again — and we become partners. Lovers.

I learn her secret but I love her anyway. Simple as that.

One day, we get a call to the Safari Pet Store way out on Blue Dia-mond. B&E. We respond.

A trap. They've lured her to the store. Their plan to recover her is simple. An enchanted leopard will eat her, and they'll take her back in the cat. After a ceremony. They need to have her body and spirit on site for the ceremony. All this afterlife shit involves ceremonies.

Ellie is fast, smart. Smarter than your average zombie or demon or spawn of Hell.

Me too. I kill her first. Because I love her, see.

It foils their plot and they go back to Hell with the cat; but here I am, holding my dying Ellie, crying like a baby.

I beg her not to die, *beg* her. Or un-die. Whatever.

I say if she dies, I'll kill myself. Ellie knows more about death than I do and she's horrified. Still, I insist.

She doesn't want to go back, I refuse to let go, so we make a pact. Even if I don't understand what's happening, I swear I'll do anything to save her.

"Anything, Al?" Blood seeps down her chin.

"Anything!" I wail. "*Anything!*"

Our bargain is made.

She does a quick chant, a make-do ceremony. She shoots me. Part of the ceremony. What the Hell; I'd shot her.

She explains later. Ellie is undead among the living. I'm unliving among the dead. Both stuck in between. We need each other. We have a deal.

She does it because she doesn't want to go back and because she doesn't want me to go forward. She loves me as much as I love her. No sacrifice too great, see?

They keep coming back. Won't give up. There's a contract.

They use one ploy or another, one cult or secret society or coven or cabal or another, like this bunch in Area 51, I now remember, to lure Ellie to where they can do a damn ceremony.

Ellie animates me in my crypt, I come out and we try to beat the bastards away.

My memory loss? Part of the deal. We know, Ellie and me, that if I remember as I lay in my crypt, remember as she wakes me up to help fight them off again, that it would hurt me so bad I'd freeze up and might not be able to do it.

I'd lose her. She'd lose me.

Our bargain. I forget between gigs. She *can't* forget — that's her pain. We save each other, time and again, as best we can.

For love. We can never hold each other, not happy-ever-after. But our love persists. And transcends.

Well, complicated, but what the Hell. You play the hand that's dealt you.

Here we are, once again — the twentieth time. Or is it the twenty-first?

Ellie climbs atop the altar and lays on her back, and the henchfiends reform in a brown-robed and Marine uniformed circle around her to chant demon shit. At the last second, Ellie mutters, "Episode 88," and I suddenly remember and I spring to action.

Cue final fight scene music, and I cut a rope conveniently hanging right over the altar with a jagged — well, some *prop*, okay? — and a big crate falls — don't ask me how it got there, but they used this schtick back in *The Mark of Zorro*, 1920, Douglas Fairbanks. It works, trust me.

Music up under as I Judo-chop a dozen armed and fanged monks and Marines and at last we go mano-y-mano, hero and chief baddie, me and Pressy, in a fistfight for Ellie's soul.

I win.

It's in the script.

I suddenly remember *that* part too, even as I stand over a defeated, fanged Pressy-demon, ready to whack him — where the Hell did I get a *baseball bat?* — on his head.

Of course I drop the bat and he gets away. For the sequel.

"I remember," I say, my voice faint.

Yes, Ellie and I have a deal. The demons keep coming after her, and I keep rescuing her, saving her soul at the last second, but the baddies keep getting away.

It's been going on for —

"I *remember*."

— oh, how this part *hurts* —

For ages.

"I'm sorry, Al." Ellie gets up from the altar, shirt torn enough to give viewers a hint of breast, but not too much.

Ages.

Now, it's Las Vegas. It had been London; and before, Rome; and before, Babylon.

"It hurts," I say.

And before —

"I know."

Back and back and back and back.

"Please make it go away."

All the way back.

"*Please.*"

To the beginning.

"Please make it go — "

She does. We have a deal.

Ellie grabs my immobile, shocked spirit, does her magic shit, guides me back to my coffin, tucks me in, chants her chant.

I start to forget, starting with the back stuff.

Something hurts, about going back, but I don't remember.

It's something *bad*, I think.

"Al?"

"Yes?" I'm lying down. In a coffin?

"Do you remember me?"

A woman's voice. I don't know where it's coming from, but it's pretty, the voice.

"No." I don't know where I am.

"What's your name?"

"My name?"

The voice says something I don't understand. Doesn't matter. I'm tired.

I sleep.

DON'T TOUCH

Carey dumped the loot on the living room floor with a clatter. Silverware, knickknacks, painted ceramic eggs, and other artsy-fartsy crap.

Ben bent over the take, pudgy hands braced on knees. "Wow, this stuff looks rich. Where'd you get it?"

Carey parked his weary bones on the old sofa, pulled off his gloves. "Remember the chick I've been hustling? Her old man is chauffeur for David Trent."

"*The* David Trent? No shit?"

"Weaseled my way into her heart, her pants, and her dad's rich boss' alarm system." Carey picked his nose, then hefted a cigar-box sized container. "Got into the rich guy's library. I found this."

"Is it special?" Ben sat on the sofa and reached for the box. Carey pulled away.

"He had it in a vault, under tons of cement and steel." Carey turned the ornate box in one hand as he lit a cigarette with the other. "The alarm setup was incredible. Proximity, heat, video, motion. Guards and dogs. The works."

"But you got it."

Carey puffed, the cigarette clenched in a smoke-filled, toothsome grin. "Am I the best or what?"

"Don't keep me in suspense, man. What's in it?"

Carey stubbed out the cigarette on the sofa arm and flicked the butt across the room. He studied the box. Oriental hieroglyphics in ivory, onyx, maybe gold leaf, he thought. Intricate scenes of royalty having fun. Mother of pearl. The box itself would bring a good price. Persian?

"Whatever it is, Ben, it's worth a fortune."

"So, open it."

Carey nodded and pried at a simple clasp lock on the box lid. Ben moved closer, smelling beery.

A hard, waxy lump encased the lock. "Tar, maybe." Carey pulled out a switchblade and pried at the lump. "Or old wax."

"The old kings used to seal messages and stuff in wax."

The wax pinged off the latch, flew across the room, and bounced on the threadbare carpet. Carey lost his grip on the box as the wax popped off, and the box fell to the floor. "Shit." The latch opened and something fell from the overturned box.

"That was easy." Ben reached toward the box.

"Don't touch." Carey intercepted him with a rough grip on Ben's upper arm. "It's mine."

"I wasn't going to touch it." Ben held up a folded piece of paper. "This was in the box too."

Carey picked up the object.

Ben unfolded the note and read.

The object Carey held looked like a fist, cut off at the wrist, with the middle finger extended, the others folded. "Heavy. It's a glove." Carey tugged on the stiff old-leather. "An old gauntlet."

Ben read silently, lips moving.

"There's something inside the glove." Carey gritted teeth as he tugged. "Maybe gold."

"Uh, hey, Carey?"

"Yeah?" Carey jerked on the leather and it came off with a dusty, ripping sound.

"Who was King Midas?"

"Old fairy tale. Whatever he tou

READ DIRECTIONS
CAREFULLY

S omebody stop that man," the little wizard cried as the subject of his concern stepped into a cab and pulled away from the curb into downtown traffic. A few people on the busy sidewalk looked quizzically at the anxious figure in the garish purple robe, pointed purple hat, and horn-rimmed glasses, but most ignored him.

"What's the trouble, Mack?" A tall, beefy cop intercepted the wizard as he was about to step into the street.

"That young man," the wizard gestured frantically. "I just sold him an invisibility potion —"

The cop snorted. "No law against that. Ought to be, if you ask me, but there ain't."

"You don't understand," the wizard panted. "I made a mistake — "

"What? You didn't overcharge him enough?"

"Please, officer. We've got to stop him. As soon as he drinks that potion, he'll —"

"He'll disappear and him and his other invisible high school buddies will sneak into the girls' locker room. Look, Mack, we was all kids once. Even you, I bet."

"But that's just it. He won't disappear — "

"We talking consumer fraud here, Mack?"

"Please, you must listen. You see, I reversed the formula, got it all wrong. It was an accident, but — "

"But what?"

"When he drinks the potion, he won't disappear, but the rest of the univer

SIDE EFFECTS

The TV commercial from the living room intruded on Mac's gloomy musing before his blank computer screen. He couldn't concentrate. He hadn't written anything all day.

" — stuck on that new novel?" the announcer said. "Do we got the novel solution or what — at Jerry's Alchemy Mart! New! Writer's block potions now in stock! All potions made while-you-wait by our staff of trained, professional alchemists, supervised by Jerry himself! All natural ingredients, safe on the ecology! Don't forget a love potion for your anniversary! Custom orders too! All major credit cards accepted! At Jerry's — "

Mac had written on his screen: "Lance turned to Cerise, his deep azure eyes burning with desire . . . writer's block???Jerry's Alchemy Mart . . . they didn't repeat the goddam phone number!!!"

"Mildred," he yelled into the living room, "did you get the number on that commercial?"

She yelled back, "You can't hold it in or what?"

"What the hell's that have to do with anything?" He walked into the hallway. As usual, Mildred sat in her terrycloth bathrobe, hair in curlers. Eating Dorritos, drinking a Bud. She looked Sunday-morning awful. It was two o'clock. The apartment was a mess.

"The commercial," she said. "For adult diapers. You know, the kind — "

"I meant the other one. The Alchemy guy, Jerry something."

"Oh, yeah. 555-1666."

Mac ran back into his office in the spare bedroom and wrote down the number.

"How'd you remember?" he yelled back at Mildred over the TV volume, which she'd jacked back up.

"Easy. The last three numbers. Six-six-six. Number of the beast. Get it?"

"I got it, twit," Mac muttered under his breath.

*

It was Sunday, but Jerry's Alchemy Mart's free store-side parking lot was full when Mac arrived just after three. He parked his '72 Pinto station wagon in the "Customer Parking Only" area across the street at Duke Miller Pontiac Used Car Lot.

Customers jammed the store. A former Safeway supermarket, it had aisles and aisles packed floor to ceiling with bottles, cans, flasks, boxes, and cartons in every size, shape, dimension, and color Mac could imagine. He began at one end of the store and read the marquees above each aisle. Love Potions, Good Luck Charms, Easy Money, Lotto, Voo Doo Accessories, Cosmetics, Intelligence Enhancement, Books/Scrolls/Magazines . . .

He walked down the Books/Scrolls/Magazines aisle, scanning titles. "Tarot for Investors." "Sorcerer's Apprentice Monthly." "Scryer's Digest." "Philosopher's Stone Magazine." "The Weekly Wizard." Nothing on writing.

"May I help you, sir?" a whiny falsetto voice said. Mac turned around to find the voice's source and saw a large woman with a full shopping cart glaring at him.

"S'cuse me?" he said to the woman before she turned with a huff and pushed the cart down the aisle, ample buttocks swaying in pink polyster pants like two pumpkins in a gunnysack.

"Oops," the falsetto voice said. "Sorry." A little man materialized where the woman had been a moment before.

"I forgot I was invisible," the man said. "Can't help the customers if they can't see you." He fluttered a hand as if brushing away flies. "But it cuts down on shoplifting."

The man wore a floor-length, satiny purple robe decorated with large yellow stars, circles, moons, hearts, and other garish symbols. He wore a pointed hat of the same material. Horn-rimmed glasses accentuated large doe-like eyes and a weak, apologetic smile framed his narrow face.

"Yeah, well, maybe you can help me — "

"Jerry." The little man extended a soft, pale hand. Mac touched it, Jerry pulled it away demurely and returned a coquettish grin. "And you are?"

"Mac Smith. I'm a writer — "

"Oh, how wonderful."

"Yeah. Look, mister — "

"Jerry. Just Jerry. I own the store."

"Yeah. Look, uh, Jerry, I caught your commercial on WZOT about the writer's block potion."

"Oh, indeed. Our newest product line. All natural ingredients, guaranteed. Made right here in the store."

"Yeah, well, whoever I just called said you had loads of the stuff. I can't find it."

"Can't find it?" Jerry looked aghast. "Gracious me, whyever not, Mr. Smith? It's right behind you."

Both looked at the rack behind Mac, filled with paperback books, magazines and scrolls. No writer's potions.

"Oops." Jerry gasped. "Sorry." He produced a wand from a quiver on his belt and waved it at the scroll rack, muttering an incantation. The scrolls disappeared and in their place a crystal ball display materialized. On the shelves sat hundreds of crystal balls in many sizes, with wooden mounts, wire holders, leather travel cases, owner's manuals, and accessories.

"Oh, dear." Jerry replaced the wand with another from his quiver. "Ditto the 'sorry' bit. Inventory wands are tricky sometimes. Especially at Christmas and Back-To-School."

He flourished the new wand like a swordsman with a rapier, danced a dainty jig, and jabbed at the crystal balls. The display changed into an aisle filled to capacity with rows and rows of flasks, bottles, canisters, vials, and jars.

"There you are." Jerry gave a delicate bow.

"Geez, there's so many." Mac read labels. "Faulkner, Hemingway, Plato, Twain. You have a whole shelf of Shakespeare."

"Prolific writer, he."

"So, it's just done by author?"

"And by title."

"Oh?"

"Look here." Jerry took Mac's sleeve and tugged him a few steps down the aisle, which Mac now saw stretched to infinity both ways. He saw no other customers.

"I won't have any trouble getting out of here, will I?"

"Guaranteed, Mr. Smith. Book titles are on this shelf."

Mac read labels. *Gone With the Wind. Huckleberry Finn. Tale of Two Cities. War and Peace* was in a gallon jug.

"I don't get it, mister, uh, Jerry." Mac scratched his bald spot. "How does it work?"

"Well, suppose you want to write a novel like *Moby Dick*. You just take a teaspoon from the jar of *Moby Dick* — be sure to follow directions carefully. Our warranty doesn't apply if you don't — and your book will be like *Moby Dick*."

"You mean, *just* like *Moby Dick*?"

"Well, not exactly. Depends on how strong you mix the potion, how much you take, phase of the moon, your sign, physiology, and so on. There'll always be a little of you, of course, in whatever you write."

"So it — the book I'd write — would be like *Moby Dick* but not *exactly* like *Moby Dick*."

"Exactly."

"I think I get it," Mac said. "And if I want to write like, say, Mark Twain, I'd take a bottle of Twain and my stuff would sound witty like his, right?"

"Exactly."

"And maybe for philosophy I'd take a little Plato, maybe for social commentary I'd do some Dickens or Steinbeck, and for pithy prose, like Hemingway — "

"Exactamente."

"And if I wanted to write short stories — "

"Depends on what style you want, of course. We have O. Henry, Jack London, Faulkner. We have Edgar Allen Poe, Ray Bradbury, Asimov, if you're into fantasy and so on. You name it. Poetry too. Horror, if you like, but the taste — "

"Hold on. Do you have bottled Herman Melville?"

"Of course. We have them all."

"Then what if I mix a bottle of *Moby Dick* with Herman Melville? Can you mix potions?"

"You can mix authors and book titles, but it's not recommended. Side effects, you know."

"Side effects?"

"A good gulp of Poe, for example, and you turn maudlin. Three fingers of straight Hemingway and you contemplate suicide. Overdose on Twain, your hair turns white and you crave cigars." He tittered. "What would happen if you mixed Poe and, say, 'The Pit and the Pendulum?'"

"Yeah, right." Mac shook his head. "It's incredible. How do you do it? If you don't mind me asking."

"Not at all. Of course, I can't tell everything. Patents, trade secrets, and so on."

"Sure. I understand."

"We start with a book," Jerry whispered, leaning toward Mac. "Through an exclusive chemical process, we separate the paper from the ink, recycle the paper, and process the ink alchemically. The ink, of course, has all the writer's words. And how, you may ask, do we condense a writer's essence into a small flask with just the ink to convey his words?"

"Yeah, okay. How?"

"That's the part I can't tell."

"Oh? How come?"

"Because," Jerry whispered, "it's magic." He tittered.

Mac nodded.

"Well," Jerry said, clasping his hands, "what can we do for you today, Mr. Smith?"

Mac sighed. "Look, uh, I write novels. Romances, but I use a pseudonym, a woman's name — "

"Yes, yes, I understand."

"Well, I'm stuck. I never used to believe in writer's block. Now I got it bad. And I got this deadline . . ." Mac mumbled to a stop.

"I understand." Jerry clucked his tongue. "Really, I do. That's why we began our special service. To better serve the American literary community better."

Mac stifled a grimace at Jerry's awkward grammar. He remembered the TV commercial.

Jerry smiled and blinked. "Well, perhaps what you need is a little *Gone With the Wind*, or perhaps *Rebecca*. What do you say?"

"Well, it's a Gothic — "

"*Rebecca*."

" — but it's set in the deep South during the Civil War."

"Then *Gone With the Wind* it is. Wise choice. Movie rights, sequels. I can see it now, Mr. Smith. Fame and fortune is just a teaspoon away."

Jerry tugged Mac a few steps down the aisle as he scanned labels, mumbling. At last he said "Aha!" and pulled a wine-shaped bottle from a shelf.

He held it out like a wine steward. "Voila!"

"Yeah, right." Mac read the label. "Take one teaspoon as needed before meals. Use only as directed. Keep out of reach of children and non-human species, especially elves. In case of accidental overdose, contact an alchemist or sorcerer immediately. Do not induce vomiting."

"Our emergency 800 number is on the label," Jerry said. "Do you like it? The bottle, I mean."

"Yeah, right. How much?"

Jerry shook another wand as if beating away a cloud of tsetse flies. A checkout stand with a cash register appeared in the aisle. Jerry consulted a price list on the register.

"Twelve ninety-five, plus tax," he announced.

Mac bought the bottle.

"Paper or plastic?" Jerry asked.

"Paper."

Jerry put the bottle in a brown paper sack and twisted the top around the bottle neck.

"Would you like us to deliver?" he asked.

"Deliver? One bottle?"

"No extra charge."

"One bottle?"

"It wouldn't do to accidentally drop and break it after you've left the store. We don't guarantee against breakage. What if you got mugged, gods and goddesses forbid, or in an accident?"

"Deliver? How would you — "

"Why, magic, of course."

Mac laughed. *Why not?* If he had to carry the paper sack past Mildred, she might look up from the TV and pester him with stupid questions. *She'd want a snort.* With the store's magic delivery, he could sneak it into his desk drawer, past Mildred. She'd never see it.

Mildred never went near the desk. Not even to clean. *She never cleans.*

Mac agreed to delivery, if the bottle could be sent right to his desk drawer. Jerry agreed, flourished another wand, and the bottle disappeared from the checkout stand.

"How do I get out of here?" Mac eyed the endless aisle.

"No problemo." Jerry pulled out yet another wand and assumed what looked like a karate stance. He snapped the wand toward each aisle end in two quick thrusts with two wimpy grunts.

It started to rain.

"Oh, dear." Jerry muttered an apology as he dug among the wands in his quiver, thin hair matted, thick glasses askew.

"Aha!" he said at last. He tapped Mac on the forehead with the wand he'd found and Mac stood in the Books/Magazines/Scrolls aisle, a big woman with an overstuffed cart glaring at him.

"'Scuse me," Mac said. He weaved through the crowds toward the exit.

Mac hesitated outside his apartment door. He couldn't hear the TV. *Mildred must be asleep.* But he didn't hear her snore.

But then, as he was about to turn the door knob, he heard her voice. He pressed his ear to the door and listened. He couldn't make out the words but it sounded like she spoke in a thick Georgia accent.

Mac swore under his breath. Mildred had gotten the *Gone With the Wind* bottle, probably drank it.

He felt like going back to the store for a refund. "Guaranteed," the little wizard had said. He'd delivered the bottle to Mildred's lap instead of the office.

Then he smelled perfume and smiled. *Gone With the Wind*. A romance. *Okay, why not?* It had been a long time.

He opened the door and called out. "Honey, I'm home."

"Mellie, you just — " she said. Nobody else in the room.

Mildred turned from her imaginary companion and focused blazing eyes on Mac. "Damn Yankee, you're not goin' to get your hands on my dead mother's earbobs, y'heah?"

Right book, Mac thought as she took out a pistol and shot him. *Wrong scene.*

AN ICBM FOR STEPHANIE

If my Dad hadn't of built that intercontinental ballistic missile in our back-yard, I'd of never gone out with Stephanie Lazarrini. We was even going steady for a while, me and Stephanie, practically a whole summer.

Now, she won't even give me the time of day.

But I got me an idea on how to fix that, let me tell you.

Used to be, everybody had a tank or at least an armored personnel carrier in their driveway and maybe some light artillery on the patio. Dad got our first howitzer when I was in kindergarten.

But we Williamses was the first ones in the neighborhood to have our very own ICBM.

Now, everybody does. These days, behind just about every fence in West Valley City — and in Riverton, Bluffdale, and Midvale too — you see nose cones sticking up out of silos. You see more radar dishes than TV satellite dishes anymore.

Some folks even have two, and multiple warheads are a yawn. Heck, they got used ICBM lots down on State Street. But then — we're talking before my freshman year, remember, prehistoric — only governments had anything that could destroy whole cities. Now, like I said, even my Grandma has one. And she's almost 80!

My Dad built it, mostly. But I helped. We were going to build a swimming pool, but, well, he just got carried away, everybody says.

"One thing led to another," Mom says and shrugs when folks come over for dinner or whatever and ask what happened, "and before you know, there it was. You know how these do-it-yourselfers are. Men! He just figured wrong and dug more hole than he needed, then ordered up enough cement to line it with."

She imitates Dad's voice pretty good and scratches her head where Dad scratches his bald spot. "'What the heck, Helen,' Fred says. 'Let's put in a silo for an ICBM instead, what do you say?' Just like a man, you know? 'Johnny,' I says to my son, 'you keep an eye on your Dad so's he don't hurt himself.'"

Sometimes I'd get to tell the company about how I helped build the actual missile itself and back up the dump truck even though I don't got a license and about all the awesome power tools we got in our garage and how I got an A in chemistry and a B+ in math and got to use my computer to help build the warhead and stuff.

Of course, I don't tell everything. I may be a rocket scientist, but I'm no dummy.

No, I just go along, keep Mom happy. Nod my head, say "yes'm" when I'm supposed to. It wouldn't do to let on she wasn't the only one who could manipulate Dad.

Anyways, about Stephanie, before we got the ICBM, and how I got to go with her.

She's the prettiest girl at West Valley High School, I swear. She was a freshman at the time. I was just an eighth-grader at West Valley Junior High, and she was taller. She lived down the block, on the corner where you turn to go to school. Kids cut across her Dad's lawn, and he'd come out and yell sometimes. I did too for a while, cut across the Lazarrini's lawn I mean, hoping to catch a peek at Stephanie before she went to school, which sometimes made me late for first period. Miss Weston. English. Gag me.

But I stopped cutting across the lawn when I learned that Stephanie thought guys — especially junior high guys — were dorky for doing it. I didn't want her to think I was a dork. Not that she ever thought of me at all, back in those days. She'd hang out with her girlfriends and talk about Malcolm Coldwater, who was a junior then.

"Malcolm this and Malcolm that," she'd say and she'd sigh like he was some kind of rock star or something. Big jerkoff if you ask me, pardon the language.

So, here I am with what my Mom called a "crush" on Stephanie who's got a crush on "Malll-colm (sigh)." What am I going to do to get my only true love to go out with me, let alone notice I even exist?

It was Valentine's Day that I got this idea. I timed it just right so's I could slip her this neat card I made and get a few seconds alone with her, sort of. I rehearsed what I'd say a million times the night before, so my homework didn't get done. But who cares when you're in love?

Anyways, I catch her just at the crosswalk in front of where she goes down this way to high school and I go that way to junior high and I sidle up to her, not nervous or nothing, but I dropped the card anyways into this mud puddle and I didn't get to say nothing to her and she didn't even see the card, cause she started across the street with her girlfriends before she could even notice me.

Dang, pardon the language.

But I heard her say to her girlfriend Patty as they walked across the street how she thought "Malll-colm (sigh)" was cool because his Dad had a swimming pool and how anybody who didn't have one was probably a real dweeb.

I spent all that day trying to figure out how to talk Dad into building a swimming pool in the back yard. I got a D-minus in a Social Studies quiz that day but it don't matter because I figured out how to talk Dad into doing it. That night, I did it, talked him into it, I mean. I'd tell how I done it but a guy doesn't want to give away all his secrets, you know.

So the next day, I'm telling everybody I can think of that might tell it to Stephanie that we're building a swimming pool and you know what? After school, on the way home, she comes up to me — and speaks to me!

"Hey, Johnny," she says in that sing-songy way that just melts my heart right into my tennies. I mean, she was *so* cool. She kind of twists a lock of her long black hair in one finger and she kind of looks at me out of the corner of her eye, batting her eyelashes, smiling. I got to tell you, I was sure glad I went to the bathroom after seventh period or I'd of wet my pants right there, for sure!

"I heard your Dad's building a swimming pool," she says, and I got to lean in real close to hear her cause she's talking real soft and low, you know what I mean, and she smells *so* good. I nearly forgot to answer.

"Yeah, sure," I says. Then I blurt right out, "You want to come over some time?"

And she says, "Maybe."

She says maybe! Can you believe it?

But I don't say anything because I'm stunned and all, so she walks off with her girlfriends and I hear her say (cause I'm sort of following, but they don't notice) as how when "Malll-colm (sigh)" is gone, and she can't use his pool, she'll be able to come over and use mine.

"Everybody's got a pool," I hear one of her girlfriends say, I forget which.

"Uh-huh," Stephanie says, "but when Malcolm is gone, Johnny's pool will be the closest."

"You're not going to go out with John Williams, are you?" Patty says.

"No way," Stephanie says. "My Malcolm's got a license and he gets to drive his Dad's tank."

I was flabbergasted. She was planning on just using me as something to do between dates with "Mal —

I broke out in zits before I got home, I swear.

What could a guy do? The only way I could think of to beat ol' Malcolm was if I got my very own tank. But after Dad committed to building the swimming pool (and I still ain't going to tell you how I talked him into it), he wasn't about to change his mind and buy me my own tank, no way. You know how Dads are, once they get their minds made up. I could still maybe get him to buy a used tank next year, but I couldn't get my driver's license till my junior year anyhow.

By then, Stephanie would probably already be married.

What was I going to do?

It was Saturday morning when I was watching Roadrunner cartoons that I got this idea. The coyote was trying to catch the roadrunner and he strapped himself to this rocket and I got to thinking —

I got on my computer and did some figuring. I spent all that weekend — didn't even go to the mall — working on how I could get Dad to screw up and dig the swimming pool too deep, and order too much cement and stuff, and get him to decide that we ought to make it into a silo for an ICBM instead.

The hard part was waiting until that summer when we got started on the pool before I could put phase one of Operation Stephanie into action. Waiting is not cool, but you can do it when you're in love.

Getting Dad to screw up on the digging part was easy, and the cement. Dad, when he was building something, he always did his figuring on a piece of wood with a big old yellow pencil he stuck behind his ear that he sharpened with a knife, or sometimes his teeth. Anyways, I just distracted him, erased his figuring while he was out of sight, and wrote in some new figures, and he never even knew the difference.

As for getting him to decide that he should cover up his mistake by deciding to make it into a missile silo instead, I ain't saying. I just used some adult psychology. Someday, I may want to sell the idea to the Pentagon, write a book on how to manipulate Dads, or something.

Once I was sure we were going to build us an ICBM missile silo of our very own in our back yard, complete with missile and warhead, I moved on to phase two of Operation Stephanie.

I arranged to be there in the mall that weekend right when her and her girlfriends were talking. Naturally, she talked about Malcolm.

"I'm going out with 'Malll-colm (sigh),' tonight," she bragged. "We're going to the Redwood Drive-In to see *Night of the Living Dead*."

All her girlfriends were jealous, I could tell, especially when she said, "We get to go in his Dad's tank."

I could of puked, I swear. But I kept my cool, you should of seen me.

"Bet his Dad has to drive you," I says, egging her on.

"No way," says she. "Malcolm, he's got his own license."

"I'll bet his Dad's tank don't have any weapons."

"You don't know anything," she said, like I was some kind of dork or something. "It's got a machine gun and a cannon in front and everything."

"Uh-huh," I said, real cool like. "Bet you don't get to fire it."

"Oh, for sure," she said. "You're just jealous. For your information, I get to fire the machine gun at the movie screen during intermission."

"So Malcolm's got a tank, huh?" says I.

"Uh-huh," says Stephanie, real bored like.

Then I says, quiet and cool, "I got an ICBM."

You should of seen her eyes! They got as big as a frisbee, I swear.

She actually canceled her date with Malcolm, and we went out that weekend. We went to the mall, did some miniature golfing, we held hands and — well, I ain't going to tell everything we did. We started going steady Monday morning.

Boy, what a summer. Going out with Stephanie, building the silo with Dad, making the missile and warhead in the garage. Did I have me a term paper on "What I Did For My Summer Vacation" or what?

For a while, when we were the only ones who had their own ICBM, it was really neat. All the guys wanted to come over. Girls would come on to me, even when I was with Stephanie. I couldn't wait till school started. I'd be the most popular freshman in history.

It wasn't even August before other people started building ICBMs. Like the Coldwaters, ol' Malcolm's folks.

A few weeks before school started, the worst thing in the world happened.

"I guess I can't go to the movies with you this Saturday, Johnny," Stephanie said that fateful day. We was waiting for the bus outside the skating rink where we'd spent the afternoon. She looked bored or something all day, and I couldn't figure what was wrong. She wouldn't hold my hand or nothing, and she looked nervous.

"How come?" I asked, trying to not let it show, you know what I mean.

"I can't lie to you, cause that wouldn't be nice. Besides, you're okay. For an eighth-grader."

I was practically a freshman, but I let it pass. "Yeah, I guess so," I said, and my old heart was beating like the drummer on KISS. I couldn't figure out what she was saying.

"I'm getting back together with Malcolm," she said just as the bus arrives. "His Dad's building this neat missile with multiple reentry warheads and — " She sighs like she's in love or something. Then she gives me back my friendship ring, and I knew my life was over for good.

Not to mention the zits.

I haven't spoken to Stephanie since. It's been practically a week. She doesn't call, and I can't come up with an excuse to call her or anything.

For the longest time, I couldn't figure out what to do. But I had to do something. School starts next week, you know?

Then I'm watching this old movie on channel seven when I get this idea. The movie is called *The Time Machine*, by H.D. Wells or somebody. It's about this guy from the 1800s or something that invents this time machine and goes forward in time. When he rescues this future woman from drowning — I got me this idea —

I figure I'd best hurry cause I'm not the only guy that saw that movie.

Us Williamses were the first in the neighborhood to have an ICBM. I figure we can do it again, be the first, I mean. And won't old Stephanie's eyes pop out when she finds out what I'm building in the garage?

If nothing else, it ought to get me an A in metal shop.

HOW I SAVED ELVIS' BUTT —AND FREDDIE'S TOO

They was a time I thought Elvis Presley was the coolest guy ever. But I learned me about the King personal and he wasn't as cool as I thought. In fact, Elvis, he was a dork.

I know. I stole my dad's time machine once, and me and my best buddy Freddie, we met him, the King, I mean. For real.

Criminy, what a dork. But I saved his butt anyway, cause, after all, he was, like, the King.

I chanced getting grounded for an entire summer for stealing the time machine, but it was worth it cause while I saved the King's patootie, I saved my buddy Freddie's butt too.

See, me and Freddie (guys also call him Saggie cause he has this droopy face and he looks like a hound dog), we was bored stiff one day and didn't have nothing to do. It was two weeks into summer vacation, and we'd went camping with our parents (gag me) and got kicked off the soccer team and seen all the new movies and tagged the fences over at the new houses being built on Redwood Road and so on, so we was bored Big Time.

"I know," Freddie says.

"Like what," I says.

"We could take your dad's car. Go cruising."

"Gimme a break," I says. "It ain't even lunchtime yet, the car's right out front where everybody in the whole entire neighborhood could see and my mom's home. Might just as well go down to juvie hall and turn ourselves in."

But I didn't dampen Freddie's spirit. I like him cause he's got spirit, but he gets in trouble sometimes and I get caught too when I'm with him. But a guy's gotta do something when he's bored, you know what I mean?

So we took my dad's time machine.

It was parked in the garage, which is by the kitchen where my mom hangs out, but we got that figured. Mom, she was making a cake or a casserole or something that smelled pretty good, but what we did, we stole one of the ingredients, baking powder or something, while she wasn't looking, so she couldn't finish what she was cooking and had to go out to get some more at the store right then cause she's all, "If I don't get this in the oven quick, it'll like fall down." So I guess it was a cake.

Anyways, out she goes in dad's car—dad, he was zonked out in the upstairs bedroom, tired from doing some time-traveling the other day, and he got home late. Or something. Anyways, he gets home from the office late a lot, and it was Saturday, so we didn't expect him to get up for at least a couple hours. Sure, mom would be back in a minute with the baking soda or whatever we took—we hid it under the sink, next to the garbage can—but by then, we'd be off to the twentieth century for three days of fun and we'd be back in two seconds flat.

You can do that with time machines—go away for a few days and still come back a few seconds after you left. It'd be cool if you could come back a few seconds before you left but you'd get into what dad calls "a time paradox," or "time paradise," or something. Anyways, you can't do it.

And dad says you can't go back to when you was younger neither. You got to go back to before. More parabox stuff.

Another thing. Dad says people can time-travel all they want to cause people back in time, they can't remember after when they seen people from the future. They forget. More parallax stuff. So you can do a lot of stuff back then! Cool, huh? Which is why you got to have licenses to time-travel (which I can't get until I turn a junior. I'm just a sophomore now, but I got me a learner's permit.)

So off we went. I programmed the time machine to take us back to the twentieth century, my favorite time in all history, I swear. I wanted to see Elvis perform on the Ed Sullivan Show. I knew the date (Sept. 9, 1956) and "the spatial coordinates" (Another of my dad's big words. It means where you go.) which was New York City and everything, and I'd watched my dad fire up the ol' time machine a few times, so I knew what to do.

You should of seen Freddie's eyes bug out when I popped the clutch and we squealed into the parking lot right outside the studio where they did the Ed Sullivan Show. We materialized by this parking lot guy. His eyes went real big, he shook his head, and took out a bottle he had in his coat pocket and threw it in a garbage can. I bet it was beer or something maybe stronger which they drank in the olden days. Then he goes "Okay, if you guys are, like, real, you can park your jalopy anywhere you damn well want to," or something. (Excuse the "damn." He said it, not me.)

So we did. Parked the jalopy, I mean. In a spot in front of this sign that said, "Reserved. Prosecutors Will Be All Like Towed Away at Violators Expense and Stuff" or something.

"What if they tow your dad's time machine," Freddie says.

I swear his eyes got as big as a pizza, he was so scared we'd get stuck in the twentieth century. I told him as how that couldn't happen cause of another of dad's paraflexes says you just plain ol' don't get stuck when you don't belong. Kind of like a safety valve, I guess. Anyways, I drove the time machine fast and I guess that scared him too. He looked pretty green like he was ready to toss his cookies. I was scared too, a little, cause I never drove alone before, but I didn't let on. Somebody had to be leader, you know?

Anyways, I gave him my Mr. Cool shrug, something I learned from watching old Elvis movies, which I got a whole collection of, and he bought it. Sometimes I think my buddy is a dork, but what can I say? Friends are friends.

So we parked, and we went into the studio.

Now, I ain't letting on how we got into that studio. It's not like they wasn't cops all over and screaming groupies like you never seen trying to get in, cause that's what it was like. But I got ways, let me tell you. Maybe that's how come Freddie stuck with me, cause I got us in. And I ain't telling how. I still use it to sneak out of algebra, second period, sometimes. I may want to write a book someday.

Anyways, we got in the studio, like I said. And we turned down a hallway and bumped right into Elvis.

Himself.

I swear.

Knocked him over on his butt, and us over on our butt too. And there we was all laying in the hallway, me and Elvis and Freddie. You should of seen us!

Then, Elvis, he pops up, says "S'cuse me," goes on past us in a big hurry and goes into the men's room, and you could hear him barfing his guts out a mile away.

Me and Freddie, we look at each other and wonder if maybe we was seeing things.

But no. In a minute, out of the john comes Elvis, wiping his chin with a paper towel and apologizing for knocking us on our keesters and stuff.

"That's okay, Mr. Presley," I says, trying to sound cool. Freddie, he just stood, mouth open like a teenybopper. Geez.

"We just snuck backstage to get your autograph," I says.

"Oh, that's mighty nice of you," the King says. (Can you believe it!) And he invites us into his dressing room so he can sign autographs.

And we follow him, Elvis Presley, the King Himself, right into his very own dressing room. I could of died!

Me and Freddie, we didn't have us nothing to get autographed, and nothing for Elvis to autograph it with neither. No pen, nothing. But it didn't differ at all.

No.

Cause, you see, when we got ourselves into Elvis' dressing room, right there at the studio where he was about to go on stage for the Ed Sullivan Show, that's when I learned the King, he was a real dork.

Bumping into him in the hallway didn't count because people can bump into other people all the time and not be dorks. Just try getting from third period English in Mr. Steskal's class down the hallway full of freshmen to gym without getting a tardy slip and see what I mean!

And him throwing up, I figured, was maybe just too much pizza or whatever. (I think they had pizza in the olden days.) So that didn't make him no dork.

What made Elvis Presley the dork he was was right in his dressing room, he bust out crying like a baby.

"I can't do it, boys," he says, big ol' gobs of tears rolling down his cheeks. "I can't, I can't, I can't," he goes on and on and on like my mom's lectures about cleaning up my room or something. Geez.

"Can't do what?" I says, finally, cause Freddie, he's still standing there with his dumb mouth open not saying nothing. Somebody's got to be the leader, you know?

"I can't go out there," Elvis says, pointing to where I guess the stage must of been. "I can't face all those people."

"But Mr. Presley, sir," I says. "You got to go on. The history books says you went on. I got a tape of you doing the Ed Sullivan Show. You got to go on. You're the King."

"I ain't king of diddly," Elvis says, shaking his head.

"But you done it before. How come you can't now?"

"I had medication before," Elvis says. "Something I took to keep my breakfast down, quiet down the butterflies." (Elvis ate butterflies for breakfast? I didn't get it, but I didn't say nothing.) "But I'm all out of the pills. See?"

He points to a bottle laying on his dressing table with the lid off and cotton stuffed in it and I figure that was the pills he took so he wouldn't throw up. It looked empty, but I didn't check. I took his word for it. He was Elvis.

Then he gropes for a tissue, all teary eyes so he can't see, and Freddie hands him one, and he says thanks and looks at us, for the first time, I guess.

He looks at Freddie and sniffles and says "I done wrote a song about you." Cause some guys called him Saggie, like I said, remember, cause he looked like a hound dog and I bet you saw that one coming, didn't you?

Anyways, Freddie and Elvis and me, we laugh cause it was funny and it felt nice to see the King smiling instead of crying like a kid that just dropped his ice cream cone.

Then, Elvis, he turns to me, frowns, cocks his head, squints and says, "You look kind of like me."

Well, me, I known that all my life. I been doing Elvis impressions since I was six. Good ones too. My dad, he says I'm the spitting image. I comb my hair just right, cock my hip just so, and you can't tell the difference. Except maybe I'm shorter and I don't got to shave yet.

Now, you're getting way ahead if you think you got figured out what happened next, and you'd be right too, cause that's what did happen. I went on stage and did my Elvis impressions and Elvis, he stayed backstage and barfed his guts out and was happy as a clam cause he didn't have to throw up in front of a million people, live on the Ed Sullivan Show. And Freddie, he watched backstage. I even signed me a few autographs.

That's it. That's how I saved Elvis' butt.

I done it more than once, let me tell you, cause, like I said, one of the time travel paraboxes is olden time folks can't remember nothing after you're gone back to your own time. So I go back to when Elvis is doing a show here and there and get to stand in for him whenever he's feeling blue. Except after 1969. The King, he got fat and I didn't look like him no more so I stopped doing Elvis impressions.

I like to think Elvis would have lived to be maybe 50 years old if he hadn't of been using medication, if he'd of let me do shows for him instead. But I couldn't of been there all the time. I mean, I had homework, yard work, and stuff to do, and dad got the time machine now and then, so I couldn't be time-traveling all the time, could I? So it ain't my fault Elvis died. I did the best I could and I had a pretty good career, let me tell you.

But there's more.

Remember ol' Freddie, I said I saved his butt too, didn't I? Well, I did.

After that first show, the Ed Sullivan Show, I was pretty happy, getting a chance to do my Elvis impression live and to sign autographs and stuff. But Freddie, he was ol' Saggie, drooping like a hound dog, right after. Wouldn't say nothing, and me jabbering on and on and on about how cool it was to be Elvis. He didn't even get all bug-eyed when I almost ran over a bag lady in the time machine before we de-materialized and came back into our own time.

"What's with you?" I says and Freddie, he just shuffles his feet, stares at the ground, and mumbles something about me having all the fun and he never gets to do nothing.

As if he didn't get to watch. Geez.

Anyways, I figured out if I could do it, Freddie could too. Go back in time and do an impression, I mean.

Now, Freddie, he's my best friend, but he's ugly as a cold anchovy pizza, I swear. He couldn't of imitated a rock star like Elvis or a movie star like Sylvester Stallone if he tried. No, Freddie, he was my best friend, but he didn't want to be no star or nothing.

But I figured a way for him to have as much fun time traveling as I was doing Elvis impressions. I did it cause what are friends for?

Did I tell you Freddie, he was short, maybe four feet ten or so? That's okay, cause he was just fourteen, but guys gave him a hard time anyways and it bummed him out. If he wasn't going on and on and on about looking like a hound dog, he was going on and on and on about being short.

Did you ever hear of a guy name of Napoleon Bonaparte?

THE GEEZERS

Across the street from Mrs. Lena Bartlett's apartment, in the cozy little park where she took her twice-daily walk with her Pekingese, Cato, four teenaged punks were beating the shit out of Mr. Lee, the grocer.

Lena called the police right away, of course, when she heard the awful music from the teenagers' truck. Then she looked out the window.

Immediately, she wished she'd called The Geezers instead.

It was just after ten p.m., a warm August night, and the streets were empty enough to afford Lena an unobstructed view, through her barely parted lace curtains, of the mugging in the park not far away. The imitation gas lamps that flanked the walkway through the center of the park illuminated the old Oriental lying curled in a ball, being kicked by the punks.

Lena had good eyesight, considering her age. She saw a large boy who looked like he wore a porcupine on his head. One emaciated kid wore a tattered black t-shirt over his bony chest. Another kid was medium build, with a large scruffy beard and puffy biceps covered with tattoos. The fourth was a rather pretty black girl with lots of frizzy hair and a skirt so short Lena blushed. Except for the girl, all wore jeans and boots.

All took turns kicking their victim.

And laughing.

And playing that obscene hippie music loud enough to wake the dead.

The awful music came from speakers that looked like two giant black refrigerators mounted upright in the bed of a well-polished, candy apple red pickup truck with lots of shiny chrome. The truck sat on the park side curb between Lena's house and the park. The music — or noise, rather — was so loud she couldn't hear the TV news or concentrate on her knitting. So she called the police.

Lena hadn't seen the gang or their truck before. A new menace to the neighborhood. Damn.

Mrs. Costello's cocker spaniel, loose again, barked at the hoods from the other side of the park and bounded toward them, stubby tail wagging.

Frightened by the barking, the gang bolted to their truck. Lena ducked back behind the lace curtain. They sped away, tires squealing, howling like coyotes and tossing beer bottles as they went.

Damn cowards, Lena thought. Afraid of little Muffin.

Except for the barking dog, the night was once again still.

Mr. Lee lay still.

Maybe he's dead, Lena thought, venturing another peek out the window. She had seen dead people before, not counting her own Augie who died of a heart attack in his sleep one November night fourteen years ago, as she slept, unknowing, next to him. Mrs. Van Winkle, for instance. At 101, she was the oldest person at the Golden Gate Senior Citizen's Center where Lena went every Wednesday afternoon to play bingo. She fell dead right in the middle of a game last year. And that paperboy, whatsisname's grandson, run down by a garbage truck last spring almost right in front of her apartment. There were more, but the thought made her uncomfortable, so Lena brushed it off and sighed, concerned about poor Mr. Lee, lying in the middle of Burgess Street Park, probably dead.

"Oh, damn," she said to Cato, "those damn gangsters have killed him. Damn, damn those kids."

Her anger didn't include her neighbors, all hiding behind their pulled blinds. She knew they wouldn't intervene in the assault on Mr. Lee. Lee probably knew it too, even as the punks beat him. Most neighborhood residents were old, like her. Or scared. Or both.

Still, it wasn't fair, damn it.

The two officers who finally responded twenty minutes too late were polite and young. Both refused her offer of oatmeal cookies and milk. One sat at the kitchen table pretending to take notes in a tiny notebook, while the other, just a little older, stood by the window watching the ambulance crew haul Mr. Lee to the hospital.

"Lee'll be okay, Mrs. Bartlett," Officer McEwin said from the window. He had beefy round shoulders, stringy red hair, and a pulpy red nose. "It wasn't all that bad. Besides, it looks like he knew how to keep from getting the shi — er, getting hurt too bad."

"You were going to say 'getting the shit kicked out of him' weren't you, Officer McEwin?" Lena said, stroking Cato, who sat in her lap, eying the strangers. Opposite her sat tall, dark-haired, baby-faced Officer Daniels. The young policemen dwarfed Lena. Tiny, doll-like, pale and fragile, people always treated her like she would crack if they raised their voices.

Hearing wasn't her problem. Punks were.

"Uh, well — " McEwin said, as Daniels pretended to write in his notebook, hiding a grin. McEwin blushed.

"Don't go prissy on me, Officer McEwin," Lena scolded. "I'm an old lady, pushing seventy-seven, but I'm not your mother. Those damn punks kicked the shit out of Mr. Lee, and calling it anything different won't make it hurt any less. So if I want to call it 'kicking the shit out of Mr. Lee,' I'll call it that, and if I want to call the damn punks who did it 'damn punks,' I'll call them that too, and if you don't like it, then why don't you just go out and catch them and throw them in jail where they belong, and I won't have to call them damn punks anymore, and they won't be able to kick the shit out of people anymore."

Daniels laughed, shaking his head. McEwin turned redder and shifted from foot to foot, looking at the floor.

McEwin's embarrassment and Daniels' laughter didn't annoy Lena. The boys weren't mocking her, she knew. In fact, they were kind of cute.

She hadn't expected much from them. Not that they didn't want to capture the crooks. They were just so busy that it was hard to take another mugging seriously. The police were a little cynical. She understood.

Lena had called them out of duty. When trouble came to the neighborhood, a good citizen called the cops. And the cops came, like good citizens. They did their professional, civic duty.

They asked their questions: Did she recognize any of the punk — er, perpetrators? (Yes. She described them, and the two officers nodded in recognition.) Did she see a license plate? (Yes. But it wasn't real. It was an obscene word. Both men blushed this time and Lena regretted her saltiness.) Did she hear anybody use a name? (Yes. An obscene word she decided to forget to spare the officers further embarrassment.) Would she recognize them if she saw them again? (Yes.)

And so on.

All a sham.

And a shame. A report would be filed and that would be the end of it. Lena knew the police would do nothing — could do nothing. The streets were so full of young hoodlums these days. Now, they'd found her neighborhood.

Their duty done, quickly but professionally, the two cops left. "Ma'am," they said at the door, giving a polite tap to the shiny brims of their caps and hurrying to their patrol car. Another call, another tragedy about which they again could do nothing. Professional. Useless.

Lena sighed as they drove away.

"Damn, damn those punks."

Her duty done, Lena picked up the phone again.

*

One afternoon nine days later, Lena received a gentleman caller. The man rang the doorbell and stood back a step, removing his hat to reveal a freckled, bald scalp rimmed with white hair. He was tall and rather handsome, in a weather-beaten way that Lena had always found attractive. And he dressed well, though not expensively. He wore a rather nice cologne.

"Yes?" Lena asked through the screen door.

"Mrs. Lena Bartlett?" he responded with a slight, almost military bow. She nodded.

"Col. Ephraim Hawthorne, at your service." The bow deepened.

"You're not the plumber, are you?"

"If you'll give me a moment, Mrs. Bartlett, you may find that I'm able to solve an even more disturbing problem."

"Oh, dear," she said, hugging her housecoat protectively at the base of her throat.

"I'm from The Geezers," he whispered, producing a card. His sand-gravel voice reminded Lena a little of Augie. I'll bet Col. Hawthorne smokes a pipe, she thought.

"The Geezers?" Lena said, opening the screen door. "Oh, my, my. Do come in."

He accepted fresh oatmeal cookies and milk, and made the appropriate compliments. He said a few nice words to Cato and seemed tolerant, even amused, when the tiny dog growled and hid behind Lena's leg.

"Well," she said at last, "you've certainly taken your time responding to my call."

"On the contrary, Mrs. Bartlett — "

"Lena."

"Lena. My aunt's name, by the way. On the contrary, Lena. We got on the case seconds after you called."

"Oh?" Lena's pale eyebrows rose. "I haven't seen any evidence of that."

Hawthorne explained. "You weren't meant to notice. We operate undercover, you understand, in part because our activities are, ahem, frowned upon in some official circles, if not sometimes illegal. Our methods are quite unorthodox, you may have heard."

Lena nodded, quite fascinated. She'd heard. What senior in the city hadn't?

"We also try not to alert the perpetrators that we're on to them," Hawthorne continued. "Your descriptions were thorough. We recognized this bunch right away. Our rap sheet on them is as long as your arm. We chased them out of the Heights on the other side of the river. Figured they'd go tame, but it looks like they came here instead. Sorry. Guess we were too easy going. This time — "

Hawthorne's police jargon excited Lena, an emotion she hadn't felt in a decade or more. He was rather charming. She offered to make tea.

"Thing is," Hawthorne said, "we need your help."

"My help?" Lena blushed. "I'll be damned. How can I help you?"

Hawthorne explained.

The next day, two gang members loafed in the park fishing for prospective victims. They couldn't help but overhear a loud conversation between two near-deaf seniors who were playing checkers and talking about poor Mr. Lee. The two old men said they were relieved that Lee had recovered, but were worried that he intended to go home through the park after closing the next night, just after ten p.m., carrying the day's receipts. The hoodlums didn't suspect a Geezer trap.

The next night, they walked right into it.

"Go," Hawthorne barked into his radio from his command center behind the lace curtains of Lena's apartment, which offered the best view of the operation. The gang had parked their pickup truck with the refrigerator-sized speakers on the street and had taken up a position to ambush Mr. Lee. It was a few minutes before ten.

With Hawthorne's command, several things happened at once.

Two blocks south, 81-year-old Willis Wood, a retired laborer, fell from his wheelchair in the middle of the street as he crossed it. Paramedics were called. Several nice, elderly passers-by helped divert traffic around the tragedy.

Two blocks north, 69-year-old Marilyn Parsons, an unemployed welder, accidentally spilled a grocery cart into the street. It contained all her possessions. Several seniors who lived in the area tried to help pick up her things. Her belligerence delayed the process, snarling traffic.

Two blocks east, 34-year-old Jacob Marzotto ordered his crew to barricade a section of the street they'd torn up in an unsuccessful search for the source of a mysterious odor reported coming from the sewer at that location by a caller who called himself Earl Warren. The caller was in fact Jason Marzotto, Jacob's 78-year-old grandfather.

Two blocks west, Officers McEwin and Daniels blocked the road leading to Burgess Street Park on orders from their watch commander, Sgt. Tony Lombardi. The two cops didn't question the vague orders from their Sergeant. The Sergeant didn't question the orders from his grand-mother.

"All set," Hawthorne heard over his radio from observers at the four sites.

"Go," Hawthorne said again. Lee, briefed by Geezer agents, walked into the park as planned. Lee didn't see the gang waiting. The gang didn't see The Geezers waiting.

At a narrow place along the sidewalk beside an old oak tree, Lee stopped to tie his shoe. The gang moved in. Inches away from their victim, the group tripped a snare that swung them high into the air in a rope net. Ralph "Tex" Whitmore, 68, a retired TV kiddie-cartoon show host, ignored the howls of pain and indignation as he lowered his trap and its contents to a few inches above the pavement. Mrs. Emma Nichols, 74, and her twin sister Esther, former grade school teachers, prodded the angry, tightly-knit group into submission with the needle-sharp points of their umbrellas as Lt. J.G. (USN, retired) John "Knots" Lander, 71, speedily tied all their hands and feet in intricate knots to prevent a premature escape.

Once under control, Whitmore's job ended. He dropped the group to the ground where they twisted, cursing and grunting. He retrieved his net.

The group's struggles subsided as the ropes bit into their wrists and ankles, and as their terror and pain increased with each poke of a sharp umbrella.

When the net sprung, Lena and Hawthorne had stepped out of her apartment and crossed the street to the park. Lena wore her Sunday best. She carried Cato.

"What the fuck is going on?" squealed the skinny punk, eying the geriat-ric assault force from his prone position under another punk. All the old-sters wore gray-leather jackets with "The Geezers" embroidered on the back.

"Geezers," the punk squeaked. "Oh, shit — "

Former librarian Mary Lou Becker, 93, the oldest of The Geezers, jammed a bar of soap into the boy's mouth. She shook him firmly by the ears and lectured him about the wisdom of appropriate language use, being courteous to others, and keeping his voice down. The boy nodded in terror and tried to say "Yes, ma'am," through his foamy teeth.

Lena, peeping from behind The Geezers' commander's back, prom-ised herself to clean up her own language before she met the intrepid Mrs. Becker.

Cato barked gleefully.

When 84-year-old Gus Konakis approached the big punk, tying a crisp white apron around his ample belly as he did so, the punk spat defiantly. "What the fu — "

The kid looked nervously at Mrs. Becker. She wagged a warning finger at him, he gulped, and looked back at Gus. When he saw the little round man stropping a straight razor on a leather strap hanging from his belt, he screamed and tried to shrink his purple Mohawk-coiffed head into his beefy, sweating shoulders.

"You be still. No get cut, eh?" Gus said.

The punk lay rigid as Gus gave him a quick haircut.

Then the fat barber gave the other boy, the one with the beard, a close shave. While doing so, he sang a Greek folk song and danced a little jig between strokes. When he finished with his work, Gus bowed and the now clean-shaven punk passed out.

Hawthorne approached the gang. "We'd like to retrieve our ropes now, if you don't mind," he said. "I'm sure you'll be nice and not try to leave us just yet." Gus, Mrs. Becker, the Nichols twins, and other Geezers all frowned with grim concern until the punks nodded and mumbled "Yes sir." The Geezers smiled, satisfied, and Knots retrieved his ropes.

Next, famed Hollywood clothier Mr. Henri, now retired, supervised a crew of Geezers in giving the four a new wardrobe. Off with the odd, on with the new. White shirts, narrow ties, pleated slacks with cuffs, and penny loafers for the boys, and for the girl (coyly concealed behind a makeshift curtain) a pretty, white, cotton lace-trimmed, calf-length dress with puff sleeves and tasteful white pumps. The duds, the kind of stuff nice people used to wear, had been mothballed in various Geezer closets since they were last word decades before — the 1950s, mostly.

The process took only a few minutes.

At umbrella point, The Geezers then escorted the gang into the middle of the street near their truck.

Dozens of gray-leather jacketed oldsters had gathered for the ceremonies. "Ladies and Gentlemen!" retired circus announcer J.S. Jovanovich declared into a large bullhorn. The tuxedo-clad gentleman stood atop a bright red milk box and waited for the watching crowd to hush. "Introducing! The One! The Only! Mrs.! Lena! Bartlett!"

Cheers and applause greeted Lena as she waved. Too bad Mr. Lee had declined to do the honors, but she was pleased that the little grocer had chosen her to do it in his stead.

She handed Cato to Hawthorne and strode majestically to the center of the street. There, across from the pickup truck, next to the announcer, she stopped. All around her, on porches, in windows, in the street and along the sidewalks, her neighbors, friends, and fellow seniors watched. To her left, the punks huddled and whimpered like wet puppies.

With solemn dignity, Capt. Alonzo Lopez, USMC retired, presented

Lena with the detonator. "You hold it here," he said, pointing to the handle on the box, "and when you're ready, push down hard. Okay?" Lena nodded.

Geezers passed out helmets, goggles, and earplugs to the crowd. They set up baffles to keep the explosion from damaging nearby trees and moved spectators standing too near the truck away.

"Watch your windows," one Geezer shouted to second story observers.

The four punks, dazed, became aware of the preparations being made. The big punk gaped, he gave a tiny squeal, shoved his fist into his mouth, and gurgled. The other three babbled, sniffled, and gaped.

But none moved.

At a signal, a Geezer drummer provided a drum roll.

"Readyyyyy!" the announcer announced. Lena got ready.

"Fire!"

Lena fired.

She didn't see what happened next in the blinding white flash from the detonation. The thunderclap pushed the air from her lungs, and she tasted acrid smoke.

She removed her goggles and squinted at her work. Her target had been a candy apple red pickup with two black refrigerator-sized speakers in the back, with lots of shiny chrome. In its place sat a charred hulk of twisted metal, burning, pouring mushroom clouds of black smoke into the sky.

"Well," she said, grinning, "I'll be da — er, darned."

A noise came from Hawthorne's radio. "Right," he said. He produced a whistle from a pocket and blew it. Instantly, The Geezers melted into the side streets, into doors and alleys, and disappeared. The neighbors returned to their homes and the street emptied.

"You kids don't come back," Hawthorne told the gang, "or we will."

The gang members nodded and mumbled agreement. At least for the moment, they'd had enough. Hawthorne escorted Lena back to her apartment, satisfied with the victory, however temporary it might be.

Maybe some day, he thought, there won't be any gangs. Maybe.

McEwin and Daniels had heard the explosion and abandoned their barricade two blocks away, alarmed. Their patrol car slid onto a strange scene.

In the middle of the street, four well-dressed and neatly trimmed teenagers stood, looking lost, confused, and a little scared. Nearby, what had once been a pickup truck, probably red in color, burned, sending black smoke billows into the night sky. Other than that, the street appeared deserted.

"What gives here?" McEwin said, awed by the spectacle.

"Nothing, Officer, sir," the big bald teenager said, adjusting his tie.

McEwin eyed the group suspiciously. "Wait a minute," he said, "you're the bunch that did old man Lee a couple of days back. Isn't that your truck? Come on, what gives?"

"Honest, sir," the skinny boy said, rubbing at his mouth. "Everything is okay. Really, sir."

"I think I'll go talk to Mrs. Bartlett," Daniels said, walking toward her apartment.

McEwin, still suspiciously eyeing the four teenagers, walked around the burning vehicle.

"Did any of you see what happened here?"

"No, sir," one of them said.

"An engine fire, sir," another said.

"So what are you doing out here so late?"

"We, uh — " one stammered.

"Volunteering to help the old folks," another piped in. "You know. With their shopping and stuff. Sir."

McEwin sputtered to a stop after a few more questions that prompted similar answers. Respectful, but uninformative.

Soon, Daniels returned, shaking his head.

"Well?" McEwin asked.

"She said The Geezers did it," Daniels whispered so the nearby teenagers wouldn't hear. "Shall I call it in?"

McEwin slowly took off his cap, sighed, and scratched his red thatch. Daniels waited for his older partner to speak.

The Geezers. Again. Damn.

McEwin looked around at the smoking wreckage, at the silent, peaceful street, and at the four clean-cut youngsters, oddly nervous but as respectful as a church choir.

He sighed again.

"Call in a vehicle fire," he said at last. "Abandoned, probably stolen. Now, let's see if these nice young folks would like a ride home."

GOOD NEIGHBORS

Mrs. Emily Lamb and Mrs. Mary Como were annoyed about the flying saucer that had crashed in their backyards just after dark, only feet from their respective kitchens, but even more disturbing was the fact that it crashed exactly on their mutual property line. Exactly.

The wood slat fence between their yards lay in a twisted, splintered heap under and on either side of the flying saucer. It had been an old fence anyway, getting older and more worm-eaten because Mrs. Lamb and Mrs. Como had never been able to agree on whose responsibility it was to fix it.

Now, crushed under the crumpled remains of a twenty-foot wide disk of smoking, charred metal, it didn't matter. A fence was supposed to make for good neighbors. Nobody expected flying saucers to land on their fences.

"It's no use, Mary," Emily said. "Half on your side, half on mine. Fifty-fifty, looks like. Your problem and mine, both."

"Yes, Emily, but — " Mary laid slender hands on her slim hips and sighed. She didn't want to call the police or whomever it was you were supposed to call when these things happened — the Air Force? Who knew? And she didn't really want to have anything to do with Emily Lamb if she could avoid it. She didn't want to get involved.

Mrs. Emily Lamb was loud and tacky. In her early sixties. Fat. And she always wanted to talk about her conspiracies. "Do you know what that communist you voted for is doing today?" she'd say to Mrs. Como across the driveway in the morning when she was out watering her yard, no doubt waiting to pounce as Mary stepped out the door and headed for work.

Emily Lamb was a widow, a retired electrician. She read mysteries.

Mrs. Mary Como, on the other hand, was quiet, fashionable. In her late forties, she took pride in the fact that her figure still turned an eye or two. She deliberately moved into the subdivision cul-de-sac to avoid pesky neighbors, but it hadn't worked in the case of Mrs. Lamb.

Mary Como was married, a real estate broker. She read science fiction.

The two women shared a mutual antipathy, though it never strayed beyond the bounds of civility and a common property line. Their large adjacent backyards faced a horse pasture. Another subdivision bordered the pasture about two blocks away.

Odd that nobody else heard the flying saucer crash. Or maybe not so odd, given that the Dekkers across the street were out of town and their teenagers were having another loud party. Waste of time calling the police on them again.

The Lees were out to dinner no doubt. Who knew what whatsisname, the cab driver that lived on the other side of the cul-de-sac, was up to? Who cared?

"Look, Emily, my boy and his wife and kids are coming over for dinner and I have plans. Couldn't you please deal with it?"

"You mean Iggie's actually going to pay you a visit, Mary?" Emily's voice took on its natural, cynical burr.

"Well, he will," Mary muttered. "Someday."

"Now, I figure it's on both of our properties," Emily said, "so it's both of ours' problem. Besides, my back is giving me fits lately."

"You want me to haul it off? *You* have a pickup."

"No," Emily said, "I was thinking we should put it in your station wagon and haul it to the dump."

"That's not very funny — "

"I know, I know." Emily shrugged. "The pickup's busted. Gearbox is giving me fits. I got it up on blocks in the garage."

"We should call the police, I suppose. Or the Air Force."

Emily spit. "Are you kidding? If they come, they'll make such a deal, you wouldn't believe. Make us sign security oaths. Investigate us. Follow us, tap our phones — "

"So we just get rid of it and don't tell anybody? I don't know — "

"I don't think anybody else saw." Emily looked around. "What about your husband?"

"Thomas is at a convention. In Las Vegas. Gone till Sunday afternoon."

Both women looked around the neighborhood. Except for the roar and thump of the party at the Dekkers' place, the neighborhood was quiet. It was a Friday night, which accounted for the many dark windows and empty driveways. People going out. And it was a nice night for early May, another excuse to get out.

"Nobody cares anymore," Emily said. She sighed. "Okay, I'll see if I can get the pickup started. In the morning — "

That's when they heard the sound from inside the saucer. A moan.

"There's something we may have overlooked," Mary said slowly.

"I'll go grab some tools," Emily said. "You go change into something a little more practical."

Mary changed from her skirt and blouse to her gardening shirt and coveralls. She put on her gardening shoes and went to the greenhouse to get a flashlight. Flying debris from the crash fifty feet across the yard had torn a gash along the greenhouse side. Jagged, gaping holes showed through a row of fiberglass paneling. And she heard mice over by the herbs. Again.

The new traps weren't working.

Emily was already tearing into the flying saucer with a crowbar and a hammer when Mary rejoined her.

"Stack these over there," Emily said to Mary as she handed her a strip of dull gray metal she'd pulled from the wreckage. Mary didn't like the idea of Emily casually ordering her, but she did it anyway, taking the strips gingerly in her gloved hands.

The metal felt surprisingly light. Mary twisted it. Strong.

"Gimme that light over here," Emily said. "Looks like after an earthquake or some such."

Through a tangle of metal shards, the women had reached what looked like the cramped cockpit of a small airplane, or submarine. A dense pack of intricate instruments, wiring, and equipment surrounded the pilot, who lay curled in a fetal position.

"Is he alive?" Mary whispered.

"Dunno," Emily said, her voice husky.

The figure was humanoid, clothed in a silverish fabric from head to foot. Overlarge head, tiny body, about the size of a four-year-old. They couldn't see the face.

The figure groaned and moved.

Mary gasped and retreated a step.

"Maybe the pilot's a woman," Emily said.

"Maybe," Mary said, leaning back in over Emily's broad shoulder.

"We've got to do something," Mary said.

"You thinking of taking her in? Making her a maid or something? Raising her and sending her off to college — "

The saucer pilot moaned again and lifted his — *its* head. The skin was glistening, slick, pale, and yellow-greenish, like a slug. A broad forehead accented huge black eyes. It was noseless. A thin line of a mouth split the narrow, pointed chin. Ugly. Smelled like a dead rat.

Both woman drew back and shivered.

"Definitely male," Mary said.

"Yeah."

The thing moaned again, its slit lips parting, showing a very humanlike tongue. It pointed to its side with a doll-like hand and winced in obvious pain.

"Where do you come from?" Mary said, raising her voice, as though the thing was hard of hearing.

"Hellsakes, be quiet."

"But we must find out — "

"We got to get this, this — *thing* out of our backyard, is what we've got to do."

"But this is the discovery of a lifetime," Mary said. "A being from another planet — "

"And you want to treat it like in one of your science fiction books. You think we're going to get a call from the president or something? Maybe get on talk shows?"

"So what do you want to do, Emily? Take it to the dump and forget all about it? This is important — "

The thing started to sit up.

Both women gasped, alarmed, and tried to step out of the tangled wreckage. Mary let out a little shriek as she tore her shirt on a jagged edge of metal and fell down. Emily swore and bolted for her back door.

The thing rose on its feet, babbling in whatever language it used to babble with, and took some tottering steps in the wreckage. It climbed from the heap and headed for the pasture.

"Emily, do something."

"Get out of the way, fool woman."

Emily had fetched a shotgun. She shouldered Mary aside and aimed the piece at the back of the creature from outer space that was waddling unsteadily toward the horse pasture.

"Emily, you can't — "

Mary grabbed for the shotgun and it went off with a ear-splitting roar and a white flash.

Both women fell back against the grass. They rose stiffly. Their ears rang and the air reeked of gunpowder. The Lisbons' dog was barking down the street. The Dekkers' party was as loud as ever. The rest was silence.

"Where's the creature?" Mary said, tugging at Emily's sleeve.

"Dunno." Emily grabbed the flashlight from the ground where it had fallen and walked out toward where the creature had staggered. The beam of the flashlight wavered left and right, left and right. After about fifty feet, the beam stopped.

"Holy-moly," Emily said.

"What? What?" Mary cried, running to the scene.

In the beam of the flashlight, the creature lay. Headless. The bloody stump of its neck looked remarkably bright red in the flashlight's stark beam.

Mary gasped and turned away.

"Blown clean away," Emily croaked, her voice oddly reverent. She cast the flashlight around in search of the creature's head. "Disintegrated into a bloody mist — "

"Oh, please, Emily," Mary said, fighting an urge to retch.

Emily heaved a massive sigh from her bosom and turned off the flashlight. "Mary," she said. "We need ourselves a drink."

Mary nodded agreement. Weak-kneed, she allowed Emily to lead her into the Lamb kitchen, where Emily plopped Mary into a chair. Emily opened her refrigerator, which immediately emitted a choking whine. She slapped it on its side and the whine changed pitch. "Damn motor's messed up."

She twisted off the caps from a pair of Buds. She handed one to Mary, dropped her bulk into a kitchen chair, tilted the bottle back to her lips, and took a healthy pull.

"Ahh," she said, wiping her lips on her forearm. "Nothing like a good brew to settle the stomach, make the mind work smoother. Loosens the tongue and the morals too, but that's another story."

Mary sat across the table from Emily, legs apart, shoulders hunched, bottle in numb fingers on the table, eyes glazed.

"Hey, you don't look so good," Emily said. "Take a few swigs. You'll feel better."

Mary blinked a few times, took a ragged breath, straightened her shoulders, and drew her knees together, coming to. She looked around the dim kitchen. Emily hadn't turned on the lights.

"You never invited me into your house before," Mary said.

"Never had occasion to."

Chipped Formica covered the cheap table. Worn plastic chairs, plastic dishes stacked by the sink. On one wall, in the dim light, Mary saw a line of three painted plaster ducks marching across the faded, flowered wallpaper, oblivious to their tacky surroundings.

"Nice ducks," Mary said, tilting back the bottle. It tasted sour, cold. She liked the malty bite at the back of her tongue.

"Present from my Joshua."

"Your oldest son. Right? I remember."

The two women sat in silence, except for the Dekker party, emptying their bottles. Emily belched, rose, and turned to the refrigerator to get seconds.

"Do you like wine?" Mary asked.

Emily turned, her hand on the refrigerator door. "Sure. Now and then."

"Come on over to my place. I got a nice, white, off-dry Riesling."

Emily hesitated. "Why not?"

The two women walked through the back yard, skirting the disemboweled wreckage of the flying saucer, stepping over fence splinters, and walked into Mary Como's dining room.

"You left it unlocked," Emily pointed out.

"Forgot. Had my mind on other things," Mary tilted her head toward the backyard. She turned up the lights a bit, illuminating the room just enough.

"You could have been robbed."

Emily looked around at the room's decor. The long, polished wood dining table gleamed in the soft light where it wasn't covered under a white lace tablecloth. A large glass bowl of wax fruit lay in the center of the table.

"So could you," Mary said, opening the beveled glass door on a tall wine cabinet. "Your place wasn't locked."

"Never is," Emily said, sitting in a high-backed chair. The puffy soft cushion under her butt whooshed as she settled her bulk into it. "I got nothing for people to steal."

Mary produced two wineglasses and sat one in front of Emily. She poured and sat back in another high-backed chair. She twirled the glass, and sniffed at it before taking a delicate sip.

Emily imitated Mary's moves, twirling, sniffing, and sipping. Cold and sour. But it had a nice, fruity bite to it she could almost chew.

"Never been in your place before," Emily said.

"Hm."

They sat in companionable silence, enjoying the warmth of the wine, their elegant surrounding. The Dekker party got louder.

"So," Mary said, emptying her glass in a gulp, "we seem to have a crashed flying saucer in our backyard — "

"And a dead pilot in the neighbor's pasture — "

"Who you shouldn't have killed — "

"And what?" Emily said. "Let him go and terrorize the neighborhood? You said it was important. You said — "

"I never said you should shoot him."

"He scared the living bejesus out of me — "

"Which provides no excuse for — "

"And the gun wouldn't have gone off if you hadn't — "

"So it's my fault, is it?" Mary said.

Emily shrugged and took a sip of her wine. Mary had raised her voice, and Emily didn't feel like arguing right now.

"Got any more wine?"

Mary sighed and poured again.

"Mary, if folks find out about this — "

"You're right. Especially now that the pilot's dead."

"Water under the dam. Sorry. Still, with the flying saucer sitting on both our property lines — "

"We've got to *do* something," Mary whined.

"We've got to get rid of the body. Hide the wreckage."

Both women sipped. Gulped.

"How?" Mary said.

Emily had a far away look in her eyes. "I saw something in this one mystery TV show, Hitchcock. I forget the title. But I think I got me an idea."

"Yes?"

"You got anything to eat around here?"

"What's for dinner, honey?" Thomas asked Sunday afternoon after he returned from the convention in Las Vegas.

"A surprise." Mary kissed her husband on the cheek. "And we're having company for dinner."

"Oh? Who?"

"You remember Mrs. Lamb, our neighbor?"

"I thought you didn't like her."

Mary shrugged, taking off Thomas' tie. "We got acquainted over the backyard fence this weekend. New fence, by the way."

"Nah."

"Sure. Come and see for yourself."

Thomas walked out onto the patio and looked.

"What is that?" he said, the frown obvious in his voice. He pointed at the ragged gray metal strips tacked up in a crazy-quilt pattern on uneven fence posts.

"Some metal plates Emily found. I used some of it to shore up the greenhouse too. To keep out the mice. It works."

"Mary, have you gone — "

A gate in the fence opened — a gate that hadn't existed before Thomas had left for Las Vegas on Thursday — and Mrs. Lamb stepped through. She was smiling, wearing a dress. Not jeans. A dress, and a white blouse.

She carried a large pan, big enough to hold a turkey, covered with a kitchen towel. She smiled.

"Finished already?" Mary called out. "I thought you were going to work on your truck first."

"Done. I jury-rigged some spare parts. Got the fridge working too. And plenty of time to cook. Your herbs and spices are really great, Mary," Emily said, approaching across the lawn. "Afternoon, Mr. Como. How was your weekend?"

"Uh," Thomas said, eyebrows raised in a silent question to his wife which she ignored, "fine. I guess. Yours?" He stepped aside to let Emily past. The dish she carried smelled delicious. "What's cooking?"

"A surprise," Emily said, exchanging a look with Mary.

"Yes," Mary said. "Something Emily saw on TV."

"Well," Thomas said, "it certainly smells delicious. It smells out of this world."

Both women laughed. Hesitantly at first, Thomas joined in the laughter and helped set the table.

THE THING IN EDDIE DRAPER'S BACKYARD

Prince woke up Eddie Draper just before six Saturday morning, barking like he'd just caught Jack the Ripper. As Eddie got to the door to shout out into the backyard telling the big lab to shut up, the phone started ringing.

It started ringing the same time Eddie put his hand on the back door knob to open it, the same time he saw what Prince was barking at in the backyard.

A monolith, like the one on "2001: A Space Odyssey." About nine feet tall. A cold-looking, reflectionless, flat black, faceless domino standing upright in Eddie Draper's backyard, right smack dab in the middle, aligned with the north-south property line, facing the house. Or facing the Brewster's place, depending on your point of view.

"I'll get it," Eddie said to Prince, reaching for the phone. "It's for me."

"Are you planning some kind of party, Eddie, or what?" Tom Brewster growled over the phone. Eddie could see Tom standing in his bathrobe on Tom's patio across the fence just beyond the monolith, talking into his cellular. Eddie could see the Coulsons too, next door to Tom's house, peeking out their kitchen window at him and the monolith.

"No, Tom. Nothing like that. It's, uh — "

"What?" Irritated. "What is it, Eddie?"

Prince strained at the rope that tied him to the back porch, straining toward the monolith a few feet away from him, barking, muscles taut from nose to tailtip. If the rope broke, Prince would lurch forward and bump nose-first into the thing.

"It's a surprise," Eddie said. The truth — he was just as surprised as Tom.

"A surprise? A *surprise?* You think you're funny, or what? Look, Eddie, I got relatives coming over this afternoon. I'm planning a barbecue. I don't want to look over my fence and see that — that *thing*. I don't want to have to try to explain — *you*. You get me?"

"Yeah, I see." Eddie knew Tom thought he was a bit weird. Bachelors like Eddie didn't live in Riverdale on cul-de-sacs on Excelsior Drive in the

Pineview Estates subdivision with families all around. Neighbors in this neck of suburbia didn't stay up till two in the a.m. playing loud music, with — strange women. Giggling. And Eddie had a mustache. But Eddie had inherited the place from his mother and it was paid for.

Besides, Eddie liked living in Riverdale. Screw Tom. Screw the neighbors.

"What the hell is it, anyway?" Tom asked.

Prince had shifted his constant barking from the monolith to a spot against the back fence, behind the apricot tree, a spot Eddie couldn't see from where he stood inside his kitchen. Somebody trying to climb over his fence from the McPherson's?

Prince seldom barked. If he'd been a yapper, the neighbors would have complained, and Eddie wouldn't have been able to keep him. He only barked when people climbed over the back fence into his yard.

Or at the occasional, suddenly appearing, black monolith.

"I got to go, Tom. The McPherson kid is after my apricot tree again."

Eddie hung up before Tom could say anything. The phone started ringing again, but Eddie ignored it. He opened the back door, took a step out, and stopped, realizing all he wore was panties. He realized this at the same instant the Coulson's did. And maybe a few other neighbors.

Eddie retreated to get a bathrobe. He usually slept buff, but he'd put on the blood red silk panties last night and slept in them after Candy went home. The panties were Candy's, a gift from her. They smelled nice. They felt nice.

When he stalked into the backyard, knotting the bathrobe over his hairy belly as he walked, it seemed like the neighborhood population had increased in the last few minutes. He could see even more faces in his neighbors' windows and on decks and patios. They'd invited friends over to stare at the monolith. At six-something in the bloody goddam a.m., a dozen people gawked into his backyard like there'd been a train wreck.

Eddie didn't glance at the monolith. He made a beeline past it toward the corner where the apricot tree stood, its fruit still pale green, not quite orange yet. Just the way pimply-faced Jamie McPherson liked them when he could steal them, when Eddie was away and Prince was tied up to the porch.

Not that Prince would ever bite anybody if Eddie let him roam, which he never did because that was the cost of keeping the dog. "You keep him tied up or he goes," Tom Brewster warned when Eddie moved in three years ago. Prince didn't mind. Eddie took Prince for walks in the hills often.

"And he better not be a barker, either," Tom had said.

Well, Prince *had*n't been.

But it wasn't the McPherson kid who'd climbed over the fence, who crouched beneath the apricot tree, aiming a camera at the thing in Eddie Draper's backyard. It was some reporter guy, taking pictures. Crouching because maybe he didn't want to get his slacks wet in the morning dew on the lawn.

"Hey, you," Eddie snapped as he approached the guy, fists bunched. The reporter had been so intent on taking pictures that he hadn't heard Eddie coming. Eddie startled him. The guy's eyes went buggy, he jerked upright, banged his head on a low tree branch, and sat down hard.

"Owowowowow." The reporter rubbed at the bruise on his head, camera swinging from the strap around his neck.

"Who the hell are you, and what the hell are you doing in my backyard?" Eddie demanded.

"You watch your tongue, Eddie Draper," Nancy Brewster said. Tom's wife stood waist high above the back fence, leaning over. Eddie realized she and Tom had dragged their patio table over to the fence to stand on it and get a better view. He didn't recognize the man standing elbow to elbow with her and Tom. The man spoke into a cellular phone, intently describing what he saw, like a sportscaster. Maybe he was a radio guy, Eddie thought.

"Yeah," Tom added, "you want my kids to learn your filthy language?"

His temper rising, Eddie wanted to give Tom the finger, but then he saw the TV camera poking over the fence on the far end of the yard, from the Coulson's backyard. He was on TV.

Or, rather, the monolith was on TV.

Prince had changed his barking target to the side gate that led from the front to the backyard, where a hand reached through the slats, trying to unlatch the gate. In fact, Prince had gone nuts — one bark at the reporter, now retreating back over the fence, one bark at the Brewster bunch, another at the TV people at the Coulson's, another at the side gate, another at the phone, still ringing.

And a few for the helicopter —

A for-hell's-sake *helicopter* hovering over Eddie Draper's backyard at six-something in the goddamit Saturday aye-bloody-em I'm-supposed-to-be-in-*bed* morning.

Over his scream of rage and frustration, Eddie also heard sirens approaching.

"What's going on?" Eddie yelled at nobody in particular.

Tom explained. "You got this thing in your backyard, is what. What I want to know is — "

"I think the city has ordinances — " Mrs. Coulson began.

"Mr. Draper, I'm from CNN. We're broadcasting live — "

"Mr. Draper, I just got off the phone with Mr. Clarke and Mr. Kubrick's lawyers — "

"Mr. Draper, we're from the physics department at the University — "

Prince's barking blended with the helicopter droning, the sirens wailing, the harsh, discordant shouts and calls from neighbors, reporters, and who-knew-who-all else. Eddie Draper stood in the midst of it all in his backyard, in his bathrobe, jaw agape on his unshaven face.

Facing the monolith.

Which had begun to hum.

Prince was the first to hear the sound. He was holding off a policeman at the side gate when suddenly his ears perked up, he cocked his head, looked at the monolith, and whimpered.

Eddie heard it next. The monolith hummed — or chanted in a ragged, high-pitched, zillion-voice a cappella chorus or whatever it was doing — and the hum got louder and louder. Soon, others heard it too. The on-lookers went silent and stared wide-eyed and gape-jawed at the monolith. The sound from the thing grew until it seemed to overtake and engulf even the helicopter.

Like the movie, Eddie thought. Just then, Eddie knew that, like in the movie, somebody had to touch the thing. That somebody, Eddie knew, was him — the thing stood in his backyard.

In the movie, when the monkey touched it, the monkey got smart, learned how to use tools, and started the human race. When Dr. Heywood Floyd touched it on the moon, it let out a high-pitched scream like a billion fax machines being dialed on the telephone at once. And then those two astronauts had to go to Jupiter where HAL went whacko and then came the psychedelic part Eddie never understood but enjoyed watching anyway.

Eddie took a step toward it. The humming rose a notch in volume and intensity. The neighbors watched.

If I touch it, Eddie thought, either I'll get very smart and me and Candy will found Homo super-sapiens or something, or the thing will let off a shriek that'll break windows in the whole neighborhood and get my ass sued. Maybe the world will change. Maybe I'll understand the end of the movie.

Who knows?

But *something* will happen.

Eddie stood within an arm's length of the monolith. The hum emanating from its flat-black face rose again in pitch and volume. Eddie reached out a hand toward it.

Prince touched it first. He lifted a leg and pissed on it.

"I'll get it, Eddie," Prince said. "It's for me."

A TAIL

Bentley Croft was the first person in Wyoming to grow a tail.

He discovered it just after slapping off the alarm on a cold Wednesday morning in March. It was 4:30 a.m., still dark, but out in the yard, Rocky crowed.

"Where in hell'd this come from?" Bentley asked Beggar, sitting up, holding the tail up between him and the dog. The big lab sniffed his master's tail tip, cocked his head stupidly, and whined.

" — since New Years Eve, when the first tail was reported," the guy on the alarm radio was saying. "Mrs. Ira Bjorkman, an Ames, Iowa, housewife, is the latest, the eighteenth known person in America to grow a tail overnight. None have so far been reported in Wyoming — "

"Give me a minute, dang it all," Bentley told the radio. He'd call the TV station over in Casper, make it official. "Right after chores. And coffee."

Bentley put his glasses on and padded into the bathroom on cold, bare feet, Beggar following. He pulled the light chain and blinked in the sudden brightness. He tried to focus bloodshot eyes on the image in the cracked medicine cabinet mirror. He yawned.

He twitched his left butt cheek and the tail he'd grown overnight snaked up over his left shoulder and hung in the air behind him, wavering like a cobra.

"I think mine is prettier than yours," he said to the dog.

The soft, rope-like tail was tan, the tip tufted with a darkish hair wad, like a lion's tail. Bentley compared the tail-hair color to his own thinning hair.

"Yeah, ain't you a hunk?" he told his reflection.

Beggar wagged his tail. Bentley wagged his. It worked, but he knocked over an empty beer bottle on the toilet seat. "I best rig this up so it don't get stepped on." He found he could twine it around his body like a belt.

He wondered how he'd learned to move the tail, to wave it, wag it, and to twitch the tip in lazy little snaps. He'd never had a tail to practice with before, but it felt like he'd known how to do it all his life. Maybe the knowledge came from watching cows and horses. He liked twitching the tip. It reminded him of a lion on the prairie, regally waiting for his woman-lion to fetch something home for dinner.

That made him feel good and he thought of Louise. He'd planned to have breakfast at the Wrangler after chores and ask her out tonight, if she was free. Or maybe Friday. Or maybe Saturday, if she had to work Friday night.

What a good-looking woman. Long legs, long hair, lots of energy. Not shy around men, and she could ride. Maybe they'd go riding on the Mesa.

"Ain't she in for a surprise," Bentley said, deciding he'd better shave.

Maybe she wouldn't like it, Bentley thought, and that made him frown.

Then Bentley wondered how he'd get it into his pants.

"Well, six and two is eight," he muttered. "Lucky I sleep buck naked or I'd've ripped my drawers."

He couldn't squeeze his bony frame into his jeans, not with a tail. He borrowed some coveralls Doc Tom had left last time he'd been out to ride his Morgan, but it was still a stretch. He cut a little hole in the backside, poked the tail out the hole, and wrapped it around his waist. It would do, but sitting down would be a hassle.

He finished chores without a hitch and got back to the house before the sun peaked over the Winds. He sipped his coffee as he hesitated, thinking about whether or not he should dial the TV station in Casper. "To hell with them," he thought at first. Then he figured maybe he ought, seeing as how they'd just find out anyway.

Besides, it might be fun, getting on TV talk shows and such like.

A girl came on the line and he talked for a while. Then they put him on the air live, with some breathless slick-talker, like a used car salesman but with a deeper voice and a waxy haircut. He hadn't wanted to go on the air, but he discovered too late that he already was. He just went along with the fast-talker, watching him on his black-and-white in the kitchen, and got off as fast as he could.

Then the girl came back on the phone and said they'd fly out a film crew later in a helicopter or something. Big news.

"Jesus H," he muttered to Beggar after he hung up. "You got a tail and you don't got to put up with folks like that. How come I do?"

He drove the pickup into town with Beggar riding shotgun. He ignored a vague feeling of apprehension, attributing it to nerves. He'd never had a tail before. That was it. Instead, he concentrated on Louise and found he felt real good, like a prowling lion. He whistled a Garth Brooks ditty.

By the time he pulled into the Wrangler parking lot, the radio station down at Kemmerer had got the story and the DJ sounded excited. "Bentley Croft, a 28-year old rancher from Pinedale, became the first Wyomingite — "

"I'm twenty-seven, dang it all. And I'm from Daniel."

Bentley wasn't surprised when he opened the cafe door to hear cheers, applause, and hoots from the cowboys, business people, and girls from the courthouse lingering over their morning coffee. It startled him though, and he grinned sheepishly.

"Hey, Ben, let's see," they called.

Bentley uncurled the tail, cocked it above his left shoulder, and waved. Everyone applauded. Bentley smiled and blushed. He hadn't gotten this much notice since he beat the crap out of Tubs Jensen a few years back.

Louise stood in the kitchen door, her hip cocked, a smile on her pretty face. She shook her head in wonder.

He sat at the counter by the door. Louise leaned over the other side of the counter and poured coffee. "Let me feel it," she said.

A few guys overheard and guffawed.

"Feel what?" Bentley said.

"You know better than to get smart with your waitress," she pouted. "Didn't your momma ever teach you?"

"Louise, I'm wondering — "

"Ben, old buddy," Jim VanAtta said from behind him, a hand on his shoulder. "Drop by the office later. I figure with a tail, I can give you a break on your insurance."

"Oh? How come?"

VanAtta looked surprised. "Think about it. With a tail to give you balance, the next time you get drunk, you're less likely to fall down and break your damn fool neck."

Bentley joined VanAtta and the chorus of laughter, though his was less hearty than the other's. When Bentley looked around, Louise stood at the other end of the cafe, waiting on Maryanne Harkness and her kids. Carolyn took Bentley's order — the usual.

He gave Louise a little "come here" wave as she hustled her order into the kitchen. She nodded and headed his way when she got back out.

"Sorry, Ben," she said, leaning on him cozy-like. "Pretty busy morning, I guess."

"Yeah, I guess. Look, I just wanted to ask if you was — "

"Ben," a voice called. It was Maryanne, waving him to her table.

"S'cuse me, Lou. I got me some rodeo business — "

"Don't worry. I'll be around."

She left to get an order, and Ben walked to the Harkness' table, careful to keep his tail up and out of the way as he passed by the closely packed tables en route.

"Morning, Maryanne," he touched his hat brim when he stood above her table. "Gina, Frank. How's school? How's Frank Senior?"

Maryanne was president of the local rodeo club and a pretty woman in her own right, even pushing forty. Bentley had to keep reminding himself that she was married, and focus on business.

"Nasty tempered, as usual," Maryanne said, nodding Ben to the empty chair across from her. The teenagers said nothing, bug eyes fixed on the tail.

He sat. "How's the season shaping up?"

"Pretty good, I guess. You still plan to ride bareback this year?"

"Don't see why not. I healed up okay. See?" He rotated his left arm to demonstrate.

Maryanne sighed, sipped her coffee. "I don't know."

"Don't know what? You want a note from Doc Tom?"

He laughed. Maryanne didn't. The kids suddenly took great interest in their scrambled eggs.

"I heard Jim," Maryanne said, pointing to the front of the cafe with her chin. "If he's right, and your tail gives you an advantage balancewise — "

Bentley's laugh died. "Aw, now what the blazes are you saying, Maryanne? Show me in the PRCA rules that says guys with tails can't ride."

"Now, Ben, don't get in an uproar — "

"Hey, Ben," Louise called from the counter. She held up a plate — eggs over easy, toast, and bacon. "This your order? You better get it before Joanie steals it."

Bentley walked back to the counter, his tail tip twitching in agitation.

"'Lo, Joanie," he said, mounting the counter stool and digging in. Louise had left to see to another customer. The cafe bustled with people walking by to drop a word at him, pat him on the back, point, and stare at his new appendage, and cluck their tongues in wonder. The parking lot was full.

"I heard about your tail," Joanie drawled. "If you ask me, it's pretty. Reminds me of my horse."

Bentley gave her a look, ready to be angry, but saw Joanie wasn't poking fun. Her smile was innocent. She was downright likable. A good hand.

Joanie worked at the paper.

"Doing a story?" he asked.

She plopped a tape recorder on the counter by her plate. "If you want to. Can you drop by the paper for a picture before you head back to the ranch? Dora's got my camera at some damn Fish and Game meeting."

He nodded. Between bites, side talk with folks coming and going, and the occasional word in edgewise with Louise, he gave Joanie the story.

"Sorry it ain't much to tell," he shrugged, sopping up egg with his toast.

Joanie returned the shrug. "A short tale?"

Bentley's involuntary explosive guffaw scattered egg bits on the counter. Joanie thumped him on the backside and left. "Don't forget," she said. He nodded, swallowed.

Louise came over. "Looks like you're a celebrity."

"Yeah, and it's sure cramping my style." He wiped his lips. "Look, Louise, I've been trying to ask you to go out."

"I don't know, Ben. With all your groupies and hangers-on, there might not be room for us two in your truck."

"Aw, c'mon, Lou — "

"Morning, Bentley," Doc Tom said as he walked in. Louise shook her head and left to pick up another order. Doc Tom sidled up to Bentley at the counter in her place.

"Yeah, Doc, about my bill," Bentley began, "I've been meaning to call — "

The doctor waved a dismissive hand. "I want to get a word in with you about your tail. Looks like you're pretty busy right now, so maybe you could drop by the clinic when you finish."

Bentley frowned. "Jehosephat, Doc, is there anything wrong with it?"

"Oh, no, probably not. All the others I've read about have been okay. But I'll bet there'll be more. And sooner or later, somebody'll break their tail and call me. Maybe it'll be you, who knows. Anyway, I'd like to take a look at yours, to be prepared."

"Yeah, well, Joanie wants me to — "

"Hey, Ben," Dale from the feed store said as he stood in the door, ready to leave, "maybe you should have Bart take a look at your tail, too." He laughed and left.

Bentley looked around. The veterinarian wasn't in this morning. Probably saw the full parking lot and decided to eat at the Stockman's. He's better off, Bentley thought. "This is too fussy," he muttered.

"I cleared a place for you, Doc," Louise called out from across the cafe. Doc Tom nodded to Bentley and made his way to the table.

A siren wail cut through two dozen conversations in the cafe, and heads turned to watch Sheriff John Schweitzer slide to a dusty, gravel-spitting stop, his lights whirling, in the Wrangler parking lot. He dashed from the car, leaving his door open, and burst into the cafe.

"Hey, Ben, there you are," the short, sandy-haired cop stopped and tipped his hat back, panting. "We got problems — " Then he saw the tail. "Holy moly, it's true. Well, I'll be danged if that ain't the weirdest — Look, Ben, I'd love to chat but we got problems out at your place."

Bentley shot off his stool, his heart in his throat. "Problems? What problems?"

"Reporters, Ben," Schweitzer said. He took a breath and wiped sweat from his brow. "Man, they're all over the place. Down from Jackson, I guess. There's one bunch in a danged helicopter, and I hear there's another flying in — "

"Are they spooking the cows?"

The whole cafe went quiet, listening.

"Some, yeah, but I got deputies out there now. But a few reporters got there before we did and left the damn gate open, and we got cows scattered all upside the road — "

"Holy moly." Bentley headed for the door. He stopped and reached for his wallet. "I'll hold your bill," Carolyn said. Bentley nodded and put his wallet away. Louise was busy.

As he ran from the cafe, right behind the sheriff, Bentley saw Gordon Phillips from over at the Lazy Bar T, grinning like a coyote with chicken feathers in its teeth and moving in on Louise. "There goes my date," he muttered.

In the parking lot, he heard an odd sound.

"Now what?" the sheriff said, squinting into the sun. A helicopter circled to land at the IGA parking lot across the street. Beggar paced Bentley's pickup bed, barking.

The sheriff got on his radio, and people came out of the cafe, the grocery store and other businesses, and the courthouse to look. Cars and trucks stopped in the street. Sirens wailed.

"Danged TV," Bentley spat, his tail snapping.

He turned to go back into the cafe. He had to talk to Doc Tom. He had thought it might be fun, having a tail. But it wasn't turning out that way. His mind made up, he went through a quick inventory of questions. How much would it cost? Would his insurance cover? Would it upset his sense of balance? He even wondered if he should be asking these questions of Bart rather than Doc Tom.

As he reached the door, he found Doc Tom just coming out.

"Doc, I got to ask you a favor."

"Oh? What is it?"

"I don't got time to discuss it right now. I got to run. But you got to help me."

"Well, sure. What do you need?"

Bentley grabbed his tail and held the twitching tip in front of Doc. "Do you know anything about bobbing tails?"

GOOD VIBRATIONS

ViceBishop John DeToulouse frowned as the transmitter booth lurched in mid-dimension. The lurch was mental rather than physical; a sudden, brief, and subtle twist a few degrees off axis. It felt as if the booth had been — *bumped* — in the vast grayness between dimensions.

Something had gone wrong. Again.

The galaxy's most important wedding waits on Kangas III while I —

Before an annoyed huff could rise to his pulpy lips, the "arrived" light blinked on the booth's inner face and the door safety latch snicked off. The interdimensional journey from his vicarage courtyard to "herenow" (*The Emperor's palace?*) took less time than the booth electronics took to report journey's end. Still, when he opened the door, he expected to see his aide, young Halbart, bowed before him, shaven head pressed in terror against the tile floor.

"What am I to do with you, Halbart?" he'd moan, looking down on the quivery, prostrate monk over his paunch, pudgy fingers intertwined. "First my burnt toast, then the missing vestment button, now the booth doesn't work. Again. Hrmp."

"I'm sorry, Your Grace — "

"Oh, go away and pray for intelligence," John would say. "I've an important wedding. Have you any idea — "

As he reached for the latch, the chamber vibrated with rhythmic thumps, as if a rude fist pounded on it.

"C'mon," a male voice yelled through the door, "you got a line up." The voice spoke Mother Tongue, but with an accent John couldn't place. Not Kangan. Not Halbart.

As John started to push the door open, it jerked outward. "I beg your — " he began.

"Yeah, groovy," a young man with a scruffy beard said. "Quit playing with yourself and split. I gotta piss so bad my teeth are floating, you dig?"

Before John could speak, the hairy man grabbed his sleeve and jerked him from the booth. John stumbled on his robes and fell into a muddy puddle. He heard raucous laughter. He spat vile-tasting mud, wiped cold goo from his cheeks.

Halbart had goofed. *Where in the Thousand Kingdoms have I been sent?*

He tried to rise, but again he caught the robe hem with a foot and plopped back in the mud. More laughter.

"Looks like you could use a toke," a female voice said.

"What?"

A young woman sat on her heels in the mud before him, smiling, holding an incense stick. "Get high," she said, nodding at the smoking stick held between thumb and forefinger.

Not a Sister. An adolescent. A broad smile and merry eyes framed with long lashes accented a flawless, pale face. Her dark hair hung long and loose. She wore a short skirt, smooth legs bare above her knees. And beneath a gossamer, white blouse —

John gasped, and the girl laughed. She shook her head and hair flowed over her shoulders, face, and —

Precious Family, what a vision of health and youthful vigor! Wherever I am, Grace has preceded!

She put one end of the incense stick to her lips and made sucking noises. The stick end glowed orange, flared, and smoke curled into the girl's nose and mouth. "Try it," she said in a husky voice, as if holding her breath. "This'll get you off." She offered the stick.

Still sitting in the mud, John took the stick. It smelled tangy, smoky — like dried chokewillow leaves, a spiritual curative on many outer system planets.

Am I in the Arm, then?

He smiled and inhaled. Tasted like chokewillow. He returned the stick and nodded satisfaction. The girl returned a beatific smile.

"Cool." She stood in a smooth glide.

John exhaled thin, blue smoke. He struggled to stand. Strong hands gripped his arms and pulled him upright. The hands belonged to the hairy-faced young man who'd pulled him from the 'mitter moments ago. The man — no; *boy* — smiled.

"Hey, man," the boy said, "I'm like sorry, you know? That you fell down, I mean. Bummer, but I had to go *bad*."

"Go where?" John asked.

"Take a leak."

John hadn't seen the boy enter the 'mitter with anything. "A 'leak?' What's a 'leak?' Take it where? Where did you go?"

The boy and the girl laughed, along with others who'd gathered to stare at John.

"The cat looks like the Pope," someone said.

For the first time since he arrived — *among the primitives in the Arm?* — John looked around. He gasped. Hundreds of people who looked like the boy and girl milled about or stood in long lines before rows and rows of 'mitters! Hundreds of 'mitters, as far as he could see!

"My Gracious Family — " John's short, round fingers fumbled for the Familia around his neck. His cheeks burned apple-red, and he puffed as if he'd been running.

Their clothes, their tongue! I've been sent to a galactic Black Worship! These booths must be connected to a thousand worlds, a thousand dimensions! All the covens must be gathered! I've stumbled upon the legendary Demon's Abode!

"Hey," the boy said, "mellow out, big daddy."

The girl stepped up, pretty lips turned down in concern. "Bad trip?" She touched John's frothy brow with a warm hand.

"Where are we?" John said, panting. "*When* are we?"

"Like," she said, "is the smell bumming you out?"

John noticed the urine odor. He nodded.

"Yeah, I'm hip, man," the boy said. "Bad vibes. Let's split upwind." Despite their heathen leanings, they treated him with the respect due a ViceBishop.

John didn't resist as the pair took him by each elbow and escorted him between the rows — *hundreds!* — of 'mitters into a grassy field toward a tree grove. He didn't recognize the trees. As the urine stench faded, so did the crowd's hubbub. A mulchy forest smell ascended. The buzz of voices from over *there* faded under a melodic din from over *there*, beyond the trees. A gut-throbbing bass, chanting, and music, but remote and indistinct.

The cabal dances at a ritual sacrifice, no doubt.

The group walked into the grove, not yet within sight of the noisy cavorting in the glade beyond. With the two young people clucking in sympathy at John, they settled outside a small conical tent under the shade of a tree where a fire smoldered in a rock hearth. The boy and girl introduced John to the group of a dozen people. Some were young and some old, but all looked alike in some way John couldn't quite place.

"Groovy," the one called The Mad Hatter said when introduced. His hat resembled the ceremonial crown worn in the puberty rites of the Mong people on Jecril.

"Far out, man," a largish woman with a ready smile said. They called her Witch Girl. Plump but pretty, she reminded John of someone he knew long ago from before he took his vows. She looked mid-thirtyish, a gray wisp in her frizzy, black hair.

She smiled, touched his hand, and held it a moment.

"Outta sight," an older man said, offering a smoke stick. Not ready to confront and maybe anger the heathen mass, John took the stick, inhaled, and held his breath in the prescribed manner. After several seconds, he exhaled and stifled a cough, which garnered smiles and approving nods.

The antibiotic nanomachines he received when he accepted the ViceBishopric scepter would counter any toxins in the smoke. Still, John felt dizzy. He felt good.

Perhaps I've found a new pharmaceutical. Some good may come from this encounter yet.

They called themselves "hippies." Some wore shirts, others were bare-chested. Some wore loose trousers, or skirts, and some wore loincloths, including one girl. Most were barefoot. They decorated their hair with feathers, beads, bands, knots, and tangles. All different, John noted, yet somehow all alike.

Their cheeks glowed, John realized, inhaling from another ceremonial stick. The glassy eyes, the ubiquitous smiles, their casual manner and loose, relaxed movements.

Yes, something in the smoke.

The Witch Girl sat close on the grass; their knees touched. She produced a damp rag and dabbed at his muddy cheeks and vestment.

They called him Big Daddy. The boy and girl he'd met at the 'mitters were Emil and Emily. John found the names funny, and he laughed.

And laughed. The titter evolved into a gutty roar as the hippies joined in.

John decided to engage the coven in conversation. *Draw them out, learn all you can. Learn the access code to this den of evil, maybe the coordinates. Then break for the 'mitters and report to the College of Sacred Inquiry.*

"Like," John said, adapting to the hippie tongue, "where are we?"

"We're right *here*, man," the Mad Hatter said.

"Big Daddy's tripping," Emily said. She turned to John. "We're at a Love-In."

"I dig. What do you do at this Love-In?"

"Love, man," Emil said. "Ain't that enough?"

"Yeah, right." Emily hugged Emil. The youngsters were mates, in fact if not yet through appropriate ceremony.

What abominable ceremony might these heathen choose to bond with each other?

The odd group gathered in a circle answered his questions with honesty, patience, and humor. John resorted to Mantras of Strength to avoid succumbing to their child-like charms.

"What's your bag, man?" the Witch Girl asked. Emily translated. Emily's beauty and kindness prompted John's most fervent Mantras. The Witch Girl prompted disturbing sensations.

"Ahh," John replied, when he understood. He thanked Emily with a nod and explained his mission. "I'm in semi-retirement, teaching dance history at the Monastery of St. Clavius on Podcairn's Planet. I'm to officiate at the most important wedding ceremony of all timespace — uh — "

John ahemed, choking back the Sin of Pride. He foresaw a long night of penitent prayer.

"The negotiated marriage between Prince Bucal of the Nestor Hegemony and Princess Koranda of the Serenity System will end the bloodshed threatening to engulf the galaxy. It could spill over into adjacent dimensions."

"Far out," someone said, slack-jawed.

"It could involve *this* dimension."

"Like, what a trip." Emil sighed.

"If I don't perform the rites, the consequences could — "

"Groovy," the Hatter said.

None had taken the cue to tell him this dimension's coordinates. John resorted to blunt inquiry.

"I'm, uh, a bit disoriented. Which dimension is this?"

"You mean, like, where are we?" the Witch Girl asked.

"And when. If you please."

In time, John learned that they were on a farm in a place called "upstate New York." Earth. The date wasn't C.E. or P.A.

"It's A.D., man, your basic Anno Domino or whatever."

The word "Earth," rather than "Earthome," puzzled him, as did the time reference. Still, John stifled elation. He had the site code if not the exact coordinates. It would do. *I must sneak away, back to the 'mitters, and report.* Night approached.

Distracted, he let the conversation drift. A bottle of a hot liquid someone called "Good Shit" passed from hand to hand. The warm afternoon progressed toward a coolish night. John found himself sleepy and at ease, even among these non-believers.

They seem harmless.

The sound the group called "rock 'n' roll" rose and faded, faded and rose, beyond the trees in the opposite direction, away from the 'mitters.

Shouts, hand clapping, and whistles punctuated the noise. John decided he must see for himself what happened at the Demon's sacrificial conclave. People had wandered throughout the afternoon and early evening to and from the glade where the music originated. They moved without hurry, without ceremony. John decided to try a stroll.

When he muttered his wish to "check out some tunes, man," the Witch Girl offered to go with him. No one objected or reacted threateningly, and John walked toward the sound on the narrow path through the trees, the Witch Girl close.

In the silence during the short walk, John sensed her attraction to him. She cleared her throat several times, found occasion to brush against him. And —

John glanced at her, exchanging a smile now and then. She smelled — groovy.

He felt an odd pressure in his chest. And trousers.

Precious Family! What's happening to me?

John bumped into a dancing couple, recovered from his dazed stupor, and apologized to the dancers, who paid him no heed. John and the Witch Girl cleared the forest and stood on the edge of a vast meadow. In the dim light of the setting sun, thousands of people milled about and huddled before a huge, raised, well-lit altar where four men moved in rhythm. They sang and slapped hands against odd devices. They made the raucous sound John had heard as a background noise all day. "Rock 'n' roll." The surging crowd cavorted in drunken abandon.

The Witch Girl, grinning, grabbed his hand, and started gyrating in a way no Sister ever did.

"C'mon, Big Daddy. Let's boogie." Her hips undulated, and John's heart pounded in rhythm to the music. His feet followed and he was swept away, dancing deeper into the crowd.

He grinned. He recognized the ritual.

This is not the Demon's Den! This is the Nimoan Courting Dance! No, it's like what the Luoban of the Yasayim System do when the male selects a female —

John's mind whirled. As he "boogied," he saw patterns in the dance reminiscent of many peoples native to systems in the Arm far from the galactic core. He'd officiated on Opus IV where the party danced just so after the ceremony. A wedding ceremony.

He tried the Opus dance — step, shuffle-shuffle, kick, step. The Witch Girl joined him, as did others. "Groovy," several revelers pronounced the new dance. Responding to requests, John demonstrated dance steps he'd learned at ceremonies on other worlds — the Two-Stepper from Bokin VI, the Thunder Hop from the Delos Colony. The merry-makers followed his lead.

After what must have been many hours, during which a large, luminous moon rose above the horizon, several fires were lit and a bank of lights came on at the far side of the field, the Witch Girl heaved a weary sigh.

"I'm beat, man," she said. "Let's bag it for the night."

"I'm hip."

They walked back toward the encampment, the Witch Girl leading John through the dark by the hand.

"You're really into dancing," she said.

"My duties as ViceBishop include mingling with natives from a thousand cultures across the dimensions. Despite my weight, I seem to have a knack for boogying."

The Witch Girl whirled on the narrow path and gripped John around his waist. "You're not fat, Big Daddy. I call them 'love handles.' I dig them." She reached up and gave John a quick kiss on his lips, whirled and continued down the path, dragging him behind.

She smelled — *groovy.*

When they reached the camp, the fire had dwindled to cinders and the few still awake spoke in whispers. Emil and Emily slept under a blanket, innocent kittens cuddling.

These are the Family's children. Not yet married, true, but none could be farther from the Demon's clutch —

The Witch Girl tugged his sleeve. She led him a few yards away from the conical tent and the fire circle where she urged him to lie down with her. In the darkness, John hesitated, but the Witch Girl's gentle persistence and his fatigue won. He sat on a soft blanket.

What are her intentions? What will I do?

The Witch Girl's seduction ritual enchanted John, which surprised him. She whispered, stroked his neck, and guided his shaky hands to her breasts. She read his unspoken hesitance, shrugged, and stopped. She giggled and snuggled against him with a sigh. They fit like spoons as they lay, like Emil and Emily fit together in their slumber.

"So you're like a priest or something?" she asked.

"Uh, something like that. Retired. Semi."

"This wedding gig. When does it go down?"

"This morning. Rather, a few hours ago, relative time."

"Bummer you missed it."

John chuckled. "No problem. I'll just recalibrate the time vector once I get back to a dimension I know, get my bearings in timespace. I assume I can use your 'mitters."

"Yeah, wow."

A long pause, then she asked, "What's a 'mitter?"

"Maybe you call them something else herenow. You have hundreds. Over there, on the other side of the grove, where I met Emil and Emily. I think Halbart — he's my aide — I think he misprogrammed our 'mitter and sent me herenow rather than to Kangas III. Poor lad's dull-witted — "

"You mean the johns?"

"What?"

"The porta-potties. You call them 'mitters?"

"You call them johns?"

"Yeah."

"That's my name."

"They're not named after you, silly."

John laughed, and the Witch Girl giggled.

She felt warm, and John knew how Emil felt.

"I'm Renna," the Witch Girl said and fell asleep. John too fell asleep, rock 'n' roll droning in the background.

I'll get to Kangas III in the morning. But for now...

Renna. Groovy name.

Morning came with the smell of coffee, soft voices murmuring, and urgent pressure on John's bladder. The Witch Girl — *Renna,* he corrected himself — sat on the blanket next to him. As he sat up, she held out a cup of steaming coffee.

"Thank you." He rubbed his puffy eyes. "I must urinate. Where — "

"That way. You remember."

"By the 'mitters?" He yawned.

"Yeah. The johns."

"That name." John stood. "Cool."

The trail through the tree grove became better defined the closer he got to the "johns." As did the urine odor.

Why are the urinals near the 'mitters? Bad planning.

John frowned as he approached the 'mitters. He saw no urinals in the area, but the people going in and out of the 'mitters — the "johns" — behaved as if going in and out of urinals. Some hopped foot to foot before they entered, others clutched their crotches in discomfort. Some adjusted their clothes as they exited.

Realization came to John in a gasp.

Family's Blood! Primitives don't transmit elsewherewhen just to piss; how wealthy these hippies are! On what poor planet in the Thousand Kingdoms do they go to urinate?

Smiling, John joined a short line before a 'mitter.

"They're called 'johns,'" he told a skinny boy who joined the line behind him. "That's my name."

"Cool."

"But they're not named after me."

"No shit."

Soon, John stood before the 'mitter door. He folded his hands and waited for the young man who'd stood in line in front of him to exit.

He read words on the 'mitter door. "Niven Sanitation Co.," it read, followed by site code "Camden, N.J." and coordinate numeric "AF19861614."

An odd grunt came from inside the box.

The door opened, and the bearded boy emerged and walked away. John entered, smiling.

His smile collapsed in confusion.

The booth had been hollowed out, the instrument panel and keypad gone. A white paper roll hung on a wire hanger against one wall. Below him, a hole opened into —

Family, the stench!

"Hey, old man," a male voice called from outside the booth, "shake it. I got to whiz."

Hands sweaty, John dashed from the booth — *the urinal!*

"Where are the 'mitters?" He grabbed the skinny hippie's t-shirt outside the booth in knotted fists.

"Hey, be cool," the boy squeaked, frightened. He struggled to untangle himself from John's grip.

John pushed him aside and went to the next booth.

"Hey, man, I'm next — "

John ignored the man in line. He jerked the booth handle toward him and a young woman stumbled out.

"Hey, what the — "

Inside was a urinal.

The next was locked and an angry voice from inside told him to do something impossible to himself. An irritated hippie mob began focusing on John.

Tears stung his eyes and his breath came in frantic gasps as he looked around.

Urinals! All of them!

"Where are the 'mitters?" he shouted.

Someone shoved him, cursing. Another shove from an unseen source knocked him down and John felt panic.

"Where have you hidden the — "

The Mad Hatter knelt before him, gripping his quaking shoulders. "Don't freak out, Big Daddy," he said. "Be cool."

"They're all urinals! All of them!"

With help from two other hippies, the Mad Hatter escorted the distraught ViceBishop back to the camp.

John had wet himself. Renna stripped off the soiled trousers and stuffed him into a colorful plaid skirt.

"I need some Good Shit," John said. Emil produced a bottle. John gulped the fiery medicine and sputtered into a coughing fit. He smoked some weed.

The chemicals over-rode his nanomeds with a gradual, soothing effect. The sympathetic expressions from hippies, and Renna's more personal touch, helped. His breathing, heart rate, and perspiration all dropped from near-fatal levels, and he became more coherent.

At last he sat by the fire, the borrowed skirt bunched at his white ankles, and tried to figure out what had happened. Renna rubbed his back. Except for Emil and Emily, the others returned to their own concerns.

"Tell me, Emil," John said, "what you saw when you entered the 'mitter yesterday, when we met."

"Just a john."

"You saw no controls, no instrument panel?"

"No. Just some toilet paper."

"Cursed Halbart." John spat, surprised at his vehemence. He mumbled a prayer of patience. "I think he realized he'd misprogrammed the 'mitter and recalled it at the instant you pulled me out — "

"Sorry, man — "

" — and just an instant before you entered."

"You mean the john?" Emily asked.

"Big Daddy calls it a 'mitter," Renna said.

"Your dimension is of pre-transmitter technology."

The three hippies sitting with him seemed to accept the notion with nonchalance. They called the trans-dimensional travel idea "cool," "far out," and "groovy."

Emil frowned. "If this Halbart cat recalled your interdimensional box thingie, wouldn't there be *nothing* in its place? Like, just a hole? Instead you got a john. And dig: how come the johns look like these 'mitter things?"

Coincidence doesn't explain all mystery. "The Family moves in mysterious ways — "

" — Its wonders to perform," Renna finished. "Like meeting you. Dig?"

As thunderstorms give way to blue sky, John's frown eased into a smile. Light shone through. Understanding. Acceptance.

"I dig," he said. "Do you dig 'interdimensional resonance'?"

They didn't, so John explained.

"Wow," Renna said when he finished, "it's like good vibes."

"I'm hip," John said. "We honor our Family, but we're responsible. We make our own future. And past."

Emil and Emily wed the next day, the Love-In's last day. ViceBishop John DeToulouse officiated. The couple wore flowers in their hair, as prescribed in the Meditationist Nuptial Canons of Regis Prime. The vows came from the Sacred Doctrines of the Risen, the Holy Faith of the Epoch Orbitals. John taught the wedding party the Bonding Circle, the communal dance he'd prepared for the Kangas III wedding.

John led the ceremony as practice for his eventual return to a familiar dimension and the ceremony awaiting on Kangas III. But he did it mostly because he suspected he'd never return; that the Family intended his "accidental" transmission to this timespace as part of a plan beyond his ken. A new Way.

Resonance? *The "good vibrations" generated herenow will resonate among the dimensions. Discontent decreases, and harmony spreads. It starts here, and I must nurture it.*

John and his wife Renna traveled from Love-In to Love-In, marrying people. The word spread among the hippies of Big Daddy's groovy rituals; he officiated at many weddings.

And he taught the multitudes to dance.

HIDE AND SEEK

H ow fortunate for you that my arrival on station is so timely," Sheldon Houseman said, his accent Oxford crisp, voice dripping with conde- scension. "I, of course, will be glad to help you capture Mr. Lloyd." His eyebrows arched regally, and he offered a smile like a prince tossing a coin to a pauper.

I don't know who I hated more — Jack Lloyd, "the greatest criminal mind of the 24th century," according to the vids, or Sheldon Houseman, "the greatest detective of all time," according to the same vids. Both were pompous asses, if you ask me. But I'm only a station security chief, a working class grunt, not educated dirtside at Oxford like these two were, not fawned over by the media, one like Robin Hood, the other like Sherlock Holmes. So don't ask me. I'd as soon blow one away as the other.

Lucky me: Lloyd would chose my station to rob, making off with the company receipts single-handed, like some damn Old West highwayman, disappearing into thin air, leaving a note on the station public screen mock- ing me personally. "Bet you can't catch me," he laughs in the note and everybody laughs with him, and I'm suddenly on the newsvids, answering reporters' questions, sweating, sputtering, sounding like I hadn't the foggi- est notion where to find Lloyd, which I didn't.

If that wasn't embarrassing enough, Houseman arrives on the next inbound shuttle. Spur of the moment thing, taking a brief holiday, and so on, he said. Just passing through. But the media were on his tail, naturally, so my boss — leave it to old "Cover Your Ass" Snodgrass — says to me "Get Houseman to help."

Yeah, why not? Like I said — lucky me.

But I really didn't have a clue where Lloyd was and I did need some help, because if I didn't find Lloyd, old CYA was prepping to scapegoat me, kick my ass into high orbit, and I'd have trouble getting a job flipping soybuns at McDougal's.

"Shoot to kill," Snodgrass hissed at me. Never mind an arrest, with the possibility of Lloyd's escape, which he'd done twice from better facilities than we have on station — or worse, the courts uncovering any number of embarrassing indiscretions on Snodgrass' part during a lengthy prosecution. Right. CYA.

I extended my hand. "I'm Norman Hansen, securi — "

"Yes," Houseman said. He touched my hand like a boxer protecting his knuckles — limp, fingers only. "Your superior, Mr. Snodgrass, so informed me."

"We think Lloyd's still on station."

"Fear not, Mr. Norman," Houseman said, sitting in my chair, behind my desk, "I'll find your fugitive. Or my name isn't Sheldon Houseman."

Vids whirred, CYA purred, and I fumed and tried to not let it show. "The name's Hansen," I muttered. But nobody heard.

After some preliminaries with the media, CYA withdrew and left me to show Houseman our security bay and its assets.

"Adequate," he nodded, hands locked behind his back. He didn't say a single word to the techs standing station in the bay, or the other security grunts who had gathered to watch. He sent an underling — his "secretary," he called him — to get some of his own equipment.

"Do you have any idea," I asked, "how long this'll — "

"An hour, perhaps." He waved a hand. "Two."

"An hour? How can you — "

"Braggadocio plays no part in my claim, Mr. Jensen — "

"Hansen. Norm — "

" — it's simply true. Mr. Lloyd is no ordinary thief, granted, but I, on the other hand, am no ordinary detective. We are alike in that respect, as in others. We differ in that I choose to exercise my genius to benefit all mankind. Lloyd opts for self-aggrandizement and enrichment."

The underling returned with a metal suitcase. On his heels, a half dozen media types with vids pressed into the narrow hallway behind our security console. "You media types are going to have to — " I began.

"I invited them, Mr. Norton. To observe."

I could see CYA standing in the outer hallway, poking his bald, sweaty head around the doorway. His shrug and smile made it clear — "It's your ass on the line, now, sucker."

Snodgrass disappeared. I nodded to my people, and they squeezed into corners and against the walls to make room for the media people.

"The authorities ought to have consulted me sooner," Houseman prattled as the vids whirred. He snapped open the silver case his secretary had brought with deft movements of his delicate hands and withdrew a few devices. Some computer interface stuff, some new stuff, things I'd only heard about on the net. Some stuff I didn't recognize at all. Very impressive, very high tech.

"I am loath to step in where uninvited, of course. I could have stopped Lloyd before he struck, prevented this unfortunate incident, but — " he shrugged eloquently. "Alas. Ego again, I'm afraid, keeps petty bureaucrats" — several vids swung toward me, to record my reaction which was not very pretty — "from doing so, before Lloyd's latest exploit. Now, they recognize Lloyd's criminal genius, as I have all along. Shamed and foiled again, they have called me."

"But would they have called," he mused, "if I hadn't happened to be on-station serendipitously? I think not. Ego again. Still, I've acquiesced to their hat-in-hand appeal, and I have set to work immediately and with my customary vigor."

He gestured to his equipment that he'd arranged on the small shelf before him in front of my security console.

"I wish you to record these events as they happen so as to benefit posterity."

He smiled expansively. Vids whirred.

"Lloyd's crimes, particularly his latest, are too well known to dwell upon here. Suffice to say, civilization itself will benefit from my work's successful outcome.

"Nor am I careless in overestimating my adversary. My respect for his genius is as great as my respect for my own. Hence, I take precaution against the possibility that he might evade my dragnet, as he has the civil authorities. I shall succeed, of course. The fate of civilization is at stake.

"Every precaution.

"Consider — today, it is possible to hide one's physical identity through surgery, genetic engineering, Nano technology, bioenhancement, and other means. One's personality may be hidden as well, disguised so only the most perceptive examiner may discover the falsehood. One's consciousness may hide within the net, flitting from point to point along the labyrinthine pathways of information, ever in motion, or hidden like some night thing in some inconspicuous device. A holo receiver, a microwave oven, a toaster may hide a mass murderer or a rapist. Beware. I once found a jewel thief's consciousness hiding in a stereo, his concealment revealed by the habit of playing the same popular tune again and again."

The reporters laughed. "What tune?" one asked. He told them and they laughed again. I didn't.

"The possibilities are endless," he said, returning to his lecture. "I will begin searching for Jack Lloyd first by eliminating routine hideouts, repeating, just as a precaution, mind you, the work already done by Mr. Nelson here."

"Hansen. Norman Han — "

"This shouldn't take long. A moment, please."

Vids whirred. Houseman did something with what looked like an ordinary hand comp. A moment passed.

"There." He handed the object to his secretary who tucked it neatly into a compartment in the silver suitcase.

"I've scoured the net for him, from the financial circuits on Earth to the communication network among the big ships and their routes among the stars. I've examined government records, private files — quite easy, really — and business transactions, libraries, inventories, AIs of all kinds. Androids. Skimmers. Kitchen alliances.

"All fruitless.

"I expected as much. From Lloyd's genius, I've expected great things. I've always expected him to challenge my own genius. He does not disappoint.

"My final search routine will now commence. Observe as I capture the man."

Houseman extended a hand palm up to his side while facing the vids, and his secretary put a device in it like a nurse handing a scalpel to a surgeon. The black box Houseman now held looked like a prototype of the advanced remote psych-probe being tested, so I hear, by SecuriTech for the Yamaguchi Mining Consortium. Cutting edge stuff, if the rumors were true.

"This search pattern counters the trick of hiding one's consciousness in parallel with a human's — in the wetware, so to speak. Schizophrenia is often no more than simple invasion of privacy, albeit a more high tech variety.

"Examining every human being in existence does not involve as much effort as the layman might expect. We've come a long way since simple computers. I'm well versed in the most advanced detection technology. This, and my own native genius, suffice to detect even the most cunning mind, like Lloyd's.

"Observe."

Silence. Vids whirred. Houseman tapped at the control panel on the black device. In a moment, a beep sounded.

"There." He smiled and handed the device to his secretary who placed it in a compartment in the silver case.

"I've eliminated nearly every human, one by one, as Lloyd's hiding place. I've also ensured that a being, once isolated as 'clean,' is not later 'inhabited' by my quarry.

"Nor am I surprised to find no trace of Lloyd among the billions of humans I've tested. From the first, I've had a hunch — the detective's greatest asset is the hunch, and I, of course, am the world's greatest — but I digress."

"The fugitive thief Jack Lloyd did not, as Mr. Jensen — "

"Hansen — "

" — earlier determined, leave the station. He is, in fact, here in this room with me right now."

A gasp emerged from the reporters and the security people before the room went dead silent. The reporters scanned each other and the security grunts watching at the edge and from the corner of the cramped room. They looked at me, at Houseman's secretary, at Houseman.

Houseman let the silence extend, savoring the drama.

"One of you reporters?" he said. Vids whirled from target to target, whirring, sniffing.

"No," he said, and you could see the tension drain from the reporters.

"One of you security people?" The vids turned on my observing, now nervous, crew.

"No," Houseman said, and one of my guys nearly collapsed, his sigh of relief cutting the air like flatulence.

"My secretary?" Vids focused on the little man, whose smug smile reflected his boss's own.

"Of course not," Houseman said with a wry chuckle. "Mr. Houston, you — "

"It's Hansen," I said. "Norman Hansen."

And I shot him right between the eyes, getting both Lloyd and that creep Houseman with one shot.

I think.

RISE ABOVE IT ALL

The children fluttering and fidgeting in a group "ohhed" and "awed," their wings humming as they viewed the image a thousand feet below in the rich California dirt.

"As seen from this angle, class, the painting resembles a horse and rider, impressionistic, but if you turn this way," the teacher demonstrated, turning herself, a delicate mid-air maneuver, "you'll see the artist has given us a rather nice original still life."

Boyd Brooks snorted. He hovered with his back to the field trip group, pretending to study a painting in a 40-acre field adjacent to the one the children looked at. The snort ruffled some feathers in his left wing and he lost a few feet in altitude straightening them out. He dropped far enough that he couldn't hear. And he wanted to hear, shameless in his eavesdropping. It was, after all, his work they admired.

But "admired" wasn't accurate. The lecture sounded like a mixed review at best. The teacher seemed ambivalent about the double-image, a style Brooks pioneered. Two years ago, he'd created a picture of Mt. Rushmore seen in one direction, Crazy Horse the other way, in a cornfield just outside Rapid City. The national attention he got from the Rushmore-Crazy Horse had led to several commissions here in the richer fields of the Imperial Valley north of Fresno.

The "rather nice" part irritated, hence the snort. Does this teacher think manipulating fields of grain and various flowers and plants is easy? Nobody credited field artists with any talent these days when it came to soil chemistry, yield control, species selection, genetic engineering —

"I've always wanted to paint," people told him at parties, always with the implication that it's easy, thus the painter is — what? Lazy? A parasite living off society's largess through art council grants and the occasional private commission from rich widows? Creativity came at too little sacrifice, most people seemed to believe. But Boyd knew how deeply into his soul he had to dig for each painting. "Oh, so you, uh, paint, do you? I've always wanted to paint."

Boyd snorted a lot.

Still, the teacher, a bookish, thin woman with slender, sparrow-like wings, hadn't flown past his work.

Boyd regained altitude as fast as he could without, he hoped, drawing attention. He kept his eyes on the adjacent painting, a rather nondescript seascape made by an acquaintance of mediocre talent whose name he tried to forget. None of the children noticed him flying to within twenty feet. Or if they did, none made mention.

Wild-eyed, wild-haired, bearded stranger hanging around school children on a field trip. No, officer, I'm not a child molester, I'm an artist —

" — double-images represented the next higher creativity level," the teacher lectured, her hands folded primly across her waist, her wings fluttering just so, "and we must recognize their artistic merit despite the fact that a trend seems to have developed — "

A trend. She was right, Boyd admitted to himself. Everyone had gotten on the bandwagon. Everybody did double-image field paintings. This last commission, the one these kids hovered over, had not come without struggle. And the last three had been for prices he'd be embarrassed to relate. But competition was tough, and one had bills to pay —

" — also must appreciate that the artist who created this work, reputed to be the pioneer of the double-image style — "

Reputed to be?

" — is not in fact the style's actual originator — "

Not in fact?

" — as you'll understand in a moment. Follow, please, class. Stay in formation."

Boyd glared at the class as they formed a flying 'v' with the teacher at the head and flew toward the low, yellow hills to the east.

Not the originator? Boyd felt a chill as he watched the group fly away.

So many artists worked the fields. There were more aspiring artists than there were fields to work. And everybody did double-images. One had to be creative to survive, let alone prosper. One created because one loved art, not money. And those few in it for the money imitated the creative ones, following on the tail feathers of the great artists.

Deep down inside, Boyd had feared his work was — pedestrian. He feared that he lacked the creative spark that would help him rise above his competitors. So the inspiration to create the double-images, to be innovative, had elated him beyond measure. The commissions and the money had come, as he knew they would. But it didn't last. The culture vultures descended in flocks to imitate, fouling the air of interest in his own work.

The notoriety of being the creator of double-imaging would get him a job or two, now, and it would have to suffice. But what if he didn't originate the style, as the teacher had said? What if someone else had beaten him to it?

But how could that be? He, Boyd Brooks, was the acknowledged pioneer of the style. If he lacked creative talent, he at least had that innovation to fall back on, come hard times.

How close were those hard times?

Could the teacher be mistaken? Not likely, Boyd admitted. He didn't own a TV, didn't read newspapers — wasn't net-linked at all. He scoffed at the faddish, pop-consumer culture promoted by the mass media. He rose above it all.

So, what if somebody had come along before him and —

Maybe it had been on the Internet and he'd missed it. But wouldn't he have heard, from colleagues, from patrons — from somebody?

Boyd felt suddenly suffocated with foreboding, a fear of insignificance, of anonymity, the taste coppery on his tongue.

The class flock had crested the nearest hills, about a mile away. Boyd flapped after them.

They hovered above orchard land, oranges and lemons and grapefruit. The growth cycle for citrus was so long that no artist, as far as Boyd knew, had used the area as a canvas. All it lent itself to was trimming the treetops, maybe dying the leaves. Craft work, not art. Aesthetically too crude to merit the effort, like sketching, and too expensive. What could warrant interest here?

He moved in closer, listening.

" — appreciate the subtlety of his work in genetics engineering, and, further, the artistic commitment in attempting a work the rewards for which would not see fruition — literally — for many years — "

Boyd almost fell from the sky as he gazed below. There in an orchard, framed in the standard 40-acre square, he saw Van Gogh's "Starry Night." The giant, odd-shaped fruit on the trees, all clustered and arranged in the necessary order for the proper effect. And the trees. Each tree stood at subtly varying heights, so the shadows produced when the light was just right —

He followed the class as it dipped for a lower altitude, to catch the light at a slightly different angle, and saw —

"The Last Supper."

It was all too much for Boyd. His wings folded, and he plunged. For a moment, he felt like keeping the wings folded, ending it all, diving right into Christ's eye.

But the moment passed. Whatever kept starving artists going back to their fields day after day, adjusting salinity in a patch of soil here to get the right tone, spraying to attract a certain insect to a certain row of grain there — whatever made a person an artist — prompted Boyd to spread wings at the last moment, and, again, rise above it all.

Still, he'd fallen so close to the ground, he couldn't resist a petulant kick at a tree, knocking a few genetically altered fruits to the ground, distorting the picture a bit. Let him be arrested for vandalism. He'd paint the jail walls.

No hawk-winged cop swooped to intercept him, so Boyd flew back to his own canvas across the valley to give it another look-see. When he arrived a few thousand feet above it, he found some viewers hovering, staring down, some with cameras.

He eavesdropped again.

And discovered they were looking at the other painting.

" — certain evocative quality, I think," one owl-like fat man said to a dovish woman companion. "And notice the depth of the water depicted. You can almost feel the spray — "

And no one — absolutely no one — hovered over his painting.

Dozens of people in the sky at various altitudes, alone and in flocks of two, three, or more, and not one — not a single one — hesitated over his painting. They all flew past.

" — if seen in the afternoon, as opposed to the morning, the rendering alters, as though swallowed by the sea — "

Boyd had turned toward the couple, a curse burning in his throat, something vulgar and threatening, something to make them flap away in horror, maybe even prompt them to call the police. But the shout died stillborn, replaced by yet another idea.

He'd thought the idea for double-imaging had been his own. As brilliant as it seemed, it had in fact originated with the artist, whose name he did not yet know, who'd grown the orchard across the valley beyond the hills. And when word got out, Boyd realized he wouldn't be able to give his work away.

But a new idea was forming. He flew home, his mind in a whirl. If he sold everything he had, he might be able to afford the equipment he needed.

Still, it was a gamble. In the old days, field painting hadn't been as popular as now when so many people had wings. The medium had become crowded as more and more people took to the air. But the first artists who'd worked in grains and flowers reaped a remarkable following, their paintings selling for more and more each year, their talents in demand.

Those years have gone forever, Boyd mused. But to be a pioneer: that's the ticket. So double-imaging was passé? Maybe this time —

Boyd had heard about the new cities under the ocean, just off Catalina. People with gills breathing water, a new fad, diving, swimming, and cavorting like porpoises under the salty waves.

The cities lay just above acres — miles — of coral forests and seaweed beds yet untouched by artistic hands.

Pioneering artistic hands.

AS WE KNOW IT

But, Jarrin, if you don't attend the Gathering this year, it'll be the end of civilization as we know it." Maurim's holo projection of herself was as a pretty, young woman with long, metallic-silver hair. She wore a gossamer, lacy, black gown. She paced back and forth along a beach before a vast ocean as she spoke to Jarrin's holo image. She made gritty shushing noises in the sand with each agitated step of sandaled feet, but the sound failed to annoy Jarrin as she'd intended.

Instead, he looked as bored as ever. He yawned, a white hand covering pale lips on a delicate face. "My dearest Maurim, how you do carry on. Civilization, indeed. Six humans inhabit the entire universe and you — "

"Five humans and one android," Maurim said. Light years separated their consciousnesses but Jarrin's and Maurim's projected images locked eye to eye centimeters apart, each in the environment they'd chosen to inhabit at the time. She lived on an island paradise in a tranquil sea on a planet she'd created for the purpose; he in a vast marble palace afloat in the emptiness between galaxies.

"I'm not an android, my dear," Jarrin said, "as I believe I demonstrated at your birthday party. As I recall, you wanted to copulate. Again. Was I bestial enough? Too much? Pray tell, dear, what rankles?"

"You saw the mating tapes," she stamped a petulant foot. "They came from your collection. How you could act like a clockwork android without a civilized thought — "

"There you go again with your 'civilization' thing," Jarrin said.

Though perverse, annoying Jarrin was among Maurim's hobbies. Resisting her jibes was among his. Maurim smiled at her small victory, which, she knew, exacerbated Jarrin's annoyance.

"We haven't been a 'civilization' for two million years, as I reckon," he said.

"Your own emotional vacuity proves your case."

"Listen, 'dearest.'" He gave the word a derisive twist of his lip, as he'd done with the word 'civilization,' "I expect the usual callow remarks from your cohorts at the Gathering. They share your views of my incivility, I'm afraid. Why need I attend to be sneered at, pray tell?"

Maurim's image sighed as her consciousness, conferring with several dedicated AI databases, calculated a response. Jarrin could choose to discorporate, she knew, as others had done before in the past million or so years. She didn't want that to happen. Not to Jarrin. Not now.

"Never mind the others, my dear," she purred at last. "Come for me. I enjoy your little surprises even if they complain. It does relieve the boredom."

"Well, I don't know . . ."

Maurim's sensors detected a slight increase in the sexual arousal level emanating from Jarrin's image. He'd come.

The anachronistic term "year" peeved Jarrin. In fact, the Gathering took place every 1,312 years, by the old Earthome calendar. The "year" was in fact the orbital period of Kangas III around its sun in the Horiuchi system — something to do with the Gathering origin some one point three million years before when the human race numbered in the hundreds. But people still called the period a "year" to honor their Earthome roots.

Sentimentality, Jarrin huffed to himself as he got his body out of storage for teleportation. Like meeting on Earthome. Why not here for a change? Or at Maurim's place? Or Crim's, or — no, not at Bhrogig's, that simple oaf.

Jarrin's sensors checked his latest physical manifestation and made minor corrections to the epidermis his aesthetics paradigm dictated. After programming schemes to counter Maurim's expected attempts to seduce him into another act of copulation at the Gathering, he unplugged his consciousness from its AI support systems and inserted it into the body.

Teleporting to the agreed-upon meeting place on Earthome, a place called "Wyoming," Jarrin smiled. He stroked the six aluminum boxes with red bows that he carried in a plastic bag under one arm. He marveled again at the near-forgotten physical sensation of touch. He found the sensation both compelling and repulsive.

Oh, they all feign annoyance, even indifference, but Maurim isn't alone in appreciating my surprises, I know.

And for once, Jarrin was glad tradition demanded all show up with their consciousnesses in physical bodies. The word "entrapped" came to mind.

*

Maurim fidgeted with her body again, concentrating on her breasts. She toyed with a program that would allow them to change size and shape at random, but abandoned it when she remembered Lomitus had used a similar program 20,000 years before. At last, she settled on a program that permitted the breasts to phosphoresce with luminosity corresponding to the sexual arousal level of whoever stared at them. She chose a silvery shift that matched her hair and covered her hips and thighs.

She reviewed the physical manifestation she'd present at the Gathering through sensors and in a mirror. Frowning, she decided it would have to do.

She slipped a necklace around her throat and let the six finger-sized vials on the chain dangle between her breasts. This time, Jarrin wouldn't be the only one with a surprise.

She smiled, snapped her fingers, and teleported to Wyoming.

"Fashionably late as usual." Crim smiled. The little man advanced to give Maurim a hug. Her breasts glowed, and Crim's smile faded into confusion. He retreated, hugless. Lomitus offered a bearish hug, crushing Maurim's head against her own massive bosom. Nebuta, a head shorter than Maurim, chastely kissed her cheek. Both women giggled at Maurim's joke.

"I like it," Bhrogig guffawed, slapping Crim on the back. Bhrogig stood, hands on hips, two meters before Maurim, gawking at her breasts, moving his gaze from one to the other as if trying to decide which was better.

Maurim's breasts flashed like pulsars in rhythm to Bhrogig's lusty stare. She huffed and slapped at him with half-hearted effort. She found Bhrogig's boorishness mildly annoying. But since Jarrin seemed jealous of him, Maurim encouraged Bhrogig just to aggravate Jarrin.

She looked around. They stood in a wooded valley. Nearby, a narrow stream flowed away from rolling hills on one horizon into a broad, grassy plain on the other. The sky was a pale blue, empty except for a few puffball white clouds. A faint breeze swayed branches in a grove of spindly trees near the stream. Heart-shaped leaves rattled like green metal flakes.

Jarrin hadn't arrived yet.

"W-we were just saying, Maurim, uh, darling," Nebuta began, fluttering a fan, "how we live for the Gathering so we can w-watch you make, uh, fools of the men."

"Gender chauvinism, still?" Crim raised an eyebrow. "I had you confused — admit it — last Gathering as to the gender in which I chose to come."

"Crim, you twit," Lomitus bellowed, "nobody gave a damn."

Crim's narrow face reddened at the group's laughter. He sputtered, then waved a hand, and disappeared.

"H-hey," Nebuta said, "you've scared him away again. I, um, kind of like him, you know."

Lomitus sighed. "He ain't gone far. He'll be back."

"As what, this time?" Startled gasps greeted Jarrin's sudden appearance.

"Whatever do you mean?" Maurim said. Her breasts failed to light, and she tried to feign indifference.

"The rules," Jarrin said. He spread a hand, created a chair, and sat on it, crossing one leg over the other. "You know the rules say we're supposed to appear at the Gathering as we are in corporeal form."

"What makes you think Crim isn't a hermaphrodite?" Maurim asked.

"We know he's bisexual," Bhrogig said. "Eh, Nebuta?"

Nebuta giggled behind her fan.

"I did a records search," Jarrin announced.

Nebuta's giggles subsided, Maurim sighed, Bhrogig hrumphed, and Lomitus arched heavy brows in indignation.

"Ain't our privacy sacred anymore?" Bhrogig took a menacing step forward.

Jarrin refused to be cowed. "Public record, from long ago. Anyway, I logged the information into your respective databases before I 'ported here. You can read about it when you get back to your — 'homes.'" He twisted his lips on the last word.

"Still, I don't like you poking around," Bhrogig growled. Eyes narrowed, he made fists and his neck muscles bunched.

"Oh?" Jarrin said. "Do you have something to hide?"

"Why, you damned — " With his step forward, Bhrogig bumped into the force field Jarrin snapped into place in front of him. Bhrogig bounced back, hitting the ground with a grunt.

"Violence," Jarrin pronounced with a satisfied nod. "You see, Maurim?" He turned to her and pointed to Bhrogig. "Your affection for animalistic behavior is misplaced."

"It's not animalism." Maurim pointedly helped Bhrogig up.

"Whatever." Jarrin waved a dismissive hand as he stood, and his chair disappeared. "The point is, I think Crim cheated last Gathering and I demand an accounting."

"An a-accounting?" Nebuta said.

"What the hell for?" Lomitus said. "To prove what? That we're who we say we are?"

"Exactly," Jarrin said.

"And where'n hell do you draw the line?" Lomitus continued. "Is Maurim's phosphorescent titties a temporary enhancement, like eye shadow? Or does it make her — what? Less than human, by your standards?"

"Oh, please — " Jarrin began.

Crim reappeared. "Sorry. Caught me off guard is all." He managed a weak smile as he joined the group. Nebuta moved to stand near him and mustered a protective, motherly stance.

"And even if Crim, um, 'cheated' last Gathering," Nebuta said, "so what? Maybe that's w-who he is, what he's become, what he's evolved into. We all change, given enough, um, time, as you've often said."

"You know my view on that subject," Jarrin said.

"Yeah." Bhrogig thrust his chin forward. "And I'm damn tired of hearing it."

"If you believe we're evolved into a new being," Maurim said, "what does it matter then in which direction Crim has evolved, or is evolving?"

"Nevertheless, I insist on an accounting."

Nebuta and Lomitus began to protest.

"I insist."

"Oh, all right," Crim sighed. "I don't mind. I, I did cheat last time." He blushed at Nebuta's frown. "Sorry. I got involved in a project and, well, you know how it is when you get busy. You forget to notice the time. I forgot about the Gathering. When I remembered, it was late, and, well — "

"You sent a simulacrum," Maurim accused, disappointment evident. Crim nodded, refusing to meet her eyes.

She turned to Jarrin. "For once I agree with Jarrin. I, too, want an accounting."

"So, what'll it be?" Bhrogig asked. "DNA analysis, retinal scan, word association, memory tests — "

"Nothing dramatic, I assure you." Jarrin snapped his fingers and a machine appeared. The small, white box sat on a waist-high tripod. "Put your hand on top."

Crim went first. The machine glowed green at his touch, as it did for the others. When they had finished, Jarrin touched the machine and it glowed green.

"So what?" Lomitus said, stifling a yawn.

"It would have glowed red for a non-human." Jarrin snapped his fingers and the machine disappeared.

"Or w-whatever you think we are," Nebuta said.

"Or whatever," Jarrin agreed. "Run your own test, if you care. I'm satisfied we are all properly Gathered."

"I'll take you up on that," Maurim said. "You argue the Gatherings are a waste, that we've evolved beyond primitive socialization. Yet now you insist we prove we're present in our corporeal bodies. I suspect your motives, Jarrin."

"Darling, I'd welcome confirmation."

Maurim looked to the others, who nodded in agreement. She ran a simple DNA inventory, confirming the group as human.

After a while, the group conjured dinner and settled into their normal Gathering routine, sitting around a long dinner table, arguing the merits of maintaining their waning humanity versus altering themselves as desire or whim dictated. Jarrin defended the artificial evolution case, while Maurim argued for keeping the human norm, at least in stasis reserve if not in regular use. The others offered argument on one side or the other, sometimes at random. All struggled against a pervasive ennui characteristic of the last few hundred Gatherings.

"Surely you've all noticed?" Jarrin gestured with a fork. "The malaise?"

"Hell's sake," Lomitus guffawed, "I've been too bored to notice."

Everyone laughed, amusement genuine, much to Maurim's annoyance.

Maurim thumped the table. "The Gathering was created to keep us from becoming other than human. Yes, we create simulated selves when need be, encasing our consciousnesses in stasis, but we're the same beings who lived here millions of years ago. Temporary change for amusement or convenience is not evolution."

"And what else is there but amusement and convenience?" Jarrin asked. He basked in the brief silence that followed.

"W-why, then, the, um, accounting?" Nebuta squeaked. It was Jarrin's turn to frown in silence. "If, if — " Nebuta took a deep breath. "If amusement and convenience prevail, you then reinforce Crim's right to come as he wishes to come, to be as he wishes to be, rather than as he is. Come, n-now, tell us."

Jarrin waited until all eyes were on him. "I wanted the accounting because I wish my gift to you at this Gathering to be memorable beyond your capacity to imagine. In order to do that, it is imperative you be here in all your fleshy glory."

Bored shrugs and vague nods greeted Jarrin's grin. Maurim, however, felt dread stir in her. *How ironic my gift does not require their corporeal presence and his does. What can it be?*

It became time for gift giving.

"This is what I was working on when I, er, skipped the last Gathering."

Crim lifted the cover from a large, flat box he'd placed on the now empty table. The others leaned in to see.

Six potted flowers sat in the box. Their broad transparent petals waved on their long stems as if bobbing in a wind.

"They're intelligent after a fashion." Crim offered the box to the others. Each selected a flower. "They learn from their environment and evolve as their environment changes."

"Oh, dear," Nebuta sighed as her flower seemed to study her, weaving back and forth. It had turned a sky blue. "Does it speak?"

"No," Crim said. "But it will nod in agreement, or shake from side to side in negation. There is a problem, I'm sorry to say, that I haven't been able to solve."

"I think I know what it is." Maurim's breasts glowed on and off as the flower stared at them, first one and then the other, in a slower version of Bhrogig's earlier lusty gaze. The flower was a vivid red.

"Ah, yes." Crim blushed. "They have personalities. They're young, so perhaps you can mold them to suit. But I can only rule out flight, not rebellion."

Even as Crim passed out an owner's manual chip, Jarrin remarked offhandedly that Crim had offered nothing new; just a revision of a gift he'd offered at a Gathering a hundred thousand years earlier. The others ignored as best they could Jarrin's expected but dreaded "there's nothing new in the universe" remark. They knew the remark would greet, in some variation, each gift presented, except his own.

Lomitus' gift was a fist-sized cube in whose facets could be seen random scenes from classic Earthome videos.

"Go ahead," she nudged Bhrogig. "Ask it something."

"Ask it — " Bhrogig started, then grinned. "Ah, I get it. Very well, then: who wants to get laid?"

The scene shifted in the cube in Bhrogig's hand and the perfect face of 3V star Ophelia Rapturous appeared, staring at him, panting. "Take me, Bhrogig, you fool," the beauty's image whispered imitating her love scene from "Alien Transit."

The group roared with laughter, except Jarrin, who staged a yawn. The others ignored him as they tried their own cubes.

"Are, um, the interactive video images in-infinitely variable?" Nebuta asked.

"No," Lomitus said. All but Jarrin attempted to hide disappointment. "I figure you ought to be able to use it for, oh, a few thousand years, I reckon, before any one variation pops up again."

After a moment, a polite interval, the group demanded to see the next gift.

"My turn, ain't it?" Bhrogig said.

He produced a small box, pointed it upward at a 45-degree angle, and pressed a button. The blue sky changed. It became a swirling, passionate, red inferno, with fiery yellow bursting here and there, and streaks of orange clouds.

"Oh," Maurim said, "how charming."

"It's not just a light show." Bhrogig handed the box to Maurim. "Here. What's on your mind?"

"You mean it's interactive, like Lomitus' and Crim's — "

"Right. Point it up and press the button."

Maurim did and the sky became a pale blue, empty as before except for a few puffball white clouds.

"Oh, dear." She handed it back to Bhrogig. "I hope I didn't break it."

"Well, I made six of 'em." Bhrogig fidgeted with the box. "One for each — "

Jarrin snatched the box from Bhrogig's hand. "Of course it works." He pointed it up and pushed the button. The sky turned a hazy gray-brown, the muck punctuated with reddish, malignant blotches. "Maurim has no imagination." He handed the box back to Bhrogig.

"Take it home." Bhrogig handed the box to Maurim. "Point it at your own sky, if you have one. Sometimes, if you have clouds, they'll form up in patterns."

He passed out the boxes. Jarrin took his and put it in a pocket without a glance. Maurim pointed hers at the sky and touched the button, replacing Jarrin's dark overcast with her own more cheery air. Then she put her box away.

Nebuta raised a hand. "May I go next?"

She offered six miniature trees, each bearing pea-sized fruit, like tiny oranges. "Try the, um, fruit," she urged. The others, including Jarrin, complied.

They nibbled on the fruit, savoring the pulp and juice in their various ways. Except for Jarrin, whose reaction remained unreadable, each responded with polite but lackluster approval.

"Pretty damn tasty," Lomitus said.

"Yes," Crim nodded. The others agreed.

"N-now try another," Nebuta said.

They complied. Tasting the second fruit from their trees, their reactions changed. Eyebrows rose, smiles appeared.

"Why, it tastes different," Bhrogig said.

"Yes, um, each fruit tastes different from the last," Nebuta said. "The tastes never repeat."

"Ever?" Bhrogig asked above the animated chatter that broke out. "Do they have any nutritional value?"

"N-no," Nebuta sighed. She handed out chips with care instructions. "And the fruit only grows so fast, um, and you have to be sure the water and soil is mixed just right. If you have water and soil where you live. So, don't eat them all at once. If you do, they might not grow b-back."

"I fancy I'll not have that problem," Jarrin said.

"Oh dear," Nebuta said. "W-what do you mean?"

"Well, mine tastes bitter." Jarrin puckered his face.

"Consider the source," Bhrogig muttered.

"I beg your pardon?" Jarrin asked.

"What Bhrogig means," Lomitus said, "is that these here gifts are interactive. They reflect the personality of the person using it. I don't reckon your plant'll last a year, Jarrin, even if you tried to nurture it with all your might."

"Interactive?" Jarrin scowled. "That's been the theme underlying most gifts exchanged at these boring Gatherings for the past few score thousand years."

Despite herself, Maurim found him attractive even when he tried to be ugly. She absently fondled the vials on her necklace.

"Jarrin, honey," Lomitus said, "what's boring is to hear your bellyaching, Gathering after Gathering."

Jarrin stood and paced around the table at which the others sat, gesturing expansively. "Don't you see? We can't interact as humans anymore so we try to invent interactive games and baubles. It's not interaction. It's not 'relationships', no. We've evolved, you see. Despite the artificial personalities, complete with anachronisms, accents, warts, and so on, we can't interact because we're not human anymore."

"May I be allowed to present evidence to the contrary?" Maurim stood. Jarrin bowed and sat. Maurim paced to the head of the table and turned toward the others.

"At my birthday party," she began, "Jarrin and I — "

"Oh, Maurim," Jarrin groaned. "Must you?"

"There's nothing more human than love-making — "

"We copulated like beasts — "

"We engaged in sexual intercourse — "

"Her idea," Jarrin pointed at Maurim. "I didn't want to do it. I didn't like it, I assure you."

"Maurim," Crim interjected, "we all engage in recreational copulation at Gatherings. So, you and Jarrin mated between Gatherings. So? I don't see how it refutes Jarrin's premise."

Maurim let a smile ease across her face. When all eyes were on her, Jarrin's smoldering, she lifted the necklace with the six vials from around her neck. A glint of sunlight caught the vials swinging on the chain in her outstretched hand.

"My gift," she said. "Fetuses."

Gasps. Groans.

"H-human?" Nebuta asked, eyes wide.

"Human," Maurim said.

The silent, incredulous stares at the six vials in Maurim's hand lingered. One by one, the stares switched from Maurim's gift to Jarrin's slack-jawed, horror-filled face.

"No, wait." He shook his head. "I didn't. I couldn't — "

"You could," Maurim said. "And you did."

"Could what?" Crim asked. "Did what?"

"Im-impregnate her," Nebuta said.

"Did you carry those — things — in your womb?" Lomitus asked.

"But six fetuses?" Bhrogig asked. "I seem to remember my historical physiology and I recall — "

"No, idiot," Lomitus said. "She couldn't have carried — "

"Why did you?" Jarrin asked. "For the love of humanity, why did — "

"Exactly," Maurim barked, dark eyes on Jarrin. The excited babble around the table stopped. "For the love of humanity — that's why I did it. I believe in humanity, Jarrin. We know you believe our species is at an end. But as you can see, you're quite mistaken."

Maurim walked around the table, handing each person a vial as she spoke. "I put a lot of time and research into this. After all, it's been more than half a million years since a human child has been conceived. Maybe as long since human male and female sexual intercourse for reproduction has taken place. In the end, I found I needed little artificial enhancement, biologic manipulation, or AI reprogramming to conceive. The main ingredient was sperm, which I suspected Jarrin possessed. I was right, as you see. The hardest part was seducing him. His convictions run deep, but he can be aroused."

Maurim stopped and stood behind Jarrin. His ragged breath came in harsh, quick huffs, his chin lowered to his chest, eyes unreadable. Maurim reached over his shoulders and put the last vial a few centimeters before his clenched hands.

"I rest my case." She stood back a step.

"Well," Bhrogig stammered, "what are we, uh, that is — "

Lomitus finished his thought. "What the hell are we to do with these — things?"

"Nurture them." Maurim sat. "Implant them in your womb and give birth. You can do it, you know. If you want to. Raise them. Create a family — "

"Family?" Crim asked.

"Ar-archaic term," Nebuta purred. She moved a little closer to Crim. "I'll explain later."

"But I can't, you know," Bhrogig stammered, "implant them. I don't have a womb."

Lomitus shrugged. "Well, you can make one. A womb, I mean. Maybe you could give the problem to your AIs, like a — what's the word? — "

"Nanny?" Nebuta offered. "Baby-sitter?"

"Cloning's also possible," Lomitus said. "The point is — "

"The point is — " Jarrin spat, words like acid, anger barely under control. The group went silent and all turned toward Jarrin. He stood again, pacing back and forth.

"The point is," he continued, "that after you create a life, any life, human or whatever, in the womb — the old fashioned way, if you like — or artificially, you become responsible. You'll become what used to be called 'parents.' Do you recall why our species stopped procreating?"

No response. Jarrin fixed his iron gaze on Maurim, and she looked away.

"I've mentioned it before," he said, "many times. Have you forgotten? Maurim didn't tell you, although I'll wager she confirmed the information in her research. Well?"

No response.

"Even that long ago, the best minds knew that our species was at an end. No humans could be found who were still totally organic, unaltered by technology. Who knows when the species really ended, when we made ourselves something — else? And who needed 'babies,'" he sneered the word, "when we can clone ourselves, when we can make companions through our bioengineer AIs? It became pointless — you see? So people stopped mating."

"Then why," Maurim asked, "have you stayed among us? Why haven't you discorporated, like the others?"

"I could have. I thought to do so often over the past few millennia. Until recently, about ten thousand years ago, I couldn't have told you why I resisted the urge that prompted most humans to discorporate in the past eons."

After a pause, he said, "Now, I know why."

"Why, then?" Crim asked.

"I've stayed alive, and I've tried to maintain my organic integrity, for one reason — my gift at this Gathering."

Jarrin passed out the small aluminum boxes with the red bows, putting them on the table. No one touched them.

"I was going to do this six Gatherings ago. Do any of you remember what I said then?"

No one spoke.

"I'm not surprised. You ignored me. I started to say then what I'm going to say now, to present this gift to you, but your banal twitter, your inattention — bordering on contempt — stayed me. As did another thought. Do you know what Gathering this is?"

Silence.

"The one-thousandth. Think of it. We've done this exactly one thousand times. I'm glad I looked that up six Gatherings ago and waited. The ninety-fourth Gathering was of no consequence. But the thousandth! Auspicious! What symmetry, eh, Maurim? Elegant, don't you think?"

Maurim stifled a yawn.

"As you know," Jarrin continued, "I'm a student of Earthome history, back when we called it 'Earth,' before the migration, particularly 'The Atomic Age.'"

"We've all studied history," Bhrogig said.

"Yes, but out of boredom, I suspect. As a hobby. I, on the other hand, studied with a mission. At first, I sought an answer to why we exist. I hoped to answer your question, Maurim: why should we go on? Why should I? I didn't know."

Jarrin sat on the table edge, one leg swinging. "In my search, I found an old formula. The one used to make an 'atomic bomb.' Who remembers what that is?"

Realization dawned on the group, and their faces darkened with horror. Yet, Jarrin noticed with grim satisfaction, Crim gingerly touched the box, fascination obvious. Nebuta cocked her head in curiosity, humming. Lomitus drew the box a centimeter toward her. Bhrogig twisted his fingers in the bow, brow furrowed in thought. Even Maurim put forth a hand to touch the box in front of her, before she withdrew it stiffly.

"An atomic — " Maurim began.

" — bomb," Jarrin finished.

"Programmed to explode when you open it," he added.

Fingers eased away from the boxes.

"Boom!" Jarrin grinned. "Happy millennium!"

"But why?" Crim asked.

"Answer that question for yourself, Crim," Jarrin said. "Do you really want to carry on? Do you? I think not. Year after year, Gathering after Gathering, our very existence maintains the illusion that there is some reason for being. Why not end it? Especially now, at this magically auspicious time? I think you will each choose, before the next Gathering, to open the box — and discorporate."

"No," Maurim said, "I think not. If we haven't yet — and, like you, we could have — then we'll resist your gift, all of us. Even you, Jarrin, will resist."

"And wait for Gathering number one-thousand and one?" Jarrin frowned. "Perhaps I'll open mine now and discorporate us all."

Gasps and wide eyes marked each face, except Maurim's.

Jarrin smiled. "No, I've given this a lot of thought, a lot of analysis, since I decided to do this. And I believe the reason none of you has discorporated in the past ages — the reason I haven't — is because we haven't had the means to do so presented to us in a manner that would make discorporating an imperative. Simple boredom, you see? Simple lack of creativity has kept us from finding a mechanism to end our own lives. Don't believe me? Then why, ask yourselves, the dismal gifts handed out each year, the boring attempts to create life? We aren't clever enough — or courageous enough — to find a means to end it. We're too programmed to continue this meaningless, self-involved farce we call 'life' to do anything creative about it. You see?

"And the anniversary! It gives it a special meaning we won't otherwise experience until," he shrugged, "maybe the ten-thousandth Gathering?"

"Or do we continue, rather," Maurim mused, "because a mechanism is built into our genes to sustain life?"

"No," Jarrin said. "History tells us our species destroys, not creates."

Maurim held up her vial in a small fist. "Here is creation. New life. A new start for the human race. I think even you, Jarrin, will choose to nurture it."

"I'll choose the box," Jarrin said.

"Why not open your damn box now, Jarrin," Lomitus asked, "if you're so determined to end the species?"

"You know the answer, I'll wager. Self-destruction must be a personal choice. None has the right to force discorporation on another who doesn't wish it."

"Then w-why the accounting?" Nebuta asked.

"Free will, again," Jarrin said. "If one of you opts to open the box now, here, then I'm wrong. The option has to exist, so the accounting."

"Creation, too, is a matter of will," Maurim said. "I could have grown these fetuses myself, but it wouldn't be the same. It's now up to each of you, as individuals."

"I want to thank you, Maurim," Jarrin said. She raised questioning eyebrows at him. "You've made this an even more interesting Gathering than I'd planned. I intended to give us all a choice — to discorporate or not. A millennial celebratory Big Bang for each of us. But you have modified my intent. You've improved the sport of it. Now instead of choosing between ending and continuing, we'll choose — "

"Yes," Maurim said. "Between ending — and beginning."

"But, um, w-what if some choose discorporation," Nebuta said, "and others choose procreation?"

"My wager," Jarrin said, "is we'll all choose one or the other, not both. The symmetry, you see."

"I agree," Maurim said. "One option — and you know which one I favor — represents the optimum for us all. We'll all need to think about it for a while. But in the end — in the beginning, I mean — we'll all independently make the same choice. The right choice."

"Well," Bhrogig sighed, "this has been an interesting Gathering, maybe the most interesting in human history."

"Because it's the one-thousandth," Jarrin said, "and the last."

"No," Maurim said. "Because it's the first."

ACING ANTHRO 201

I almost quit school midway through astrophysics after I got a D in planetary construction. The Asteroids; they were supposed to stay together. I don't know what happened.

In the first place, there was Becky Lynne, the prettiest girl in the whole freshman class at Celestial University. Ahh. How would I ever get a chance to go out with her if I dropped out? I know I was shy at the time — couldn't build up the courage to ask her out, but believe me, I wanted to. My hormones went wild at the thought of her. But she never noticed me.

I thought. Back then.

I didn't want to go home a failure either. If I didn't graduate, I knew I'd end up a cometmaker like my dad, a middle level management type commuting to the cometworks in the Oort Cloud with all the other cometmakers, making comets millennia after millennia. Make a comet, fling it into orbit, make another comet, fling it into orbit. Dirty, frozen gas balls, one right after the other.

I watched my dad, over the millennia, turn into a dirty, frozen gas ball himself with the constant drudgery, the numbing sameness of the work. So I stuck it out at C.U. and I'm glad I did. I finally got Becky Lynne's attention — and a lot more.

Professor Larsen didn't have to talk about it in front of the whole class, about the Asteroids, I mean. But she did. "Kenneth," she chirped, glasses sliding down her beak nose as she spoke, "planetary cohesion is among the most basic of principles and one must conquer the basic principles before one moves on to greater endeavors vis-à-vis astrophysics in general, and planetary construction in particular, mustn't one?"

Some kids snickered.

Becky Lynne looked away.

Prof Larsen hates me.

Then she goes on to talk about Becky Lynne, who did Saturn. "The Rings are a fascinating touch," she cooed, hands clasped in rapture. "They demonstrate a mastery of the subject matter one would naturally expect because Rebecca Lynne is an astrophysics major. The subtle, even artistic, interplay of cosmic forces evoke poetic imagery that yak, yak, yak, blah, blah, blah, etc."

Becky Lynne got an A for Saturn.

I didn't dare raise my hand and wonder aloud whether Becky Lynne had been tinkering around ahead of schedule with making moons, our next unit, and maybe she'd messed up on the cohesion part and decided to cover it up by making rings.

I still hoped Becky Lynne would get around to noticing me, even though she hadn't said a word to me all semester. But asking her out continued to be Out Of The Question. I wouldn't have been able to handle it if she said "no." And saying she'd, well, "fudged a little" on the assignment would make me look jealous, unfriendly. I didn't want her to think that.

Besides, it probably wouldn't change my grade.

We did moons next, as I said, and I figured if I could get an A in that unit, I could salvage my GPA and I'd be able to continue fall semester. Maybe by then, I'd declare a major. Whatever I declared, it wouldn't be astrophysics.

Prof Larsen built the Moon to show us what she wanted us to do. Since she only had six students in the class, she skipped Mercury and Venus and started assigning planets from Mars out. I got Mars. Becky Lynne got Jupiter.

At first I planned on making an ice moon about a third Mars' diameter, something substantial with a hefty magnetic field, but it would look too much like Earth's Moon and I believed Prof Larsen might down-grade me, suspecting I was trying to kiss up to her. Then I figured if Prof Larsen wanted "subtle, even artistic, interplay of cosmic forces," maybe I'd just make a couple small moons (slightly misshapen for character) and set them in a fast, low orbit to give them a presence in the Martian sky. That sounded good. So, I made Deimos and Phobos.

Becky Lynne, meanwhile, went nuts with Jupiter, filling the Jovian sky with moons, more than a dozen by the time I quit counting. Moons in different sizes and shapes. She'd overdone it, I could see, letting her ego loose. Overkill. Surely, I'd get a better grade on this unit than she would.

So, I felt elated, anticipating a good grade — I'd settle for a B — when Prof Larsen started inspecting our projects.

She started with Mars and worked outward. She peered at Deimos and Phobos over the half-glasses perched on the end of her nose, "hmm"ed now and then, and scribbled on a clipboard. When she finished, she gave me a curt nod and moved to Jupiter.

When she skirted the Asteroids, giving a disdainful sniff in passing, I got a peek at her clipboard. She had things on it like Number of Satellite Unit(s), Mass(es), Orbital Eccentricity(ies), Albido(s), Relative Distance(s) From Host Planet, Surface Features. That sort of thing. I didn't see all the criteria she had listed, but I know Atmosphere(s) wasn't on the list. That was our next unit.

She gave Becky Lynne's hodgepodge of satellites whizzing hither and thither the same routine she gave my moons. Peering, "hmm"ing, scribbling, then stiffly nodding and moving on. She did the same at Saturn (which also had a lot of moons, which made me suspect that Jonathan Biggs, who did Saturn, had copied from Becky Lynne), Neptune, Uranus, and Pluto; Biggs, Marylou Snipes, Wesley Dunhaven III, and Morgan Frelander, respectively. It looked as if she'd grade this unit with such scrupulous fairness that I began to wonder if my earlier conclusion about her hating me had been an error in judgment on my part. In fact, I began calculating my new, higher, and more respectable GPA.

I shouldn't have. Figured my new GPA, I mean — or altered my perception of Prof Larsen's hatred for me.

She did it again. In front of the class. Embarrassed me.

No use trying to hide it. It's right up there for all to see. My moons, my beautiful twin moons, delicate light pinpricks dashing through the Martian sky in "subtle, even artistic, interplay of cosmic forces" were retrograde.

Everybody else's moons went *this* way around their planets, mostly. Mine went *that* way. After Prof Larsen pointed out my error, much to my classmates' general merriment, she seemed to have spent her venom, and when she came to other faults in the heavens (like mine and in some cases, in my opinion, even greater), she underplayed them with a dismissive wave of bony fingers and a lilt in her wispy voice that infuriated me.

It made me mad. Another D. It was outrageous. But what could I do? Point out mine weren't the only retrograde bodies in the heavens? "Yes, Kenneth," she said when I confronted her after class, keeping her annoyance barely under control, like I was questioning her inspired wisdom or something, "what you say is quite true. Quite, I'm sure. But observe the degree to which the error you've made in this respect, unwittingly, as you admit, dominates the heavens of your planet. Whereas, errors in other planetary systems, if indeed such they may be called, pale by comparison given the overlying fact that yak, yak, yak, blah, blah, blah, etc."

I should have been discouraged. I should have quit right then. But the more I thought about going back to the Oort System, about slaving my life away in the cometworks, about not ever having a chance to go out with

Becky Lynne (who still hadn't spoken to me yet), about the injustice of it all, the madder and madder I got and the more determined I got to show Prof Larsen — to show them all — I wasn't hopelessly stupid. I could get good grades; I could get my degree. I had to.

So I calculated and figured I could squeak by if I did well on the next unit, Atmosphere.

I studied — oh, how I studied. Nuclear and plasma physics, electrical storm dynamics, elementary and advanced atmospheric chemical composition, moisture and acidity, solar and cosmic radiation, relationship between weather patterns and air currents, the entire panoply of the electromagnetic spectrum as it relates to atmospheric dynamics. The whole nine billion yards. I studied — I *mastered* — it all. I was ready.

Prof Larsen hates me. She said the selection of planets for the atmospheric unit was random, but I know otherwise. I got Jupiter because Prof Larsen hates me.

Jupiter, the solar system's biggest planet. You'd think, at first glance, a hot giant, almost-star, like Jupiter would be easy to do — a few gigabillion tons of methane and a few noble gases, pressurize, and that's it. But its enormous surface area magnified the likelihood of error, any error, getting out of control and ruining the entire atmosphere. I was doomed.

Becky Lynne drew Saturn.

Now, Saturn and Jupiter are enough alike that whatever works atmospherically on one will likely work on the other. I think. Anyway, I decided to spy on Becky Lynne and — I'll admit it, I was desperate — copy her homework.

She did an excellent job. The upper stratospheric clouds, pole to equator, both hemispheres, played out in wide bands of different colors, harmonious blends, subtle, haunting, beautiful. It looked flawless, to me.

So, I tried what she'd done with her Saturn on my Jupiter. She'd finished quite fast — after all, astrophysics was her major — which meant I had plenty of time to do it right, to check and recheck my figures, compositions, and conclusions before the assignment came due.

I finished fast too. I was checking a border between two distinct cloud bands near my equator — which is quite tricky, keeping one coherent cloud band distinct and separate from an adjacent band and keeping them in constant motion relative to each other and the planetary surface drag — when Becky Lynne came up to me. And spoke.

Ahh.

"Hi, Kenneth," she said. I hadn't seen her coming up behind me. Her voice in the stillness of near-Jovian space startled me, and I spilled a few billion deciliters of frozen argon gas into a highly eccentric orbit.

"Oh." Yes, my voice squeaked through two octave changes. "Becky Lynne. How are you? What brings you, uh, I mean — "

"I finished early and thought I'd see how you're doing."

"Oh." It's amazing how inarticulate I'd suddenly become considering the countless hours I'd spent, I'll confess, daydreaming about talking with Becky Lynne. Alone. "Oh," I repeated, if for no other reason than to confirm to the most beautiful woman in the freshman class at Celestial University that I was a hopeless, socially inept dolt.

She laughed.

But she didn't laugh at me, I could tell. And it was beautiful. Her laugh, I mean. Beautiful.

She hovered in the same orbit I occupied, maybe a few kilometers higher, the light from Jupiter giving her skin a fresh-washed glow. And her eyes caught the light and sparkled like stars. And she looked —

The term "subtle, even artistic, interplay of cosmic forces" came to mind.

Right then, my mouth open, my eyes bugged out shamelessly staring at this vision of perfection sharing an orbit with me, I decided my major. Anatomy.

"I saw you watching me do Saturn." She smiled. "You were stealing my homework, weren't you?"

I stammered something inane, something I hoped she hadn't heard.

"It's okay." The heavenly music in her voice convinced me anything would be okay, if she said so.

"You mean, you aren't going to tell on me?" There, I'd uttered a clear, complete thought; a coherent sentence, however stupid. I felt proud.

"Oh, no." She drifted closer. I know she couldn't hear my heart beat in the vacuum, but it felt as if she could. "I wouldn't do that. In fact, I kind of like you."

I barked a nervous laugh and my jaw dropped open even more, as impossible as it seems. I blushed and stammered and giggled and made a few foolish gestures, I'm sure. Anybody monitoring that section of space would have registered the creation of a new star, I radiated enough heat.

I was in love.

Simple as that.

And the amazing thing — so was Becky Lynne. With me.

Becky Lynne was in love with *me*.

Ahh.

We talked in orbit, holding hands, coy in these early hours of a relationship that seemed (we both believed) destined to last as long as the Universe existed. We laughed at my shyness; we laughed at the fact that Prof

Larsen considered Becky Lynne "teacher's pet." We laughed about the Asteroids, and we laughed about Deimos and Phobos, and we laughed about the satellite clutter buzzing around Jupiter.

It seemed to last a billion years, but in fact, our sojourn lasted only a few millennia. It ended when Becky Lynne happened to look away from my rapt stare and glance at the planet surface below.

"Oh, my," she gasped and I tore my gaze away from her perfect face to see, on Jupiter's surface —

— A huge red spot, a boil in an equatorial cloud band, swirling like a gigantic whirlpool, sucking the symmetry from my homework, dooming me to another D, if not an F.

I raved, I'm afraid, my passion for Becky Lynne momentarily forgotten. It took a while before I noticed how calm she was. If she loved me, wouldn't she be distressed on my behalf, share my grief? But no. She looked amused.

"I don't get it." I put my hands on my hips and glared at her, hurt. It looked as though we were about to have our first quarrel. "Why are you laughing?" She didn't exactly laugh, but it was close enough.

"I think we can fix it."

It took me a moment to absorb what she'd said.

"Fix it? Fix what? Fix *that*?" I pointed at the planetary pimple.

"No, silly. Fix your grade."

"Huh?" I don't care if I ended up a brain surgeon, no matter what I did or said, it would always look inane in her company. She did that to me.

"Look." She took my hand and I felt my heart melt. "Prof Larsen thinks I'm teacher's pet, right? So I'll just tell her how impressive I think your, uh, artistic effort, or whatever, is and she'll give you a better grade."

"Think she'll go for it?"

She shrugged perfect shoulders. "What do we have to lose?"

We. She said "we."

I watched Becky Lynne chatting with Prof Larsen a few decades later — they crossed orbits in the hallway near the ladies room (the one at Earth's L-5) and I saw them chatting but I couldn't hear them. But their expressions told all. She bought it. Prof Larsen, I mean. I'd get a good grade.

And it came to pass.

I got an A.

But Prof Larsen still hates me, I can tell. After she inspected the atmospheres, she lectured the class, as usual, about why she graded one way or the other. I know all the profs didn't grade that way, didn't tell everybody what grade they got and why they graded that way in front of the whole class, but she did it. And I don't think she did it as a "constructive critique," as she called it. I think she did it so she could cause me grief because she hated me.

"The source of the creative eye is a wonder." She fluttered eyelashes, sighed, and waxed poetic. "If not for Rebecca Lynne's artistic deportment, seeing beauty in all she surveys, it's possible the anomalous aspect, not to say 'artistic flare,' of the Jovian atmosphere Kenneth created, might have passed our notice. Indeed, the rendering yak, yak, yak, blah, blah, blah, etc."

Was I the only one who noticed she didn't say, "You did a nice job, Kenneth?" No. Instead, she praised Becky Lynne for noticing that I'd done something right.

But I still got an A.

And sitting there in the final few decades of astrophysics class, looking across the room at Becky Lynne, I felt sure, during summer break, I'd lose my virginity. At last.

But it didn't come to pass.

I tried. Oh, how I tried. But when we went out together, we almost always ended up at a party or something where it was impossible to be alone for long.

And I discovered that Becky Lynne was "saving herself for marriage," as she put it.

I got an idea, a plan, a way to solve my problem.

"I thought we were going to take the same classes together, Kenneth." It was right after we'd registered. Becky Lynne looked dejected, lower lip protruding a fraction of a centimeter in a pretty, petulant pout.

"Well, yeah." I shrugged. "Except for this class. It's a surprise."

"A surprise?"

"Yeah. Wait'll you see my final project."

Becky Lynne shrugged and seemed to lose interest.

We didn't get to go out much during fall semester because we were both so busy with classes. Oh, we held hands as often as possible, met for lunch on the quad in good weather (old Professor Maxwell Hammerstein made the local weather. He liked cumulonimbus cloud formations, so weather was always an iffy thing at C.U.), and now and then we got to make out, but money was tight so we didn't go on any formal dates.

We shared a few classes. Primeval biology turned out to be pretty fun, making viruses, microbes, and simple one-celled animals in Earth's primordial soup. Later we got to make more complex organisms and eventually fishes. Then we progressed to amphibians. At that point, our class split and a few bio diehards stuck with the sea while most students, including me and

Becky Lynne, moved on to land. We were all looking forward to making mammals and getting into the unit on Man.

Anthropology 201, the Creation of Man.

"Aren't you excited?" Becky Lynne squeezed my hand in the corridor right after we got our final grades for Primate Evolution, the so-called "Monkey Business Class." She got an A, and I got a B.

"About Anthro 201?" I shrugged, feigning casual disinterest. "Yeah. I guess so."

"Creating an intelligent species? The very beginning of civilization, the initial spark itself? Being there, taking part? You're not excited?"

I shrugged.

"Kenneth, you're positively weird." Still, she smiled at me and went her way. She went off to her class on Primitive Languages, and I went on to my own class, Agriculture.

I hung back in Anthro 201, not joking around like the other kids. I did well enough on my assignments, getting passable but not spectacular grades. Becky Lynne told me one day that I seemed to be smiling a lot lately and she asked why.

"Oh, you'll see."

"When?"

"Last day of school."

"Kenneth, you're definitely weird." But she smiled and squeezed my hand.

On the last day of the semester, the Garden of Eden lay before us, complete. We'd all collaborated, of course, on creating Adam and Eve, and they stood to one side, shyly answering questions and accepting everybody's wishes for a good life and prosperity and so on. They were a beautiful couple. I did Adam's nose. B-minus; a bit large. Becky Lynne did Eve's hair in near-perfect imitation of her own. A-plus.

"Okay, Kenneth, time to drop the other shoe." Becky Lynne took my arm and led me down a path away from the others crowded around Adam and Eve.

"Okay, here's the deal," I said. "Ag 201 students collaborated on the foliage in the Garden, you know, as a class assignment."

"Uh-huh."

"We've provided for significant biological diversity. Plenty of grasses to hold down the soil — "

"And for the ungulates to graze."

"Bushes and shrubs for variety and — "

"And for small animal nesting and nourishment."

"Flowers for a touch of color and — "

"And to sustain the birds and bees."

"You made a few of the animals, I gather?"

"So everybody had a part in creating The Creation. But the way you've been smirking for the last few hundred thousand years, you'd think you did it all by yourself."

"Yes, everybody had a part in creating The Creation. And for the most part, none of us can say with any certainty which part, exactly, we created individually. I guess that's the plan, isn't it, to avoid any ego problems? Team effort, that sort of — "

"It seems to have worked."

I stopped Becky Lynne in the shade of a tree. "But if you look closely, you can see individual touches here and there — "

"Like the Asteroids, Deimos and Phobos, Jupiter's Red Spot."

"And even here, right in the middle of the Garden of — "

"No, not here, Kenneth, I think. The curriculum was made to avoid such individual enterprises. We all know that."

"Not so. I managed to — "

"You cheated?"

I smiled. I didn't speak. Instead, I turned to the tree, plucked a fruit, and handed it to her.

"Kenneth, you shouldn't have."

She bit into the fruit.

Ahh.

SNOWFLAKES, ONE BY ONE

\

Outside the monastery's walls, the snowfall called "Winged Fleas Cavort" became the snowfall called "Butterflies at Play," a prelude to the snowfall called "His Image Incarnates." Inside, the tour group got around to Emil Levina's table. That's when Emil saw someone in the group who startled him so much he dropped a snowflake on his table and uttered an involuntary gasp. His hearts stopped, as he was sure others had noticed his sacrilege.

A snowflake, spilled and ruined in the Hall of His Image Recounted. Horrors.

There were about a dozen in the group touring the monastery, Church of the Search for His Image Regained. The group was led by Comrade Gabro, who his Comrades of the Search called (behind his back), "The Well-Nourished One."

Emil didn't shift eyestalks from his task of cataloging snowflakes, of course, when he first saw the group enter the Hall. Inattention to one's duty was a sacrilege. Besides, he and the two hundred and sixteen monks in the cold, cavernous Hall of His Image Recounted could see from the corners of their eyestalks. The monks had long become accustomed to the monotonous cataloging of snowflakes in their billions, sunrise to sunset, decit after decit, yosim after yosim, each monk at his station in neat row after neat row from one end of the large, high-ceilinged room to the other, one snowflake at a time, with one tentacle, one eyestalk, and one part of the brain. The devotional search routine thus accommodated, that left the other tentacles, eyestalks, and brain-half at ease for daydreams and other entertainment.

Behind the appearance of machine-like industriousness in the Hall, an appearance the monks dedicated themselves to maintaining, almost as much as they dedicated themselves to The Search, they carried on elaborate conversations, debates, jokes, discussions, fantasies, and such. They did it with footpad taps, small tentacle gestures, and eyestalk flicks too fast to be detected by outside observers. And they did it all so silently, so subtly, that not only did the tourists never notice, but the Abbots at their floor monitors just off the Hall proper saw no deviation from the norm on their screens. If they did, they never let on.

At first, it looked like the usual thrice daily tour group. Six or seven appeared to be human, there was a Belarite triple, the middie's birthsac bulging with fetus, and a pair of Varois — twins, or perhaps clones. And one Amuno, a female. The female looked to Emil so much like his beloved Kistra that he lost composure for a moment and dropped the snowflake.

The snowflake, harvested from a recent "His Image Incarnate" flurry, slipped off the transfer tray between the collection bin and the input bay of Emil's terminal onto the table. It fell a half dozen centimeters, made not a sound as it hit the cold, hard table, landing almost flat and intact. Still, as far as Emil's hearts were concerned, it might as well have exploded. His involuntary intake of breath had been noticed. Derras, "Too Tall For His Hair," working at the table across from Emil, glanced up, a flick of one eyestalk, the glance there and quickly gone.

Emil scooped the flake onto the transfer tray and processed it. Had Gabro noticed, or a tourist? No, Emil assured himself, they hadn't. They focused on Gabro's chatter.

" — each terminal inputs optical and dimensional data, as well as weight, chemical composition, and fifty-nine other criteria from each individual snowflake into the mainframe, where each image is compared to all others that have been entered into it for the past seven hundred and five yosim, local reckoning. In human reckoning, that would be — "

But it wasn't Kistra in the group. Of course not. It was just an Amuno female. Kistra waited in an upstairs room, room number seven, second door to your right at the top of the stairs, in a brothel a few minnim's slide from the monastery, a brothel called by the sign above its door, "Gentlemen's Rest," but called by the Comrades (but only in whispers) "Where Warm Tentacles Caress."

"But what happens if you find a snowflake that matches one you've already cataloged?" the female Amuno asked. Not Kistra's voice.

"Ha!" A human snorted. "You know what the odds against that happening are?"

"We do," Gabro interjected, tentacles folded over his chest just so, a tolerant lilt in his voice. "We calculated those odds when we began our Search so many, many yosim ago. While the odds haven't changed, our dedication to finding that One Flake hasn't wilted since either."

"Hrmp," the human said.

"But what happens if you do find the snowflake," the Amuno repeated, "the one that matches another?"

Gabro spread tentacles in an expansive gesture. "Then our Search will be over. It will be the signal for the Universe to freeze over in a solid icy — "

"But what if we don't believe in your frozen savior," the annoying human said, "your, your, whatsisname — "

"But He believes in you," Gabro crooned. "Amuno, Human, Varois, Belarite, they are all precious in His sight — "

"Hrmp."

"Snow falls on the entire surface on Frysm, did you know that, my good sir or madam or other?" Gabro focused eyestalks at the human, tentacles knotted on hips, patience on the brink. "The entire surface. No other planet in the galaxy is so blessed with His Presence Manifest as are we on Frysm. Even to the Haylf Mountains on the equator, a snow we call "His Whispering Breath" falls at least once a yosim."

"Hrmp."

"He froze to death for your sins, sir or madam or other," Gabro hissed, wagging a tentacle at the human. He leaned forward on the balls of his footpads, a belligerent stance the human seemed not to notice.

Suddenly he stopped and tilted his head as if listening.

Gabro's monitoring Abbot, Emil thought, admonishing him through his earpodpiece for his near-outburst, telling him to get back to the program.

Gabro smiled and gestured toward Emil. "The Search continues," he said, inviting the tour group to observe Emil at work, doing his part in the Search.

"Comrade Levina," a tiny voice said in Emil's earpodpiece, "our visitors would treasure forever, as we do, seeing your legendary industriousness at full capacity."

Emil acknowledged the vigilant Abbot's admonition with a silent nod of a stalk toward the monitor and returned full attention to his duties. His tentacles blurred as he processed snowflakes, one at a time, swiftly, deftly, "At One With the Oneness," as the saying went.

Despite the cold of the Hall, perspiration formed on Emil's round forehead. His startlement at seeing the female he thought was Kistra had interrupted his routine vigor enough that it had come to the attention of the Abbot monitors.

Mud and slush, he swore. He resolved to complete his shift without a single thought about Kistra, about what he would do to her at his next decit off, and she to him, about her lustrous tangle of nape-hair, so thick, so soft, so tasty —

The tour group moved on, and Gabro's voice became an indistinct buzz fading into the background. The Hall hummed with keyboard clattering, input bay panels opening and closing with tiny plastic taps, the hissy breath of two hundred-sixteen devoted monks, their robes rustling as they moved snowflake by snowflake through their duties.

Grasp snowflake in collection bin with transfer tray probe. Lift transfer tray to terminal input bay. Insert tray. Tap "analyze" key. When signal flashes red, tap "retrieve" key and remove transfer tray. Make visual check to ensure tray is dry. Repeat process.

Again and again and again.

Do this for eight youris a decit, with a fifteen minnim break three times a decit, five decits a wennik, a hundred and five wenniks a yosim, with three wenniks off each yosim to go sliding down Broniker Skiway or skating across Icejat Bay, or visiting a brothel where Kistra waited —

Emil sighed. Just three youris left until his shift ended and the wennikend began. Two decits at large. He'd take his hard-earned tabbits, minimum wage, and go sliding into town. To see his beloved.

The visual stimulus of Kistra's beckoning tentacles formed before Emil's eyestalks, and he shut off his conscious mind and settled deeper into automatic. His tentacles did their routine processing thing while his mind did its thing to Kistra.

Then something happened.

At least Emil thought something happened. What he thought happened was a light on his terminal screen began flashing — amber, amber, amber, amber — like a clot of defiled snow. The warning light had gone off.

The light.

"When the light flashes on your terminal," an old Abbot whose name Emil had long forgotten had told him and the other acolytes training for their part in The Search so many, many yosim ago, "you will know it is time. *The* Time. Of course, it must be double-checked by the monitoring Abbots, but it is the sign we seek. When the light flashes, The Search is over. It means our computer has found a match. The snowflake you just inserted into the terminal analysis bay has been matched perfectly with another snowflake the dimensions of which had been entered into the computer's memory from some other terminal who-knows-how-long before. Imagine, Comrades; two snowflakes exactly alike, just as He foresaw, just as He promised. And you, blessed above all Comrades, save His own frozen Self, have found it. Imagine."

The blinking stopped.

Had Emil imagined it?

"Comrade Levina," the monitoring Abbot's tiny voice chimed in his earpodpiece, "you appear flushed. Are you all right?"

"Why, yes," Emil began. "That is, I — " But he realized that he sat motionless, not processing snowflakes. In blasphemous idleness. Something was wrong. Emil sensed a few eyestalks from nearby Comrades darting quick glances at him.

Had he seen the light? Or just imagined it?

If he'd seen the light, why hadn't the monitoring Abbot mentioned it? And why had it stopped flashing?

If he hadn't seen the light, what did that mean?

"Comrade Levina," the monitoring Abbot's voice dropped to an I'm-very-concerned-about-you tone, "kindly shut down your terminal and bless me with your presence in the office."

Emil complied, aware that eyestalks across the width and length of the Hall darted his way in surreptitious, gossipy glances, some scornfully, some amused, some concerned, and a few fearfully.

Emil shut down his terminal, left his table, and slid between rows and rows of tables, Amunoed by monk after monk busily Searching for the one snowflake — The One Snowflake — like the one he, for a glorious moment, thought he'd found. Found and then lost to — what? Hallucination? Fatigue? Brain tumor? He hadn't even had time to savor the moment to which he had dedicated his life. It came and went, in a flash.

He left the Hall and went to the office, knowing he had just become the subject of gossip among the monks in the Hall. Their footpads and eyestalks would be tapping and vibrating frantically about "The Undertall One," as he knew some called him (behind his back). "What's wrong with him?" "Did you see him go stiff? Like he'd frozen to death." "Are they going to reassign him?" And so on.

Emil himself had engaged in similar discussions on the Hall floor when a monk shut down his terminal mid-shift and left the Hall, eyestalks downcast. Speculation as to why, what shortcomings of the monk in question had prompted such unusual activity, always provided a much-welcomed diversion from the monotonous routine of the Search.

Sometimes the monk in question had eaten something over-ripe in his last break and had suffered an urgent need to eliminate. Even that provided occasion for gossip, and embarrassment for the afflicted monk.

Now and then, the monk who shut down mid-shift didn't return to his terminal, either later that decit or the in following wenniks.

The monks never discussed what happened to those others. An unspoken rule of the Hall declared those who disappeared in such circumstances didn't warrant further notice. And if a little apprehension about what had happened to them, why they never returned, existed among the remaining monks, that was never discussed either — also part of the unspoken rules.

In the office, Abbot Jessib Lalac waited, tentacles folded across his chest and a beatific smile on his face. The Abbot gestured a graceful welcome to Emil and ushered him down a long hallway, into a conference room Emil had never seen before.

He'd seldom been into the busy office, hub of Search Operations, let alone deep into its far recesses, where he now sat. He and the Abbot who the monks called "He Whose Voice Induces Sleep," (but not so he could hear), sat alone in the large conference room, the bustle beyond the door a dim hum. They sat at opposite ends of a huge table dominating the room.

"Well." Abbot Lalac smiled across the table. "And how are we liking our part in The Search, Comrade Levina?"

"Uh, most well, dear Abbot." Emil tittered, nervous. "I'm liking it, uh. Quite. Good. Sir."

"I'm ever so glad to hear your say so, Comrade. Finding devotees for The Search is a never-ending search in itself. You have no idea what we in Administration go through in our — "

Emil nodded in agreement, and the nodding became a rhythmic counterpoint to the Abbot's monotonous prattling. It had a hypnotic quality, the Abbot's voice did. Emil found himself saying, "Yes, yes indeed," in answer to the Abbot's question about his age.

Embarrassed, Emil resolved to stay alert. But a minnim later, he answered "Of course, just as you say," to the Abbot's question about how long he'd been in The Search.

Whatever the reason for the meeting, Emil decided with stoic resignation, he'd probably miss it. If he hadn't already.

" — So you agree then that a rest of, say, two wenniks, would suffice? If you take my meaning?"

"Yes, yes, of cou — " Emil leaned forward, alert. "A rest? From my duties?"

"After a brief medical examination, of course. It may be simply a matter of fatigue, I'm sure, still one never knows, does one? 'The body grows cold from the inside out,' as the saying goes. Not that I suspect anything like a, say, a tumor," the Abbot laughed and waved a dismissive tentacle, "but one never — "

"Tumor?"

"Perhaps a vision problem. Easily correctable."

"Uh, I'm not sure — "

"Of course, you probably wouldn't notice. That's why we monitor you. Or a vitamin deficiency or something like that."

"Vitamin deficiency?"

"Easily dealt with. Dietary supplements, you see. I myself take daily doses of vitamins Q and P, did you know?"

"Dietary supplements?"

"Fit as an iceboat, I am." The Abbot thumped his chest, coughed once weakly, and chuckled. "So, you agree?"

"To two wenniks off? Two wenniks away from my terminal?"

"With pay, of course. And fear not, my good Comrade, about your terminal. Our technicians will check your terminal to make sure it is not at fault. Oh, we take care of every contingency. Every contingency, I say. Terminals do go bad, I'm afraid. We don't like to advertise the fact, and I'm sure we can count on your discretion, don't you agree? This conversation is private, if you take my meaning. Wouldn't want the laity to suspect — "

As the Abbot prattled, Emil began to understand what was happening. He understood not by what the Abbot said, but by what he didn't say. The Abbot was a good bureaucrat. That's why his own higher-ups, "The Skis," as the monks called them (but not in earpodshot), chose him for the task.

As soon as the amber light blinks on a terminal, He Whose Voice Induces Sleep shuts it off, summons the monk Amunoing the afflicted terminal, and gets him out of circulation as quick as you can say Jole Frysm.

Why?

Because Church interests are best served by the Search, not by the Finding. If a match is found, then —

That couldn't be it. Could it? One Searches to Find and thus Fulfill His Prophecies.

Yes. But Emil *had* been daydreaming. About Kistra.

So, maybe he'd hallucinated, or the terminal malfunctioned. Whatever, it required immediate intervention, because —

" — because," the Abbot droned, "if that happened, where would we be? Don't you agree?"

"Where, indeed?" Emil hadn't heard the Abbot. Again.

"No, indeed. If that happened, we would be — we would be, uh, well, up to our tentaclepits in mud and slush, excuse the language, but it's the only way to describe what could happen if we found a matching snowflake and didn't realize it. Because of a terminal malfunction. Or whatever. You know. If you take my meaning. Do you agree?"

Emil nodded, afraid to open his mouth. Two wenniks, paid.

"So, it's all settled then, I take it? If you take my meaning, don't you agree? Perhaps you'll want to go ice fishing on Snowspire Lake or sledding across the Blue Gopf Basin. Perhaps you'll find diversion closer to home, say, a friend you know in town? Someone you could visit, take your mind off The Search? Something like that, perhaps? Whatever is your wont to do, I envy you, dear Comrade." The Abbot stood and the meeting ended.

The smiling, prattling Abbot escorted Emil from the conference room, down a hallway and out a door he'd never noticed before, let alone been through. It led not back to the Hall floor, but out the other end of the office, near Personnel, where his paycheck waited and a security monk showed him the door, gently but firmly. Out the back way.

He stood beside the iceway behind the monastery in the full flurry of the snowfall called "His Image Incarnates." Traffic along the iceway was heavy.

Emil looked up. Billions and billions of snowflakes fell on and around him. Some fell on his eyestalks, and he blinked.

Emil extruded his tongue and allowed a few flakes to settle on it. He withdrew the tongue and sucked the snowflakes that had fallen on it, trying to taste each one.

What if one of these snowflakes is The One?

Emil shook his head.

Nah. Not likely.

He sledded into town. His beloved Kistra waited` and he'd just got paid.

SCRATCH, AT THE DOOR

Scratch held the door to the Seashell Inn ajar and stood, one foot inside the tavern, the other on the rough-hewn boards outside, boards worn shiny by so many customers' feet over the years. He was alone, his customers gone. He had to decide whether to join them or stay.

The Inn — his home — beckoned with comfortable aromas — varnished tables, polished brass, mulchy sawdust floor, tobacco smoke. But the foul reek of buckberry juice, still damp on the blue spiral shell doorknob, burned his nose hairs.

Outside, the boojnut forest stretched in a green carpet, rolling to the horizon. Not far away, smoke curled above swaying treetops. It was a boojnut beer brewery and Scratch's mouth watered as he recalled that long unsavored brew.

He looked from one to the other. Inside — home and comfort. Outside — dreams realized.

Once the door closed, behind him or in front, there would be no turning back.

To go or stay. The others chose. So must he.

On his way to open up the Inn that morning, Scratch decided to walk along the seashore and gather change. Among the flotsam left by the tide, he found some clang shells, two mugwump shells, and a few brother-of-pearl bits.

Besides the regulars from the nearby village of Burning Stump, Scratch never knew what the day would bring. The road by the Inn followed a north-south course paralleling the western coast. Travelers of all kind came. Their needs varied, and Scratch tried to be prepared. He kept in stock a variety of the exchange media his customers preferred.

His pouch at last clattering full, he turned from the beach toward the path that wound among the grassy dunes, up and down and between them, inland toward the east and the Inn not far away. As he turned, the rays from the just-risen sun caught a glint of something in the kelp at the tide line.

Perhaps it's treasure. He turned the leaves aside with his boot, found a spiral-shaped shell, milky blue, like glass.

He picked it up, turning it to catch the light, cooing at its beauty. Clang and mugwump shells and brother-of-pearl made good spare change, but spiral shells were another matter. Rare. Scratch had never seen one so pale, so blue.

You're pretty, yes, but what are you worth?

He put the shell in his back pocket.

He walked to the Inn on the narrow pathway flanked by sand castle parapets half collapsed and long abandoned. The dune crickets sang about Pink Rabbits. Scratch whistled along, his pace in counterpoint.

It's going to be a good day. I can feel it.

Long ago, the Seashell Inn was a boojnut storage shed. Boojbeetles wiped out a whole year's crop, and the farmers' co-op that owned the place had to sell. Except for some trees at Sir Duncan Peese's Estate, no boojnuts grew anymore.

Scratch owned the Inn. He brewed beer out back, reputed the finest for miles around, but nothing like the legendary boojnut beer, as Scratch admitted. Customers also liked his tea, root beer, and yak milk.

Scratch was short. On his toes, he could just see his tabletops. He lacquered his thin, black hair and parted it down the middle. Fussy, he was always cleaning or polishing. His tiny eyes flitted constantly, scanning the room to ensure all his customers' mugs, flagons, and glasses were full.

The Inn stood west of the village, near the sea.

A huge elm tree stretched branches across the road and the front of the Inn. Under the elm at the hitching post near the door stood two droopy horses drinking from a water trough. Travel gear clung to their backs.

Their dusty riders, the day's first customers, stood nearby. Scratch nodded to them as he unlocked the door.

"Good day, gentlemen," he said.

"And to you, sir," the two strangers said in near unison.

The door hinges creaked as Scratch opened it. The two strangers entered after him, and the door swung shut.

*

Scratch opened the Inn door, and Burning Stump stirred. Fires sparked in kitchen hearths, drowsy shopkeepers coughed and yawned, a tap dance rhythm clanged from T.D. Tinker's blacksmith shop. Pink smoke belched from Doc Tay's bathroom.

A dog barked.

A wagon suddenly slid around the town square corner so fast it almost tipped over. But the two wheels that briefly lifted into the air crashed back to the ground and the wagon sped on. The two double-horses, with braided tails and manes (trademarks of Sir Duncan Peese's stable) galloped full tilt, their four tails and four manes snapping like flags, heading straight for doormaker Thadius McNatt's shop.

Burning Stump's residents had just roused, except Doc Tay who'd been up all night. They made breakfast with hooded eyes, dragging steps, and yawns. Thad still lay in bed, one bony, pink foot probing for the cold floor, the other ready to follow, when he heard the wagon rumble around the square.

He leaped up, ran downstairs, and swung his door open just as the wagon, its brakes screaming, stopped in front of his shop in a dust cloud.

Thadius muttered something irreverent. He sneezed and stroked his full beard with brisk, irritated strokes.

The ruckus drew Thad's neighbors. Many lived behind or above their shops, like Thad. A dozen faces peered around partly opened doors from this shop or that, facing the square. Like Thadius, many wore nightgowns, but unlike him, some backed their curiosity with caution: a blunderbuss in window maker Clarence Parsaval's steady hands, a shotgun held nervously by storekeeper Jason Popolot, a sword here, a crossbow there.

But there was no cause for alarm. Werewolves, nightmares, or goblins hadn't invaded. No earl or duke had come, and no parade was pending. It was just a Sir Duncan Peese employee returning a door to Thadius McNatt for repair.

The villagers grumbled in their various ways and resumed their interrupted routines.

Thad's long, white brow bobbed to keep the dust from his tiny, deep set eyes. He had a single eyebrow, running uninterrupted over his knife-thin nose across his long face. White hair topped his otherwise bald head like goose down. His beard was dusty and white.

He was as thin as a door seen edge on. His bony, pink feet were bare, and his toes twitched as he studied the wagon.

He sneezed again. The two double-horses snickered.

"All right," Thadius said, "you know the speed limit."

"Uh-huh," replied Chadwick, Sir Duncan's stable boy, as he hunched over the wagon's reins, "but you know it don't apply to no wagons carrying doors that need repair to your doorshop."

"What's wrong with the door?" Thad sighed.

"Sir Duncan says the squeak don't sound eerie enough and he wants a muffled thump, not a ominous slam." Chadwick heaved his bulk off the wagon and walked to the back.

Sir Duncan had achieved over the years a well-haunted estate. Almost. It disappointed him that no real ghosts inhabited its many halls and chambers. He'd advertised to correct the defect without success. Still, it had all the other amenities. It had fog, eerie sounds, musty odors, bats, hidden passages, spooky lights, and creaky doors, clattering shutters, rattling chains. He delighted in accuracy and wouldn't accept an underdone odor or sound, texture or taste. If a door didn't sound right, back to the shop it went.

Thadius didn't mind the repair work that came with Sir Duncan's hobby. One seldom argued with him; he paid well in huge tubs of chestnuts, acorns, and pecans from his estate. When especially pleased, he paid with boojnuts.

"He's got enough ominous slams, you know," Chadwick said.

"I should. I built them."

"But he didn't want this one to have no ominous slam."

"He should have told me."

"Didn't he?"

"No."

"Oh. How come?"

"I don't know," Thad shrugged. "He just said he wanted it especially eerie. But it isn't eerie enough either?"

"Unh-unh. But he likes the wood, the color is okay, and it knocks with a nifty thump, and it's cold to the touch, damp, musty, and stuff, but — "

"Not eerie enough."

"Uh-huh."

Thad sighed. He walked behind the wagon to get a better look at the heavy door. He dreaded the effort needed to move it into the shop and onto his workbench, but he began to appreciate the creative challenge. The muffled thump was no problem, but where to squeeze more eerie?

Well, Thad thought, shivering, might as well do it.

"Let's move it inside, then," he said.

"Okay." Chadwick leaped into the wagon bed. It rocked under his weight, and the loose brakes squeaked.

Grunting, they maneuvered the door into the shop.

The door straddled two wooden benches in the room's center, surrounded by saws, drills, hammers, and other implements on rickety shelves, stacked in corners, and lying willy-nilly about the shop. Thad paced beside the door, examining it while Chadwick sat on a box in a corner.

"I'll have no trouble replacing the ominous slam with a muffled thump," Thad said. "I have a good muffled thump in the back that'll fit, with a little trim. That's no problem. It's the eerie I'm worried about."

"Don't you got any?"

"It's not that." Thad stopped pacing and dropped into a battered, paint-freckled rocker. "I keep lots of eerie on hand because I know Sir Duncan uses a lot. The problem is a technical one, Chadwick. You wouldn't understand."

"Try me," said Chadwick, who made up for what he lacked in intelligence with a desire to be helpful.

"The problem is how to put in more of what's already there without taking out what you don't want to not have in."

"Uh-huh."

"You see, Sir Duncan orders the best doors, my deluxe package. There's no room for changes. Every nook and cranny is filled to capacity — color, sound, taste, odor, size, texture — everything you can put into a door is there, and at a fair price, too. There's no extra space. It's jammed full."

Chadwick blinked and picked his nose. "Uh-huh."

Thad sighed. He drummed his fingers on the chair arm, making little dust puffs. Chadwick rocked back and forth.

Thad paced again. "How far must the door open?"

"Gee, all the way, I guess."

"Are you sure? All the way to the inside wall?"

"Uh-huh. He even got this little rubber stopper for the door knob to hit on the wall."

"Good," Thad said, clapping his hands. "If you'll just fetch me a pencil over there," he pointed to a near-collapsed shelf, piled with nails and screws, "I think I have an answer."

"What is it?" Chadwick asked, brushing hair from his eyes as he dug among the rubble for a pencil.

"All I have to do is expand the effective magnitude door-swing radius a few degrees and I can use the resultant space differential to integrate the extra eerie squeaks."

Chadwick didn't understand, so he just said, "Uh-huh. When can I come and pick it up?"

"Tomorrow at sunup. Meanwhile, can you drop me at the Inn on your way home?" Thad pulled a pencil from his pocket, a blue one, like the one stuck behind his right ear. "I feel like calculating over some boojnut juice."

"Okay," Chadwick said, giving up his search for a pencil.

Thad grabbed some paper made from door shavings, a few calculating devices, and several whistles and animals he'd carved to use to buy boojnut juice. Scratch, at the Inn, liked the whistles. He joined Chadwick.

The double-horses sighed and bent their shoulders into the long trek home, anticipating lunch. "Stop by the Seashell Inn first," Chadwick told them as they trotted back around the square. The double-horses nodded.

A squeaking door and singing crickets announced Thadius McNatt's entrance to the Inn. The door swung shut behind him. The two strangers glanced up. They were deep into twin cider mugs while Scratch enthralled them with the tale of his narrow escape from two werewolves among the sand castles. In the far corner, a few weary, old bearded faces could be seen through the smoke-haze, hovering over mugs of ale.

Thad wore a long nightgown under his coat and carried papers, an abacus, and carved wooden animals and whistles. He had a long, blue pencil stuck behind his right ear.

His eyebrow twitched, and he muttered in thought.

He sat at his usual table by the front door, sneezed, and began scribbling figures. Scratch interrupted his narrative and brought Thad a pitcher of boojnut juice.

The weary, old bearded faces in the corner continued to provide atmosphere and color to the place.

And the crickets sang on.

Jack Ratchett, not quite human, was a constable. This morning, he was a frustrated constable. He was frustrated because nothing happened all night in Burning Stump, and nothing frustrates a constable more than nothing happening.

Dawn broke, and nothing continued to happen.

Ratchett shifted his weight to lean against the town's only parking meter. He decided to try yet another olfactory sweep. He stuck his blunt snout up and sucked in huge gulps of air, sifting the molecules for law violators. Nothing.

He turned up his hearing aid. Just dune cricket song.

Ratchett twiddled the left stem of his long handlebar mustache, the chrome hand-clutch at the end glinted. Again, he radar-scanned the streets facing the square and those off it to the north, south, east, and west. His wrist-radar screen revealed all peaceful, legal, and . . .

Something was happening. A green light speck appeared on the radar screen — coming from Sir Duncan Peese's Estate. Ratchett's pulse quickened. He leaned forward on his rubber wheelfoot, gripping the clutch handle on his left mustache.

"Chadwick, no doubt," he muttered, "with a door for Thadius McNatt." He snorted. "So I can't give him a ticket, but," he patted the shirt pocket under his badge to make sure his ticket book was there with a gnarled pencil stub he used to write tickets, "with stealth, I may catch him breaking a law."

Ratchett recalled the thousand laws he'd memorized. He nodded, satisfied he had enough material.

The dot on his radar screen grew to a blotch. Sixteen hooves beat a rhythm, getting louder, closer. Soon, the wagon thundered into view across the square.

The double-horses galloped to the doormaker's shop. Legal.

Ratchett moved away from the parking meter into the deeper concealment of a nearby boojnut bush. He started his motor.

At last, Chadwick and McNatt set out in the wagon around the square toward the Seashell Inn and the Peese Estate beyond. The wagon lurched away at breakneck speed, all quite legal, with Ratchett not far behind, alert.

After a brief stop at the Inn, Ratchett decided duty and boredom compelled him to follow Chadwick all the way to the edge of his jurisdiction.

Chadwick set out at a brisk but legal pace, the double-horses trotting, their long braided manes and tails bouncing. Their clipippity-clopoppity and casual horse-to-horse-to-horse-to-horse chatter echoed off the trees along the lane a few miles outside town. The stout tree trunks squatted under gnarled, intertwined branches, blotting out the stars by night and the sun by day.

The leaves whispered in a breeze, shadows flickered, and Ratchett shivered.

Suddenly a Pink Rabbit ran across the road before the wagon. Its eyes glowed, long ears waved flag-like, hind legs kicked, and it bolted off. The double-horses, discussing lunch, didn't see it pass less than a wagon's length ahead.

Whether Chadwick saw was beside the point. His failure to stop broke several criminal codes concerning the rights-of-way accorded to Pink Rabbits.

Ratchett sprang into action, his duty clear.

Doc Tay experienced a long-awaited epiphany.

"Geronimo!" he cried.

"Eureka!" would have been more appropriate, but the physician's excitement was nonetheless genuine.

At last, he'd made —

THE DISCOVERY!

That's what he called it, always capitalized, with an exclamation point. Even in his dreams, it always looked that way. But for years, it had been just a dream, unattainable. Yet here it was. He mouthed the words reverently.

THE DISCOVERY!

He fought an urge to dance, sing, or do something demonstrative. Instead, he stepped back and admired his genius.

Night after night he experimented and calculated. A carnival of light, sound, and odor emerged from his cottage. Iridescent oranges, blotchy purples, and flashy pinks vied for dominance behind his tiny bathroom window. Sometimes a gurgling, clinking, or muffled explosion, accompanied by incantations in Latin or Greek, filtered into the air. A pungent odor, like boiled shoe leather and sulfuric acid, permeated the atmosphere near the cottage.

THE DISCOVERY!

His thin hands trembled as he held up the flask of pink liquid, marveling at its luster. It resembled a weak boojnut juice, and smelled foul. Still, it radiated power, mysticism, and wisdom. It was the nectar of youth, the secret of the ages, the magic elixir, the philosopher's stone, the Holy Grail of scientific inquiry —

THE DISCOVERY!

He sat the vial on the toilet seat and wrote in his journal.

He paused in mid-scribble and frowned, puzzled.

He glanced at the flask and muttered.

"Calculations, calculations!" he said.

He calculated. His blue pencil whipped across yellowed journal pages. He paused, and thought. Rechecked his figures. Consulted an astronomical chart. Altered some figures. Frowned. Consulted a large book written in Greek. "Aha!'d". Recalculated. Picked his nose.

He laid the heavy journal down. He was getting nowhere.

"This is getting me nowhere!" he muttered.

He paced from the bathtub to the door by the sink, five little steps. His hands clasped and unclasped behind his back.

At last he stopped at the small window over the toilet and stared out. He listened to the crickets sing their rabbit song. He heard laughter at the Seashell Inn.

Doc Tay was a regular at the Inn. Several times a week, most often in the morning hours, he took his calculations there. He went there when his tiny workspace began to reek of the unsolvable, when his ponderings of the great universal questions began to give him a headache, when he became thirsty.

Now, he was thirsty.

With a decisive nod, he grabbed his journal, the flask, some books, a broken slide rule, an out-of-tune flumommeter, and a pocket aughtoscope, placed a floppy hat on his head, and headed for the Seashell Inn.

"You broke the law, Chadwick," Ratchett said, reaching for his ticket book.

Chadwick's stomach growled. He'd skipped breakfast. He and the animals looked forward to a hot lunch.

"You don't really have to give me no ticket, do you Constable Ratchett, sir?"

"I wouldn't give you a ticket if I didn't have to, if you hadn't broken the law. Besides," Ratchett said, still smiling, and opening his ticket book, "it's my job."

"Sir Duncan ain't gonna be happy," Chadwick said to nobody in particular, his hope fading further.

"Yep." Ratchett began to compose the ticket.

Chadwick sat rocking back and forth, tapping his foot.

What happened next resulted from Chadwick's twitching foot releasing pressure on the already-loose brakes, barely holding the wagon still on the slight incline on which it had stopped, and from the double-horses, bored and hungry, choosing that instant to give the vehicle a slight tug as they reached for a few boojnuts on a bush at the road's edge. At that moment, the wagon rolled forward an inch, Ratchett's foot, resting on the greasy hub of the wheel, slipped, and he fell.

He yelped more in surprise than pain.

Chadwick dismounted the wagon. He didn't know what to do, but he felt at ease making noises that sounded helpful.

"Are you okay?" Chadwick asked as Ratchett stood, wobbling.

"Of course I'm not," Ratchett said, feeling around his pulpy body for bruises.

"Oh."

"I've bumped my head and wounded my dignity."

"Oh."

"And I've lost my ticket book." Ratchett crawled under the wagon to look for it.

"Oh." Being helpful, if not too bright, Chadwick got down to help look for the book.

He found it.

"Here it is," Chadwick said, holding it up. It had fallen near the double-horses' heads.

The double-horses hadn't noticed the ticket book lying nearby. Their roadside snack had been only briefly interrupted by the fuss beyond their braided tails; they were unimpressed with the constable's unfortunate acrobatics.

"Ah," Ratchett said, rolling a step forward. As he extended a fuzzy hand to grasp the book, one double-horse grabbed it from Chadwick's hand between its teeth and ate it.

"Uh-oh," Chadwick said.

The double-horse spat out a few staples and burped.

Ratchett bristled. His brow knotted, and his fuzz stood on end. He turned toward Chadwick, then stopped. The constable looked puzzled, then frustrated. Then he bid Chadwick a curt good day, turned on his wheelfoot, and sped away.

Chadwick stood a moment, brushing hair from his eyes, blinking at the dust, astonished at the constable's sudden departure. A possible reason occurred to him, and he grinned.

Chadwick guessed that after the double-horse ate the ticket book, the constable searched his mental log of legal lore and found no law against double-horses eating ticket books. And Ratchett had just one ticket book with him.

He went on his way, his mood brightened.

Squeaking door hinges and a cricket chorus accompanied Doc Tay's entrance into the Seashell Inn. He wore his usual — a floppy felt hat and whatever seemed to be handy when it occurred to him to put it on. His shirt had two buttons gone and holes in the elbows. His pants' knees and bottoms were threadbare, and his fly was open. He wore shoes two sizes too big, and his socks didn't match.

He walked almost sideways, juggling papers and books in his arms, with some help from his chin. Hooked between one thumb and two fingers dangled a flask of pink liquid that resembled weak boojnut juice, and smelled foul.

He glanced up once, as if to assure himself that he had indeed arrived at the Seashell Inn, and moved to a table near the door. He dumped his armload, careful not to spill the liquid. Several papers and one old book fell to the floor. He picked them up and sat down, arranging his stuff about him.

Scratch continued to entertain the two travelers at the bar. He showed them the hides of the werewolves he had met among the sand castles and had conned into killing each other rather than him. He excused himself when he saw Tay enter and got off his stool.

More calculations, thought Scratch as he carried a yak milk pitcher to Tay's table.

"More calculations, Scratch," Tay said.

"Yes, and what'll you use for pay today?"

Doc Tay often forgot to take money with him when he went out, but he always paid in time, so Scratch wasn't distressed. A regular at the Inn, Tay often paid by curing the flu, mending a broken leg, or fixing the elm outside.

Tay motioned Scratch closer. Scratch was used to intrigues — he moved to within conspiratorial whispering range.

Tay's glare swept the Inn for eavesdroppers. He noted Thadius McNatt scribbling and muttering to himself at a nearby table, the two strangers at the bar examining the werewolf pelts, and a few weary, old bearded faces in the far corner.

Convinced no one listened except Scratch, Tay pointed to the flask of pink fluid and gave Scratch a wink to indicate the secret of the ages sat within his very grasp.

"What is it?" Scratch whispered.

"The secret of the ages is within your very grasp," Doc Tay said, and winked again.

"Oh. Do you drink it, or do you bathe in it?"

Doc Tay frowned. "I'm not quite sure yet. Give me some time to calculate, and I'll let you know."

"If it doesn't work, I'd accept your pocket slide rule."

"It's broken."

"Still . . ."

Tay agreed, Scratch nodded, gave the table a quick wipe, and walked back to his conversation with the two travelers.

"Calculations, calculations!" Tay muttered as he began calculating, sipping his milk.

Creaking door hinges and singing crickets interrupted Scratch's tale of adventure. He and his two-person audience turned to see Constable Ratchett push through the door.

Burning Stump's finest eased his bulk into his usual chair at his usual table. He broke his glazed look for a moment to give Scratch a faint nod.

Scratch returned the gesture, excused himself from the travelers, and fetched his new customer his usual order — a steaming mug of herbal tea.

Ratchett sipped in bliss and eased deeper into the chair.

Scratch returned to the bar.

"Of course it's genuine," Scratch answered one of the travelers' questions. The traveler examined a werewolf skull. "I may be short in stature, but I am tall in integrity." He huffed out his tiny chest. "I am a businessman." But the travelers were customers, so he tempered his indignation.

The traveler shrugged as if unimpressed and passed the skull to his partner, who eyed it. Scratch dismissed their caution. Clearly, places still existed where his honest reputation had not yet reached.

The first traveler was tall, slender, and bearded. He wore a tattered, faded, weather-beaten hat, a black cape, and a leather patch over his left eye. The second traveler was tall, slender, and bearded. He wore a tattered, faded, weather-beaten hat, a black cape, and a leather patch over his right eye.

Scratch knew travelers' ways included a reluctance to reveal their names, or much else. It was unbusinesslike to ask. He called this pair Left-eye and Right-eye.

But Scratch's guests didn't shy from asking him for details about his surprise encounter with two werewolves among the sand castles, their plan to eat his meager flesh, his clever conversation with them, their turning on each other as a better dinner candidate than he, their demise at their own jaws, his taking them home, tanning their hides, bleaching their skulls, and showing them to strangers like them, and their good fortune in having an opportunity to buy a genuine werewolf skull.

So Scratch repeated for them again and again every detail of the story they asked for while they probed the skull's huge teeth, eyed its deep eye-sockets, held it up to the light, tapped it between where its ears used to be, and did all they could imagine to prove they weren't being fooled by a three-and-a-half foot tall bartender, who, whatever his faults, nonetheless served a quality apple cider.

"I'm a wee touch puzzled about one thing," said Right-eye.

"What, pray tell?"

"Well," said Right-eye, scratching his beard, "it's sure a right nice adventure you had yourself with these werewolf fellows. Makes a mighty well-told tale, a right nice addition to a right nice place, keeps the customers entertained. So I'm just kinda wondering why you'd want to sell the evidence to such a story to a couple of passing-through strangers?"

"Yeah, how come?" Left-eye asked.

"Because I am a businessman," Scratch said. "Businessmen sell things. Have you experienced otherwise?"

Both admitted they hadn't, and Scratch saw it was time for price haggling. He soon found the two were barely well-to-do, their shabby attire an affectation. But with two mugs of cider offered on the house, they reached an agreeable price.

Right-eye and Left-eye brought out small leather purses from which they counted out bits of garnet and jade to pay for their new treasure, each contributing exactly half the agreed-upon price. Scratch provided yet another round of on-the-house cider, and the three exchanged grins as well as money, skull, and businesslike handshakes.

The deal done, Scratch surveyed the Inn. He saw an empty glass at Thadius McNatt's table and excused himself to refill it with more boojnut juice. The travelers began to discuss how they would transport the werewolf skull. They had wrapped it in a cloth fragment that might have been a battle flag but smelled like a handkerchief.

As Scratch poured from a pitcher into Thad's glass, Thad nodded thanks, felt about on the table for another whistle or a carved animal to pay for it with one hand, continuing to calculate with the other. His calculating hand stopped calculating when his searching hand came up empty. He frowned.

"I seem to have run out of money, Scratch," he said.

"Hm," Scratch said. He thought for a moment. "How about a quick fix on my front door? The hinges squeak."

Thad nodded agreement and rose to attend to the front door while Scratch returned to his bar. Halfway there, Scratch noticed Constable Ratchett had run low on tea. He fetched a fresh pot. The two travelers still discussed how they would transport their skull and ignored Scratch as he stepped around the bar to get the tea.

As Scratch poured the constable's tea, Ratchett probed his pockets with a puzzled look.

"I seem to have run out of money," he said, embarrassed.

"Hm," Scratch said. "How about your badge?"

Ratchett nodded, removed the badge, and handed it to Scratch, who took it with grave dignity.

Scratch headed back to the bar.

He stopped halfway there and scanned the room, checking to see if all his customers had enough of their favorite beverage. Doc Tay did not.

As he fetched more yak milk from behind the bar for Tay, Scratch noticed the two travelers' talk had become heated. He sensed they verged on arguing, so he resolved to take his time in delivering the milk to Doc Tay, and perhaps stop to chat with Constable Ratchett until the travelers' voices softened.

He poured Tay a fresh glass of milk. The physician frowned and looked puzzled.

"I seem to have run out of . . ."

"Don't tell me."

". . . ideas," Doc Tay said.

"Oh," Scratch said as he accepted the broken slide rule in payment. The travelers' argument grew louder.

Tay suddenly brightened and returned to his calculations.

Scratch couldn't see above the table edge at what Tay was doing, but he was curious. He was also anxious to postpone as long as possible the need to return to the bar and the arguing travelers. He coughed and asked, "How are you?"

"Fine," Doc Tay said, not looking up, calculating.

"Got it figured out yet?" Scratch asked, glancing over his shoulder at the now red-faced travelers.

"Fine," Doc Tay said, calculating, calculating.

"Tickle your chin with a feather?"

"Fine."

Scratch began to saunter back to his bar. Halfway there, he decided to chat with Ratchett. He walked over.

"So," Scratch said, "how have you been?"

"I don't want to talk about it," the constable snorted, gulping his tea, and sinking back into his chair.

Scratch took the hint, and finding no other way to avoid getting too close to the now loud travelers, he went back to his post behind the bar on a high stool which formed a point of a triangle with the two travelers on the other side of the bar.

"But my saddlebags are full of holes," Left-eye shouted.

"That's why our grub's in mine," Right-eye said. "No holes."

"But that's why we ought to put it in your saddlebags."

"But it's full already. Yours is empty. Put it there."

"Can't put it there. Too many holes. It'll drop out. Your bag doesn't have holes in it. Put it there."

"I'll put it up your nose."

Left-eye and Right-eye swung a right fist and a left fist, respectively, at the same time, missing each other. Scratch was not so lucky or so fast. He took both punches on his tiny chin, did a backward somersault, and landed with a crash among many bottles, glasses, and bar paraphernalia.

Right-eye peered over the bar and said, "Oops."

Left-eye grinned sheepishly and shrugged at Ratchett as the constable rose to investigate. McNatt glanced up from his work at the door and shook his head, annoyed. Doc Tay got up from his calculating to offer his medical advice. Several weary, old faces in a far, dim corner did nothing, continuing to provide atmosphere and a bit of color to the Inn.

At that moment, McNatt, crouched at the front door, reached behind him to take a drink of his boojnut juice while he pondered the best way to fix the door. He grabbed, unseeing, not the fresh boojnut juice Scratch had just poured for him, but rather Doc Tay's flask of liquid that resembled weak boojnut juice and smelled foul, that Tay called THE DISCOVERY!, and that sat on the table edge, inches from Thad's table and his boojnut juice. Doc Tay, busy tending to Scratch's aches, didn't see.

Thad sneezed. He didn't notice the foul odor as he gulped down half the flask.

Across the room, Doc Tay said, "Try to sit up, Scratch."

Scratch said, "Oh."

Right-eye said, "Oops."

Left-eye shrugged.

Constable Ratchett snorted, "Broke the law."

The weary, old bearded faces in a dim corner did nothing.

Thad McNatt thought, *Hm. Interesting. Very interesting.*

Doc Tay thought, *What a thing to happen. Just as I almost have the equation solved. I hope nothing's broken.*

Right-eye thought, *I'm going to get a ticket.*

Left-eye thought, *We're going to get a ticket.*

Constable Ratchett thought, *How can I give these two a ticket without a ticket book? How embarrassing. I guess I'll just have to throw them out the door instead.*

The weary, old bearded faces continued doing nothing.

Thad thought, *What I could do with this door! Look at the color, the texture, the surfaces! Magnificent! Incredible! This is more than a door, it's challenge incarnate, a creative opportunity, clay waiting for the touch of genius! And to think I wanted to be a ceiling painter!*

He stood back and viewed his new canvas, breathing deeply, his eyes bloodshot. He drooled. The dented, tarnished door handle caught his eye, and he frowned. *This will never do. Not on my masterpiece.* He looked around the room.

He saw a spiral seashell lying under a chair and picked it up. *This will do*. He held it up to the light.

He'd found the shell that had, until seconds ago, rested forgotten in Scratch's back pocket. It had popped from Scratch's pocket into the air when the two travelers hit him. It had bounced off the ceiling, landing under a chair by the door where Thad found it.

"I'm afraid I have to throw you fellows out," Ratchett told the travelers with grave authority. The two looked at each other glumly, resigned.

Scratch sat up, rubbing his chin.

"Are you okay?" Doc Tay asked.

Scratch nodded. "I think so," he managed between clenched teeth. He stood shakily.

McNatt replaced the old door handle with the blue shell and stood back to study the effect. "Still needs something," he concluded, looking around again. He saw the now half-empty flask containing Doc Tay's DISCOVERY!, and he reached for it.

From across the room, Doc Tay finally noticed what had been happening to his precious fluid and called out, "Wait a minute!" He was too late, as Thad splashed the stuff on the door, doorframe, and the pale blue spiral-shell doorknob, chuckling with manic glee, spittle on his lips.

Scratch handed Ratchett's badge back to him. The constable grabbed the two travelers by their collars and walked them to the door where he nodded to McNatt to open it. McNatt returned his nod without understanding its meaning and continued to admire the damp, subtle blue stain on the door.

Ratchett started to say something to McNatt when Scratch stepped up and opened the door.

Ratchett threw the travelers out with practiced efficiency. He wiped his hands, nodded his thanks to Scratch, who closed the door again. McNatt looked on, grinning, entranced with his masterpiece.

Half a step back toward his bar, Scratch stopped and gasped. "Did you hear?" he said, louder than he'd intended. Everyone turned to look at him.

"Hear what?" Ratchett asked.

"The silence," Scratch said.

"It hasn't been silent in here all day," Doc Tay said. "I know. I've been trying to calculate in all this noise."

"What silence?" Ratchett repeated.

"When the door opened," Scratch said. "It was quiet."

"I fixed those squeaky hinges for you, Scratch," McNatt said. "Isn't it wonderful?"

"Not that," Scratch said. "The crickets. I didn't hear crickets singing when the door opened."

"But the crickets always sing," Doc Tay said. Ratchett hushed him, and everyone listened. Through the closed door, faint but clear, crickets sang. The Pink Rabbit Song.

"There, you see?" Ratchett said.

"Now try it with the door open," Scratch said. Everyone looked at him, puzzled. They gathered closer to the door as Scratch swept it open.

No one spoke.

Beyond the door, instead of crickets singing, tall pines hissed as they swayed in a gentle breeze. Instead of sea-salt, the aroma of pines permeated the air. Instead of day, it was dusk. Instead of the dunes with the ocean beyond, a pine forest spread across gentle slopes. A mountain ridge hugged the horizon, blue in the distance and snow-capped.

Instead of a rough dirt road by the Inn, there spread a broad highway, paved in red stone. Instead of an elm, a pine tree. Instead of two weary travelers on weary horses, two noblemen dressed in silks and bright, embroidered scarves stepped into an elegant carriage aided by footmen.

Scratch let the door swing shut.

Thadius McNatt, Doc Tay, Constable Jack Ratchett, Scratch, and the few weary, old bearded faces who'd come from their dim corner into the center of the room, all looked at each other with awed expressions.

And through the closed door, the group in the Seashell Inn heard crickets singing in the dune grass.

Scratch reopened the door. This time beyond the door they saw a jungle. Insects buzzed, the air smelled of sweet fruits. Two hunters guided two camels laden with gear down a path through tall trees shrouded in vines and moss. Monkeys and birds hooted and chattered in the green canopy above them.

Opening the door, then closing it, opening it, closing it, open, closed, open, closed —

The huddled group saw deserts, cities, forests, plains, swamps, grasslands, oceans, mountains, castles, glaciers, busy markets, and a kaleidoscope of people and animals.

At last, Scratch closed the door. Outside the Inn, crickets sang. Inside — silence.

Ratchett went first. He approached the door, and Scratch opened it. Ratchett stood on the threshold like it was a diving board, studying the panorama before him.

Highways jammed with vehicles as far as the eye could see crisscrossed one another in all directions. Horns blared, engines rumbled and rattled, each separate voice adding to the din. The hazy air smelled like oil and hot metal.

Violators fled flashing red lights and screaming sirens.

"Looks like a few folks are breaking the law," Ratchett snorted. Just then, a truck cruised slowly by. The truck sign read "Acme Ticket Book Co."

Ratchett patted his badge to make sure he had it, hiked his belt up over his stomach, and rolled through the door, which swung closed behind him.

"And to think I did this with my own hands," Thadius McNatt said as he stepped toward the door.

"What do you mean, *you* did it?" Doc Tay said, with a step toward McNatt. "*My* formula made this possible."

"I don't recall hearing your contribution to my calculations of the physical parameters of structural deficiencies of this portal . . ." McNatt said, belligerently.

"Clearly, the time-space continuum distortional phenomenon we now observe is consistent with my formula's chemical properties . . ." said Doc Tay as belligerently and at the same time as McNatt spoke.

Before the two could escalate either a vigorous scientific discussion or a brawl, Scratch opened the door and stepped back. Barkeeper, doormaker, and scientist all gaped.

Across the dunes at the cliff edge stood a large, majestic castle. Long, gaudy flags and bright banners snapped in a sturdy breeze from towers, parapets, battlements, buttresses, and bridges. The afternoon sun glinted off well-polished armor as knights patrolled the ramparts.

Windows and doors adorned the castle — hundreds of them.

"Do you do windows?" Doc Tay asked.

McNatt didn't answer. He focused on a huge drawbridge as it lowered to admit a carriage into the courtyard. He gasped in sympathy as massive door hinges groaned in rusty neglect.

"Poor baby," he said. He gathered his calculating devices and other doormaking paraphernalia. He left, his mission set. The door swung shut behind him.

"My turn," Doc Tay said. "What do you expect we'll see?"

"A university named after you?" Scratch ventured. "A fountain flowing with THE DISCOVERY!?"

Tay shrugged and nodded to Scratch, who opened the door.

Across the road, ancient and prestigious Doc Tay University, with its vast ivy-covered halls, dominated the landscape. Fresh-faced, bright-eyed students carried armloads of books down broad sidewalks. Large open lawns rimmed each building, bordered by trimmed boojnut hedges.

The fountain in the foreground sprayed in gentle gushers a now familiar pale pink liquid. DTU's founder struck a dramatic pose in marble in the fountain center.

"Somewhere on this campus is a physical science laboratory that, despite high caliber state-of-the-art equipment, is at sea with confused but enthusiastic students who need guidance in their struggles to uncover nature's secrets," Doc Tay said. "And I know who can help them." He walked through the door.

The door closed behind him, and the bustle of campus life was replaced by crickets singing in the dunes beyond the road past the Seashell Inn. The Pink Rabbit Song.

The group of weary, old bearded faces retreated a few steps and huddled. They muttered, shuffled, chattered, shifted from one foot to another, snorted, spat, gestured, scratched themselves, picked their noses, shook, and nodded their heads.

Finally, they approached Scratch. One whispered to him. Scratch nodded and opened the door. The group peered with grave intensity at the scene before them.

It was a warm spring day.

Before the Inn ran a broad road paved in red stone. A wagon had stopped in the road a few feet away, its rear axle broken, and several large wooden casks spilled into the street. A bluish liquid seeped from one cask into a gutter. A stout man with stringy red hair cursed as he struggled to set up a jack. Two double-horses harnessed to the wagon watched, bored.

Several weary, old bearded faces shook their heads and clucked in sympathy. Some sniffed the air, savoring the heady aroma emanating from the casks.

The gents nodded, muttered, and decided. They shuffled through the door, headed for the stout wagon man and his labors. As they left, they mumbled good-byes, tested the air with tongue or finger, rolled up their sleeves ready for work, and smacked their lips anticipating a refreshing reward.

The door closed, and the Inn lost its atmosphere and became less colorful.

The crickets outside sang.

Scratch stood frowning at the door, hands on hips. The barrels from the overturned wagon had born the Imperial Wojatake Winery crest. *They produce a fine wine in the Wojatake Valley, full-bodied and spirited*, Scratch thought, getting up on a stool and donning a hat and coat. He liked the bluish wine. Especially with fish. *But it doesn't travel well.*

Scratch carried a small satchel to the door where he paused, looking around the Inn with undisguised affection. He'd bought the place when it was a boojnut storage shed. He'd made a life at the Inn.

But I miss boojnut beer. He turned and opened the door.

It didn't surprise him to see the boojnut forest, though its lushness and rich aroma stunned him. He saw what looked like a small brewery in a clearing not far away. He hesitated.

The thought came unbidden and unwelcome — *If I leave, who will care for the Inn?*

He looked around. He propped the door open with a chair, walked behind the bar, and wiped it.

He swept, dusted, washed glasses, straightened tables, chairs, and pictures. He cleaned the bathroom, the mirror over the bar, and the spittoons.

In time, the aroma of boojnuts drew him back to the opened door, where he stood gazing into the woods scant yards away and back into the tavern — his home.

In time, he chose.

TO SEE CLEARLY

Squire Algernon Eppingham hit Duncan Quimm on his head, which sent Quimm, arms windmilling, into a display case of tiny glass animals.

Except for an alert glass double-horse that scuttled away in time, the critters exploded into fragments that filled the air in the windowmaker's display room like a glittering mist. Quimm pulled his opponent off his feet, and the two continued to beat each other. They rolled, grunted, and groaned in a tight, frantic ball of fists and feet, punching and kicking, knocking things over, frightening innocent glass animals, until —

"Gentlemen, gentlemen!" Clarence Parsaval cried from the door of his back shop. "I'd be pleased to know what's going on here."

The big windowmaker filled the door, bald head touching the top, broad shoulders touching each side. His round face gleamed with sweat.

The two fighters halted in mid assault, like clothed and bloody mannequins, and looked up at the windowmaker. Then, expressions unchanged, they resumed combat.

In the brief instant they hesitated in their mayhem, Parsaval recognized them.

The tall, beak-nosed scarecrow biting his opponent's ear was Duncan Quimm, pigkeeper. The shorter, stout, well-dressed man with the hairpiece askew, gouging his opponent's eye, was Squire Algernon Eppingham.

"Oh dear," Parsaval moaned.

If it had been any other two fighting in Parsaval's New and Used Window Shoppe display room, the windowmaker would have grabbed both by their collars and tossed them gently but firmly through a window into the street. But the Squire was Parsaval's richest customer, and his landlord.

The Squire owned several shops on the square in Burning Stump. With the windowmaker's shop, he owned the doormaker's shop next door and the doorknob shop next to that, a few other businesses, and some homes. He lived in the biggest one. He spent lavishly. One order from Eppingham often paid the monthly rent.

And Quimm, while just a pigkeeper, had no less importance to the Parsaval family welfare; he was an influential member of the Agricultural Amalgamated Association, the farmer's co-op. The farmers were frequent clients — his bread and Yakken butter. The group met after evening chores at the Seashell Inn to gossip and drink boojnut juice. If Quimm started berating Parsaval at the Inn or at the AAA Union Hall, his clients might go elsewhere.

Parsaval had done jobs for both recently, and both owed him. The rent was due. His display room was a mess, except for one tiny glass double-horse, cowering in a corner. In a glance, he estimated the loss at —

"Oh dear, dear — "

He mentally counted his blessings to counter his distress, and stepped into the fray. He lifted the two off the floor, one in each massive paw, and separated them, doing so with as much deference as he could manage. Parsaval's shaggy eyebrows, puffy jowls, and broad mouth bobbed in a cacophonous display of mixed emotions, clashing between frowns, sheep-ish grins, and gaping horror as he looked from one to the other.

"Ease up, sirs, would you please?" he begged.

Both continued to cuff and grab at each other, dangling and twisting at the ends of Parsaval's arms.

"Squire Eppingham, sir — ouch — Duncan, my good fellow — ow — " Parsaval took a few blows and kicks.

"If you mean His Lordship," Quimm sputtered, "'bandit's' more like it."

"Speak for yourself, pig-brain," Eppingham snarled.

Soon Eppingham and Quimm stopped sputtering and snarling, and dangled like wet sheets from Parsaval's outstretched arms. At last assured they wouldn't resume their brouhaha, Parsaval released them, directed them to neutral corners of the room, and stood in the center, ready to intercept any breach of peace.

"I would be pleased to know what the fuss is all about," he said. "I would also be pleased to accept any assistance offered in paying for — " he gestured at the gleaming landscape of glass shards littering the usually immaculate floor. "As for cleaning it up, well — " he shrugged.

Both spoke at once. Parsaval flapped his arms, shushing them, and gave Eppingham the floor. "Alphabetical order, if you please," he said to mollify Quimm.

"Duncan, I'm right sorry I tried to bite your nose off," Eppingham mumbled, shuffling his feet. "I guess you were just handy for biting."

"Likewise," Quimm nodded. "Bit angry myself. Needed to hit a body. You were handy. I'll pay for to buy you a new ear. Sorry."

"Parsaval," Eppingham said, "it's you I'm really ticked off at. You see, the window you sold me is all messed up. I want it fixed — quick."

"But, sir, your maitre d'hotel assured me — "

"Tarnation, Parsaval. That little ferret ain't got the brains of chuckleweed. I wish you'd waited for me to get back before you let that snotnosed half-wit sign off on the deal."

"Oh, dear — "

The day before, Parsaval had filled an order for a picture window at Eppingham's posh restaurant, expanded to include a second floor. The restaurant, the Blue McGregor, stood on a hill east of Burning Stump on the Dainty Run. It catered to a high-class clientele, offering cloth napkins, real silver silverware, a string quartet, and snooty waiters.

The window would be the final touch on the second floor addition, offering guests a grand view to the west of the town, the sand-castles beyond, and the ocean on the horizon. It offered a tranquil ambiance for which the be-furred, be-jeweled, and be-moneyed customers would pay a premium.

The new dining room grand opening would occur the next day.

Parsaval made and hung the window as instructed, he thought. But Eppingham had been called out of town on some business deal. Eager to get on to his next job — a window for Duncan Quimm — he got Eppingham's maitre d'hotel, an efficient, well-polished man named Henri le Clerk, to approve the finished task.

Parsaval didn't understand all the man said, but it sounded like, "Nice work," or something similar, so he'd accepted le Clerk's serpentine signature on the order, left a copy at the cash box for Eppingham to see with a personal note ("My Dear Sq. Epp.: Please call at Your soonest convenience to confirm Your Pleasure with the Window. Your faithful Servant, P."), and hurried to Quimm's more fragrant but less pretentious place.

Quimm also wanted a window. A nice view of the rounded, forested hills to the east, he said, for his pigs. The peaceful view would help them relax so they'd eat more, get fatter faster, and be ready for market sooner, he said.

How convenient for Parsaval that the restaurant and the pig sty were a stone's throw from each other. The two, separated by the road, some trees, and a prevailing wind that carried the sty odor east and upvalley, away from the restaurant, were in symbiotic relationship. Quimm raised pigs, and Eppingham bought them.

For the second time in one day, the man who ordered the work — in this case, Quimm — was also out. Quimm was at market, or something, a drab, shapeless, ageless woman he took to be Quimm's wife, daughter, or mother told him. It wasn't clear who she was, or what she'd said, since she talked with her mouth full.

Still, it was late afternoon, dinner would be ready at home soon, and he thought he understood the order well enough. These considerations helped still his disquiet over the unusual circumstances, occurring twice in a day. He finished the job and wrote a note, like the one that he'd left for Eppingham, that he wedged in a crack in the window frame. He didn't try to find the woman to give her the note. She'd disappeared back into Quimm's ramshackle house after mumbling at him.

Parsaval had whistled a happy tune as he walked home.

Early the next day, while in his back room firing up his furnace, he heard the little bell above the front door announce with a brassy tinkle his first customer. Parsaval smiled. Two commissions done the day before, and the day's first customer minutes after opening — things looked prosperous.

"One moment, sir — or madam," he called out.

As he dabbed at his sweaty forehead with a cloth and wiped his hands, preparing to greet his customer in the front display room, he heard another tinkle announce yet another customer.

His smile broadened.

But just as he was about to part the curtain between the back and front rooms, he heard the tumult of a fistfight and the crash of shattered glass and display cases.

Eppingham framed the scene in the air before him with his hands. "Imagine," he said, "you set yourself on down in the swankest eatery north of Big Stick and south of God's Eardrum, get catered to by a herd of snooty waiters, with a string quartet instead of a squeezebox serenading you. Real cloth napkins, silver silverware, all the highbrow stuff. You order up a big old plateful of ham and eggs, or pork chops — or even pork and beans — and then you take a gander out the window."

Eppingham took a ragged breath and wailed. "It's the wrong view! Instead of facing west down the hillside toward town and the sea, the window faces east across the road — toward — toward — " he pointed past Parsaval at Quimm and stammered to a halt.

Parsaval groaned. He turned to Quimm and frowned.

"I'd be pleased if you'd tell me, Duncan, I didn't install the wrong view for your, er, pigs."

"Druther," Quimm said, anchoring fists on hips and thrusting knobby elbows askew. "Don't see much choice."

Parsaval sighed. "And what, precisely, sir, is the impact of my unfortunate error?"

"Didn't matter before. One-story café 'cross the road, trees in the way, folks couldn't see my place. Squire builds a second story. Folks can see over the trees. Worse, pigs look up out their window and see folks eating pork at the restaurant. Pigs are sensitive creatures. Smart too. They get queasy. Won't eat. Can't sell skinny pigs."

Eppingham snorted. "It don't bode diddly if your pigs get fat. If my customers — used-to-be-customers, I mean — get gut-sick when they sit down to chow, seeing where their meal comes from, still on the hoof, I don't need to buy any because ain't nobody to eat 'em. So it don't matter one way of the other."

"Well," Quimm said, rubbing his long chin, "if you don't buy any of my pigs cause they fright your customers — "

"Maybe even close the joint — "

"Not sure if I can pay my bills — "

"Boarding up the window wouldn't cover my losses — "

"A moment," Parsaval said, "gentlemen, please. Do I understand you can't — that is, you won't, er, pay your — "

"Bullseye, Parsaval," Eppingham said.

"E-yep," Quimm agreed.

Parsaval moaned. Eppingham didn't need to frame the picture for him. He saw it clearly, saw the Squire demanding the rent immediately — "or out you go," saw Quimm at the Seashell Inn — "Poor service, e-yep. Can't be trusted, that one."

He added the cost to the damaged display goods and cases —

"Oh dear, dear — "

Quimm and Eppingham left after Parsaval promised to make good — somehow. He had no idea how he'd do it, and he walked home in gloomy silence.

Parsaval tried to present a cheery front before his eight children — soon to be homeless, poor dears, he told himself — and his wife — soon to be kitchenless. His lackluster attempt went unnoticed. The children played as usual, and his wife bustled about the kitchen, making dinner, little Tim-

Tim anchored on a broad hip. She interrupted her off-key humming now and then to gently scold one child or another over some breach of kitchen decorum or another.

Ah, dinner. The thought of a Mama-cooked dinner brought a warm smile to Parsaval's face. He eased his bone-weary bulk further back into his chair, closed his eyes, and inhaled the fragrances from Mama's kitchen. He smelled corn covered in fresh Yakken butter, carrots, sweet potatoes, boojnut tarts for dessert, fresh bread and honey, and —

Pork chops.

"Oh dear, dear."

"Dinn-errr's rea-dyyy," Mama sang. The children hurried to their places around the huge table, giggling and jostling. Parsaval smiled at his wife at one end of the table from his place at the other. She returned a beatific smile.

When all were seated, the room went silent, except for little Tim-Tim in Mama's lap, fussing for a nipple. Parsaval ahemed and muttered a prayer. "Oh Lord, bless these eight good children (mutter, mutter) and bless this food that we, er — ahem. Ah, Lord, bless this food — "

Parsaval sneezed, Clarence Junior said "Amen," and the family dug into the feast with their usual zest. They were good kids, Parsaval reflected, raised by a good Mama. They didn't deserve to be brought to poverty by a poor excuse for a father.

Gloom weighed on Parsaval as he watched the clatter and shuffle of his family eating. They were about as well mannered a bunch, he thought, as any other children. Certainly they didn't behave like a herd of, of —

Parsaval sighed, sat his fork down, the meal untouched.

"Too dry, dear?" Mama cooed. "I'll eat it, then, and get you another. I'm famished." She rose, little Tim-Tim on one hip, and started around the table.

Parsaval shook his head and found a weak smile. Mama sat back down with a thump as he jabbed a ragged piece of meat into his dry mouth and chewed.

"Rough day at work, then?" Mama asked.

Parsaval frowned, nodded, chewed.

Mama's responding smile was as radiant as Parsaval's frown was dismal. "Well," she said, "we'll talk later. Now, let's eat." She set to with gusto.

"By the way," she said as she dished herself more potatoes, "it's nine."

"What's nine?"

"Your blessing. You asked a blessing for eight children. You should have asked blessing for nine. Not eight." Mamma giggled, patted her ample stomach.

"Oh dear, dear."

Mama's maternal glow kindled in Parsaval both despair and determination to mask it. His food went down like lumps of slag past a smile he welded on.

"It's called 'taters,'" John-John said, sticking out a little pink tongue at Missy, his junior by a year, "not 'po-TAY-toes.'" They sat across the table from each other. Mama's arrangement kept them from physical combat at dinner, but their vigorous verbal exchanges didn't flag.

Mama stood at the counter, back to the table, spooning dessert, and the children were getting restless, eager to resume their play outdoors.

"'Taters' is uneducated," Missy said, dismissing her brother with a wrinkled nose in near-perfect imitation of her older, almost-grown-up sister Lulu. "You're supposed to say 'po-TAY-toes.'" She stuck out her little finger daintily for emphasis.

"You don't know nothing."

"Do too."

"Do not."

"Do too."

"Not."

"Too — "

"Now, you two behave, or you get no tarts," Mama threatened sweetly. They gave her a quick glance, decided the threat lacked sincerity, and resumed their discourse.

"Where'd you hear such a dumb thing, anyways," John-John asked, twitching a foot.

"What's it to you?"

"Bet from one of those dumb girls you play dolls with. Bet you got it from Franny, that fat pig — "

Parsaval winced.

"Did not."

"Betcha."

"Not so. For your information, smarty, I got it from Mr. Joshua Eppingham, whose papa happens to be the Squire, and he knows a lot about po-TAY-toes cause he owns this restaurant — "

Parsaval's involuntary sigh was monumental. It stopped Missy in midbrag. She and John-John, several other children, and Mama turned to look at his sagging face.

Mama immediately stomped to her beleaguered husband's defense. She marched to the table and plopped Tim-Tim without preamble on Lulu's lap. Then, wordless, she lifted John-John's chair with him in it and turned it away from the table, its back to Missy. She walked around the table and did the same to Missy's chair, placing its back to John-John.

She stepped back, put a hand on a hip, and glared at the two children. "I'll not have you two fighting at the table and upsetting your father's digestion," she said, wagging a creamy spoon, "after he's put in a hard day. If you can't look at each other without fighting, then you'll just sit back to back until you can behave. Do you understand your Mama?"

The two nodded, contrite, at least for the moment.

"Yes!" Parsaval shouted, jumping up, "I understand!" He kissed and hugged his startled wife and children. "I understand! I understand!" he told each in turn, even little Tim-Tim. He left the dining room, laughing till tears came, and headed back to the shop. He forgot his coat and dessert.

"You done me and my customers proud, Parsaval," Eppingham said, thumping the windowmaker's back. "Business is booming."

"E-yep," Quimm nodded. "Pigs are happy too."

"I'm grateful, gentlemen," Parsaval said. "Your prompt payment was most appreciated. And for the display room. And this dinner. It's, well — "

He stammered to a halt and jammed a huge forkful of pork chop into his mouth, chewed, and nodded in satisfaction to his two companions. They sat in a window booth on the Blue McGregor's second floor, enjoying themselves. Happy customers ate, drank, and spent money.

And the view through the large window was breathtaking, the perfect tranquil ambiance.

"Nothing better for the digestion than watching folks enjoy dinner," Eppingham said. "Even if it's just us we're watching."

"E-yep," Quimm agreed.

Parsaval nodded, mouth full.

The replacement window Parsaval had installed in the second floor dining room at the Blue McGregor presented the merry diners a view across the road and above the trees of another restaurant where well-groomed, rich diners also enjoyed themselves — and looked out their window at the diners in the Blue McGregor, whose contentment reflected theirs exactly.

"And how's farming out your way?" Eppingham asked Quimm.

"Pigs are happy. Eating more. Getting fatter, quicker. Best thing for 'em — looking out that window you put in, Parsaval. Seeing other pigs looking back at 'em, eating proper."

"Switching windows was smart, Parsaval," Eppingham said.

"Not just the window," Parsaval corrected. "The views."

"Brilliant, any way you look at it," Eppingham said.

The three laughed at the joke.

"How about you, Parsaval?" Eppingham said. "How's business out your way?"

The windowmaker smiled, teeth exposed between puffy jowls, and told them about his ninth blessing.

PLAN 9 FROM PLANET HOLLYWOOD

Eliot Hollingsworth looked into the dresser mirror and did not see Bugs Bunny. Instead, he saw Elmer Fudd.

Fudd.

Elmer Doggone Fudd.

He tried to say, "Eh, what's up, doc?" to complete his daily morning ritual, but it came out, "Gwacious, dat's a dweadful woad of cawwots."

He tried a laugh. "Huh-uh-uh-uh."

Wrong laugh.

"Dis will wiwwy wuin my day." Annoyance made his weak Fuddy voice squeak even more.

A glance down at his roly-poly body sent bile to his throat, and he looked away. The smell of fresh carrots in the bowl on the dresser amplified his nausea — Fudd's reaction, not his. Eliot liked carrots. Fudd hated them.

Deep inside, where he was Eliot Hollingsworth, he still *felt* like Bugs Bunny. He'd morphed into his favorite Warner Bros. cartoon character six thousand years ago, moved here to Planet Hollywood, and had never had a problem.

Until now.

Services started in half an hour, and Bugs Bunny looked like Elmer Fudd. What if he'd gone On The Air without checking his image? What if, for some reason, this particular day, he'd skipped his morning ritual, a lifelong habit, hadn't seen the offensive image, and had gone in front of billions of faithful, worshipful viewers all over the galaxy?

His too-round shoulders shuddered. He couldn't continue the blasphemous thought.

Spontaneous morphing.

It had never happened to him before. Never in six thousand years. He'd risen slowly but steadily from a common acolyte among billions of common acolytes to his current lofty position as Fourth Assistant Associate

UnderHigh Priest in Charge of Saturday Morning Worship Services, rotating vacation relief shift, and never in all that time had he ever experienced a spontaneous morphing. If anybody discovered the lapse, Eliot could kiss goodbye his dream of one day becoming First Assistant UnderHigh.

Why today of all days? Today the First Assistant was at the dentists, and Eliot was on call. He was to administer the Services rituals as Saturday morning cartoon show host for the galaxy. Spontaneous morphing was morally reprehensible, but spontaneously morphing into Elmer Fudd was, was —

The word "blasphemy" came out in his thoughts as "bwasphemy."

He shuddered again, concerned that the mirrored image reflected his true, inner self. He pinched his button nose in disgust. "How atwotous."

Eliot screwed up his face and grunted in concentration, willing himself to morph back into his beloved Bugs.

Nothing happened.

Eliot's failure didn't particularly surprise or annoy him. He hadn't needed to consciously morph from one image to another in six millennia, since he took his Oath of Fealty.

He tried again, harder, grunting aloud and mentally straining.

Elmer Fudd still looked back at him in the mirror.

Eliot tried again, harder.

Fudd.

The finger-in-the-light-socket trick didn't work either.

"Maybe something's wong with the miwwow."

On the back of a spoon, in a pie plate, on Fudd's shiny hunting boots, on the doorknob, in a glass of water. On every reflective surface he could find in his room, Eliot saw Fudd.

The stage manager knocked on the door and called out, "Twenty minutes, Mr. Bunny."

"I'll be weady — " Eliot stopped. "Okay," he said.

The door was still closed. "Are you all right, Mr. Bunny?"

Eliot quickly grabbed the water glass, tipped it to his mouth, and started gargling. "Unh-hunh," he gargled, "I'ng ogay."

The stage manager went away.

Desperately, Eliot tried one more time to morph into Bugs and failed.

Long, long ago, Eliot remembered, he'd suffered from stage fright. Besides boredom, it was one reason he morphed into Bugs. The Rabbit feared nothing, so neither had Eliot Hollingsworth.

Until now.

Had his long-forgotten stage fright been this intense?

He checked and confirmed he hadn't pissed his pants.

Fifteen minutes to showtime, and Bugs Bunny was Elmer Fudd. *What to do, what to do?*

"What would dat waskewwy wabbit do?"

Desperation and fear prompted an experiment: he tried to morph into Daffy Duck. No good.

"Dwat the wuck." He moaned and paced, mincing little steps on big feet, trying to think.

A light went on over his head.

At least that still works, he thought.

In his closet, he found some old socks and a bag of cotton, some thread, and a needle. He set to work making a Bugs Bunny costume, the way prehistoric, premorphing humans might have done it. Poor old humans, living their miserable lives in the bodies they were born in. Mayfly lives, short, brutish, and unimaginative.

"But they did make pwetty good cartoons." He laughed. "Huh-uh-uh-uh."

He cut and sewed and sewed and cut, his swiftness fed by panic. He waddled to the mirror to see the result.

Grim.

The stitches looked like something from a Frankenstein cartoon and the costume fit like Tweety Bird might fit in a Sylvester the Cat suit. It looked — comic.

"Oh, gowwy, gowwy, gowwy." And only ten minutes to showtime.

He began stuffing clothes, towels, bedding, and his pillow into the make-do costume to puff it out, shape it up. Not enough.

"Five minutes, Mr. Bunny."

With a cry in his throat, Eliot wadded up pages from his priceless collection of antique, real-paper comic books and finished stuffing the costume.

He stood before the mirror.

The costume was good enough, he decided at last; he looked like Bugs Bunny. "But I don't sound wike dat wabbit for diddwy."

"One minute, Mr. Bunny."

Thinkthinkthinkthink . . .

The light over his head went on again.

Eliot yanked out one of the costume's two front teeth, and tossed it aside. One-toothed, he went out to face the cameras.

*

Things did not go as planned. Thirty seconds into Services, the producer called for a commercial break, and Eliot was hauled off.

The Warner Bros. Most High Inquisitor had traded in his original cartoon name for one he liked better, now that he was in charge: Major Rooster.

"Siddown, son," the rooster said, nodding his floppy, red topknot toward a chair in front of his desk, "make yourself – I say make yourself at home. I don't stand on ceremony here, no sir. Keep it casual, the way I like it, like in the old days, back on the farm. You ever been to a farm, boy? You'll have to talk louder, son."

"Weww, actuawwy — "

"Get to the point — the point, I say." The rooster's beak turned down and his eyes narrowed. "Boy, did anybody ever tell you you look like—" he looked at a paper on his desk and reading glasses appeared on his beak as he read, muttering.

Eliot fidgeted. His feeble try to morph out of Fudd failed as he expected and he shrugged, resigned.

"Say, wait just a doggone minute here," Rooster said, "ain't you the one, I say, ain't you the Assistant Blah-de-blah that spontaneously – that's what it says right here, and you know I wouldn't make such a thing up, no sir — "

Eliot nodded vigorously, hoping to speed the official inquiry along, take his punishment, and be done with it.

"Speak up, son, I can't hear you."

"Huh-uh-uh-uh — "

"Don't give me that doggone Fudd jabber. Gives me a headache. I know what you're going to say."

Rooster kept talking and talking. Maybe this was part of the punishment? Eliot's awareness faded in and out.

". . . tell you why, son, if you'll just be quiet and listen for a second — "

"Weww — "

"— so we keep our shapes so the great unwashed out there in videoland, whether they be Warner Bros fans, or whether they favor our colleagues at the Disney Studios — why heckfire, boy, even Walter Lantz fans — all of them need guidance to know what the Sam Hill to look like when they get bored looking like their own selves and want to be whatever plonks their twanger — "

"Weww — "

"— and if spontaneous morphing ain't bad enough, you got to go and get yourself stuck — *stuck* is what you are, take a look at yourself, go on ahead and look."

"Weww — "

"You keep interrupting me, son. But you're right. Good thing we got to edit that broadcast. Be a doggone shame if it went On The Air, you in that ridiculous get-up, all moth-eaten and droopy. What made you think you could get away with it?

"Now you're wondering whether I'm going to make you clean the henhouse with a toothbrush for a thousand years or such deviltry. Well, I ain't. If you'll just stop your doggone yammering, I'll tell you want I'm gonna do . . ."

It took Eliot Hollingsworth a thousand years after he was ex-communicated to leave Bugs Bunny behind and adjust to never being able to morph out of Elmer Fudd. Still, it took another thousand years before he stopped trying to say, "Eh, what's up, doc?"

In another thousand years, he began to stop missing Planet Hollywood, and a thousand years after that, he started to like the desert planet to which he'd been exiled. Planet Wyoming, they called it.

A thousand years later, he met another Fudd, wandering around lost and lonely, exiled as he'd been to Planet Wyoming. A thousand years later, he met another. Then another and another.

Hundreds of them.

Thousands.

Millions.

They called themselves "Stuckies."

All the Elmer Fudd Stuckies exiled to Planet Wyoming milled around aimlessly, passing endless days in boring pursuits — Trivial Pursuits as often as not — without coherent goals, aspirations, ambitions.

Leaderless.

Eliot Hollingsworth passed the millennia with such thoughts among his brothers, his fellow-fallen.

On Planet Hollywood, among his peers there, his highest aspiration reached only to First UnderPriest. Here, among his fellow Fudd Stuckies, he more than aspired. He *achieved.*

In time (a long, long time), the former Assistant Associate UnderWhatever (he'd managed to forget the exact title) promoted himself to the rank of the OverPriest, First and Only, His Fuddness.

In time (a long, long time), His Fuddness, the former Eliot Hollingsworth, stood alone on the edge of a high, flat mesa on his desert planet and gazed out. He looked down to his devoted armies of Fudds in the valley below, marching to and fro in clompy hunting boots, stubby shotguns bobbing on their shoulders, in tidy little rows.

He looked up at the garish pink lights of distant Planet Hollywood, "The Planet That Never Sleeps," and thought how unfortunate were those on that planet, and in the galaxy in general, those who didn't know the blessings of Stuckness, of Fuddness.

He looked up, and made plans.

PATIENT ARE
THE SCAVENGERS

The 10:55 a.m. shipment of dead people bound for Hell was late. The highway that stretched between Las Vegas beyond the eastern horizon and Hell beyond the western horizon lay empty as far as Buzzy could see from his perch atop a dead cottonwood. The two-lane asphalt road cut through flat desert, a straight gray ribbon laced with white stitches down its center. No clouds marred the sky's puke green hue. No wind. The hot air shimmered.

Buzzy's stomach growled.

"Scavengers don't whine," Vernon, Buzzy's wingmate, said. His wings shuddered pointedly as if to brush off the offense.

"I wasn't whining," Buzzy whined.

"Scavengers are patient." Vernon bobbed his wattle but said nothing more.

A sulphurous glow stained the Hellward horizon, while to the east, neon brilliance marred the horizon beyond which Las Vegas lay unseen.

"It's after six," Buzzy said. And the 4:55 shipment had been late too.

"I know."

"We haven't eaten since — "

"I *know*, dammit." Scavengers could go a long time between meals, but Vernon's stomach rumbled anyway. "Look, something's wrong. The shipments are never late."

"What do you suppose — "

"How the Hell should I know? I'm going to see what I can see." Vernon spread his wings and rose.

"Me too," Buzzy said, and rose in Vernon's wake.

Buzzy didn't want to expend energy to fly. It had been almost two months since he'd had a decent meal. Back then, a pleasant cloudless Sunday it was, a baby had slipped through a tear in a corner of the tarp that covered the pile of dead people just as the overloaded truck hit a pothole. The tiny tad fell onto the pavement and bounced — *squish, squish, squish* — leaving a trail of yummy entrails.

But it wasn't enough nourishment; maybe only six or seven pounds of meat, split between the two scavengers.

Nothing since except for a couple of crickets, a spider, and one little mouse.

Dead people bound for Hell were Buzzy and Vernon's main source of sustenance.

The drivers were sloppy, tossing the tarp covering the heaping mound haphazardly, so sometimes dead people fell off the truck, especially when the truck was overloaded, and sometimes they didn't. When dead people fell off, the drivers never noticed, but Buzzy and Vernon did.

A sharp-eyed scavenger could spot the twice-daily delivery trucks miles away from the old cottonwood, even farther if he caught a thermal and got higher, but why bother? The trucks passed by *right here*, heading to Hell. Follow for a few miles — don't get too close to Hell, no sir, as it was too damn hot there — and wait for dinner.

Empty trucks came back.

Now, both the a.m. and the p.m. shipments were late.

Vernon's patience flagged, so he climbed up to see farther. Buzzy wasn't going to let Vernon get the jump on him if Vernon saw something and got the juicier parts first, so up he climbed too, wings spread to catch the heated air.

Sensing they'd reached as high as the thermal would take them, Buzzy and Vernon hovered for a long time, scanning the eastern skyline. Nothing.

"I'm going in to take a closer look," Vernon said even as he dipped his beak toward the city.

"Wait." But Vernon was already going.

Buzzy watched till Vernon became a dot in the neon smudge of sky he flew towards.

The humans in Las Vegas had guns; they used them; Buzzy had heard stories. Humans had killed off everything, almost down to the last mouse and snake.

Buzzy wondered what humans ate.

Buzzy and Vernon had tried vegetarianism, but it didn't answer. They were equally loath to attack each other; they were scavengers, not predators. Besides, it was too much work.

But humans had no such scruples. Which is why there was almost nothing left to eat. Except dead people bound for Hell.

It was dangerous to fly close to the city. Humans killed. But Vernon was *that* hungry.

Buzzy sighed when Vernon's dot disappeared over the edge of the world, and he slipped slowly after his wingmate.

He'd hang back a safe distance, wait for Vernon to come back and report. If he came back.

A dire vision entered Buzzy's mind as he flew slowly closer to Las Vegas: what if Vernon gets injured, flies back closer to me, then dies —

No. If humans kill Vernon, he'll die among them, not get a chance to fly back to the desert. Damn waste.

Buzzy kept a wary eye on the city's dim spires, closer now than he'd ever flown. He hovered and waited till dawn, when he sensed a commotion. Then he saw a dot approaching.

Vernon.

"Well?" Buzzy asked, as Vernon fell into orbit with him.

"Trucker strike," Vernon said, "or something like it. Who knows how long it'll last."

"I'll be damned."

They flew in silence all morning, scanning the desert floor. Maybe a cricket or cockroach would show up.

"So what do we do?" Buzzy asked. He was so nonplussed by the news that he didn't bother to ask Vernon how he'd survived his close encounter with humans.

Vernon didn't answer. They slid from the sky later that afternoon to the cottonwood, there to wait for developments.

They looked around for sustenance and saw none.

Two weeks later, still with no dead people trucks in sight, Vernon said, "To Hell with this. I'm going to go into town."

Vernon rose into the air and Buzzy rose after. "Wait, the humans, they'll — "

"I'll come in high. It's night. Humans never look up."

Buzzy rose to his wingmate's side. "But — "

"They must be stockpiling the dead people somewhere, for when the strike ends. In a warehouse maybe."

If the humans' dead people storage warehouse was as poorly maintained as their delivery trucks and highways were, there might be spillage. Dinner.

But danger.

"Vernon — "

"I'm damn hungry, Buzzy."

"But — "

"Well, aren't *you?*"

"Well, yes, but — "

"Tell you what, Buzz. I die, you eat. Deal?"

Buzzy hesitated only long enough for Vernon to turn his beak toward him and add, "Well?"

"And if — "

"Yeah, right," Vernon said. "And if."

They flew onward silently, toward Las Vegas and the possibility of a dead people warehouse spillage — and live humans, with guns.

They approached cautiously but soon discovered there was no need. Humans milled in haphazard knots in the brightly lit streets below: a riot. Staccato pops — gunfire — and the occasional explosion punctuated by human screams. Acrid smoke rose from several fires, helping to obscure the two scavengers circling above The Strip. No humans looked up.

Under cover of a massive, black smoke cloud billowing from a burning casino, Buzzy and Vernon descended till they rested atop a huge roller coaster.

They looked down on chaos. Riot. People killing one another. Dead bodies lay scattered in the street and on the sidewalks, the scent of fresh death rising in tantalizing wafts.

"How can they get any work done in all this?" Buzzy said. He was thinking that the humans were so busy killing each other that they didn't have time to truck the bodies to Hell.

"The waste," Vernon said, a whine in his cracked voice, "The insane *waste*." The bodies would rot, unless —

Vernon folded his wings.

"No, Vernon!" But Buzzy was too late. Patience cast aside, Vernon had already dived to the street below and the banquet of dead people.

And armed humans.

Buzzy dived after.

Vernon had chosen to fall onto the exposed stomach of a blood-soaked body lying on the street and began pecking at its entrails. Buzzy joined him. Humans milled about, shouting and running and shoving and shooting. They ignored the scavengers.

"I'm not dead," the human on which they dined muttered through bloodied teeth, a pained grimace on its face. It feebly tried to push Vernon away from its exposed gut.

"Oh, shit," Vernon said and spat out a length of intestine in disgust. "You scared the Hell out of me."

Buzzy gagged and threw up. They were scavengers, not predators.

But the human's efforts to stuff its entrails back inside its rent abdomen quickly grew feeble and it slumped back dead. Buzzy and Vernon ate, content.

The humans running to and fro ignored them. One even jumped over them, rushing headlong somewhere.

Finally, Buzzy belched and nudged Vernon. "Let's get out of here."

"Yeah, let's."

They rose straight up, a bit sluggish from a few pounds of fresh meat weighing them down. Atop the roller coaster again, they settled to digest in leisure. From below, the smell of smoke, burning gasoline and fresh, dead people, and the sound of gunfire and screams rose up.

"We were lucky," Vernon said.

"Yeah, but maybe not next time."

"Yeah. What if they keep this up — "

"Yeah, what if."

The killing meant a banquet, if you didn't get killed yourself, but *what if?*

Buzzy imagined what would happen when the last human killed off the second to last human: no more food — *at all.*

It could happen. These were, after all, humans.

"We've got to do something," Vernon said. He belched.

They sat in silence for a long time, thinking, digesting.

"I got an idea," Buzzy said.

Given the scavengers' lack of opposable thumbs, it took a lot of planning, imagination and clever strategy to capture the human pair. And it took a lot of time. But scavengers are patient.

Luckily the humans, one a male and one a female, could survive on vegetation because by the time Buzzy and Vernon caught them and caged them, they were probably the last humans alive, anywhere.

Buzzy and Vernon watched their captives through the bars of the bear cage at the Las Vegas zoo they'd appropriated for the purpose. They'd studied human behavior since the night their scheme hatched. They studied how humans ate, communicated, clothed themselves, defended themselves from predators, and how they slept.

How they mated.

"How long do you — " Buzzy started.

The humans in the cage were mating.

"A while," Vernon said.

"Well. Scavengers are patient."

CHARLIE'S IN THE BOTTLE

P op.
Charlie disappeared.

He'd been sitting at a table by the Lucky Nickel Saloon front door, where the batwing doors swung open on dusty Second Avenue, Laramie, Wyoming Territory, U. S. of A., arguing with Banky across the table. Then Banky said something that sounded Chinese, Greek, or maybe Irish and —

Pop.

Charlie disappeared.

We found him quick enough. He was in a gin bottle on the table where he'd been sitting, an empty bottle, luckily, as Charlie couldn't swim. I imagine swimming in gin might be just as irksome as being disappeared, shrunk, and popped into an empty gin bottle. But since these things had never happened to me, I couldn't say for sure how Charlie felt.

He stood in the bottle, cupped hands to his mouth, and shouted something up. Everybody had become quite agitated when Charlie disappeared and even more so when they discovered him in the bottle. They were as noisy as a pugilist crowd, except for Banky who had passed out. I hushed everybody so I could hear. I cleared out some earwax with my little finger, bent to the bottle mouth, and listened.

"Say again, Charlie."

"Get me out of here, Tom," he yelled.

Nobody else in the room heard him but me since he was so tiny, a half-inch tall, and thus endowed with tiny lungs. He sounded like a flea might sound if a flea took a notion to talk.

The men in the saloon stood back, giving Charlie, the bottle he was in, the table on which the bottle sat, and under which Banky lay unconscious, plenty of room. Maybe they thought if they got too close, they'd get sucked into the bottle too. The same thought had occurred to me, but I figured Charlie was no bigger than a ten-day mustache hair because Banky said something magic. And since Banky had passed out, I figured it was safe.

Of course, I kept one wary eye on Banky laying in a sodden lump under the table. If Banky so much as broke wind, I intended to be in Cheyenne before the smell hit.

Well, if it hadn't been something political that riled Banky enough to shrink his buddy, since Banky was a Democrat and Charlie a Republican, it would have been baseball. Baseball was big in Wyoming at the time. Banky and Charlie loved to argue about anything, but politics and baseball occupied them mostly.

But nevermind why Banky shrunk his buddy. How the blue blazes, excuse my French, were we going to help poor old Charlie?

Getting him out of the bottle wasn't the problem. He was tiny enough he'd drop right out if we upended the bottle. Getting him unshrunk was the problem.

I relayed Charlie's reasonable request to my colleagues in the Lucky Nickel Saloon. It was forenoon and the only gents in the room besides Charlie and Banky were me and Casper, plus Mick the barkeep and a fellow named Sam Something, a newspaper reporter biding time waiting for an eastbound train. Jack Thatcher hadn't arrived yet.

"Well, it's obvious, ain't it?" Casper intoned. He was an ex-Indian fighter, now a one-eyed gambler, but not a good one.

"What?" Mick asked.

"Well, we got to wake old Banky up and get him to say what he said that got Charlie in this fix, but say it backward so poor Charlie can get out of it."

"One problem," the reporter named Sam cautioned.

"What?" Mick observed.

"Fellow's passed out," Sam indicated. He tugged at his mustache and relit his cigar. "Whatever your friend here — "

"Banky," I informed the gentleman. "Short for Bancroft." His discourtesy could be forgiven, as he wasn't a regular.

" — Banky," the reporter fellow resumed. "He said what he said, not under the influence of alcohol, I assure you gentlemen. No. Rather, he was under the influence of spirits of another kind. Spirits from beyond the veil."

"What?" Mick required.

"Spiritism?" Casper put in. "Well, haw."

I stayed shut up, as did the unconscious Banky. If Charlie could hear the reporter pontificate from his vantage in the bottle, he didn't say. And if he did, we couldn't hear.

"Spiritism," the reporter confirmed, nodding his shaggy mane sagely. "I've seen it on Mississippi riverboats and on wagon trains, seen it from Saint Louie to New Orleans, from the Potomac to the Sacramento. I've seen it from the bayou to the boardwalk, in the mining camps and among the Indians. I've seen it from sea to shining sea — "

"What then," I requested to forestall what seemed to be the first leg of a long, windy story, "do we do?"

"What?" Mick inquired.

"Sobriety," Sam declared, "would be unproductive in this case. No, sir. You must induce Mr. Bancroft to consume more gin to reproduce the state he was in when the spirits used him to abuse the unfortunate Mr., uh, Charles — "

"Charlie," I informed the gentleman, whose pompousness had begun to rankle. "Mr. Charles Enright, whom we call 'Charlie.'"

"Indeed," Sam conceded. "Charlie. No offense meant, sir. I'm only trying to help."

"Well, let me get this straight," Casper interjected. "We wake Banky up, get him drunk and, what? Let these, uh, spirits, speak through him again?"

"It seems the solution," Sam declared.

"Well, what if these spirits put somebody else in the bottle with Charlie? Maybe me or maybe even you?"

Sam shook his head, frowning. "Consider what Banky said the second before Charlie disappeared *here* — " he pointed to the now-empty chair where Charlie had 'popped' out of thin air " — and reappeared *here*." He gestured toward the bottle in which Charlie had sat down. Charlie looked forlorn.

"Well, I don't recall rightly what he said," Casper admitted.

"What?" Mick inquired.

"Sounded to me something like — " and here Sam made noises that sounded Italian but without the vigorous hand wiggling.

Pop.

Casper disappeared.

We found him in short order, in the bottle.

"Oops," Sam commented.

"What?" Mick offered.

I turned on the reporter with murderous intent but before I could thrash him, it came to me to ask how he knew the exact words Banky, who had begun to awaken, had used to shrink Charlie.

"A good memory for details," Sam muttered, chin bobbing in distress. "It's an asset in my profession. When one can't take notes in the field, memory must suffice. During a battle, for instance, or while astride a horse being pursued by a band of blood-thirsty savages across the plain, or on a tall ship during a blow, I find it — "

"Nevermind all that," I insisted. "What're we going to do to get him back?"

"What?" Mick queried.

Sam looked quite sorrowful. "I'm truly sorry, sir. I had no idea that repeating — "

"Nevermind all that." The fellow was much too windy for my taste. "Can you undo it?"

At that point, Charlie swayed through the front batwing doors, collar askew, suspenders hanging, hair tangled, looking disheveled but quite the old Charlie we knew before he got shrunk.

A closer look at the bottle on the table revealed Casper inside, jumping up and down and shouting his flea-sized lungs out, but no Charlie in the bottle. No, Charlie stood amid his back-thumping, relieved, welcoming cronies, which now included Banky, who had emerged from his slumber to stand pasty-faced and as wobble-legged as a newborn colt.

Sam looked somber, as if he'd et something disagreeable or Mexican. As for me, I was relieved right enough to see Charlie out of his fix, but distressed that Casper was now in the same fix, and I had a few questions for both Banky and our visiting journalist. I suspected Sam hadn't been candid with us in the few minutes in which we had become acquainted.

"I believe, sir," I confronted Sam, "you have some explaining to do."

My tone suggested seriousness, and the others in the room — Mick, Banky, and Charlie — quit their fussing and paid attention.

"What?" Mick prompted.

Sam ahemed and shuffled feet. "Well, I didn't exactly say exactly what Banky said when he said what he said that put Charlie in the bottle — "

"But what you said put Casper in the bottle," I pointed out.

"And got me out, I reckon, at the same time," Charlie contributed.

"Yes," Sam conceded, "the phenomena appear linked."

"And something else," Charlie offered. "When Banky said what he said and I ended up in that bottle, I had me the worst cold I've had since my days in Saskatoon, I swear. But I don't now."

"You figure I cured you or something?" Banky inquired, voice slurry, like he was talking Swedish or gargling or suchlike.

This prompted vigorous verbiage among all present, except for Casper who we couldn't hear and Mick who just said "What?"

During which exchange Sam allowed as how the incantation Banky incanted, and which he'd confessedly botched, sounded Hindoo to him. Banky admitted he'd seen a VooDoo Negress that a.m. to treat a painful ingrown toenail and left a dispute over the fee unresolved. As a result, although she had cured his ailment, the woman may have also cursed him.

Whereupon Charlie reminded us, it may not have been a curse.

"What?" Mick wondered.

"I had this cold afore," Charlie recalled. "Now I don't. I think getting shrunk and all made my cold go away."

"But when you got unshrunk," Sam noted, "Casper was. Shrunk, that is."

We stood in silence for a moment taking in the implications. Casper could be heard stomping around inside his bottle like a fly against a window.

"One way to figure it out," Sam decided.

"What?" Mick asked.

"Repeat the experiment."

"But how?" I wondered. "You confessed that what you said that shrunk Casper and deshrunk Charlie wasn't exactly what Banky said in the first place to shrink Charlie — "

"For which I'm mighty sorry, old friend," Banky apologized, a sob in his throat.

"Banky, my good man," Sam patted Banky's shoulder in an annoying, paternal gesture, "can you remember what you said to Charlie when he, uh, you know — "

"Not a blamed word," Banky uttered. "I was drunk at the time."

"Charlie, can you remember — "

"Not word for word, I reckon," Charlie shook his head. "But close enough to try. And if it'll save our friend Casper there in the bottle, I'm willing to give it a try."

I suspect Casper heard this last, as his head commenced to frantic bobbing up and down and I could hear his squeaking agreement in a fairy voice.

I bent my ear to the bottle. "I figure you got to be looking at whoever gets popped," Casper called out to me.

I gave him the okay sign and told the others. They already had that part figured.

We all gathered around Charlie, except for Casper. The swaying Banky, the bewildered-seeming Mick, Sam with stogie ablaze, and me, Tom Dooley, we all stood shoulder to shoulder in solidarity with Charlie as he tried to recall what Banky had said.

All I got was mumble, mumble, you low-down no-good yakity-yakity, yellow-bellied, son-of-a so on and so forth, blah, blah, blah. And such like. I had the impression Charlie was making up what he said he remembered Banky say, and it didn't resemble at all what Sam had said he'd remembered Banky saying when Sam had said what he said Banky said.

Pop.

Mick disappeared.

And Casper fell down from midair and broke a table, and Mick was in the bottle and Casper tried to stand and shake off the spittoon in which he'd lodged a boot when he fell.

"Well, it works," Casper declared. He shook the spittoon off with a jerk, flipped his eye patch up on his forehead, and blinked.

"Well, it works," he repeated.

If Mick said "What?" nobody heard.

"Well, I can see," Casper cried out in joy.

And he could. Since that time his rifle backfired poking his eye out, Casper hadn't seen anything three-dimensional. Now he saw as clear-eyed as Annie Oakley.

Backslapping and raucous yipping commenced to celebrate Casper's good fortune.

Which abated as the assembled realized with chagrin that Mick was now in the fix Casper had been in and Charlie had been in before Casper.

"If Mick is to resume his rightful place behind the bar," I submitted, "one of us will have to say some magic words — "

"And it doesn't seem critical who says it or what they say, exactly," Sam interjected. "At least for it to work."

" — and put another of us in Mick's place."

"Well, I'll bet Mick can hear as good as I can see," Casper stated.

After some discussion, we decided I would say what I recalled the others having said and pop the reporter into the bottle, as he suffered from a condition about which true men are reluctant to refer even among each other.

So I said my say, we heard a "pop," Sam appeared in the bottle on the table, and Mick came walking through the back door from the alley where he had reappeared. And, yes, Mick could hear quite well. Rather than say "What?" all the time, he took to saying "Pipe down" a lot.

Sam turned his tiny back to us in the bottle, unbuttoned his tiny fly, and inspected his tiny problem. He yelled something up to us that we couldn't hear. So I bent my ear to the bottle mouth and heard him say, "I'll have to try it out to see if it works, but I think there's hope. I'm grateful."

I relayed his comment to the others in the room who nodded in silent acknowledgment.

"Now get me out of here," Sam yelled, flea-voiced. Sam had to catch a train, he reminded us.

But who would say the incantation and who would go into the bottle in Sam's place?

In our subsequent conversation, I came to realize my compatriots had taken as much a dislike to our guest as had I. We'd been too polite and too busy with our own concerns to tell him he was a lout and ought to seek companionship elsewhere while waiting for his train. But now he wanted out of the gin bottle, and the question became who disliked him least so as to allow himself to get put into the bottle for Sam's benefit.

I don't recall who noted I hadn't had a turn in the bottle yet.

Not me. I felt no need to see the world from the bottom of a gin bottle, and I felt as healthy as a muleskinner and in no need of medication, magical, or otherwise. And besides, I felt forced to confess, I didn't like this Sam Something, reporter, enough to undergo the experience. No, sir. Not me.

My companions seemed likewise reluctant to volunteer.

We discussed Sam's predicament and our difficulty in coming to grips with it for a while before we noted a new presence in the saloon. Jack Thatcher had arrived, taking his usual seat.

Mick had been so involved with us in Sam's dilemma that he hadn't noticed Jack limp in, pull his own pitcher, grab a mug, and squat. Besides, hearing was a new thing for Mick and he likely didn't know what "Jack arriving" sounded like. But Jack spoke up right enough, reminding us of our responsibility to guests.

"Say," he called out, tapping his cane against the table for attention, "what are you all doing that's so all-fired important you forget to say hello to your friends? Or at least a regular customer, such as I."

We stared at Jack as if he had spoken Chinese. Then we stared at each other, and at Sam, who'd gone quiet in the bottle.

"Well, how's the leg?" Casper inquired.

Jack shrugged. "Could be better."

Us boys had a lot to think about. We might could make a buck or two off this, somehow. We'll have to find somebody who didn't mind spending time in a gin bottle, but Laramie has a few saloons. That won't be hard.

But first —

Mick did the honors.

Pop.

QUEEN O' THE DRAGONS

Mick was in love and not just a little. Every night after closing the Lucky Nickel Saloon, he took his profits and ambled down to Dolly's Boarding House for Ladies and partook of the entertainment offered there by a certain Miss Emma Drummond, late of Saint Louie and points east.

"She's the prettiest girl in Wyoming Territory," Mick reminded us often, in case we regulars forgot. He had a photograph taken of her. She looked like a lady in the picture, all gussied up in petticoats, a bustle, toting a parasol and suchlike.

Us regulars daren't tell Mick what we thought. Even mud fence ugly, with a mustache better than Mick's, she looked as tolerable as any girl in Laramie in the entertainment trade. And Mick'd win no beauty contest himself unless he competed with mules. So, it didn't seem proper to opine unasked.

One day Mick came late to open, and we regulars got close to calling the sheriff to see if he'd fallen down an outhouse somewheres. But no, up he comes, finally, droopy-faced like somebody shot his favorite dog.

"What gives?" Casper asked in brotherly concern.

"Yeah, what?" Banky added.

"My life is over," Mick pronounced. We waited for him to drop the proverbial other boot as he set up for the day and he sighed a powerful lot of heavy weight sighs. But there was no egging him on. He worked at his own steady pace.

At last, he informed us. It seemed as how he'd asked the light of his life for to marry him, and she turned him down.

"But why?" Charlie inquired.

"Yeah, why?" Banky added.

Seemed as how Miss Emma wanted Mick to pay off her contract to Miss Dolly first.

"Well," Casper put in, "we could help you. Pass the hat, so to speak. How much does your lady owe?"

"Yeah, how much?" Banky added.

Mick said and us who'd had breakfast near lost it.

"There's more," Mick noted, his countenance bleaker than any I'd seen outside a funeral home.

Given Mick's last news item, nobody wanted to hear, but he said anyway. "She wants me to give up the saloon trade and take up homesteading."

In the silence which ensued, you could have heard a cockroach fart.

We liked Mick right well enough, and if he took a fancy to a soiled dove, we figured more power to him. A man needs companionship. Besides, if he took a notion to marry such a one, that was okeydokey too, even if she demanded he become frugal in the process and do something noble like rescue her from some onerous contract. It might do Mick good to do something noble for a change. T'would keep him from going to hell for watering his whiskey.

But abandon the saloon business?

They'd build a cobblestone road twixt Laramie and Cheyenne afore us boys would cotton to such like. I saw my compatriots frown, shoulders hunched, brows furrowed, trying to figure how to talk Mick into accepting fate.

"The Lucky Nickel won't make you rich enough, I reckon," Charlie commiserated, "to buy out Miss Emma's contract, let alone give up the business. Too bad."

"Yeah, too bad," Banky added.

We all nodded agreement.

Besides, none of us could get credit anywheres else.

Mick just shrugged, saddened. He dusted off his picture of Miss Emma which he kept behind the bar to moon at.

Somehow we had to get him quit from thinking of Miss Emma, or the worst would happen. Mick was a clever enough businessman and no mistake, and if he set his mind to it, he'd figure a way to make his stake soon enough. I had to confer with the boys and see we got cleverer quicker.

I had no sooner thought up this thought when the day's first unregular customer sauntered in.

T'was a cowboy, judging by the chaps, dirty boots, and spurs, and just in off the trail, judging by the smell.

He toted a fair-sized canvas bag in one hand. In the other, he dragged a rope with a leather loop on one end across the sawdust floor. He moseyed to the bar and ordered a beer.

"I'm seeking a buyer," he announces, bold as a politician. He held up the loop connected to the rope on the floor.

"What's for sale?" I wondered.

"Yeah, what?" Banky added.

"Why, this here dragon," he responded, nodding at the loop he held up.

"Dragon?" Mick questioned.

"Well, I don't see no dragon," Casper noted.

"Me neither," Charlie joined in.

"Of course you don't," the cowboy agreed. He snorted and spat. *Ping.* "It's an invisible dragon."

I'd never seen a dragon before, let alone an invisible one. And I'd traveled some too.

We all sat or stood jaw-dropped, gazing at the place the fellow said his dragon sat.

"It don't bite none," the cowboy assured us in a whiny voice. He leaned away from the bar and reached over, rubbing a hand through the air just in front of the belt-like leather loop I now recognized as a collar, but one which could have hung loose on a Clydesdale's neck.

The cowboy held the collar up so a guy couldn't tell if he just held up the collar or if there was indeed an invisible neck through it, a body on one side sprawled on the floor and a head on the other side. The rope affixed to the collar drooped down to coil on the floor next to the cowboy's boots. He'd put the tote bag on the floor next to the leash.

The cowboy spat again. *Ping.* He was a good shot.

"I don't trade in livestock," Mick declared. He'd been polishing the same shot glass since the cowboy, who said his name was Slim, proposed to sell the dragon. "I prefer money."

"Reckon you do," Slim drawled, unperturbed. He puffed up whisker-specked cheeks preparatory to another shot at the spittoon fifteen feet away. *Ping.*

He gnawed off a thumb-sized bite of plug with yellow teeth and commenced to vigorous chewing again. We waited for him to speak. Me standing next to him, Mick behind the bar, Charlie over by the piano, Casper and Banky playing cards at their usual table, we all waited, polite-like. It was mid-morning and Jack Thatcher hadn't limped in yet.

"But this here dragon," Slim imparted, "ain't no regular dragon. No sir. I got her down to Utah, a place called Goblin Valley. S'posed to be haunted, I hear tell. Nobody goes in there but Indians, Mormons, and other crazy folk, so the dragons what live there, they prosper." He leaned over the bar to Mick and added in a stage whisper, so we all could hear, "This here dragon is the queen o' the dragons."

"Do tell," I stated. As Slim was a few sheets to the wind and still upright, I took him for neither Indian nor Mormon, but what remained made his story somewhat plausible. Just a little.

"We had us some royalty in the Lucky Nickel once," Charlie observed. "Some Russian duke or other. Or was he Polish? Or was that some other saloon?"

Now, Mick, he was a right smart businessman as I said, and I figured his poker face for a prelude to a boot in Slim's fanny, on account of if I saw the cowpoke's flim-flammery then surely Mick did too. Mick could tell from a snake oil peddler when he saw one, and I knew from embarrassing personal experience he could spot a marked deck across a smoky room.

But no. To my surprise, Mick looked halfway interested. "Queen o' the dragons, you say?" he asked Slim.

"Yessir." Slim focused his sales pitch toward Mick.

I have to admit it got me powerful puzzled watching Mick polish that damn shot glass so hard the rag frazzled.

"Well, what can you do with a dragon?" Casper inquired. He blinked his one good eye, stood from the table at which he'd sat and inched closer to the critter. I expect Casper'd want to pet it, invisible or no, animal lover he is, but for fear he'd lose a hand. A one-eyed gambler is handicapped enough.

Slim laughed and tobacco juice sprayed. "What can you do with a dragon?" he repeated. For a moment, in which Banky unbuttoned his coat so he could grip his Colt if the need arose to shoot varmint, we thought Slim had insulted Casper, who wasn't bright but a good friend.

But no. Slim commenced into a windy narrative of dragon-owning benefits. Dragons, he informed us, made cracker guard animals, as they didn't cotton to rustlers nor coyotes. They made better beasts of burden than mules as they weren't as stubborn nor noisy and didn't kick. Like goats, they ate what you gave them, and not much at that, and they could go days without water like camels if the need arose for them to cross desert. They weren't as skittish as some horses when it came to fording rivers or suchlike. They had a way with sheep that made most dogs look lazy. They calmed nervous cows in storms better than an army of drovers.

"And they don't smell," he concluded, by which time Banky had joined Casper a few feet away from the critter in question. Charlie had come over too.

"See?" Slim stood over the dragon and inhaled. Charlie, Casper, and Banky did the same.

As Mick continued to look intrigued, I guess I was too. And if Mick had gone tetched in the head, so be it. I'd play along. He was a good barkeep and friend, and I'll be the last fool to tell him he'd gone plumb loco. I hadn't told him so when he first declared his love for Miss Emma Drummond and I wasn't about to start.

And Banky was a tad more temperamental with that Colt than my nerves could tolerate, which helped convince me to join in. He and Casper were tight, which didn't bode well for anyone who crossed Casper. So I stuck my nose over the collar, inhaled a draught, and reported I couldn't smell the dragon either.

"Can't see it, neither," Charlie mumbled.

"Yet another advantage," Slim exclaimed. "Imagine sneaking a dragon into a boarding house or a train. Wouldn't rile the dragon none, but folks in the vicinity would raise cane. Futhermore, folks can steal horses, but what fool'd try to steal a dragon they can't see?"

It appeared to me as if Mick slipped yet another notch toward being full bore hoodwinked by Slim's flim-flammery. In my effort to avoid offense to him and my compatriots, I'd gone along with the sham too far to counter developments now with a dose of reality. So I stayed shut up. I reckoned it wouldn't hurt Mick a heap if he owned an invisible dragon. Sure he'd be out maybe a few bucks or a few drinks, but I'd seen him overcharge the occasional greenhorn or Chinaman, and the drinks were watered down anyway, so it all evened out.

Besides, it'd serve to distract him from Emma.

Slim also pointed out the dragon didn't bark and was house broken, as evidenced by its silence and lack of dragon shit.

By the time Slim talked Mick into paying five dollars and free drinks for the dragon if he threw in the collar, leash, and tote bag, I was in too far to buck, and mighty chagrined about it. I resolved to lose a few dollars to Mick in our next poker game to make up for my complicity.

In the tote bag, Slim uttered, lay rags for polishing the dragon and other useful equipage for the care of one's dragon.

We looked inside the bag and found what I took to be the usual old clothing items, bits of hardware, used utensils, saddle soap, and such stuff as one might expect among a cowboy's possibles. I stayed shut up, even when the boys in the bar nodded acceptingly as Slim pointed out how the bent metal fork he'd taken from the bag could be used for dragon grooming. He even demonstrated. He got down on the floor and extracted a splinter from the dragon's foot.

"I don't see no splinter," Charlie muttered.

"Ordinary splinters don't bode diddly to invisible dragons," Slim countered. "Invisible splinters give 'em fits."

By and by, Slim took his leave. He stood at the door, smiled us a so-long smile, and spat.

Ping.

"Well, where ought you to put the beast?" Casper wondered.

"Yeah, where?" Banky added.

"Leave it to me," Mick declared as he sauntered around the bar and took the dragon in leash by one hand and the tote bag in the other and went into the back room, his quarters. "Mr. Bancroft," he communicated as he left, "please be so kind as to tend while I'm away."

Banky nodded, went around the bar, put on an apron, and affixed on his face a poor imitation of the stony frown for which Mick had acquired considerable notoriety.

We could hear shuffling, tapping, and thumping from the back room and occasional cursing in Mick's voice. We heard nothing from the dragon.

Just then, Jack Thatcher limped in.

"Afternoon, boys," he waved his cane, plopped into his usual chair close by the bar, and stretched out his game leg. He gave a puzzled look at Banky when the latter brought a pitcher. Jack inquired as to Mick's whereabouts.

"In the back tending to some business," Banky responded.

Jack took a pull at his beer, wiped the froth off his mustache, and coughed. "I reckon you-all've had yourself a mighty frisky time today."

"Well, what makes you say so?" Casper inquired.

"Yeah, what?" Banky added.

"I saw that cowboy fellow leaving the Lucky Nickel. He was laughing fit to bust a gut. Are you-all going to let me in on the joke or what have you?"

I looked at my companion's faces and realized they too had seen through the scam the cowboy named Slim had played on our friend Mick. And as I had done, they too had played along to avoid embarrassing Mick.

It took a few minutes to extract the information that they too went along with it because they each figured everyone else had bought into the scam, and they didn't want to hurt anybody's feelings by pointing out how foolish they were. Why, they even thought I'd been hornswoggled too, a little.

"Fact is," Jack pointed out over his mug rim, "you all figured you each one was the onliest one not taken in." He laughed. "Now I see why that poke was laughing so hard. He humbugged you all."

When no one joined his jollity, he sobered up right quick. "What?" he inquired.

I nodded my head toward the back where we could still hear Mick fussing with his dragon.

"We wasn't took," Charlie declared, voice lowish, as if Mick might hear. "But Mick, he's out five bucks."

"And a couple drinks," Banky observed.

"It gets worse," I realized, as the notion occurred to me.

"Well, how so, Tom?" Casper demanded.

"Yeah, how?" Banky added.

"That cowpoke'll go to every bar in Laramie and brag up as how he pulled the wool over Mick's eyes. Mick'll be the laughing stock of the West."

"It ain't right," Jack insisted. "Not atall."

"There's more, Jack," I continued. I told him how Mick had proposed to Emma Drummond and how she'd turned him down, conditional-like, saying she wanted him to buy out her contract first, then quit the saloon business and homestead.

"Ever since he got amored of his lady friend," Jack declared, "Mick acts like somebody shot his lead duck."

"It just got as worst as it can get," Charlie added. "I calculate Mick'll be out of business by sundown, and his lady love will give him the boot soon thereafter."

We all agreed. Banky began fingering his Colt as if fixing to drill him a cowboy or a whore and couldn't decide which. But he wore Mick's apron and tended Mick's bar, which occasional duty he took serious, so no gun-play seemed in our immediate future, lucky for Slim or Emma.

"This morn, I worried we'd lose Mick to wedding bells," I recalled, "and see the end of the Lucky Nickel to boot. But now it looks like we'll see the end of the Lucky Nickel and ol' Mick won't win his true love's heart neither in the process."

"I'd druther lose the Lucky Nickel," Charlie maintained, wiping away a tear, "than lose my friend to a broken heart."

We all agreed, but no solution to our new dilemma seemed imminent.

"What'll we tell Mick?" Charlie wondered.

"If anything," Banky put in.

"Well, we got to tell him something," Casper declared.

"Yeah," Jack decided. "T'wouldn't be right not to."

We heard the door to the back open, and Mick reentered the bar. He appeared to be toting firewood or suchlike.

"I'll do what's right," I informed my friends, stiffening myself to the disagreeable task. They looked relieved I had volunteered. I didn't blame them diddly.

As I approached Mick, he handed me the contents of his arms. "Careful," he warned. "Paint's still wet."

He'd painted up some signs.

"What in tarnation?" I exclaimed.

"I recognized that fellow just in here," Mick announced as he escorted his dragon over by the piano.

"You did?" Banky asked.

"Yep. Howdy, Jack."

"Morning, Mick."

The piano sat on a kind of raised platform, sort of stagelike. It wasn't like I'd seen at real show houses, but it kept the occasional drunk from tripping over the piano player, when Mick could afford one in his employ.

"You recognized him?" I persisted.

"Yep."

He tied up the dragon's leash to the piano and plopped the collar on the piano bench.

"Well, do tell," Casper insisted.

Mick put a rope thing around the piano stage area, a sort of courtesy barrier, like I'd seen at shows when they want to keep folk in lines or see they don't jump out at dignitaries or celebs. As I recall, Mick won it from a banker in a poker game or somesuch. Anyway, it looked velvety and classy.

"Please hand me the second sign there," Mick requested of me. I put the signs down on the bar, next to where Mick had put the tote bag with the dragon maintenance stuff in it.

"Yep," Mick continued. "I recognized the sidewinder. Fellow name of Slim Yonkers, out of the Lazy Bar J up toward Tie Siding way. Sneaks into town of an occasional Saturday night and stops by Miss Dolly's, as is a cowboy's wont to do. Now, I'm not opposed to a hand taking his recreation as he sees fit, but this one, well — "

"Well, what?" Banky demanded. He took off Mick's apron, handed it to Mick, and stepped away from behind the bar.

Mick tied his apron on over his paunch and continued. "This fellow has taken a shine to my Emma. More than a regular fellow ought. More than just a little." You could see murder in Mick's usually unreadable eye, and Banky's gun hand twitched in sympathy.

"You want me to speak to him?" Banky offered.

"I got me another plan," Mick countered. "Gather round."

We did and Mick explained his plan.

It added up to this: if we went along, he'd insist Emma let him keep the bar open. We dithered a tad at first, but then he offered to tear up our bar tabs.

We joined his army. What are friends for?

*

Dragon's Eggs, the signs all over the bar read, *.50 cents ea. cooked as you like 'em.*

Hear the Queen o' the Dragons Play, the sign at the roped off area around the piano read. *Donations Gladly Accepted. Do Not Touch.*

We'd spread the word around town quick enough. The bar had filled up no later than lunch and had stayed so into the dinner hour and on. Banky had abandoned his table to help Mick behind the bar and business appeared brisk and steady.

A dandy, just off the train, sidled up to me at the bar, and peered at my plate, a wondering look on his face.

"S'cuse me," he drawled from under a white mustache and around an odorous five-cent cigar, his white eyebrows like thatch over his eyes. "I'd be obliged if you could tell me what's going on here."

I put down my fork, finished chewing, wiped my lips with the napkin tucked neath my chin, and regarded him. "Why so?"

"I'm a journalist," he confessed, hooking thumbs in his vest. "Looks like an interesting story. I wondered if you'd share it with me."

I pondered the dude's inquiry a moment as he introduced himself as Sam Something, on his way to San Francisco.

I told him the story and recommended he find Slim Yonkers from the Lazy Bar J to confirm it, as he was the one who found the queen o' the dragons in the first place. I felt sure if the reporter interviewed Slim, the cowboy'd give credibility to the tale, as Slim'd be lynched if he asserted contrary words, thus irritating the good folks enjoying Mick's hospitality.

In answer to his question about the silent piano music, where the donation tin filled steadily, I pointed out as how invisible dragons made invisible music, which fact is known even by Indians, Mormons, and other crazy people. He wrote it all down in a little notebook.

He bought me more invisible dragon eggs, scrambled as I like them, as we'd agreed he'd do in exchange for my story.

"How d'you know if they're undercooked?" he wondered.

Mick didn't hear, nor did Banky, or I would have feared for the reporter's life. "Mick's reputation as a cook is as great as his reputation as a bartender," I pontificated.

He nodded, satisfied at my sincerity, wrote down my words, and searched for other folk to interview in the crowded room.

Miss Emma Drummond showed up close on to sundown, as she'd heard about the doings over to the Lucky Nickel. I watched she and Mick confer in whispers at the end of the bar. I couldn't hear, nor could the other regulars. But we all watched the exchange as best we could.

Miss Emma seemed a might perturbed at first. I reckoned by her expression that, though she was delighted with Mick's apparent business success, she stuck by her guns on both the buying of her contract and the quitting of the saloon business in exchange for her hand.

Mick snuck her a quick gander at the roll of greenbacks he'd stashed in the moneybelt he always wore, and her eyes sparkled. I knew of an instant Mick had won the day and he'd gotten her to let him keep the bar. She smiled and sat demurely at a table two gentlemen had vacated for her benefit.

As she waited for the invisible dragon eggs she'd ordered, she tapped a dainty foot in time to the invisible piano music played by the invisible Queen o' the Dragons.

Everybody in the place was either fooled, seemed like, or drunk, or maybe they were all going along, pretending, just a little. But it wasn't until near closing when Mick sauntered over to the piano and whispered something to the invisible dragon that I began to wonder.

Just a little.

THE PROBLEM
WITH MERMAIDS

The world is a strange place, except for the Lucky Nickel Saloon, where nothing much ever happens. Which is lucky, all in all, as us regulars like it tranquil.

Take Dan Murphy, for instance. A body expects Dan to ride in to Laramie now and then and pass the time of day telling whoppers. We always listened proper, for he told the best fish stories in Wyoming Territory.

But when he let on he'd caught a mermaid on the Medicine Bow, we gave him what for. The result, I declare, was *not* tranquil.

Dan didn't appear at the time in a tale-telling mood, but we cranked it from him. Looking back, I reckon he just dropped by to wash down some dust — he looked a bit road-weary — but we got to egging him on and he let spill. Telling tales was such a habit, it was hard for him not to. I could see he wanted to swallow the words back right off, but too late. First he allowed as how he'd been fishing, then "I got me this mermaid," he uttered, then looked like he said something he hadn't ought.

"Well, what kind of bait did you use?" Casper inquired, eyebrow wiggling above his eyepatch. "Worms, or did you offer to take her dancing?"

We all bust a gut laughing, including a newspaper fellow, Sam Something, who'd stopped to wet his whistle while waiting for a train to go back east. We could poke fun at Dan, we knew, being friends, even though at first glance you'd figure Dan for an ornery cuss, as he sported a perpetual glower on his dark, bearded face like he'd et something disagreeable or Mexican. He had one black eyebrow above beady black eyes. That and the fact that he and an ox could play teeter-totter made him a force to be reckoned with.

We took Dan lightly on this particular tale, which we soon found we ought not. Dan did not favor us with so much as a grin. No, he just scrunched over the bar, shoulders arched like a steel bridge, and glowered into his mug. Mick also didn't laugh as he never laughed at paying customers before they'd paid.

"Well, I knew a girl once who ate worms," Casper offered from over by the piano where he worried a gin bottle. "Boy howdy, could she kiss. But her breath left much to be desired." His attempt to lighten up the situation fell like a dead pigeon.

We intended our laughter to be good-natured, but Dan didn't see it. He took a lungful of a sigh, downed his brew in one gulp, wiped the foam off his formidable black mustache, slammed the mug down, and stalked out, toward his wagon, hitched out front. He looked neither left nor right as he did so and he looked none too happy.

"Hey, Dan, old friend," Banky expressed in alarm as he followed the man to the batwing front doors, "what gives?" Dan had that red-eyed, frowny glare which might indicate imminent gunplay on a lesser man.

"You figure Dan'll come back guns a-blazing, Tom?" Banky inquired of me.

Banky was a tolerable crack shot with his Colt which he always carried, and as Dan couldn't shoot worth diddly, it wasn't his life for which Banky feared when Dan stalked out. No sir. But Dan had had a snootful and when he did such, he was apt to strap on his rusty piece and ventilate the local woodwork. Dan couldn't shoot, but that wouldn't stop him from trying if he'd been righteous annoyed.

"Well, uh-oh," Casper observed. "Should we hightail it out of here and hide until the fireworks is over?"

Mick slapped down the mug he'd just pulled for Sam in front of the man with a solid smack and gave Casper a sternful eye. Our taciturn Irish host wouldn't close for man nor Indian, no matter how riled either was.

"Should we go after Dan and try to humor him?" I wondered.

Banky spat. *Ping.* "I reckon he's had time to repent, or arm himself, if he be so inclined." He unbuttoned his vest to facilitate more ready access to his Colt. The gesture was reflex, no doubt. As he and Dan were as tight as two mice in the same spittoon, he wouldn't kill Dan for firing first, but he'd no doubt fire a few rounds to scare Dan back into sober contemplation of more agreeable options.

"Maybe he won't come back," Mick suggested. "His tab is pretty steep."

"You don't suppose he's planning to pay you with pickles." Banky stood near the batwing doors peering into the street. "Or with crackers." He spoke without turning. We sat or stood at no good vantage to see what Banky saw as the Lucky Nickel was bereft of windows.

"Well, what?" Casper declared as he sauntered over to peer over Banky's shoulder. I joined them as did Sam. Mick stayed at the bar.

Dan had pulled a canvas tarp off his cargo on his wagon. Roped upright on the wagon bed sat a wooden barrel, a big one.

I saw water splash over the barrel rim and I suspicioned its contents.

Sam ran knobby fingers through white hair, nodded toward the wagon, and commented, "Boys, that ain't pickles nor crackers. It's a fish barrel."

I thought Dan might ask that we step outside to see the evidence of his fish story, but no. We got back away from the door so as not to impede him as he unloaded the cargo. Us boys, being polite, and so as not to affront Dan's pride, refrained from offering to help lift the barrel off the wagon and tote it up the steps into the saloon.

Which he did with much splashing, facial contortions, admirable grunts, and such English language usage as would awe a muleskinner. When he finished, Dan wiped his brow on his sleeve and sighed as if he'd just suffered the annoyance of some mild but necessary exertion.

He stood beside the barrel, knobby fists anchored on hips, around which I noted with relief nary gun belt nor gun, and glared at us, one by one.

"Y'all took me for a liar, din't y'all? Well, I won't tolerate it. Which of you gents will be the first to step up and see for hisownself?"

We each took a gander into the barrel. When I took my turn, I confess I didn't know what to expect. I didn't expect to see a yellow-haired girl, maybe fifteen, sixteen or so, quite naked, sitting under water in the bottom of the barrel. We don't see many females in the Lucky Nickel. I'd never seen a white girl out West over eight years old shirtless, except whores, let alone under water in a barrel in the Lucky Nickel.

I might have been tempted to stare at her chest above her crossed arms, as she seemed unabashed to be uncovered. But her scowly demeanor tempered all lusty thought. She wouldn't meet my eye and she looked as sulky as a housewife with muddy bootprints on her parlor rug.

Meanwhile, Dan glared at me as if to say without saying that he disapproved of me looking at what he'd invited me to look at. I guess the glare come of his upset that we'd called him a liar, as our laughter implied. I felt mighty chagrined.

And you'd figure any normal person sitting under water in the bottom of a barrel might elect to sit cross-legged in the confined space, if they chose to sit at all. But no. The female in the barrel sat with her tail curled around her hips.

From the waist down she was fish, and it wasn't until I noticed her tail aflutter in the water, the way an impatient young lady might flutter a fan in agitation waiting on a late-arriving gentleman caller, that I noticed a fishy odor.

After we'd all had our look, we stood away from the barrel to give the lady a little privacy. We didn't want to be so ungentlemanlike as to stare, especially under Dan's glower.

"Well, she's a mermaid for certain sure," Casper pontificated, quiet and breathless. The eyebrow above his eyepatch wiggled snakelike.

"I warrant we owe you an apology, Dan." Banky rebuttoned his vest over the Colt and extended his hand to Dan in contrition. Dan took it and shook it, ever the gentleman. We all took turns offering handshakes in apology, then nursing the appendage thus wounded in Dan's iron grip.

"I see a problem," Sam observed, thumbs anchored in his white vest.

"What?" Banky wondered. Spit. *Ping.*

"Yeah, what?" Dan added.

"Have you had occasion to speak to your, er, catch?"

"What do you mean?" Dan asked.

"When you caught her, did she say anything? Tell you to go about your business and leave her be? Anything like that?"

"I recall being a touch distracted at the time." Dan took off his hat and scratched at his thick hair, a patch of prairie grass after a big blow. He seemed reluctant to go on.

"What did she say?" Sam persisted.

"I think, Mister Reporter, sir, that words between a fisherman and his catch ought to be free from public scrutiny."

"He means he ain't going to say," Banky interpreted.

"But you reeled her in anyway, didn't you?" Sam pressed.

Dan stared at the floor, mumbled, and shuffled foot to foot as if he had to pee. We feared for Sam's safety for a spell, but Dan didn't throttle the nosy little man. Besides, he didn't have his gun, which he preferred to fists. In time, Sam pried from Dan a truth any man'd be reluctant to reveal to even his best drinking buddies.

Dan Murphy had used a net. He'd *netted* the mermaid.

His shame was palpable. Dan was the best fisherman among us, despite tales tall enough as to impress Jonah, and we were all tolerable good even with a pole, some string, and a bent pin. We couldn't meet his eye for a long time, but I resolved to make up with him as he owed me two dollars.

"Why was the lady in the Medicine Bow, after all?" Sam wondered.

"Yeah, why?" Banky joined in.

Dan glared, arms crossed and lips shut.

"We know the mermaid is not native to these parts, am I correct, gentlemen?" Sam continued.

"I've never heard to the contrary," I assured him.

"Gentlemen, I've traveled the world. I'm familiar with the customs of a hundred foreign countries. I have encountered tales about mermaids in twenty foreign climes. And as I am fluent in a dozen languages, I feel that if we can persuade our guest to surface, perhaps we can solve the problem."

"Well, how do we get her to come up?" Casper pondered.

"Oh, all right." Dan looked as if he itched to toss his beer mug across the room or chew it, whichever. Instead, he gulped down its contents and walked over to the barrel. "If y'all'll hush a bit, I'll fess up and solve your wondering."

Dan leaned over the barrel, took a breath, held it in puffy cheeks, and stuck his head under water, much of which splashed over the sides. Bubbles rose and a body might have thought Dan and the mermaid conversed as we heard odd sounds emerging with the bubbles. They sounded argumentative.

At last, Dan surfaced, drippy as a bird dog after a good hunt, and demanded, "Okay, y'all turn your backs now."

"What?" Banky inquired.

Dan bunched fists like two nine-pound hammers and gave us a glare as brooked no dispute. We turned our backs forthwith.

In a moment we heard more splashing, then what sounded like a woman — or a lady, but we couldn't tell as the words were muffled and indistinct, whispered, nor was I sure if I heard any cussing in the utterances — and Dan's voice whispering, only it sounded more contrite than I'd ever heard from Dan, so I figure he was talking with the mermaid who, as far as I could tell, had risen from the barrel for what purpose Dan had yet to reveal. Still, I kept my back turned so as to comply with Dan's wish and to avoid embarrassment to the mermaid by staring at her chest as I'd done when she sat in the barrel sulking.

"Okay," Dan announced, "y'all can turn around now."

We did and saw Dan standing shirtless, sopping, and hairy-chested beside the barrel in which we could now see the mermaid wearing Dan's wet shirt as big as a tent on her.

A body might have figured we looked upon a gal standing in a barrel if not for the fact we'd already seen she had a tail where other folks had legs.

The mermaid looked terrible put out, as well as sad and shy.

She'd moved a gob of wet blonde hair off her forehead and although she looked downcast, we could see how pretty she was.

"Boys," Dan announced, "I'd like you to meet Miss Elizabeth Suzette Cockette."

We all nodded and howdied. Casper doffed his hat, and Banky buffed his boots on his calves. He didn't spit.

"Lizzy," Dan continued, addressing the mermaid, "these here are the boys."

"How-dee, zee boys," Lizzy the mermaid howdied in what sounded to me like a French accent. Or maybe Greek.

We did personal introductions during which we all bowed or nodded and said our say, all somewhat uncomfortable in the presence of a young girl-woman — I still hadn't figured out for sure yet which, except she was a mermaid — whose upper torso we'd just had a gander at.

"And now, for the problem," Sam interjected. He'd been the last to be formally introduced to the lady-woman-girl mermaid and he did so with the dignity one expects from a fellow who'd interviewed queens, Arabs, and potentates in far lands and who'd traveled even more easter than Saint Lou.

"If you ain't the most nosy critter — " Dan began to fume. The mermaid lit into him in French or Greek or whatever, and Dan, to our surprise, listened. After a few seconds of high-velocity jabber, Dan's shoulders hunched, his head bowed, and he began shuffling his toe in the sawdust, hat in hand. We got the message the mermaid was giving him a tongue-lashing that sounded powerful enough to melt the varnish off the bar.

He muttered in mermaid-talk, which surprised us all again, and nodded. He sighed and faced us.

"Now, boys," he informed us, "Lizzy ain't never been in a bar before, and she's a might put out."

"But that ain't your problem," Sam persisted.

Once again the mermaid intervened, preventing Dan from bashing the soda crackers out of Sam Something. To our amazement again, Dan answered in mermaid gibberish.

"What're they talking?" Banky asked, in general.

"French," Sam told us she spoke, as did Dan.

Just then a commotion in the street interrupted Dan as he was fixing to explain what the blue blazes was going on, including as how he knew how to speak French.

We crowded toward the batwing doors where we saw, coming at us, the sheriff and the strangest entourage I'd ever seen.

The folks with the sheriff looked as if they'd escaped from a circus. Among them stalked a tall man, must have been seven or eight foot, a lady who made the term 'stout' seem an understatement, a woman with a beard thicker than Dan's, one person who looked both man and woman, a slick, mustachioed fellow in tails and a top hat I took to be a circus ringmaster, and a three feet tall fellow toting a shotgun twice as long as he was tall.

None toted a rope, but they looked awful lynch-mob like.

"Now," Sam declared, hiding behind the bar, out of the line of fire, "*there*'s a problem."

With a glance at Lizzy's gloomy countenance, which matched Dan's, I finally figured what Sam'd figured.

Runaway lovers, Dan and his mermaid. And here come pa with the shotgun. Or somesuch. There was more to it, no doubt, but like as not, I was close.

"You're in a heap of trouble, Dan Murphy," Banky declared.

"Don't I know it," Dan answered, but he looked at Lizzy when he said it, not at the mob.

"Zere would no a problem be, mon cherry," Lizzy glared at Dan, hands on her hips, "eef to me you 'ad listened." In my mind's eye, I visualized a rolling pin in her dainty fist.

"If you hadn't jumped in the crick — " but Dan's protest fell beneath the onslaught of the mob's entrance.

Everybody talked at once. The ringmaster demanded somewhat of Lizzy in stern, fatherly, French tones. The dwarf threatened Dan with his shotgun and a flea-sized squeaky voice. Dan ignored him as if he were a toddler wielding a slingshot. Several ladies in the entourage, including the person whose sex appeared in open dispute, descended on Lizzy like a pack of wild hens, yakking and fussing.

The sheriff tried to hush everybody and get them to talk one at a time. As usual, nobody paid him much attention.

Mick looked as happy as his otherwise taciturn features allowed to see such a crowd in the saloon so early in the day and no shots fired yet.

Folks came in off Second Ave wondering what gives.

Dan took it quiet, arms folded, glowering, as did Lizzy, a tiny imitation of Dan's glower on her wet, pretty face.

Sam observed the folderol from behind the bar, where I hunkered along with Banky, Mick, and Casper.

I'd seen a circus before, but never in the Lucky Nickel, as far as I can recall. 'Twas a sight and no mistake.

Sam whispered into Banky's ear. Banky frowned suspicious and put a hand over his Colt as if Sam had asked to borrow it or somesuch else improper. Which, in a way, I soon discovered, Sam had done.

After more whispers betwixt the two, which I strained to overhear but didn't, the light dawned on Banky, his eyebrows rose, and he nodded agreement. Whereupon he spat — *ping* — withdrew the Colt, and fired a shot at the ceiling.

Nothing prompts attention as a shot fired in a room full of arguing people. Folks scattered like flushed quail. The hens flustered and fainted, as evidenced when some chairs by the fat lady thunderously collapsed. The sheriff drew a pistol and while looking around for someone to cuss at, dropped the piece and ducked as it discharged. The bullet tore the heel off the tall guy's boot, and he fell from over *there* to over *here*. I wanted to yell "timber" as he fell but didn't.

I saw Mick's lips move, assessing the furniture damage as his hands protectively surrounded his exposed glassware.

In the ensuing silence, Sam Something, back-east reporter and world traveler, expert in mermaids, French, and who knows what all else, took a stance on a chair and waited for everybody to pay him attention. Which we did, by and by.

"It looks," Sam pontificated, "like we got a problem."

"Well, you keep saying that," Casper responded, annoyed.

"And I mean to solve it before my train arrives," Sam countered. He took out his pocket watch, flicked it open, gazed at it, clicked it shut, repocketed it. "One hour."

For a time everybody talked at once again, until Sam gave a nod to Banky, who fired another shot into the ceiling. Everybody shut up again, and Sam continued.

He sounded more like a lawyer than a reporter as he proceeded to question the witnesses present and in jig time, figure out what the Sam Hill was going on.

It seems Dan had gone down to Grand Encampment a few months back to visit kin and, while there, he took in a circus. He fell in love straight away with one of the attractions, one Miss Elizabeth Suzette Cockette, mermaid, which love she returned.

But the star-crossed lovers parted on account of Dan's commitment to a job in Laramie and hers to the circus, which had a schedule to keep. They parted with heartfelt promises to meet again and, well, get together, so to speak. Exactly how that would be done wasn't specified in Sam's interrogation, but I do admit to my own curiosity.

Not a week past, Dan heard the circus was swinging back along the Union Pacific from Sacramento, through Salt Lake City, then through Laramie and points east. Sam himself had seen the show in question in Carson City and knew of the mermaid. His trip east paralleled the circus', more or less.

"Now comes the part where the two lovebirds decide to elope," Sam related. "Stop me if I get this wrong, son," he suggested to Dan. "You and Miss Cockette decide to elope at Medicine Bow on account of, Miss Cockette, your guardian, the ringmaster here, whose name I've forgotten — sorry, sir — would disapprove, as you well knew, on account of your age. Anyway, you set out and you start talking about marriage with Dan, and Dan says something like, 'What the goldurn hell you talking about? Marriage? Whatever for?' Like as though the subject had never come up before betwixt you, which maybe it hadn't. And at this point — correct me if I'm wrong, Miss Cockette — you take umbrage, get angered, and jump out of the wagon and dip into the crick from whence Dan is obliged to fish you out. How'm I doing so far?"

"I didn't say 'goldurn hell,'" Dan protested. "Something near like it, but I don't swear in front of a lady. No sir."

"And even zoe 'is mine 'e changes," Lizzy observed, "marry heem weel I no."

"She says she ain't going to marry him," Banky interpreted.

"*Now*, we're at the real problem, ain't we?" Sam intoned.

Further interrogation, Sam officiating, ensued during which the dilemma became clear — Lizzy wanted to marry Dan, Dan was reluctant to get hitched, the ringmaster-guardian wanted what he called "justice done of his little girl, if required," and Mick wanted somebody to pay for the broken furniture.

At some point, Sam took out his pocket watch, frowned, and yelled above the hubbub. "Is there a preacher in the house?"

A body would've thought it unlikely there'd be a preacher in the Lucky Nickel, but it had been an odd day. The circus was in the saloon, so why not a preacher?

He stepped from the crowd of townsfolk attracted by gunshots and the to-do. Reverend Avery Morgan, he declared himself, and though I don't recall ever breaking bread or getting drunk with him, he seemed a right nice fellow.

"Your Reverendship," Sam proposed, "would you be averse to marrying Dan Murphy, citizen of Laramie, to Lizzy Cockette?"

The all-hell which broke loose at Sam's question ended abrupt as Banky added another hole in the ceiling. I foresaw the need for some carpentry atop the Lucky Nickel before the rainy season set in. Anyway, quiet followed.

Sam got down from the chair and had a whisper conference with the ringmaster, with Dan, with Lizzy, and with the preacher. And with Mick.

Then Dan had a whisper talk with the ringmaster, with Lizzy, with the preacher, and with Mick.

Then Lizzy had a whisper chat with the ringmaster, with the preacher, with Dan, and with Mick.

Then — well, then, so on and so forth.

It came to pass we had a wedding in the Lucky Nickel Saloon. Dan Murphy got hitched to Miss Elizabeth Suzette Cockette, and she became Mrs. etc. The women folk, circus and townie, bearded and clean-shaven, skinny and not, and even the semi-woman, all had theirselves a good cry. The menfolk drank a lot but didn't get in too many fights. Nobody got killed.

Sam disappeared in the fuss after the wedding to catch his train before I could ask how he managed to keep everybody happy meeting their various and contradictory needs.

The circus bunch left in a flurry of singing, gunfire, and carousing the like of which Laramie hadn't seen since they hung Big Nose George. I discovered too late Dan Murphy had left with the circus along with his bride.

In fact, I found myself alone in the Lucky Nickel except for Mick who stood behind the bar, whistling an Irish ditty, as happy as a cowboy on Saturday night.

"What gives?" I asked.

He stopped whistling long enough to look at me like I'd just asked him how many boots he wore on each foot.

"I mean," I clarified, "how come Dan went along with getting hitched? I thought he was averse to the notion. What swung him, so to speak?"

"Couple things. First, I forgave him his bar tab."

"You *what?*"

"He brought enough business in today to make up for it."

"Huh. But I never figured Dan to be the kind who'd run away with a circus."

"You figured wrong. Seems as how Sam knew the circus had lost their strongman in a bar fight back in Winnemucca. Sam suggested the circus hire Dan as their strongman. This pleased the ringmaster as he got to keep Lizzy on — he was fearsome she'd leave, you know — and he got his strongman in Dan."

"Huh. So Dan wanted to run away and join the circus?"

"Truth."

"That answers for Dan and the ringmaster and the other circus types, right enough. But what of Lizzy? I mean, she told as how even if ''is mind 'e changes, I marry 'im no.' Or somesuch."

Mick took in a powerful big sigh and leaned on the bar, wonderment on his otherwise stoic countenance. "You ain't going to believe this," he warned.

"I've seen a mermaid in a barrel in the Lucky Nickel, a naked one. I've seen me Dan Murphy talking to a mermaid in a barrel with his head underwater in the Lucky Nickel. I've seen me a circus right here in the — "

"You ain't going to believe — "

" — I've seen a wedding betwixt a mermaid and Dan Murphy — "

"Ain't going to."

"Huh." I shrugged. "If you say so."

"Remember the problem to which that reporter fellow kept referring?"

"Yep. I never heard what it was though. Did I?"

"He told me afore he left."

"What?"

"Mermaids are kin to fish."

Mick let me chew on that a spell, no doubt enjoying the consternation which unfolded on my face.

"Lordy," I gasped, awed. If I'd been chewing at the time, I'd swallowed my plug for certain sure. "Say it ain't so."

"It's so. Lizzy talked Dan into giving up fishing."

"Huh," I declared, flabbergasted.

"Truth. He was that much in love." Mick's tone reflected his awe. He shook his head, went about his business, cleaning glassware, whistling and suchlike.

And when, a few days later, a cowboy entered the Lucky Nickel Saloon hauling a dragon on a leash, we threw both cowboy and dragon out into the street with nary a word.

Yessir, the world is a strange place, except for the Lucky Nickel, where nothing much ever happens. Which is a lucky thing, all in all, as us regulars like it tranquil.

THE GRIM REAPER
DROPS BY

It was still forenoon, and nobody else in the Lucky Nickel Saloon but us regulars, when the Grim Reaper pushed through the batwing doors.

Outside, the August sun beat down relentless on dusty Second Avenue, Laramie, Wyoming Territory, U. S. of A. Inside, it was cool and tranquil, which is how us regulars like it.

"What'll it be, stranger?" Mick the barkeep asked without looking up from his glass-buffing duties at the bar.

"Whiskey," a voice from the bottom of a grave demanded. "Bring the bottle." The batwing doors squeaked shut behind him as he entered and took a table.

At which point Mick looked up at the stranger, as did we all — me, Banky with gun-hand aquiver near his ever-ready Colt, and Casper with his one good eye. Charlie lay passed out, and Jack Thatcher hadn't arrived yet.

"Lordy be," Mick muttered and crossed himself, a good Irishman. "It's the Banshee."

"Well, what tribe is that, Tom?" Casper inquired of me. His good eye watered from the jalapenos he'd been munching and he couldn't focus worth diddly, which makes it hard to tell the Angel of Death from an Indian.

"Ain't no tribe, Casper," I informed him. "It's trouble for certain sure."

Casper blinked, focused, and exclaimed, "Well, I'll be left for dead." He wiped his sweaty forehead with a trembly hand.

"Reckon I ought to persuade him to skedaddle?" Banky offered, as he crouched in his ready-to-shoot stance.

Mick considered, sucking on his teeth and tugging at his prodigious black mustache. "Don't guess you ought, Banky."

"Whyfor not?"

"The feller ain't totin' iron, for one."

Gunless. Indeed the feller looked like a Spanish monk, all decked out in a dirt-brown robe from head to foot. The robe hood was so big a guy couldn't see the face hidden deep within, which was maybe a good thing, as what we could see of his parts like to make your skin crawl right off your body. Which may have been what had happened to our guest. The hands protruding from the huge robe sleeves were naught but skeletal appendages.

Bones, just bones. Skinless, like his feet, sticking out from under the tattered, dusty robe fringe. Yet the hands twitched with such animation as one sees in a guy impatiently waiting for a barkeep to fetch up his drink. As we discovered was the case in this instance.

"I believe I just ordered a whiskey," the voice, like a cold wind at midnight, recalled.

"'Sides," Mick went on, "gunplay this early might retard the day's commerce a touch."

I figured gunfire might lure in a few customers, curious ones, who otherwise might not be thirsty, but it was Mick's bar so I didn't say squat.

"I believe I just ordered — "

"'Sides, we ain't made the feller's acquaintance yet."

" — a whiskey, bring the bottle." He tossed a dollar on the table.

"'Sides, he paid in advance." Mick brought a glass and a bottle and scooped up the dollar, which he examined as he returned to the bar.

"Well, 'scuse me." Casper sidling up to the stranger. "You look like, uh, that is, uh — "

"Who's going to get killed?" Banky interjected.

A skeletal hand grabbed the bottle and splashed a shot into the glass. The other bony hand brought the glass into the dismal, dark cave of the stranger's hood and the hood tipped back a tad. We heard gulping noises emerge from within. Soon the glass emerged, empty, slapped on the table with a wet smack, and the feller intoned, "I am the Grim Reaper and I have come."

"We got that part figured out, Mister Reaper, sir," I agreed, "but what we ain't got figured is whyfor."

"I am the Grim Reaper and I have come," again came the sepulchral retort, a touch whiny.

Just then Charlie woke up.

He struggled to the semblance of an upright stance, shaky as a snake with a crutch, and tried to focus on the Reaper.

"Land O' Goshen," Charlie uttered when he saw. Then he eyed the near empty gin bottle he held and raised his arm as if to cast it away. Instead, he shrugged and gulped the gin. "Mick, how about one on the house," he said tearfully, "on account of it's a going-away present?"

Mick didn't have time to ponder his friend's request for Charlie passed out again.

Banky drew lightning quick and aimed his Colt Grim Reaperwards. "Charlie's my friend, you no-good, dirty, rotten, dadgum, low-down, yellow-bellied snake in the grass — "

The Angel of Death waved a dismissive bony gesture as if to say it wasn't Charlie for whom he'd come. "I am the Grim Reaper and — "

"We got all that part," I repeated. "What we want to know is whyfor have you come."

"Yeah," Banky demanded, squinting down his sights. "Who you come to reap?"

The Grim Reaper held up a bony finger as if to say "Hold yer horses," removed a notebook from his robe and flipped it open. "I've come for — "

Just then Jack Thatcher hobbled in through the batwing doors. He stood and wiped his sweaty face with a bandanna and put it back in his pocket. Then he saw. He took one look, eyes bugged out. He pointed with his cane and insisted, "Why you, you — you're — "

"I'm the Grim Reaper and I've — "

Jack Thatcher screamed and lit out, leg, stump, and cane flying every whichaway.

"Now you've gone and done it," Mick growled. "Jack Thatcher's a regular and a friend. Pays his bills, usually, and today's payday and now you've chased him off."

Knobby shoulders shrugged inside the Reaper's robes. He inserted another shot into his hood cave and, I reckon, took a drink. Leastwise the glass emerged empty.

"Well, what ought we to do?" Casper wondered.

"I figure I know what." Banky fired six rounds from his Colt at the ghoulish figure so fast it sounded like Spanish castanets. We expected we'd be engaged in grisly mop duty, but no. The wall behind the Grim Reaper was newly holed and splintered, but Banky's target remained unshot.

"Huh," Banky remarked as he blew smoke from the Colt barrel and reloaded. He'd been but four paces away when he let fly. "Do you reckon I stood too close?"

Mick gestured to us for a huddle. We grouped at the bar, beyond the Grim Reaper's earshot — if he had ears.

"What ought we to do?" Mick asked.

"I figure gunplay ought to bring in the day's business," I offered, "but that," I nodded at our visitor, "would spoil their thirst for certain sure."

"Reckon you're right," Mick agreed. "We got to do something, or I'm bankrupt."

"Well, what?" Casper demanded.

"You don't figure I can earn my daily bread off you regulars, do you?"

Mick continued. "I mean, you pay your tabs on time, most often, but it ain't your trade I depend on. I require the occasional passing through cowboy or townie or stranger for my income."

"Why don't we just ask him to leave?" I suggested.

Casper, Banky, and Mick shrugged.

Mick sauntered over to the Grim Reaper's table. "Beggin' yer pardon, Mister Grim Reaper, sir." He cleared his throat. "Me and the boys was wondering, that is, I run a tranquil place here and it might not be as exciting as you're used to. Anyway, uh, we was wondering if you mightn't choose a more raucous saloon in which to wait for your, uh, charge. Or whatever you call 'em when you come for 'em."

"Client," the Grim Reaper intoned. "I provide a service."

"Yes, well, that's nice," Mick agreed. "But we was wondering — "

The Grim Reaper held up a bony finger to interrupt. He removed his notebook again, flipped a few pages, and read to himself, I reckon, moving a fingerbone along the page. At last he flipped the book closed and repocketed it. "Nope," he insisted, graveyard-voiced. "This here's the place."

Just then Jack Thatcher hobbled back in with Preacher Avery Morgan in tow. I knew of Morgan, though I'd never had the chance to break bread nor get drunk with him. Still I heard he was both a devout man of God and not a temperance fool, bless him.

"Welcome, uh, Brother Morgan." Mick spat on his hand and offered it to shake. Brother Morgan extended his hand. Then he saw the reason for his presence.

"Is that," he pointed, "is that, is that — "

"Reckon so," Banky confirmed.

The preacher took a breath and declared his intentions. "Brother Thatcher brought me forth to exorcise the demon. And even though this ain't exactly the House o' God, I 'spect y'all're decent God-fearing gents, leastwise when you ain't too liquored up. Tenny rate, it don't bode well for decent folk to have such as him in our midst."

We all agreed, and Mick offered the preacher a drink to steel him to the disagreeable but necessary task ahead. The preacher nodded gratitude and proceeded to fill up his courage.

It soon became remarkable how much courage it took to fortify him. "Wrestling with Satan's minions is thirsty work," he informed us, "and requires a great deal o' fortification."

He added, "'Sides, it's hot outside."

I could see Mick calculate his on-the-house preacher fortification costs versus the lost trade the preacher's exorcism would restore, and how long it'd take before one canceled the other's benefit. His mustache danced on his upper lip like a cat in a hot skillet. Then his eyebrows climbed back up his forehead far enough to merge with his receding hair, he went all goggle-eyed, and exclaimed in horror.

"Well, what?" Casper inquired solicitously.

"Bankruptcy," Mick managed to gasp. "Dire and imminent."

"Exactly what," I posed, "does that mean to us regulars?"

"Closing the Lucky Nickel," Mick gasped. He looked pale.

As did we all.

"Reckon you best get to exorcisin'," Banky prompted the preacher at gunpoint. I didn't figure Banky would really ventilate him, but you never knew. The situation was dire.

So we had ourselves an exorcism in the Lucky Nickel. The preacher chanted in Latin, I guess, and danced around as if his boots were on fire. He chucked holy water, I guess, Grim Reaperwards, and waved his arms around as if conducting the Mormon Tabernacle Choir or swatting away flies.

Nothing.

The preacher stood afore the Reaper, panting, sweating, defeated. "How come you ain't been vanquished?" he asked.

The Grim Reaper shrugged. Then he crooked a finger at the preacher in a come-here gesture. The preacher looked around at us. He met nary an eye as we all found other places to look — I discovered I needed to clean my fingernails — so he recast his weary glance at the patient, robed skeleton at the table.

Reluctantly, he stepped forward and bent an ear to the cave of the Reaper's hood. We heard the buzz of his graveyard voice whisper to the preacher but strain as we did — Jack Thatcher lost his balance from leaning over and fell down — we couldn't make out a word.

Presently, the preacher stood, gasped like a caught trout, and muttered, "Boys, I'm moving to Boise." He marched to the door. "Right now."

Heading out the batwing doors, he bumped into a dude walking in. The dude dressed in a mostly white suit with a white vest, black string tie, and mostly clean boots. Just in off the westbound train, he announced himself as Sam Something, a newspaper reporter on his way to San Fran.

"I heard about the commotion," he declared around a smelly five-cent cigar and a thatchy white mustache. "I got time to kill during the dinner stop, so I figured I'd drop by and have a looksee. Hot, ain't it?" He wiped his brow with a kerchief from his hind pocket.

Mick set up the stranger with a whiskey and told him about the other feller across the room, including the part about how he expected bankruptcy if the Grim Reaper stayed too long.

Sam moseyed over to the table, drink in hand. He bent at the waist and gazed up into the deep pit of the Reaper's hood. He ahemed. "Pardon me, Mister Reaper, good sir. I'm a reporter and I'd like to interview you. Would you be averse — "

"I'll have another bottle of whiskey," the Grim Reaper said to Mick. He tossed a dollar across the room, and Mick caught it with an overhand grab.

Mick shrugged and brought another bottle.

Sam Something, passing-through reporter, snorted. "I never thought I'd see the day." He walked away from the Reaper and back to the bar. "Everybody wants to be in the paper."

As we discussed our dilemma, a number of folk dropped by. They'd caught wind of our predicament, as had Sam, and had stopped by to see for themselves. A few gawkers tried to see who or what resided inside the deep cowl. None saw.

Mick bravely fought back tears as he explained the Grim Reaper'd drive away customers and he'd be forced to close. Many a toast got lifted in salute to the soon-to-be shut Lucky Nickel, and many a sad tear spilled on the saloon floor.

And, as it was a hot day, yet more people came in, took a gander at the Grim Reaper, and ordered a drink and commiserated with Mick's dire straits.

"I got it," Sam hollered, finger upthrust for emphasis.

"Well, what?" Casper prompted.

The crowd fell silent. "I've traveled thither and yon — worldwide, that is, and I've learnt the ways of many a heathen race. The Hindoo of Hindoostan, the pashas of Pakistan, the Turks and bearded shamans of the vast steppes of Asia — "

"What's yer point," Banky urged.

Sam eyed the Grim Reaper across the room. The crowd had given him a wide space around the table at which he sat, alone, nursing his second whiskey bottle.

Sam whispered and those assembled leaned in to hear. "Voodoo," is what he said, and commenced to explain a ritual he said he'd learned in the steamy jungles of Siam.

In a moment, the rapt listeners, who had formed a circle four or five bodies deep around Sam, parted to allow the reporter to pass. Sam walked up to the Grim Reaper and the crowd moved across the room, re-forming around the two.

Sam commenced to gibber and holler and dance up and down as if he had a frog in his drawers. The Grim Reaper sat and sipped his drink, I suppose, in silence.

Grim silence.

At last, sweaty and panting, Sam gave up. "Dunno whyfor it don't work." He shrugged, and somebody brought him a drink.

It had gotten on to late afternoon, hotter than a two-dollar whore. Sam had become so entranced in the local situation he decided to linger until the next train came through. More folk drifted in off Second Ave to see what's up.

Mick set 'em up as fast as they ordered, sniffling and forcing a smile as he told his customers about his pending unemployment. The floor got down-right slippery wet with tears.

The Grim Reaper finished his third whiskey bottle as the sun set. It was standing room only in the Lucky Nickel. Somebody had dusted off the old piano in the corner and attempted to play tunes on it, somebody else fell off a table on which they'd been dancing and broke an arm (Doc Tom was present and semi-sober), the entire Ladies' Temperance Union stopped by, singing hymns to celebrate the saloon's pending closure, and Charlie regained consciousness.

When Banky decided to do some target practice, shooting cockroaches on the wall, the Grim Reaper stood.

He hadn't stood since he'd sat down that morn and ordered his first bottle. Not even to pee. And when he did stand, the saloon, its walls vibrating with the hoot and holler of four score conversations, got real quiet.

The Grim Reaper looked around at the patrons. The grim patrons looked back. Silence continued.

At last, the Reaper sighed, wind through a fresh grave, and sauntered to the bar, the crowd parting as he passed.

"Barkeep," he announced, "I'll be moving on." He walked to the batwing doors, where he stopped and looked back.

"Whyever for?" Mick wondered, brave smile wavering a tad.

"Well," Casper upped, "ain't you going to, uh, you know — "

"Ain't you going to reap nobody?" Banky finished the question. "Ain't that what you come for?"

"I am the Grim Reaper and I have come," he raised a fingerbone for emphasis, "*for a vacation.*"

He sighed and shook his big hood. "Noisy and rowdy I can get any day on the job what with wars and shoot-outs and baseball and Congress and such like. I came here because I heard talk — even in Hell, I heard talk — about how tranquil the Lucky Nickel Saloon, Second Avenue, Laramie, Wyoming Territory, U. S. of A., was."

He pushed open the batwing doors. "Barkeep, yer reputation is much overblown. You are not as advertised."

He left.

Presently, the crowd thinned out. Mick lit a few lamps and bid a few customers good night, those sober enough to bid him good night in return. The last unconscious patron got hauled out before dinnertime.

Sam Something went off to find a hotel room, muttering that his voodoo must have worked, but with a delayed reaction.

Soon, nobody remained but us regulars.

"Well," Casper winked at Mick, "I reckon you'll be glad to see that reaper guy," he tilted his head at the door, "*gone.*"

Mick buffed glasses behind the bar, frowning.

"Yeah," Banky added. "And nobody got killed today."

Mick sighed, buffed.

"And being shut of him," I concluded, "you won't have to close up."

Mick nodded, buffed. His lower lip trembled.

"I shudder to think," Jack Thatcher shuddered, "of the Lucky Nickel closed on account of him."

Mick sniffled and wiped his nose.

"Imagine," Charlie imagined, "that feller chasing away all your customers. Maybe even us regulars. Imagine — "

Mick bust out crying. Great gobs of tears rolled down his round, red cheeks into his beard and his big shoulders shook with sobs as he buffed the glasses.

The tranquil ambiance for which the Lucky Nickel, Second Avenue, Laramie, Wyoming Territory, U. S. of A., had come to be known throughout the West and in Hell itself, had been restored when the Grim Reaper left. I figured Mick would be happy to have his reputation back unsullied.

But no. Mick's weeping and wailing went on until us regulars tired of it and left to get some peace and quiet. And when we did, Mick just cried even louder.

Darned if I can figure out whyfor.

A SPIDER POOR COWBOY RAPT AND WIDE LEMON

Not until the stranger hunching over the bar reached for his whisky and his hand passed through the glass did I figure out why he seemed so peculiar. He wasn't there.

"Now, ain't that amazing?" said I to nobody in particular.

At least, he looked mighty insubstantial. I could see the batwing doors of the Lucky Nickel Saloon through his scarecrow-thin torso, the hitching post beyond, and Laramie's muddy Second Avenue beyond that. He looked to be no more than a suggestion of a man, something somebody thought up and then decided "nevermind" halfway through.

"Do you not see what I don't see?" said Casper, whose one good eye watered. He took out his glass eyeball, buffed it on his sleeve, and put it back in and blinked. It didn't help.

"Reckon I don't." Banky flicked his vest away from the handle of his ever-ready Colt, in case whatever strangeness was going on required gunplay. Mick the barkeep's lip twitched causing his formidable black mustache to tickle his nose and make him sneeze, but otherwise he remained his stony-faced self. Charlie lay passed out under a table by the piano, and Jack Thatcher hadn't arrived yet.

Nobody else in the bar — it was still early — except us regulars, and the stranger who wasn't all there.

"Well," Casper intoned, "I guess now I've seen everything. Or not, if you take my meaning."

"Reckon I do," Banky responded. He bent at the waist, examining the so-far silent stranger's feet. They did not touch the floor. At first glance, the toes of the ethereal appendages seemed to be anchored under the brass bar rail as if to keep their owner from floating away, off to Heaven or wherever. But no. Banky pointed out the toes didn't touch the bar rail underside — the stranger floated twixt floor and rail.

The stranger made another attempt to grab the whisky glass. His hand passed through, and he sighed. It sounded like a cold wind in a graveyard.

"Beggin' your pardon, guv'nor." Mick cleared his throat. "I notice yer having a bit o' trouble graspin' yer drink."

The stranger looked at Mick with sad, see-through eyes and nodded his see-through head.

"You'll pardon me, sir," Mick continued, "if I remark that you seem a tad, uh, insubstantial, so to speak."

The stranger nodded again. His sigh was so cold I buttoned the top button of my coat.

"And," Mick continued in his methodical Irish way, "if I offered you a hand and, like, poured the drink down yer throat, it'd probably go right through you like Texas chili and splash on the floor undrunk. Am I right so far?"

The stranger nodded again. I could see a tear in one eye.

"And how did you intend to pay for your drink?" Mick got to the point. "I mean, if substantial things like drink go right through you, and you can't take hold of a whisky glass, I'll wager coin'd drop right through yer pockets."

The stranger looked puzzled for a moment. He pulled his pockets inside out, and as Mick predicted, they were empty.

It's downright embarrassing to see a grown man cry, whether he's all there or not.

Mick offered the stranger a bar towel to wipe his eyes, holding it out so the stranger could drip onto it. Banky turned away and busied himself refilling his lip with chaw so as not to see the stranger's wimpy display of emotion. Casper polished his eye again, I got a coughing fit, Charlie remained passed out, and Jack Thatcher hadn't arrived yet.

In due time (I reckon t'was in due time — I'm not conversant as to what constitutes "due time" for ghosts) the stranger quit snuffling. Mick tossed the soggy towel aside and reached to pick up the stranger's whisky glass.

Banky, ever quick on the draw, intercepted same, downing the contents in a gulp. "Waste not, want not," he pontificated, wiping his lips with the back of his non-gun hand. He tossed a nickel on the bar.

"I'm sorry, bartender." The stranger spoke at last. He sounded hollow-like, as if he spoke from the bottom of a well, and mighty contrite to boot. "I've never been dead before and I, I — I'm sorry."

Mick's formidable shoulders lifted an inch, his taciturn way of accepting the apology.

"Well, stranger," Casper piped up, "how'd you happen to, uh, you know — "

The stranger peered at Casper with watery eyes and frowned, puzzled. Casper shuffled, head-bobbing, tongue-tied.

"Yeah," Banky intervened, "how'd you get kilt?"

The stranger uttered another graveyard sigh, parted his vest, and displayed the .45-caliber sized hole in his shirt, beyond which his heart no longer beat. Through the hole, I could see Charlie waking up.

"My name's Butch Parker," the stranger began, "late of Medicine Bow." His tale unfolded and we learned thus:

Butch foremanned at the Lazy Bar-K cattle ranch between Rock Springs and Reliance. He was on his way home after selling a herd back in Kansas City. But when he got off the train to stretch his legs in Laramie during a dinner stop the night afore, somebody jumped him to take his poke. He protested the robbery and his assailants did him in with one shot.

"I come to and stood over myself, realizing I'd been kilt. Saddened me good and proper." He nodded toward the now empty glass. "I needed that drink."

"So you chose to get drunk at the Lucky Nickel," I remarked. "Heard about us down the line, did you?"

"No. You was just closest."

"Well, tarnation," Casper gasped, good eye twitching. He ran out the back door into the alley behind the Lucky Nickel. In a second, he ran back in. He walked up to the stranger and looked him right in the eye, blinking. "That's you out there, all right. Well, you — you're dead."

"Reckon I know that," the stranger — Butch — confirmed.

"I thought I heard a shot this morning," Mick recalled, "just as I opened up."

Banky crouched, flint-eyed, gun hand ready. "Why those no good yellow-bellied, low-down, dirty, rotten sons of — "

"What do we do now?" I wondered.

"We're a tad late, helpwise," Mick observed.

Silence ensued.

At last, Butch piped up: "Mind if I stick around and, you know, sort of haunt your place?"

Mick's jaw dropped open, and he stammered something that sounded like he was strangling on a lump of Miss Emma Quill's Boarding House's almost-mashed potatoes. Casper's glass eye almost popped out, and Banky almost dropped his gun.

Charlie, who'd just resumed consciousness, appeared over my shoulder and peered bleary-eyed at Butch. He focused at last, and pointed. "Tom, it's a gho-gho — "

"A ghost," I finished. "His name is — "

But Charlie didn't stay for introductions. He ran, suspenders flapping, still clutching his empty gin bottle, into the street, screaming like he'd been scalped.

"Now, you understand, Butch," Mick explained, "why I'd druthern't have my saloon haunted. Charlie's my friend, and he pays his tab, now and then. I reckon he'll go drink someplace else now, where there ain't no ghosts."

"I'm sorry," Butch squeaked. He sighed, as broken-hearted as a mamaless calf. "But I got no place else to go."

Just then, Jack Thatcher arrived. "Say," he said, as he hobbled in, "I just saw Charlie running — " Then, eyes bugged out, he pointed at the ghost with his cane and commenced to jabber and drool. "A gho — gho — " and so on, before he took flight — foot, stump, and cane flying every whichaway, like a hog skittering on ice — for a more agreeable locale.

"And Jack Thatcher," Mick said, pointing, voice raised, "he's been steady custom since '78. That's two of my regulars — "

"I said I'm sorry," Butch insisted, "but I got no other place to go."

"You mean to say," Mick inquired, "you're going to stay here whether I like it or not?"

"Ghosts are supposed to haunt places, ain't they?"

"Well, yeah, but — "

"I told you, I got no other place — "

"Land O' Goshen." Mick threw up his hands. "I'm arguing with a dead man."

"Well, maybe we should go get the sheriff." Casper blinked. "And the coroner. We got us a dead body in the alley needs burying."

"Right," Banky said, quick as ever, striding to the door, "maybe if we bury Butch here, his spirit will go away." He gave the ghost a dirty look as he departed.

"I'm sorry — " Butch began.

"Oh, shut up," Mick finished. Mick sauntered over to the end of the bar, summoning me and Casper with a twitch of his burly head. We huddled out of Butch's earshot.

"Boys," Mick whispered, "I reckon I'm in a fix and no mistake. If this ghost insists on staying, I won't get no paying customers. I mean, you guys pay your tabs come payday, usually, and all, but — "

"Well, I guess I know what you mean, Mick, old friend." Casper frowned. "Ain't nobody but us regulars in all Wyoming Territory, I reckon, would stay put in a saloon frequented by a ghost. I mean, us regulars, we know you. We wouldn't take our custom elsewhere, come hell or high water. But other folks — "

"You're in a heap of trouble, Mick." I shook my head. My payday wasn't due for two weeks yet, and I already owed Casper two dollars. No, the Lucky Nickel didn't earn its keep, meager as it was, from us regulars — me and Casper, Charlie, Banky, and Jack Thatcher. It depended on the custom of passing-through cowboys and miners, the odd townie, and business folk that traveled by train or hung around the station a block and a half west of the saloon. They sure as shooting wouldn't cotton to a ghost at their elbow, weeping in its beer.

And it wasn't as if Mick didn't like ghosts. His liberal reputation earned praise from San Francisco to Chicago. He served Indians, Chinamen, and the occasional Mormon just like he would any whiteman, watering down their liquor not much at all.

"Well, we can't throw him out," Casper pondered. "He's too insubstantial to grab a holt of."

"We sure can't scare him off," I added. "He's the ghost."

"Maybe burying him'll do the trick," Mick muttered. We all went about our business, Mick figuring his losses, Casper polishing his eye, me drinking the day by. And Butch, weeping ghostly at the bar.

We passed the hat and coughed up fifty cents each for a nice pine box to put Butch's body in. We got Preacher Avery Morgan drunk enough to officiate at the burying in the pauper's field on the other side of the tracks, but burying Butch Parker didn't answer.

Butch attended his own funeral and cried and carried on such that the preacher ran off scared — we hadn't gotten him drunk enough. Me, Mick, and Casper finished the praying as best we could, being inexperienced in the practice.

Then we did the shoveling.

And Butch, right after the burying, went on back to the Lucky Nickel, took his place at the bar, staring sadly at the empty shot glass Mick put before him as sort of a monument to mark his spot — as if somebody would want to take that stool — and resumed his graveyard moaning and weeping.

Banky glowered at him. "I thought burying you would make you go away."

Butch shrugged and wept.

Come the third day of practically no business in the Lucky Nickel, except us regulars — free drinks persuaded Charlie and Jack Thatcher to resume their custom — when a dude walked in.

Sam Something, the fellow introduced himself, a newspaper reporter on his way to San Francisco, whiling the dinner stop away soaking up local color.

"I heard about your ghost away back in Saint Jo," he said, puffing on the five-cent cigar clenched between his teeth. He anchored thumbs in a white vest and bobbed his white eyebrows.

"What of it?" Mick snarled. His usual placid demeanor had begun to crack under the pressure of his pending poverty.

"I'd like to interview the fellow," the reporter said.

Butch almost stopped crying for a moment as he overheard.

Mick shrugged. "Suit yourself."

And Sam Something did. He sauntered over and took the stool next to Butch and commenced to interview the spook. We couldn't hear what they said as Sam spoke low and Butch replied in kind. Now and then, the two would turn to look at us most peculiar-like, as if examining a herd of two-headed lambs. Now and then, Butch would take to weeping and moaning plenty loud, and Sam would try to pat him on the back only to jerk away amazed as his hand passed through the skinny ghost's back. Then Sam'd shake his head in wonder and continue talking to Butch, taking notes in a little notebook.

Soon, the reporter stood. He extended his hand as if to shake with the ghost, momentarily forgetting Butch's insubstantiality. Butch broke down in another boo-hooing fit, Sam shook his head and came back to sit with us live types on the other side of the room — we gave Butch a wide birth, leaving him alone in his misery.

"Boys," Sam said, "that's the saddest ghost I ever seen." He tugged at his shaggy, white mustache and relit his cigar.

"Well, how many sad ghosts have you seen?" Casper asked.

Sam ignored Casper. "And I know what to do about it."

"You do?" Mick all but sat in Sam's lap, so evident was his interest. We all paid attention as the reporter explained.

"Turns out Mr. Parker ain't Christian, y'see. No sir. He's Hindoo."

"Well, he don't look Hindooish," Casper observed.

"And he requires a proper Hindoo burial to lay his soul to rest. I've seen the ritual in my extensive foreign travels and I believe I know how to do the honors."

It took some doing to get Butch Parker's body dug up so we could rebury it proper and Hindoolike. It wasn't because anybody cared one way or the other (he was, after all, in the pauper's graveyard). In fact, Preacher

Morgan was glad to pitch in once we got him good and drunk, to which condition he was not averse when we told him what we had in mind.

We couldn't find the body.

It had rained like a cow pissing on a flat rock the night Sam told us what needed doing and he agreed to stay a few days to help us in the doing thereof. The rain had washed away the grave markers and fresh dirt, and we couldn't figure under which mud hole slept Butch's body, whose ghost took the dismal development as tearfully as we'd come to expect.

After we dug up and re-buried three suspects (us regulars dug and Sam supervised on account of he had a bad back) we finally come across the right cadaver.

Then we performed us a genuine Hindoo burial ceremony.

Except for Sam who complained of a skin condition, we all had to wear dresses for the ceremony. Kilts, Sam called them, and he said the burying priests in Hindoostan all wore them. We got some help from Miss Dolly, who ran Miss Dolly's Boarding House for Ladies a block down Second Ave, and the ladies of the entertainment trade who resided there.

The required sandals were make-do, throw-away hide clumps from Joe Meecham's Tannery tied on with twine. We wondered how the Hindoos managed to ride a horse wearing dresses and sandals, but we didn't say diddly. If it meant getting shut of our haunt, we'd go along.

But it was a trial and no mistake.

I'd worn facepaint once when I got drunk at a Shoshone hunting camp, but I don't recall ever being drunk enough to wear flowers in my hair.

I figure the dance step Sam taught us might come in handy some day when I had to scare the hell out of a griz bear, but I was too stewed to remember all the words to the song he taught.

Just bits and pieces:

"As I wig doubt inner stretch of tomatoes,
A sigh weak down in tomato and hay,
A spider poor cowboy rapt and wide lemon,
A ripped and wide leanin' ass goldish decay."

Or somesuch.

All us regulars took part as substitute Hindoo priests, as Sam insisted was needed to properly lay Butch to rest.

The ceremony, held on a hill within rock-throwing distance of the Lucky Nickel, began at high noon of a Saturday, and attracted quite a crowd. We were so intent on doing the ceremony right we paid no nevermind to the snickers and guffaws from the gawkers.

And right as the last shovelful of dirt fell on the Hindoo grave of the late Mr. Butch Parker, his shade vanished in a silent puff of not-there-anymore-ness.

Which event Mick greeted with a nod, Banky touched off a few rounds in the air, Casper whooped and his glass eye popped, Charlie regained consciousness, and Jack Thatcher took off his wooden leg and did a one-legged backward somersault.

We all got out of our Hindoo costumes and got into our regular duds and went to the Lucky Nickel to get drunk. Mick did a brisk business, what with all the gawkers and on-lookers who'd tagged along to help celebrate.

At the bar, I sidled up to Sam Something. "You know, I felt right silly wearing that stuff you said we had to wear."

"Do tell."

"And that dancing and carrying on you said was required."

"Indeed."

"And the warpaint and suchlike."

"What about 'em?"

"Tell me true," I leaned in, whispering so nobody else could hear, "did we really have to do all that stuff to get rid of Butch's ghost?"

Sam's thatchy white eyebrows rose into his thatchy white hair and he uttered a snort that, at first, I took for derision. "Whisky for this man," he called to Mick, "as much as he'll take afore passing out."

"Mighty kind of you, Sam, uh — "

"You are a right smart gent, I declare." Sam patted me on the back. "The reward is justified. As is the truth for which you've asked. And here 'tis.

"Your ghost weren't Hindoo atall. I made up all that."

I had "You what?" in my throat ready to come out when I realized maybe I didn't want anybody else to hear what Sam had to say. So I just nodded for him to go on, as he did, thankfully not too loud.

"I made it up because of the way you yahoos in this here saloon treated the man, not letting him haunt your joint like he asked. After all, the poor cowboy had no place other to go.

"And I knew him, or knew *of* him. Feller name of Ben Killpecker owns the Lazy-Bar-K where Butch foremanned. I know ol' Ben from way back. Figured I could do a favor for the deceased cowpoke and my ol' buddy in one swell foop and give you n'er-do-wells a lick or two while I'm about it.

"Now, ain't you chagrined?" Sam smiled in triumph.

And chagrined I was. The joke was on us.

"But it worked," I pointed out. "Butch's ghost got."

"I told him it'd work, and he believed me, so it worked. I told you I'd traveled some. T'were no lie. The foolishness folks'll believe and how powerful such belief can be — ain't it amazing?"

"Still, Mick's regained his lost custom," I mused as much to myself as to Sam.

He dismissed this with a backhanded gesture and a puff of cigar smoke. "Look around at who's laughing at who."

I looked around. The bar was crowded and Mick was earning his keep to be sure, but folks pointed and laughed at him and us regulars when they thought we weren't looking. Banky was getting suspicious that something was amiss as he'd unbuttoned his vest and his gun hand twitched spastic, but he couldn't find anybody to shoot at as the laughers got mighty cautious in their merriment when it came to Banky.

"I dunno," I said, pondering the situation.

"Well, don't let it get in your craw," Sam said. "These folks'll move on after they've had their laugh. This joint won't be open a week from Sunday." He took out a pocket watch, eyed it, grunted, clicked it shut, and repocketed it. "Train leaves in a few minutes, so I'll bid you good day."

He stood to leave. "Oh, one more thing."

"I'm not sure I want to hear — "

"His assailants didn't get Butch's whole poke. He'd stashed a good portion of it before and told me where at. I dug it up and I got it in my bag now. The money is my reward for helping him get revenge on you boys."

With that, Sam Something, newspaper reporter, strode off, laughing.

And I got me an idea of how to salvage something from what might otherwise be the Lucky Nickel's last few days.

Rumor spread quick around Laramie, and in time throughout Wyoming Territory, that Butch Parker's murderers hadn't got his whole poke. Rumor says he'd stashed a good portion of it before and told us regulars at the Lucky Nickel, in gratitude for our hospitality (for where else would a ghost find such hospitality but at the Lucky Nickel?) where it was at. Rumor says, if you drop by and buy one or more of the regulars a drink or two, or three, you might get somebody to loosen their tongue enough to tell you where the treasure is stowed. You might could even buy yourself a map. Or two.

Now, ain't that amazing?

THE VAMPIRE WHO
DOTED ON HIS CHICKEN

A feller parted the batwing doors of the Lucky Nickel Saloon, letting in a bucketful of snow and a cold gust off Second Ave, Laramie, Wyoming Territory, U. S. of A., holding a chicken in his hand, and he looked bewildered. The feller, I mean, looked bewildered. The chicken looked dead.

The feller looked preacher-like, clean-shaven, and gussied up in a black frock coat, boiled shirt, and string tie. Hatless. He wasn't a preacher, though. He held a chicken in hand instead of the Good Book.

The chicken, your regular white bantam, hung upside down, feet grasped in the feller's bony fist. A white feather drifted floorward.

The feller, tall and rail-fence skinny, all knees and elbows, blinked somber-faced in the dim light — the saloon was bereft of windows — as if he wasn't sure where he was at.

'Twas a tranquil though cold winter day. Me and Banky and Casper sat at table playing poker, matchstick stakes as we were broke as usual. We sat close to the potbellied stove so we could shove sticks in as needed because 'twas colder than a banker's smile. Blizzard been going on three, four days. We'd caulked the wall gaps as best we could with gum and chaw and spit. Helped keep the heat in, but it kept the smell in too. You don't want to know.

Still, 'twas tranquil enough.

The guy wasn't armed, so Banky made no move for his Colt. Casper didn't bother to look up out of his good eye, so I figured he was trying to fill him an inside straight. I held me two aces so I didn't look much neither.

Mick, our taciturn and Irish barkeep, stood behind the bar buffing a shotglass with a snotrag. Charlie lay asleep under the piano, and Jack Thatcher hadn't arrived yet. I expected he might not arrive at all, as the storm was hefty.

Nobody else was present as 'twas a Tuesday noon, a week and a half till payday, and this blizzard afield, as told.

Mick upped "Help you?" just as Sam Something pushed through the doors, puffing like a locomotive making a seven-degree grade. Sam was a back-east dude reporter who stopped by from time to time to wet his whistle between trains and whose family name I never cottoned proper. He wasn't a pest, much, nor a damnfool. He played lousy but enthusiastic poker and paid in cash, so we let him be a semi-regular.

"*There* you are," Sam declared. He patted the feller on his bony shoulder and snowflakes fluttered to the sawdust floor. "See you found it." He waved a hand at us as if we was medicine show displays. "Yessir, these here are the regulars of the Lucky Nickel — "

"Is that a cooking bantam?" Casper took out his glass eye, puffed a garlicky breath on it, and buffed it on his sleeve.

"Well, sir," Sam responded, wiping snow off his white mustache, "you see — "

"We-all ain't had dinner in a day or so," Banky informed. "On account of the storm and all. Supplies are scarce."

"Well, sir — "

"We'd be pleased to help you cook up your hen," I offered.

"Well, sir." Sam looked at the guy. "Ain't for me to say."

"How's about it, partner?" I quizzed.

The guy looked puzzled, and Sam spoke in Persian or Polish or Pakistany, dunno which, but it wasn't American nor even Mexican. The guy responded likewise, and Sam reported: "He says, sure, you can eat the chicken, but he gets to guzzle down his share first."

"Huh?" we all inquired.

"Just fetch up a skillet," Sam retorted. "This won't take but a second."

Sam and the feller and the chicken sat at a table, also close by the potbellied stove, and the guy wrung the chicken's neck. We all stood around watching. Sam and his friend both smelled pepperminty, freshly shaved, I reckoned. The chicken smelled like a chicken.

Then the feller did something I never seen in all my days, and I've had me a few days, and seen me a few things, sober and not. He cut the chicken's neck with his jackknife and held the cut to his lips and sucked the blood outten the chicken. Slurp, slurp, slurp. Eyes closed, he looked as content as a newborn calf at titty. Sucked on that bantam, slurpslurpslurp.

Casper's eyeball popped out and he caught it afore it went clattery across the sawdust floor, Banky drew reflexively, Mick grunted in bewonderment, and I was impressed too. Charlie slept, and Jack Thatcher hadn't arrived yet, so I don't know how they took it.

At last, "Ah!" the fellow sighed, and set the bloodless chicken down. He muffled a satisfied burp with a pale fist, set back, and smiled like he'd just et a home-cooked Thanksgiving dinner and got the wishbone. Real tranquil.

You can disbelieve this next part if you want, since Sam was as apt to make stuff up for entertainment purposes as the next feller, but we listened to his story, as 'twas polite to do so, and we didn't guffaw a bit.

Here's what Sam told: the feller, whose name we finally took to be "Count Wreckala," was a foreign royal feller, and what Sam called a "vampire." Thought he'd said "umpire" at first and that got us off on a tangent, but we got back in the saddle pronto. Seems as the Count dotes on blood, his favorite food, and he can't stomach meat nor potatoes, poor guy.

Worse, Sam related: Count Wreckala dotes on folk's blood.

"You mean — people?" Casper asked.

Sam nodded, and the Count looked embarrassed. He didn't speak American, but I reckon he understood well enough.

"But he sucked up this bantam," I pointed out.

"Reformed," Sam informed. Seems as how the Count aimed to reform of sucking folks' blood on account of his neighbors took exception to the practice and threatened a necktie party — this was back in Hungary or Roomany or one of them European places — so he skipped town, resolved to mend his ways afore he did a mid-air ballet under a cottonwood. He come out West, sampling alternate fare, and found bantams right tasty and nourishing. Sam met him outside a poultry farm in Saint Jo.

"He's wanted in six states for chicken thievery," Sam declaimed, "so he's on the lam. Looking for a spot to light where folks ain't apt to shoot nor stretch him. I'm resolved to assist, the comradely thing to do, but I'm short of notions, and this storm — "

"Stuck, then?" Banky.

"Tracks are blocked a spell. Then — well, dunno what then."

Just then, Jack Thatcher arrived, snow and wind in his wake. We brought him up to date as we husked the chicken and set plates and forks. Sam ordered up a bottle and kindly shared as we was all broke, as told. Count Wreckala sat, elbows and knees askew, smiling content as a canary-fed cat. Burp. Tranquil.

Dinner got cooked up pronto; roast chicken smell replacing unwashed body smell in the saloon.

"Eat up good, boys," Jack saluted us with a forkful of chicken liver, "cause this might be the last bite we get till spring thaw."

"Huh?" Us all again. Except Charlie, asleep.

Jack told: as he made his way to the saloon, he got turned around in the blow, and entered the telegraph shack two blocks over by the railroad station instead. There, he heard the storm was getting worst instead of petering out and no supplies was coming for a week.

And we was bereft of supplies, foodwise.

At this news, Banky drew, Casper took out his eye and buffed it, Mick polished glassware, scritchitchitch, and I was concerned too. Sam wrote in his itty-bitty reporter notebook, and Count Wrackala smiled and burped. Charlie slept.

We set aside a slab of chicken for Charlie. When he woke up, he'd be hungry as well as thirsty, and we was comrades, after all. We ordered another whiskey bottle; Sam paid, bless his heart, and we drank slow, as it was going to be a long day.

Long week.

We'd et just now, sure, but how long afore we required more fuel? Whereat was we to get said fuel? As I told, the pantries was empty. Not just the saloon storeroom shelves, but the whole town. We was in dire straits for certain sure.

Except, I pondered, for the Count. Hadn't Sam told us the Count doted on folks' blood? Sure, he'd reformed, but what if he ran out of chicken and had to rely on —

"Um, Jack," I wondered. "Seen any chickens about?"

"Nor dogs nor cats nor horsehide nor flesh of any sort. The whole town's bust. This here chicken — burp, 'scuse me — is the last of the foodstock betwixt Cheyenne and Grand Encampment, so I heard in the telegraph office."

"Uh, Sam," I continued wondering, "what if — "

I couldn't finish the thought. Imagine your very blood the only food source for a hundred miles around. I stoked the stove, but still felt as cold as a well digger's pale patootie.

Well, no point in dragging out this part, so here 'tis: the week drew on, we boiled Jack's wooden leg and chewed it for sustenance, and as feared, by and by, the Count got hungry too.

We could chew our boots and belts and holsters to last out another couple days, as needed, but the Count required blood to keep bellybutton and backbone apart. We had us no chickens to suck on, but there was folks.

"What ought we to do?" Casper bemoaned.

'Twouldn't be neighborly to let the Count starve to death, but who among us, starving too, would offer up our very blood?

We drew straws is what we did.

Charlie lost. We'd included him in the drawing even though he was asleep at the time as 'twouldn't be neighborly to leave him out, would it? Anyways, he got the short straw.

Just in time, as the Count was woozy and near to buzzard bait when he crawled under the piano and bit Charlie on the neck.

"Don't you drain our buddy," we warned.

Slurp, slurp.

After a short time, the Count burped, smiled, and curled up under the piano next to Charlie to take an after-dinner nap.

He snored. From both ends. From the nether end, he was eye-wateringly odiferous.

Now, I reckon he snored whilst asleep in the week he was with us, and passed wind. We couldn't go nowheres in the blizzard and had to sleep right here, close by the stove, and all of us curled up in a ball to keep warm, but nobody heard him snore afore as we was all asleep at the time. Nor smelled him, praise Jesus.

But we heard now. And smelled. And fainted from the gassy venting, mostly.

Charlie woke up. He looked a tad pale and woozy.

Maybe Charlie had woken those other times the Count had fallen asleep, but we didn't know for sure neither, because, as told, we was asleep them times.

"Gosh," Charlie yawned, "he snores loud enough to wake the dead." Charlie had nasal restrictions; he couldn't smell diddly.

Come to think of it, nasal problems probably explained whyfor Sam could pal up with the Count while the lack of nasal problems explained whyfor those foreigners wanted to string the Count up. Sucking blood was a bad enough habit, but — well, you get my drift.

The storm abated two days later, a supply wagon got through, and we all ate hearty. The tracks got cleared and Sam left with the first westbound U-P, but the Count didn't go with him. No sir, Count Wreckala's days of running from mobs with pitchforks and rope are over, for he has gainful and welcome employment right here in Laramie.

Go down the alley betwixt Grant and First toward the stockyard, behind Miss Dolly Dubois' Residence for Refined Ladies, and listen up. From the ladies' backyard, where they got a henhouse for breakfast eggs for the ladies and their guests, and choice white pullets for dinner, you'll hear, louder the closer you get, a sawmill buzz, the foreign royal making it asleep and content in a cozy little hut they built for him.

Coyotes nor wild dogs nor chicken thieves bother those bantams. None dare get too close unless you're desperate hungry, crazy, asleep, or got nasal problems.

They pay the Count in a chicken now and then, as needed, which he sucks out and offers the leavings to his new friends.

Burp. Tranquil.

MR. GIBBER
SAVES THE DAY

T'wasn't long after Mick opened the Lucky Nickel Saloon for the day that us regulars started up our daily poker game. Matchstick stakes as we was all bereft of funds as usual.

T'was a tranquil October morn, dry, cool, and not much wind to stir up the dust — Hallowe'en that very eve — and what better way to pass the time than poker with your mates? Me — I'm Tom Dooley, at your service — and Casper and Banky, playing cards. Charlie lay passed out under the piano, and Jack Thatcher hadn't arrived yet.

T'was not long afore Banky wiped me out, so I moseyed over to the bar to bum a few sticks from Mick and run up my tab a tad futher. That's when I found out things in the Lucky Nickel Saloon, Second Ave, Laramie, Wyoming Territory, U S of A, weren't as tranquil as one might suppose.

"Mick," says I. "I wonder if — "

"I reckon." Mick nodded at a jack-o'-lantern on the bar Charlie'd carved last night afore passing out. Inside, Mick put lucifers for smokers to light up stogies with and for us boys to use for poker. I took out ten sticks, and Mick made a note on a paper scrap with a pencil stub he kept in his apron and tossed the note in a ceegar box he kept under the bar for his receipts.

He sighed a sad sigh like somebody stole his jackknife, and I wondered what gives so I asked.

He upped, "I got two quarters, a dime, four nickels, and six pennies in my box. Plus IOUs."

"So?" I inquired. Sounded a fortune to me.

Mick's black beard twitched, all scattery like the fur on a cat with his tail caught in a door.

"That's all of it," he lamented.

"All of what?" I wished he'd get to the point.

"What I got to pay the mortgage with. Due tomorrow." Then he told me how much he owed, and if I'd had chaw, I'd've swallowed it certain.

"That much?" I gasped.

Mick nodded. He looked toward the batwing doors. A wagon rattled past down Second Ave. A mule brayed. Early, no traffic, and not hot enough to encourage much thirst quenchery, and prospects did not look good for more business that eve neither, Hallowe'en or no.

"Wait a minute," I demanded, of a sudden grasping the hind end of the tiger, "you don't mean — "

He nodded. He *did* mean.

I couldn't get my mind wrapped around the Lucky Nickel being closed, and it made me dizzy to think on it.

Mick was smarter than a tree full of owls when it came to business. He'd relieved temporary financial woe with a marked deck, a shell and pea game, and a scam involving an invisible dragon, and I expect he'd already dismissed similar remedy. Iffen he was baffled, our predicament loomed even more dire.

Us regulars would rescue Mick, in the financial sense, but we were broker than him. None of us even had a ceegar box to put in the money we didn't have. Those IOUs us owed Mick gave no succor as nobody had a payday afore that mortgage came due.

None of us could get credit elewheres.

"I'll tell the boys," I assured Mick. He couldn't've told them hisownself on account of pridefulness, and it stressed him so to put a dozen words together in the same week. "We'll think of something," I offered.

I sat, dealt, poised to relate Mick's woes and ourn to the boys, but kept my peace for now as I held me two aces.

Just then, into the saloon stepped Sam Something, a reporter feller from back East, and a world traveler to boot, and whose proper name I never did fix, but I never tried hard to, and he had a guest in tow.

Us boys looked up from our card table, but nobody paid heed. Mick also looked up, frowny, from behind the bar, buffing glasses. Here was possible paying customers, not early tricky-treaters, but Mick was too dispirited to appreciate.

"Gibber, gibber, gibber," Sam pronounced to his friend, hands aflutter, as they stepped inside and the batwing doors squeaked shut. So it sounded. I don't speak gibberish nor Mexican nor Irish. Just American. The feller seemed to savvy.

The feller stood two heads taller than Sam, not skinny though a tad pasty-faced. He dressed regular in a Stetson, flannel shirt, Levi's, and braces, brogans worn but semi-clean.

Sam Something inhaled past his white mustache as if sniffing new-mown clover or roses or a lady's parfume instead of beer-soaked sawdust on the floor, us regulars two weeks from our next bath, and sundry odors common to your basic neighborhood tavern.

"And these here," he gestured like we was medicine show exhibits, "are the boys."

The feller squinted at him, and he upped, "Oh, sorry. Gibber, gibber." The feller smiled and nodded.

Us regulars bothered to look up again, but still nobody stood or offered neither howdies nor shakes. We held cards, me two aces, and I reckon Sam savvied poker etiquette enough not to press. I didn't know if his friend did or not.

The feller smiled, nodded, waved.

Casper took out his glass eye and buffed it on a sleeve as he nodded, Banky whose gun hand twitched by his ever-ready Colt but no more than usual nodded, and myownself also nodded howdy. Charlie didn't hear, still passed out under the piano, and Jack Thatcher hadn't arrived yet.

"And Mick," Sam indicated, "the barkeep. Gibber."

Mick nodded howdy. Frowning.

We didn't reckon too ill of the little reporter for barging in like he owned the place as he was a semi-regular, stopping now and then when his train laid over a spell, taking notes in an itty-bitty notebook, asking damn-fool questions "for the newspaper." We didn't mind folks making fools of theirselves in the Lucky Nickel as long as they didn't make fun of Jack Thatcher too much, didn't spill their whiskey on folk's cards, and didn't break glass nor wind, much.

Something odd about Sam's feller, though. Clean-shaven he was, and pink-skinned, and his dome as slick as a baby's butt.

"Gibber, gibber," he told Sam. It wasn't Irish, as if so, Mick would have savvied.

They left us, sauntered barward, yakking in Turkish or Chinaman, and us regulars resumed our game.

I won my hand and then relayed to the boys what Mick had told me about the pending doom of the Lucky Nickel. As I told, I watched Mick take an IOU, not coin, from Sam and serve up two frothy mugs of beer. Mick was as stony-faced as ever as he did so, but even from across the room, I could see a tear in his beady eyes.

"Well," Casper got down to business, "what ought we to do?"

"I'll bet we could get his landlord drunk," I suggested.

"*She* don't drink," Casper informed. He'd learned, don't know how, that Miss Dolly Dubois, famous as the propriatress of Miss Dolly Dubois' Residence for Fine Ladies down the street two blocks and hang a left toward the stockyards, held the Lucky Nickel's mortgage. Unlike kind-hearted Mick, she ran no tab for man, Indian, nor Mormon. Cash up front was her motto.

"Hows about maybe she has an accident?" Banky twirled his Colt and didn't drop it.

"Nah," Casper responded. "Might not be healthy. She packs heat." He pointed to his upper thigh. "Holster about here. Derringer. I seen it. Once. She ventilated a broke poke."

We all paused, imaginizing some skinny cowboy, running down an alley, longjohns aflap, the lady aiming at the miscreant's derrière from fifteen paces. *Pow*. Made me shudder.

"Well, what ought we to do?" Charlie had awoke and crawled out from under the piano. He'd pulled up a chair at the table and he'd heard enough to know trouble brewed, and he hadn't had his first drink of the day yet.

"Dunno," we all commiserated.

Just then, in walks a guy. He looked the cowboy, tall and rail-fence thin, with flannel shirt, denim trousers, and dirty boots, but he didn't smell cowboyish. He'd been barbered and slicked up recent, judging by his waxed mustache and pepperminty odor. The barber had took off a bit too much atop though, and the feller's head seemed covered with peach fuzz. Still, he looked hairy compared to the gibberish feller.

He toted a Colt tucked into his pants pocket.

He held the batwing doors open and peered in, Adam's apple abob on his chicken neck, judging, I reckon, if the Lucky Nickel was worthy of his custom. Then he nodded to hisself and entered.

"Well, I'll be," Banky muttered, and his gun hand twitched, reactive, more than usual.

As the stranger sauntered barward after a quick peep our way, and Mick greeted him with a customer-welcoming smile, Banky lay down his cards and motioned me and Casper and Charlie to lean over the table and conduct a whisper conference. "Know who that there is?" he whispered. Banky'd had onion for breakfast.

"No," we admitted.

"That there," he pointed with a thumb over his shoulder, "is none other than Maurice Epstein."

"Never heard," Casper countered.

"Me neither," Charlie dittoed.

"Ditto." Me.

Banky snorted, exasperated. He was not a patient soul. "You ain't never heard of Maurice 'The Best They Is' Epstein?"

"Oh," Casper ohed, "*that* Maurice Epstein."

"Still ain't never heard," Charlie affirmed.

I "dittoed" again, and feared Banky would blow a valve, but he informed, one eye squinty, "They say he can do anything better'n other folk. Fastest on the draw, better at poker and bronc busting. Arm wrassle, foot race, hunt, womanize, spit, whistle, whittle, knife throw, hog wrassle, lie, fart, you name it. Better'n anybody."

"Huh." Casper glared through his good eye at the guy who held up the bar a few paces from Sam and the bald feller.

"Huh," me and Charlie dittoed.

"Yes, sir," Banky related. "Works at the Killpecker spread running errands. Mostly he lays about, accepting challenges, taking bets, and such to make hisself and his boss rich."

"Is he faster than you?" I asked. "On the draw?"

The gears in Banky's head needed oil as I heard them squeak like a mouse drowning in a spittoon. "Hmm," he pondered. He scratched his whiskers and eyed our famous guest.

"What're you thinking?" Casper, Charlie, and me asked.

He told.

We got ourselves up a shooting match then and there to take place afore the Lucky Nickel, right on Second Ave, as soon as folks had their bets down, which got done soon enough.

Jack Thatcher arrived, and curious folk from thither and yon likewise, folks Charlie and Casper and me had rounded up by running up and down the Ave, nosing into bars, and yelling what gives. Folks came, yappering and laying down bets.

It took a tad to set up the contest rules, what they'd shoot at, how they'd figure who was fastest and such. Reverend Avery Morgan, who I'd met once or twice but had never broke bread nor gotten drunk with yet, officiated and held our notes, as the most sober among the crowd and the least untrustworthy.

Banky and Mr. "The Best" Epstein stood across the street from the Lucky Nickel so they could see up above on the false front where it said in big white letters LUCKY NICKEL SALOON. They'd shoot the "O," Banky the left and Epstein the right.

The foreign feller asked Sam what gives, I reckon, as Sam told him in gibberish. The two watched, the bald feller's head a-gleam in the noonday sun. Neither bet. I wondered how much reporters make. Sam scribbled lickety-split in his notebook.

Epstein and Banky faced their targets, got ready, and Jack Thatcher took off his wooden leg and dropped it, and when it thunked in the dirt, the two commenced shooting.

His Reverendship judged, and fairly, that Epstein had won.

"Uh oh," we-all concluded as Mick went back into the Lucky Nickel to soak woe in an IOUd bottle of his own backroom rotgut.

Us boys went inside and huddled in the corner by the busted piano and tried to figure what happened.

"I got outshot," Banky confessed, voice quivery with chagrin. He swallered a stout and much-needed toot from a bottle we'd just IOUd.

"Mick'll lose the Lucky Nickel," Casper determined, buffing tears from his eyes, glass and real. Charlie and Jack Thatcher and I dittoed.

Sam and the bald feller gathered in intent converse on t'other side of the bar. They didn't have money nor sense, so we paid them no heed — we had a *real* problem.

On the sidewalk out front, Epstein collected his due in coin and paper, pocketing same till he bulged like a corn-fed hog.

Mick stood behind his bar, figuring his losses with his stubby pencil. A few folk come in and Mick served them up as they required, glum as a mamaless calf. He dropped a few coins in his ceegar box, but you could see it didn't suffice.

The other boys noticed too, and Casper ups with, "Well, what ought we to do?"

"Get drunk," Charlie decided, tooting from our bottle.

Sudden, Mick stands up on a stool behind the bar and ahems. He didn't have to ahem as we all gandered his way. We'd never seen Mick on a stool afore. He was tall already.

When all and sundry in the Lucky Nickel had hushed and even Epstein from t'other side of the batwing doors had espied something afoot inside and come in to figure what, Mick spoke thus: "I challenge you, Mr. Epstein, sir, to a wrassling match."

We got ourselves up a wrassling match then and there to take place afore the Lucky Nickel, right on Second Ave, as soon as folks had bets down, which got done soon enough.

Rev Avery hadn't got too drunk since the shooting match, so he officiated the match.

It took but a tad to work out rules. The bets got steeper, and more folks had come by in the last hour to see the show. Some folks reckoned Mick so stout and Epstein so skinny that Mick would whup the stuffings out of Epstein.

Mick stripped shirt and braces, and Epstein did the same, but it took him longer as he had booty to get unhooked from.

Jack Thatcher dropped his leg again, and the boys let fly.

They wrassled late into the afternoon.

Epstein won.

"Well, what ought we — " Charlie began, but Banky told him "Shut up," and he shut. You'd of figured a buggy had run over Mick's dog the way the gloom hung in the Lucky Nickel, but not all were gloomy. Epstein was as happy as a coyote in a hen house. He sat at a table by the broke piano, counting loot. To add insult to injury, he didn't buy nobody no drinks atall.

We boys IOUd another bottle and sat as saggy-faced as Mick. Sam and friend come over to our table.

"What gives?" Sam asked. He didn't know the Lucky Nickel was set to close because Mick was broke, which shouldn't of surprised as nobody had told him.

"Huh," he announced, when told. "I wonder if we can help?"

"Go ahead." I nodded toward Mick. "Replace your IOUs with your poke. I expect Mick'll be grateful."

Sam shook his white-haired head and told how little reporters get paid. I never expected I'd reckon cowboying as a gravy gig, but I did then.

Sam took out his pocketwatch, studied it, and declared: "I reckon we *can* help." He closed the watch and put it away.

"Gibber, gibber, gibber?" Sam queried the bald feller.

The feller pondered a tick, then retorted: "Gibber, gibber."

"There, you see?" Sam noted to us boys. "We can help."

"How so?" Banky asked. We all dittoed.

"I have forgot my manners," Sam recalled. I didn't say "It's about time," but I thought it. "I ain't introduced you to my companion yet, have I?"

We all said no and he introduced us. It sounded like "Mr. Gibber," and we shook hands and howdied.

Then he explained how to save the Lucky Nickel.

We got ourselves up a beard-growing contest then and there to take place afore the Lucky Nickel, right on Second Ave, as soon as folks had bets down, which got done soon enough.

Took us a tad to get up to a trot, though, as Epstein was skeptical. "This foreign feller is bald as a cue ball," he determined, after a close look-see. "Is they some tricky-treat here or what gives?"

"No trick," Sam assured. "Mr. Gibber's from Hungary." He anchored thumbs in his vest, bobbed bony elbows and thatchy head as if that answered.

"Well, I'm from tired," Charlie offered and yawned.

"And I'm from confused," Casper admitted.

"In Hungary," Sam continued, "they believe if a feller soaks his skull in good whiskey, his hair'll grow something awful. Why, if Mr. Gibber elects, he can raise a head of hair t'would make even Mick gawk in admiration, and quick too."

The guffawing and pushing and sundry raucous horse-play in reaction to this notion was as if Sam had declared horseless carriages could fly. Epstein scoffed first and biggest.

"Well, haw!" He laughed and slapped his knee till dust flew. "Well, just haw, I say. I allow as how I could grow my hair faster than yer hungry feller."

"No, sir." Sam shook his head. "You ain't got the magic."

Then and there, the challenge got made and met. It was Epstein versus the bald feller, Mr. Gibber, in an old-fashioned, Hungarian, hair-growing contest.

Mr. Gibber, as told, was starkbald, whilst Epstein had hisself a fuzzy growth from his recent barbery. The difference, a quarter inch, got allowed as a handicap.

Bets got made among the folk attending this weirdest contest ever allowed in Lucky Nickel history.

We boys was torn betwixt loyalty to our own, even if "our own" was our semi-regular, traveling-through reporter Sam Something's Hungarian-speaking buddy on the one hand, and the evident confidence Epstein gave out on this occasion on t'other. Epstein had won twice already.

We tossed a penny, heads we bet with the house, tails we sided with Epstein, and after it fell through the slats in the floor, we decided what the Hades, let's stay with the house.

Now, your standard Hungarian beard-growing contest is a sight and no mistake. We carried out two tables and set them down in the street. We carried out two chairs and set each before same. Epstein sat in one chair afore one table, and Mr. Gibber sat in the t'other chair afore the t'other table. They faced each other at twenty paces.

Before each, we placed a clean-enough chili bowl, into which Mick hisownself poured a cup of whiskey. They'd hold their heads under whiskey for an hour, so went the official Hungarian rules Sam explained, then they'd rise up from their whiskey head-soak and stand for measuring. Whoever had grown the most hair after an hour won fair and square.

As usual, we counted on the redoubtable Rev Avery, still mostly sober, bless his Christian heart, even after such a long and exciting day, to offici-ate. Which he did with a stopwatch and a measuring stick he borrowed from a local railroad surveyor for to measure hair length with.

"On your marks!" the Rev hollered after the contestants sat at table afore their whiskey bowls.

"Get set." And they got set and folks jostled to get a better look-see.

Jack Thatcher dropped his wooden leg, folks hollered "Go!" and the two contestants dipped heads in their whiskey bowls, and the Rev clicked his stopwatch, and we all commenced shouting and whooping and such celebrating as we ain't seen since the time they hung Mule-Thief Molly.

An hour later, the Rev hollered "Stop!" and the two contestants stood upright, dripping whiskey.

The sun had gone down since the battle started and the moon had rose over the mountains, Hallowe'en eve proper. We had enough moonlight — in fact it was quite bright as t'was a full moon that eve — for a body to see okay.

Mr. Gibber had won.

Sam Something, reporter, world traveler, and Lucky Nickel semi-regu-lar, and his Hungary friend left on the westbound U-P that a.m. with their winnings. Mr. Gibber gibbered goodbyes as he let Mick touch his beard reverent-like one last time.

Mr. Gibber, the man from Hungary who showed up that a.m. bald as a cue ball, now had a head of hair thicker than Mick's. Black hair sprouted on his dome so fast you could see it grow. And his beard. And his mus-tache. And his nose and ear hairs. His eyebrows grew so long he had to part them to see.

Yes sir, down Mr. Gibber had sat, bald, then up he had stood after soaking his head in whiskey, hairy.

Mick counted real cash money into his ceegar box enough to pay his mortgage, which he set a boy off to do with a penny in pay afore breakfast. Maybe now Mick could fix up the piano and buy a few new rolls to play in it.

Charlie got drunk and passed out under the piano. Jack Thatcher won a new custom-made leg from a carpenter he'd side-betted with. Casper

bought a quart jar of new eyeballs in case he lost his favorite one. Banky
won a box of bullets. I come out ahead too, but I expect I'll blow it on
poker. Pennies and nickels, not matchsticks.

Mortgage-wise, Mick was set for now. "But what about next time?" I
asked. He just winked.

"Whyfor do you suppose," Casper wondered to us boys around the
card table, dealing our first hand of the day, "Mr. Gibber was out West?"

I looked at my mates. "Yeah, how come none of you asked?"

"How come *you* never?" Banky retorted.

"Because," I re-retorted, "I don't speak gibberish."

Charlie said nothing as he lay passed out, and Jack Thatcher hadn't
arrived yet.

"What I meant was," Casper explained, "why didn't Sam never tell
nobody how it got done? The hair-raising thing, I mean. I mean, how'd he
do it? I mean Mr. Gibber. How did he — "

"We know what you mean," I interrupted. Casper either held a flush or
had to pee, he was so yammery. "You mean how come he could grow hair
all of sudden when it takes Mick all afternoon to raise a stiff bristle. Mick
being Irish and all."

"Yeah," Banky persisted, "how come? Din't nobody ask?"

Just then, Mick walked over. "T'was the moon." He jerked a thumb
over his shoulder, behind him. "Sam said. Come up on schedule last night.
He knew."

"Huh?" we all asked.

Mick explained.

Then three cowboys pushed through the batwing doors.

"I spread a story," Mick added as the doors swung shut behind the new
customers. "T'was the whiskey, I told, did it. Didn't say diddly about no
moon." He winked and s'cused hisself to tend bar.

"Wolf?" Banky wondered. "Did he say '*who* wolf'?"

"Nah." Casper. "Where."

"What?"

"No. *Where*."

"Why, right here. Didn't you listen — "

"Never mind," I mediated.

I paid no heed to the three cowboys across the room as they doffed
their dusty Stetsons, exposing one a receding hairline, another a well-shaved
scalp, and t'other a monkish bald spot. I couldn't hear, but I paid them no
heed anyways as they chatted up Mick a spell and he chatted back. Mick
plonked four whiskey bottles on the bar and yammered about each bottle,
near like as a medicine show peddler as his taciturn demeanor allowed.

Then, after a whisper conference amongst theirselves past Mick's ear-shot, the three ordered up each a whiskey bowl, plonked a quarter each on the bar — a quarter, mind you, *each* — selected *that* bottle — don't know why one would be better than the other, but t'wasn't my business — and watched close as Mick poured, then dunked their heads in their respective whiskey bowls. Mick took out a pocketwatch.

I paid no heed. I held me two aces.

THE CLOCKWORK SHERIFF

The gunfighter's first shot caromed with a thin whine off the granite two feet to the right of the tin can. His second shot went off before he'd cleared leather and ripped a groove along his left boot heel.

"Ouch," cried Maurice "Lightning" Epstein, "The Fastest Gun in Wyoming," as the papers in Johnson County and all along the Union Pacific Railroad called him. He danced around a bit before he realized he hadn't really injured himself, then sat down with a grunt to examine the boot.

The heel came off in his hand.

He debated saving the well-worn lump of hard leather for a fix in town when he arrived in an hour, but decided against. He'd buy new boots with his first pay. Meanwhile, he'd make up a tale to explain — "This rattler, big around as your thigh, came leaping out of nowhere. I dodged quick and shot his head off just as he bit off my heel." That should do it. Maybe somebody'd give him some boots if he embellished the story enough.

Meanwhile, he'd try to avoid limping.

He tossed the heel into the sage that spotted the desert around the aspen grove where he'd camped. He'd made a quick meal before riding into town as it wouldn't do to arrive hungry. No, he had to appear indifferent to adversity. His immunity to the debilitating effects of hunger and other travails of his trade would be evident in his slow pace, steely gaze, and steady left hand, always close to the gleaming Colt .44 nestled ready in a well-oiled black holster.

Townsfolk would see the twenty notches on the Colt handle and know they'd done right in hiring him.

Lightning stood. He grimaced as pain stabbed the knuckles of his left hand, his shooting hand. It was getting worse.

He sighed as he kneaded the inflamed joints. He was still fast — *the fastest, and no mistake* — but the arthritis would erupt at the darndest times, spoiling his accuracy.

And his eyesight, fading.

"This might be my last gig, Thunder," he told his horse. "Reckon I'll end up working for the dadgum Pinkerton's in Denver, riding a desk or being a night watchman." The horse snorted in response and nodded its head sagely. "And you'll end up in a gluepot. No kind of life for either of us."

Lightning saddled up and rode toward town.

En route, he passed a recently extinguished campfire in a cottonwood copse near a spring. A wagon had been there. One woman, or a boy, judging by the small size of the tracks, and two horses, had left the site maybe an hour earlier, at sunup.

Lightning grunted. If the site was unoccupied come nightfall, he'd use it himself. It lay closer to town, a better shelter, better situated.

But no, he decided as he saw a stack of fresh firewood. Whoever set up here would be back. The camp had a less-than-temporary look. The same party had in fact, occupied it for at least a week, Lightning reckoned. He preferred to camp alone.

Lightning sighed and rode on.

He timed his arrival in the coal-mining town of Cumberland so the rising sun would be at his back. He'd appear grandly out of the sun as the town's prayed-for salvation, a foreboding image of righteousness armed with a six-gun and a reputation.

He pulled his hat over his eyes and loosened his spurs so they'd jingle as he rode, loose-jointed, calm, but alert.

But the townsfolk didn't notice him. Instead, a ruckus with the earmarks of a lynching held their attention in front of a livery stable facing the town's dusty main street.

"A lynching, for sure." Lightning nodded to himself as he made out beyond the crowd a noose being thrown over a beam extending out over the stable's big front door. The crowd of thirty or forty burly men burst into a cheer when the noose swung into place. Lightning heard above their raucous shouts what he took to be the cry of the apparent lynchee.

He frowned. Lynching didn't bother him, as such. A body ought not to take too much personal concern in other folks' business, he always believed. But if they were lynching the party they'd sent for him to subdue, he'd be out of a job as soon as the miscreant swung.

Then he stopped and stood high in the saddle, squinting. A straw dummy hung in the noose. "Something odd here," he muttered, patting Thunder's neck. The horse snorted and nodded. The cry from the apparent lynchee had a clanky mechanical accent.

Then he heard the staccato rattle of a six-gun — no, *two pistols* — firing rapidly. The suspended effigy exploded in mists of smoke, straw, and cloth as it danced and swung.

The crowd roared in triumph, hats flew into the air.

"Tarnation." Lightning prompted Thunder forward. With his bad eyesight, he wasn't certain, but from the smoke it looked like those shots had come from a hundred feet out. Whoever the shooter was, he was good — *darn good*.

"Hold it right there, mister," insisted a stout man with an explosion of rust-red hair for a beard and a shotgun held at port arms. The big man planted his feet in Thunder's path twenty feet away. "We don't cotton to gunmen in these parts."

Lightning showed the man both hands, empty. "Easy with that peashooter, friend. I ain't your nemesis."

A couple of men in the crowd turned to eye him suspiciously, but most focused their cheering attention on somebody in the stable door's shade. With his foggy vision, Lightning couldn't see the man beyond the crowd. It was likely the shooter who'd shredded the dummy to show his prowess.

"Then who might you be?" The big man sounded Irish.

Lightning summoned his practiced, lazy smile, right side of his lip lifted just so. "Name's Maurice Epstein. Most folks call me," he paused for effect, "*Lightning*."

The big man frowned. At last: "Oh, sure." He relaxed the shotgun to his side. "You're the fellow we sent for before — " he indicated the unseen shooter behind the crowd with a thumb.

By now the crowd had quieted to a rumble and most had turned from the object of their adoration to look up at Lightning, hands raised to shade eyes from the just-risen sun.

Lightning dismounted, spurs a-jingle. "I heard you had varmint trouble," he drawled. He managed to avoid tottering on the missing heel as he stood loose, more or less on his toes, feet apart, thumbs anchored in his gunbelt.

"Well, that's right, Mister, uh, Lightning, sir." A short, fat man in a cheap Sears suit stepped to the Irishman's side. "'Scuse me, I'm Fred Acliff, Cumberland mayor, and this here's Tom Murphy, town councilman and blacksmith." The stubby mayor nodded at the Irishman, who grinned.

"Acliff." Lightning nodded. "I got your wire."

"Yes, well, ahem." The mayor looked at the ground where he made little circles in the dust with his boot toe. Nobody met Lightning's eyes. "That is, things have changed, you see, since I sent that wire. We still have outlaw trouble, but, well, we don't need your, uh, help now. You see."

Lightning stood impassive, steely-eyed. Silent.

"Sure and we got us a real gunfighter now," Murphy piped up, grinning.

"We waited for you, but — " The mayor shrugged round shoulders.

Lightning cursed himself silently. If he'd been here on time. If. Well, his stirrup broke, and he fell off his horse, and sprained his ankle, and got lost and —

Two weeks late.

Lightning tried to force a contrite apology to his lips, but it didn't take. As he struggled for the right words, another man, a tiny, slender dude, stepped to the mayor's side, his little grin matching the massive Irishman's for toothsome brilliance.

Lightning squinted. The little man toted a Colt.

"*You?*" Lightning pointed, brows raised. "A *gunfighter?*"

The little man barked an effeminate laugh. "Hardly, good sir." He offered a hand. "I am Dr. Dashel Bixby Hawthorne." Startled, Lightning shook the hand. It felt soft, a clerk's hand. "The Fourth of that august lineage."

"If you're not a gunfighter, Dr. Hawthorne — "

"Friends call me 'Dashel.'"

"Right, Dr. Dashel. So if you ain't a gunfighter — "

The little man took a brisk step to one side and made a grand flourish with one hand. "Meet — *Bullseye Bixby!*"

Nothing happened.

Sounding exasperated, the doctor repeated, louder. "I said, meet *Bullseye Bixby!*"

After a second, a giant, a head taller than the tallest man in the awed crowd, strode forth into Lightning's foggy view. The giant moved with a veteran gunfighter's slow grace, hips rolling, hands at his sides. His twitching fingers hung inches from the triggers of twin six-guns nestled in twin black holsters against his thighs.

The giant gunfighter stopped twenty feet from Lightning. He cocked his head to one side like a hound-dog, listening dumbly. Then, he tipped his hat back and his elbow joint squeaked.

The gunfighter was a machine.

The machine was gleaming steel, the face a mockery of human features: two red glass orbs for eyes, a metal flap for a nose, and a riveted, hinged jaw formed a mouth cavity. No eyebrows. No hair. No expression at all.

"Your steam engine needs oil," Lightning pointed out. He realized the elbow-joint squeak was the one he'd earlier thought had come from a terrified lynchee.

"Quite," Dashel said. He nodded to somebody in the crowd and an oil can appeared. A boy, who Lightning took for Dashel's assistant, lubricated the gunfighter machine's elbows and knee joints. The giant stood motionless all the while.

"Yes, friends," Dashel went back into his well-practiced, carnival barker oration, addressing the crowd, "Introducing Bullseye Bixby! The World's First and Only Mechanical Law-Enforcement Officer! Utterly Impartial in the Enforcement of Our Community's Laws! Infallibly Accurate in the Dispensation of Justice! Fully Functional Twenty-four Hours Per Day, Seven Days Per Week, Three Hundred and — "

"But is he fast?" Lightning interjected.

"Beg pardon, sir?"

The mechanical man slowly cocked his head the other way. Lightning tensed.

"I said — " Lightning drew his Colt and aimed it at the machine. "Is he fast?" He reholstered the gun before anybody had time to twitch. His arthritic knuckles stung with the sudden move as if jabbed by a hot branding iron, but he hid the pain, teeth gritted in what he hoped the crowd took for a professional gunfighter's snarl.

The mechanical slowly cocked its head back the other way. It hadn't touched leather, let alone cleared it. It hadn't tried.

The crowd gasped.

"Land O' Goshen," muttered Tom Murphy.

"You are, uh, *fast*, Mr. Lightning, sir," the mayor said, "I concede. But we've already engaged the services of Dr. Hawthorne and his Bullseye Bixby to rid our community of the vermin plaguing us. I'm powerful sorry."

Lightning fixed the mayor with as baleful a glare as he could muster. "Now, let me get this straight. I come out here all the way from Laramie, and you tell me — "

"A tad late," somebody mumbled.

"See here, sir," the little doctor harrumphed, pointing a dainty finger at Lightning like a derringer. "I'll warrant Bullseye Bixby's reputation with my very life. My very life, I say. Why, but one month past, he triumphed over Doc Cassidy in Muddy Gap. And surely, you've heard of his dispersal of the bloody Mad Dog Kirkpatrick Gang in the legendary Battle of Ten Sleep? It was in all the papers. Twenty fierce desperadoes — "

"I can't afford no newspapers. Not on my wages."

"Oh, we'll pay your expenses," Tom Murphy said, "sure enough, won't we, mayor? And welcome you to linger a spell to boot. Rest yourself a day or two, like."

"So you reckon you made a good choice hiring this, this — *tin can* — instead of me? You reckon this thing's — "

"Bullseye Bixby, sir."

" — this addled doohickey is any rival for me, Maurice 'Lightning' Epstein, 'The Fastest Gun in Wyoming'?"

In the ensuing tension, somebody in the crowd proposed a shooting match. Lightning pondered his response, but Dashel agreed, beating him to the draw, and the whooping crowd seconded the notion.

A new dummy was hung above the stable door. The crowd cleared from between the two gunfighters, human and machine, as the two faced their target, fifty feet distant.

"Now, I'll be for droppin' this hammer," Murphy said as he stepped behind and between the two gunfighters. "When you hear it hit the ground, start shootin'. Have you got that?"

Lightning nodded and fixed his gaze on the target.

"One moment, please," the little doctor said, grinning apologetically. He took his machine aside and spoke to it quietly, earnestly. Lightning couldn't hear, but he wanted to. He pretended indifference.

The thing cocked its head dumbly, and the doctor, irritated, repeated his short speech. At last, the machine nodded, and the good doctor and the machine returned.

"We're ready now," he said. The mechanical stood at Lightning's side and faced the target. Human and machine hunched forward, knees bent, trigger-fingers twitching.

The town of Cumberland, Wyoming, went quiet. A shutter thumped against the wall of Miss Emma Drummond's Boarding House for Ladies three buildings east. A horse whinnied from the hitching post at the Lucky Nickel Saloon across the street. To the west, a dog barked.

A hammer thumped in the dirt five feet behind the two gunfighters —
— and blazing gunfire erupted.

The dummy danced and spun, shedding straw and substance as if exploding from the inside. Raw splinters cascaded from the stable wall behind the dummy, and dust and pungent gunpowder filled the air.

The shooting stopped.

Silence.

Lightning reholstered his empty Colt, nearly fainting from the pain in his left hand. He turned and tended to Thunder, leading him to a nearby water trough as if indifferent to the townsfolk's response to the exhibition. In truth, Lightning needed to soak the hand. Sometimes it helped.

The townsfolk began muttering among themselves, their awe subsiding as they examined the carnage wrought by three Colts. Behind his turned back, Lightning could hear a conversation among the mayor, the Irishman, and the tiny dude, grow from frantic whispers to muffled shouts. He tried to listen as he soaked his hand, but the words were indistinct.

Maybe I'm going deaf, too, he thought.

"Mr. Lightning, sir." The mayor, the Irishman, the dude, and several other men approached. Lightning turned, stern-faced. "We thank you for coming and we'll pay your traveling expenses, but we've decided, the town council and I, that is, we took a vote and, well, due to your, er, tardiness, and seeing as how our town will have the first mechanical sheriff in Wyoming, we figured — "

"Suit yourself." He saddled up. "But you don't owe me diddly." He turned Thunder eastward.

"Oh, but your expenses. At least let us — "

He paid the whining mayor no mind. He was burning mad, but he saw no cause to take it out on the mayor. He *did* intend to right things, in due time. He rode off, planning his move.

In an hour, he regained the campsite he'd occupied the night before, where he unsaddled Thunder. He found the boot heel he'd earlier discarded and reattached it to the boot with a couple of horseshoe nails from his saddlebags. Then he backtracked stealthily, on foot, to the cottonwood copse situated closer to town, the one he'd passed going into and coming back out of the town. The one where he'd seen a little person's prints — the size of Doctor Dashel's foot.

He crept along a reed-choked ditch toward the copse until he found a good spot to wait. A grassy nook between a thick berry patch and a big fallen cottonwood provided him with shade, concealment, and a view of the campsite fifty yards distant. He found a stout club, one he reckoned ought to serve to dismantle the infernal machine with a few good blows. Then he settled down to wait. He napped as the sun descended in the west.

An approaching wagon's wooden creak woke him. Starlight and a full moon rendered the arrival of Dr. Dashel Bixby Hawthorne IV at the campsite in silvery clarity. The mechanical man sat motionless in the wagon back as the little man set up camp.

Dashel spoke to the mechanical as if it was alive, or, as Lightning suspected, a little man sat inside manipulating it.

But the device didn't reply to Dashel's chatter, even after it rose from the wagon and walked near the fire in response to a command, repeated twice, from Dashel. Lightning couldn't make out Dashel's words. He *was* going deaf.

He crept forward so he could hear and see better. He planned to step out and, at gunpoint, hold Dashel at bay while he dealt with the machine. Then he'd expose all to the townsfolk, get the job after all.

Twenty yards distant, he saw the true face of the fraud. Dashel commanded the machine — *in Yiddish.*

Maurice Epstein hadn't heard Yiddish since he was twelve, when he'd left Chicago to go West. He'd fled his tyrannical father, who was set on him becoming a rabbi. Maurice wanted to be a gunfighter, like the ones he'd read about in the dime novels his father had forbidden him to read.

Dashel Hawthorne, British accent or no, was Jewish too. And the mechanical gunfighter was a golem, an inanimate object endowed with magical life.

Lightning sat back with an involuntary grunt.

The sound startled Dashel and his golem. They stood, silhouettes against the campfire light.

"Who's there?" Dashel demanded, Colt drawn. The giant golem drew his twin Colts, but slower. The guns aimed at Lightning.

"Easy now, feller," Lightning said. He stood, hands high.

"Well, well," Dashel said. "If it isn't Mr. Lightning, 'The Fastest Gun and so on.' Drop your gun — *slowly* — and sit there, please." He pointed with his gun to a nearby log.

Lightning undid his gunbelt and sat.

Dashel told the golem in Yiddish to put away his guns. Twice. The golem slowly complied and sat across the fire from Lightning. "You recognize Yiddish, I take it then?" Dashel said. He holstered his gun and sat.

"Yep. Been a while, though. And you do the Englishman act real good, partner."

Dashel huffed, the affront apparent in his stiffened spine and drawn-in chin. "I *am* British, my good sir. Not many British Jews, of course, but I am Jewish. As are you."

Lightning sat in silence. Dashel had started coffee, and the smell was enticing. His mouth watered.

"Can't have you ruining my plans, can I," Dashel continued as if talking to himself. "What to do, eh? Can't bribe you. Tie you up? Kill you?"

"I'd accept a cup of that coffee."

"Gracious, how uncivil of me." As Dashel rose to hand a tin cup to Lightning, he found himself staring into the stubby twin barrels of the derringer the gunfighter drew from his boot.

"Don't move diddly," Lightning warned the wide-eyed Dashel. The golem sat motionless beyond the fire, head cocked questioningly to one side. Too slow.

"What now, Mr. Lightning? Report me to the authorities?"

"You're a dadgum shyster, you and your tin can — "

"Our reputations are secure. More so than yours, I warrant."

Lightning's jaw twitched. "He's just a dumb machine."

"Wonder of the ages, wave of the future and all that."

Lightning didn't respond, thinking about the horseless carriage he'd seen in Denver, the telephone he'd used last week.

"So," Dashel continued, "what *will* you say, eh? Exactly. Will you denounce Bullseye Bixby as a steam engine? No. Nor can you reveal the man inside because there is no such man. What then? Say it's powered by magic? Reveal the spirit of a man who swapped his ailing body for this tin shell, who does my bidding in exchange for frequent oiling?"

"Hold on. That don't sound, uh, *kosher*."

"A golem nonetheless. Learned some variations whilst building railroads in Brazil. Voodoo stuff. Daddy didn't approve of my hobby. Tossed me out. Drink your coffee, good sir. It's getting cold." Dashel calmly reached for his cup and sipped.

Lightning sipped, gun still aimed in Dashel's general direction. Thinking. "Now, if I got you accurate — "

"You're fast, Mr. Lightning, I concede. But not accurate."

"No? Reckon I could ventilate you from here. I wouldn't need to be fast."

"Reckon so," Dashel said, exaggerating his British version of a Western American accent. "Killing me won't make you any younger, any more — *accurate*."

"I am *too* accurate — "

"Oh, humbug, Mr. Lightning. The townsfolk were all agog at the spectacle — three guns blazing. They didn't see who shot when and who hit what. I noticed. You *shot* first, yes, but Bullseye Bixby *hit* the target. *You* did *not*. Face it. If you fink on me, it will only enhance my credibility, not yours."

Lightning frowned, thinking. At last he put the derringer back in his boot and pressed the hot cup to his aching knuckles.

"Arthritis, I'll wager," Dashel said. "Advanced age — "

"It ain't diddly."

The two men sat in silence, sipping coffee. Lightning eyed his rival, the giant tin machine, as it sat motionless on the log across the fire from him. *Not fast. But accurate.*

"The accuracy part." Lightning pointed with his chin at the machine. "Is that the spirit inside or the machine?"

"Professionals don't tell, eh?"

Lightning thought for a while. Then: "How long'll your machine last? I heard it squeak."

"I fired the boy whose job it was to keep him oiled. Would *you* like the job?"

"You couldn't pay him anyway, could you?"

Dashel smiled, silent.

"Does it do what you say? Or can it — you know — do what it wants to do sometimes?"

"My, you're curious."

"Just thinking." Lightning stood, knees popping, and tossed the coffee dregs aside. Dashel, ever polite, also stood.

"Going, are you?" Dashel said.

"Reckon." Lightning casually picked up his gunbelt and sauntered off toward his own camp.

Thinking.

He walked the distance to his own camp, a mile or more, when he decided. He saddled Thunder and rode back to Dashel's camp.

He made no effort to be silent as he approached. Dashel, startled, sat up in his blanket on the ground by the wagon. A second later, the golem looked his way, head cocked.

"Mr. Lightning." Dashel yawned. "What brings you — ?"

"You know, it'll be a couple of days before some yahoo gets wind of your tin sheriff." Lightning dismounted and stood before Dashel, feet apart, fists anchored on hips. "He'll come riding into town, liquored up, yipping and hollering. Your doohickey will saunter into the street toward the miscreant and — *boom!* — the feller'll blow your can full of holes. So will his partner, hiding behind the batwing doors of the nearest saloon."

Dashel rose. Red, long underwear hung loose on his small frame. "D'you really think so?"

"I got twenty notches on my iron from shooting two-legged snakes. Your guy may be accurate when he clears leather, but no varmint'll let him get a chance."

"My — *guy* — can take care of himself."

"My horse is smarter than your doohickey. I got a hunch your spirit guy wasn't a gunfighter when he wore skin instead o' tin."

"As I said, I'm not allowed to disclose — "

"You fired your boy because you can't pay him. You're destitute, ain't you?"

Dashel inhaled through his nose, lips pressed together in grim silence.

"How'd you come by your spirit? Grab some drunk off the street?"

"I'm not at liberty — "

"You could fire him, like you did your boy? That wouldn't take too much magical fuss, would it?"

"It would. I'd have to transfer the spirit into another, er, receptacle. Beast, man or — doohickey. Highly involved magic, you wouldn't understand."

"So you can't do it?"

"I *can* do it, if I want to. I'm as good a magician as I am an engineer. Now, what — "

"I got me a proposition, Dr. Dashel Bixby Hawthorne."

"The Fourth."

Lightning smiled. "Let's stoke that fire, shall we?" He kneaded throbbing knuckles. "We're both at the end of the trail, in our own ways. I think we can dicker."

The mayor shook his head in amazement as he kicked dirt over the blood spot soaking into the ground. "My, my, you've sure earned your keep, Dashel," he muttered. "How'd your machine know there'd be three guys ready to jump him?"

Dashel shrugged. "He's a clever machine, Lightning is."

"*Lightning*? I thought you called him *Bullseye Bixby*."

Dashel patted his new horse. The horse cocked its dumb head questioningly, like a hound dog.

"As fast as he is on the draw?" he said. "No. Lightning he was, and Lightning he is."

CALAMITY DJINN

M arry me, or I'll shoot."
Calamity Djinn stood firm as a cottonwood, back to the just-risen sun, knee-high buckskin moccasins spread in a shooter's stance in the tall meadow grass. She aimed her Sharps, as long as she was tall, at Butch Parker, who stood across the campfire from her. Seconds before, he'd been asleep. He was awake now, his eyes riveted on the weapon aimed at him. At and up — Butch stood a good two feet taller than Calamity.

Pungent gunpowder overwhelmed the meadow's sage perfume. A covey of quail flushed in the tall grass close by, but the woman didn't flinch.

Butch could have reached out, if he'd wanted to, and stuck his finger in the muzzle, but he didn't. Nobody messed with a loaded Sharps. Or with the trapper woman some folks called Calamity Djinn. Some folks called her "Calamity" because wherever she went, calamity followed. Some folks said she was a witch, or something like it; that's where the "Djinn" came from.

Nobody messed with her, not even Butch Parker, who was big enough to be called "Porker" behind his back by his fellow trappers, and big enough that that seldom happened.

Butch flicked his eyes away from the Sharps and looked around the grassy meadow where they stood. He looked at the big dead cottonwood behind them, at the aspen and pine-covered rolling hills beyond the meadow, and the jagged spikes of the Wind River Mountains on the eastern horizon over the woman's shoulder. It looked to Calamity as if he was scouting for a griz or a Shoshone war party or something else to change the subject. But she didn't flinch.

She'd planned the ambush well. No bear for miles, and the nearest Indians she'd tracked was a hunting party moving away and north, upvalley.

"Now, Calamity," Butch said, voice molasses smooth, "that Sharps packs a kick, you know."

"Reckon I do."

"And you don't want to hurt yourself."

"Reckon I don't."

"So, if you'll just sort of — "

Butch lowered one big paw to gesture, but being nervous facing the Sharps, he did it too fast and the motion spooked Calamity, who gasped, a tad nervous too — the thought of marriage and all, at last — and took half a step back. She caught her heel on a loose rock and stumbled. The Sharps discharged with a roar, knocking her to the ground in a gunpowder-smoke cloud.

The bullet tore Butch's coonskin hat off. The slug, the size of a cigar stub, careened off a snag hanging from the cottonwood behind Butch.

The limb, as big around as Butch's thigh, fell straight down on him from twenty feet up, butt first, hit him on the head like a well-swung war club. Knocked him out cold.

Calamity tore up the petticoat she'd got a few days before from a Mormon pushcart company that had been led astray — too far north — by a drunken so-called guide named Big Nose Jack. Calamity beat the tar out of Jack, sent him on his way mostly still alive, and redirected the company back onto the Lander Cutoff, where they were supposed to be. In reward, one of the three women in the company — the one as tiny as Calamity — traded her, in secret, the petticoat for a pint of whiskey.

Calamity wanted the lacy white undergarment for her wedding night. Which she hoped to enjoy right soon with her beloved Butch.

Truth be told, she envied those Mormon women. Nine kids, she'd counted, among them. And one woman heavy with number ten.

She'd have children of her own, too — soon — by God, and by Butch Parker.

As soon as he regained consciousness.

Now the petticoat was tattered, bloody. Its cedarwood scent had been lost. She used it to staunch the blood gushing from Butch's head and bandage the wound. The blood stopped by noon, and he'd rested until sundown, and beyond, slipping in and out of consciousness.

He moaned a lot and cussed some when he woke up, but Calamity figured he'd live.

She gave him whiskey — from *his* parfleche, not hers — when his bellyaching got too loud. By midnight, he'd quieted down some but not much, so Calamity concocted a poultice made from boiled Jimsonweed she found near the creek that bordered the meadow.

She stayed up through the night, smoking her corncob pipe, stoking the fire, tossing rocks at the occasional nosy coyote, and swearing to God and the goddam Great Spirit that if Butch was still alive come morning, she was going to kill him for scaring her so.

"I almost blew your head off, you damn fool," she said. "Can't hardly marry me a corpse, now can I, huh?"

Butch snorted under the buffalo robe Calamity had tossed over him to help keep out the chill. She had hoped they'd *both* be under that robe this very night, snuggled together, enjoying the bonds of holy matrimony, but —

Preacher Avery Morgan ministered to the good folk of Three Pines, white and Indian, a half day's hike southwest, over on the west bank of the Green where they had a ferry. Calamity could have been Mrs. Parker by now, but no.

Butch snorted loud, and Calamity knelt at his side. "What?" she said.

"I don't feel so good," he said.

"There, there." Calamity stroked Butch's stringy beard with her tiny fingers, remembering her mother gently touching her cheek the same way *that* long ago, back in Missouri when she'd come down with the chicken pox. "There, there," her mother had said. Just like Calamity did now.

Back then, Calamity had no idea what "there, there," meant, but it worked. It didn't work now.

Butch's eyes popped wide, wild sparks in the whites reflected from the campfire light, as he raised up on his shoulders, stout arms twitching, spastic.

"What, Butch? What?"

Butch sighed, relaxed, and closed his eyes.

And died.

It took Calamity a few minutes to get her mind around Butch's new condition. The poultice hadn't helped. Her tender ministrations hadn't helped. "There, there," hadn't helped either.

"Well goddam you, Butch Parker, anyways."

Crickets churruped, and a coyote howled.

The night smelled of burnt sagewood, old blood, and tobacco. And Butch.

A comet passed among the stars.

Nobody saw Calamity Djinn cry. She cried till dawn.

The creekbank ground a hundred yards away afforded better digging, so Calamity decided to bury Butch there. She dug with her hatchet, and her toad sticker, and a good pole she found, and with her fingers. She dug without let up, wanting to be sure Butch was deep enough that no goddam coyote dug him up. She dug as the sun rose above the Winds, sweat soaking her buckskins, making her stink and itch.

Then, she rolled Butch's huge corpse onto a makeshift travois — he was still wrapped in her buffalo robe — and tied it down with rawhide rope. She dragged the contraption across the grassy meadow to the grave.

Beside the hole, she caught her breath before speaking. "I ain't said a prayer in thirty — I mean *twenty-nine* — years. Sorry, Lord. Been too busy, I reckon, to pay you no social calls." She sniffled and blew her nose on her sleeve.

"But I expect you know all that, about me, about the beaver trade going to the dogs in these parts — hell, fifteen years ago, and more — about me wanting to settle, have kids. About this here miserable, no good, ornery, son-of-a-bitch — "

She anchored fists on narrow hips and addressed the Winds, as if God lived there, and could hear her from where she stood a good four days west.

"Well, never mind. This here's Butch Parker, and maybe he never amounted to much — I guess *you* know — but I loved him anyway. I — I — "

She burst out crying again.

Wiping away tears, she undid the ropes that secured the robe-clad corpse to the travois and heaved Butch toward his grave.

The robe slipped from her sweaty hands, and Butch fell part way out, onto his back, feet and legs in the grave.

Cold dead eyes looked up at Calamity.

I shut them eyes, didn't I?

That did it.

"*I can't hardly marry me no corpse, now can I, huh?*" She'd said that.

She'd tried a Jimsonweed poultice and "there, there." Neither answered, but she had more tricks in her possibles sack.

Twenty years before, Calamity was named Sarah Jane Foster. Indians killed her folks the same summer she met Bob Beaumont, a handsome young fellow, son of a nearby farmer. An adventurer, Bob was. When Sarah Jane lost her folks, Bob was about to head out West, to see some land, and trap beaver in the Shining Mountains. Bereft of family, in love with Bob, Sarah joined him.

Bob fell off his horse en route and broke his fool neck. Sarah, with nowhere else to go and nothing else to do, buried him and moved on. She joined up with old Jim Bridger's outfit. When she told him her story, she got dubbed "Calamity" on the spot.

Bridger told her. "Nobody treks these here mountains without knowing how to do for their owndamnselves." With that, he'd taught her to fish, shoot, skin, fight, smoke, patch clothes and wounds, cook, and fix a fair rosehip tea.

After he taught her all he knew, he loaned her to his friend Shot in the Hip, a Shoshone medicine man. "Ol' Shotsie'll give you the lowdown on medicine manning, stuff even I don't know. Y'ever need to set your own leg, or take out a bullet or an arrow, you'll remember your lessons."

Calamity learned how to use and abuse more than three hundred herbs, roots, flowers, leaves, barks, pollens, sap, seeds, stems, stalks, and grasses. She learned how to use bear fat and wild onion to make a salve for burns, how to use badger gall and flax seed to brew a tea to cure headaches, how to use dried moss and coyote shit to staunch a wound. She learned how to cure every ailment, harm, malady, and complaint known to man, Indian, and horse.

"What else is there?" Calamity had asked Shot in the Hip when her training was near done. It had taken up the latter half of the winter and early spring her first year west of the Missouri. She was smart, a quick learner.

The old Indian, as tiny as Calamity, frowned, adding wrinkles to his leathery face. "You know everything Indians know, and everything the French and Americans know. You're a good doctor. What else is there to know?"

"How to raise the dead?"

At the time, Calamity had thought she was joking.

The batwing doors of the Lucky Nickel Saloon, on Laramie's muddy Second Avenue, swung open, and a woman stepped inside. She stood there, firm as an old cottonwood. She wore buckskins, knee-high moccasins spread in a shooter's stance. Besides the old-fashioned garb, like the old-time trappers used to wear before the beaver trade petered out thirty years gone and more, the woman toted an ancient Sharps, as long as she was tall.

The doors swung shut behind her, squeaking. It was an hour before noon, and the saloon was empty, except for Mick, the Irish bartender, and

Casper, the one-eyed ex-gunfighter, who wasn't very drunk yet, and Banky, but he was passed out under a table. Jack Thatcher hadn't arrived yet.

The woman peered around, squinty-eyed, adjusting to the dim interior.

"Lord a'mighty," Mick whispered, awe cracking his deep bass voice. His eyes bugged, and his big hands trembled. It took a lot to rile Mick, who seldom neither smiled nor frowned, even in a fight.

"What?" Casper said. He didn't turn around to see who'd come in. Couldn't see worth diddly anyway.

Mick nodded toward the door. "Know who that is?" Sweat speckled his broad forehead.

Casper turned at last. He squinted. "Reckon I don't."

"Daughter of Butch Parker and Calamity Djinn."

Casper turned back to Mick, his thin brows raised in inquiry. "What?" he said, a touch worried-sounding.

"You know the story, don't you?" Mick whispered.

The woman stalked toward them across the sawdust floor.

"Aw, that's just a fairy tale," Casper said, voice wavering, "made up to scare children and — "

"Pardon me, barkeep." The woman propped the Sharps, muzzle up, against the bar.

"Yes'm?" Mick's voice cracked again.

"I just got into town," she said, "and I'm looking for me a husband."

ABOUT THE AUTHOR

Ken Rand resides with his wife and family in West Jordan, Utah. He has three children and five grandchildren. He's written more than a hundred short stories, almost two hundred humor columns, several novels and nonfiction books, and countless articles and interviews. His web site **www.sfwa.org/members/Rand** has a full biography and bibliography. His writing and living philosophy: lighten up.

ALSO AVAILABLE:
VOLUME ONE
OF KEN RAND'S
TWO-PART
STORY COLLECTION

WHERE ANGELS FEAR

Printed in the United States
138919LV00002B/68/P